9/22/08 7:40

D0678746

Latin 251, 282, 300

THE WORLD IS THE HOME OF
LOVE AND DEATH

HAROLD
BRODKEY

METROPOLITAN BOOKS

HENRY HOLT AND COMPANY

NEW YORK

THE
WORLD
IS THE
HOME
OF LOVE
AND
DEATH

Stories

Metropolitan Books
Henry Holt and Company, Inc.
Publishers since 1866
115 West 18th Street
New York, New York 10011

Metropolitan Books™ is an imprint of Henry Holt and Company, Inc.

Published in Canada by Fitzhenry & Whiteside Ltd.
195 Allstate Parkway, Markham, Ontario L3R 4T8

These stories originally appeared, some of them in different form, in the following publications:
"The Bullies" (*The New Yorker,* June 30, 1986); "Spring Fugue" (*The New Yorker,* April 23, 1990);
"What I Do for Money" (*The New Yorker,* October 18, 1993); "Religion" (*Glimmer Train,* Spring
1995); "Dumbness Is Everything" (*The New Yorker,* October 7, 1996).

Library of Congress Cataloging-in-Publication Data
Brodkey, Harold.
The world is the home of love and death : stories / Harold
Brodkey. — 1st ed.
p.   cm.
Contents: The bullies — Spring fugue — What I do for money —
Religion — Waking — Car buying — Lila and S.L. — Jibber-jabber
in Little Rock — The world is the home of love and death —
Dumbness is everything — A guest in the universe.
ISBN 0-8050-5513-4 (hc : alk. paper)
1. Middle West—Social life and customs—Fiction.   2. Family—
Middle West—Fiction.   3. Boys—Middle West—Fiction.   I. Title.
PS3552.R6224W65   1997   97-16459
813'.54—dc21   CIP

Henry Holt books are available for special promotions and premiums.
For details contact: Director, Special Markets.

First Edition 1997

DESIGNED BY KATE NICHOLS

Printed in the United States of America
All first editions are printed on acid-free paper. ∞

1   3   5   7   9   10   8   6   4   2

CONTENTS

[handwritten top note: cuts hand / calls wife]

THE WORLD IS THE HOME OF
LOVE AND DEATH

THE BULLIES

The hard rain sounds like a heartbeat. The heavy green canvas awnings around the three-sided screened porch buck and grunt and creak; they sag with the hard rain, and they drip, and then suddenly they rise and twist and water splashes out. Inside those passionate sounds, the porch glider squeals and the wicker chair squeaks. Ida Nicholson, Momma's guest, in expensively crude, heavyish, wrinkled linen and with stylishly stately curls on either side of her head (her hair smells of hot iron even in the rain), sits with bossy nervousness in the wicker chair.

Momma has on rouge and eye shadow; and her lipstick is so bright in the damp air that it shouts in my eye. Ma's porch grandeur. She is all dressed up. Her eyes are not fully lit; they are stirring like half-lit theaters. The lights never go on, the scenes are not explained. Her nakedness of but only half-lit soul puts a disturbance into the air—I feel shouted at by that, too. Her art is immersed in darkness. The floor of the porch—concrete with an oval straw rug—smells of the rain. Lila's voice: "Ida, everything that I do on this matter, I do because S.L. loves this child—he's pretty, isn't he? You wouldn't think he was just flotsam and jetsam. You know me: I may vote Republican yet; I'm not the maternal type—the child is S.L.'s pet project. S.L. makes the decisions; if he doesn't call in a doctor because the child doesn't talk, there's an excellent reason: S.L. has thought it out: if the child is real sick, what are we going to do? How long can we keep him? Now he's doing fine. S.L.'s in no rush: sufficient evil unto the day. I can't tell you what to think, but I can advise. I recommend it to everyone, Let's live and let live. I'm not an inexperienced person, Ida; in a lot of battles, I count for more than a man."

Ida is delicately made but ungainly—that is a kind of sexual signal. It is an indication of will. Her movements and eyes are more for purposes of giving social and political and intellectual messages than *sexual* ones—this is a matter of pride as well as of defiance, a useful grotesquerie. Her alertness is a kind of crack-the-whip thing—not uncommon in the Middle West but uncommon there to the extent she takes it when she is not being folksy and Middle Western. Her style of dress, expensive and *sportif,* French, is obliquely sexual in the manner of women athletes of that day, golf players and tennis players, and is without the insolence that marks the project of the arousal of men: she is seriously chic, magisterially so, and that includes a mock dowdiness.

Lila does not try to compete with that: big-breasted Lila, in white with polka dots and a wide patent-leather belt, is sadly heterosexual—theatrical at it—but convincingly real, not even faintly a pretender. She has the gift, or art, or intrusiveness, of apparent personal authenticity.

Ida's legs are thin—toylike almost—above flat shoes with fringed shields over the laces. Lila's legs are those of a cabaret singer, in high-heeled patent-leather pumps, very plain and yet noticeable anyway. Ida has on a white-and-blue tie, Lila a white-and-black polka-dotted scarf caught with a diamond pin. Ida's "polite" inexpressiveness, a powerful quality in her, and her social rank (her position in relation to what others want from her) add up to her being *a dry person, someone with a dry wit, a wonderful person, really, and* (to go on using Momma's terms) *she was in charge. Who was I? We were nobodies.*

Ida has a pronounced quality of command—but it is not local-dowager stuff—it is *charmingly in-and-out—taking turns, fair play* (Ida's phrases)—*but* (Lila said) *she was always the referee and the judge* (of what was fair).

Ida feels that nothing in the way of feeling or intellect is a puzzle for her. Her omniscience had lapses but she did not overtly confess to them: she could not have run her kingdom then. Her confidence came from her triumphs: her sister married a newspaper-and-magazine potentate in the East (Boston chiefly). She may have influenced the policies of the newspaper. She always said she did. She was a dilettante philosopher in public conversation and good at it. Then, there were her successes in Europe—social ones, with women: the most difficult kind. She divided feelings into those of pleasure—by which she meant feelings of self-love, the acknowledgment of merit and standing, of the powers of the self—and the feelings of emergency: hurt, rage, self-pity, the necessity for fighting.

Knowing Ida meant you were playing with fire. For Ida, incoherence is ill-health: she becomes an invalid from contradiction—in herself, by others of her. The fluctuation in others of contradiction, the foreign actuality of others' thoughts, plus her ignored feelings when others show their strange thoughts, cause her *nervousness*. Ida feels as a Christian (lady) that historically the *serious* work has been done and that certain forgiveness obtains nearby for silliness—forgiveness overall and acceptance: a truce. For her, religion has altered into *manners*—through manners she has a high-speed connection to what she considers to be the tragic; and she has a tactful attachment to silliness (everything that is not tragic but is merely sad). She hungers for transcendence. This gives her a beauty that Lila is aware of, an ugly beauty of a sort, *a real beauty, the kind men don't know about: Ida is a someone.* Ida's moral illiteracy, her ethical inanity, are not anything unusual—they are the common human matter of power.

When Ida was on her high horse, you could forget she hated everybody and could do anything she liked and when she did it she didn't apologize: there was

*a lot to her. If luck had gone her way, who knows what she could have done?
She was a brilliant person who was also no good.*

Ida—this is in a moment without men in it—asks, converting her
full rank into tentative silliness, with a great deal of calm and yet nervous music in her voice, "Well, Lila—" Pause. "*What* do you think of
the rain?"

Lila sits suddenly still on the porch glider. Her face seems to recognize a great many notes and possibilities in the question—this is
sort of a joke—and she replies as if carefully, the false carefulness making an ambiguous music, "I don't mind rain; my hair holds up in the
rain. I'm lucky: I don't get frizzy."

Ida puffs on a cigarette. Momma suddenly—naïvely—poses as
someone who is not watching Ida.

Ida looks at Momma's hair—the widow's peak, the shininess above
and below and around, past the polka-dot bandanna (and its tail); and
she says, "I'm a daughter of the pioneers, Lilly. I have prairie hair—I
get frizzy; it's a bane: I'm just a workaday person—Lilly—"

That's special Midwestern talk, including Momma's grade-school
name.

Momma has a drink clasped in a ringed hand; she keeps her eyes
lowered even when her old name is uttered. Ida has a drink, too, and
a cigarette. Momma sighs: so much deciphering—Ida's clothes and
money and voice and the moment—and then Momma shifts her posture and suddenly "gives up," as if with overwhelmed innocence or
naïveté or ignorance: this is her most common tactic with a powerful
woman, to give in, give up, and not mean it: it's a kind of wit—a kind
of sexuality. Ma's face shows she decides to be *the hostess*—ordinary.
There is a question whether Ida will allow it. Will Ida insist on being
at home in Lila's house? Will she treat it like *a pigsty?* The particular
music—the cast of voice, of face—with which Ma gets ready to do
this marks her as worthwhile, as not a novice, as having social
promise: "Ida, we have some little sandwiches; Annemarie put them
together for you: she stayed away from the noisy lettuce you don't
like—I told her what you said that day at the governor's luncheon.

She made them especially for you—I told her you were coming. *You impress—her.*" Ma rose and walked across the porch—a sort of workaday hostess: a version of workaday to offer Ida a plate of sandwiches. Momma's dress has birdlike lights in it and rustlings: she is enclosed in a watery aviary of small lights and small noises. She has a sweetish, and slightly sweaty, full-bodied smell—startling. Her red mouth is, too.

Ida blinks and takes a sandwich and tilts her head like a fragile queen who yet has a sinewy strength of mind. She says, in educated, rapid, smart tones of a kind that Lila has never heard from anyone else, never heard a version of in the movies or onstage: "And you, do I impress *you?*"

Lila recognizes the *power* and feels thrilled. She feels the "class" thing her way, as beauty and as enmity—the possibility is that she will be hurt; she is game.

But (in Ida's terms) she is *infinitely sly*—Momma has her own fairly complete realm of knowledge and she has her own power: she hears not *a complete woman* (Lila's term) but *a girl bookworm* and *a woman who doesn't smell like a rose*: someone lonely, wooden, undemocratic, locally solitary—it's the Christian snobbery: that mingling of *truth* and *the ideal* (Momma's dichotomy), *the truth* being loneliness and a kind of poverty of life, of soul, and the ideal being a social reality, symbolized by Ida's Parisian suit, with its man-cut jacket and pleated skirt, the *real ideal* (Ma's term) inside the ideal being the satisfaction of the impulses of a woman of rank (in America, in imitation in this case of European examples): satisfactions, consolations, *and rank.* What Lila understood as *the ideal* was earthbound, but it was earthbound romance, self-loss—suicidal bursts of love and extravagance with money to make *a real story, a legend around here.* Not that she practiced that form of suicide, but she played at its edges. So to speak. What Momma meant by *the ideal* was the most advantageous *human* thing for a woman. In order not to be aggravated and go mad or give up: when Momma says she is not young, is not nineteen, this is part of what she means.

Ida feels herself to be a *Christian* warrior, Ida feels she is a vessel by blood, by blood lineage, for illumination and heroism as part of the matter of competing, as a mark of victory—i.e., of government. She is very stubborn about this.

Lila thinks that is banana oil.

But the fact is that at moments Ida is her ideal.

Ida knows that The Ideal Figure is *the one that gets loved* but not necessarily embraced.

Ida is impatient with reality and minds it that if you solve one problem, that does not solve all problems.

She has a very elevated notion of personal greatness as a social matter and as an aspect and reward of heartfelt, transcendent belief.

So Ida is often afraid she is being laughed at—terror and anger then display themselves at a distance—abruptly she embodies them and then drowns them in her usual courage and willfulness: this makes her vibrate and be nervous; this fills her with disgust and friendliness. (The more she is drawn to someone, the more disgust she feels. I think it is so she will not be pushed around by her feelings.)

Do I impress you?

Lila's sense of Ida's question goes deep in her: *Why Ida was asking it was the question.* Lila says, "It would hurt my pride to answer that—" Lila pauses. Really, if you have the time and a fine enough nervous system you can study what an elaborate pause it is, what detail work is in it. She says, as if she had not paused, "It would be a risk to answer that."

Her tone is ineffably muted, *respectful* daring, and with a lot of heterosexual good sportsmanship in it. Homosexual women, in Ma's experience, substitute gallantry for sportsmanship, and Ma does not like that. And Ma thinks she is attractive to Ida to the extent that she, Ma, is not homosexual. So Ma is maybe emphasizing this side of herself a lot.

Ida shivers. Ida, girlishly (but a ferocious girl), shows on her face that she *admires* Lila's courage: *it's* not *tacked down* (Lila's phrase): *nothing is said.*

Ida never—never—detaches herself from considerations of power; neither does Ma, differently, starting from a different background. Ida never associates power with evil, although she says she does, but Ma really does. Ma thinks "goodness" is consolation for not taking the risks to be bad and a leader—i.e., wicked—*a good conscience is your reward for avoiding leadership if you ask me.* . . .

Both women can be comic. Ida thinks the stuff of this exchange so far is charming: she says, "I should have worn a hat and gloves."

"Ha-ha," Momma says. "That's some song and dance—hat and gloves and pearls." But her smile indicates she likes it, too.

So far, so good, Momma feels.

Ida's sexual courage is limited—those shadowy reaches among the other's desires and gusts of feeling—the robot courage, a boy's humility is beyond her. Ida is too impatient with such *ordinariness* to know that stuff—her love of power forbids it. Lila is too ashamed of her physical self now (at the age she is) to be comfortable sexually: she would like to be like Ida.

They smile, eye each other, smile independently and at an angle without looking at each other; they sit and drink and smoke: a certain sort of physical punctuation.

Ida can sense the presence of *the other thing* in Lila—that aging sexual power—that power *fascinates* Ida and makes her a student: this is as docile as she gets, a rebellious student of Lila's sexual reality, which is, according to Momma's manner, that of someone whose duty is to be sexual—sexually generous.

Lila's rambunctiousness is Jewish *"mockery"* of that and not simple and not comprehensible to Ida. It is an ultimate defiance: a (Jewish) sacrilege. Ida trusts that Lila trades, *as everyone does,* in humiliations, that Lila's *defiance* is that of a Jewess.

Ida puffed restlessly on a new cigarette. She sucked smoke in a French manner. She eyed Lila to see if Lila recognized the marvelousness of Ida's style. She bit into a sandwich. She said, "But these sandwiches are *good,* Lila."

"Praise from *you* is praise and a half and then some—did you taste both kinds? You haven't tried the shrimp. The shrimp are from New Orleans. My momma says God will punish us for eating shrimp." Sin. A Jewish woman entering the secular.

"This is a perfect *cucumber* sandwich. I *adore* cucumber *sandwiches.*" Ida is encouraging the secular but is respectful toward religion and does not mention shrimp.

"Oh, I'm a divine housewife," Lila says, as if she weren't being shocking about what she ought to be. "I know who to hire. Have you met our Annemarie? She's a little on the fat side. But she's a very fine person—she soaks our cucumbers in milk. It's something she learned in France; she's from France. She says it gets the acid out—is that important? I don't know what *I* think of the acid in cucumbers: probably it's important to get the acid out—"

"Lila, these sandwiches: I'm your slave." (That is, *lower me to your* peasant *level: let's roll in the gutter for a while:* No more religious issues. No more social issues. Lila worries that she looks at people too darkly; but she thinks that's what Ida means by that remark—Ida doesn't mean she'll be obedient.)

Ida says, when Lila blinkingly and pointedly says nothing, "Your housekeeper soaks cucumbers in milk? I never heard of that."

Lila says carefully, without in any way denying the double meaning, "Neither did I. But I guess I go along with it."

"Really?" Ida says, looking triumphant in the face of Ma's being a riddle.

"I'm not fooling—I'm not a fooler. I'm honest—you can trust me. I'm always impressed when a woman's honest, I like to be impressive," Lila says melodiously, unmocking (maybe) or mocking.

Ida breathes slowly and eats in a way that mingles considerable delicacy with cynical doubt—perhaps about eating and chewing in general but doubt eased maybe by the *happiness* of the moment.

Lila watches Ida eat, and she says, "You'd be surprised how honest I am. I have to be careful—you know what they say? Why be a martyr? I admit I like an opportunity to shine. I like to show what I'm made of. I like a chance to rise to the occasion." The look in her face may mean she is saying she can lie, she can keep her mouth shut, she can rise to any worldly occasion, or it may mean something else: maybe she thinks two things at once and that enables her to say things that mean two things at least. She says, "But I wouldn't want to be quoted on this." She smiles—Momma had so many smiles that you might say, if you counted contexts, that she had an infinite number of them. "People don't understand always what honesty is when a woman's honest."

"I think of myself as honest," Ida says with a certain superior curvature of voice; and, having stopped eating, watches Lila through the smoke of another cigarette.

"You can say that—wherever you speak, you speak from a throne room," Lila said, leaving the question open and yet speaking more directly than before. "A woman can't say that who only has a porch. People don't mind when *you* show your colors: you have two streets in this town named after your family." It's up to Ida to speak first about the happiness of the moment and about human affection, Momma means—maybe.

The set of her pretty mouth and unlit eyes means Lila's both sad and cheerful that people sometimes think of her as a villainess (as *not honest*).

Ida has that sense of Momma as a pretty *Jewish* woman, a villainess: clever, ruthless, dishonest—foreign. What does it mean that Momma doesn't mind? Is it that she's letting Ida build up a debt and she will get even?

Ida is—naïvely—*pleased* that Lila knows Jews are unrooted opportunists, sly satirists, thieves of a sort—thieves of one's comfort with oneself and one's thoughts.

As well as of money often.

Ida says cautiously, blinkingly, now scoffingly friendly, "Everyone in town puts you on a pedestal, Lila."

"Oh, *that* kind of pedestal is *nothing*," Momma says in an old voice, watching Ida.

"No, it's serious," Ida says.

Her voice is firm—it is not her judgment so much as her temper, her nervousness, that dominates the moment.

The intelligence and shrewdness required to make one's nervousness a sign of social class and an intellectual plane of discourse and a sign of emotion mark *a leader*—this is what Ma thinks, and *leader* is Ma's term.

Lila said, "If a woman has flashing eyes, she can't joke, she can't make jokes, but name a street after me and maybe there could be a little comedy—you think a woman like me's allowed to make fun? I'm a menace. I suppose you don't know about me."

She said it in such tones that flattery of the other woman's *fineness* was intended and disparagement of her local standing in politics as a beauty worth listening to.

Her voice was musical. The voice was nakedly peeled; it gently crooned along.

Ida is abruptly amused—it is a matter of eligibility: Momma's. Holding her head and shoulders and back in a pleasantly angular slouch, Ida says, "The women in my family have a motto: that the only foolish thing is to be frightened." I.e., class equals *bravery.* So Momma to show class should offer affection first.

Momma purses her lips and says, very softly, "Well, we say nothing ventured, nothing gained in our family; it's a good idea to look before you leap." I.e., you go first: you act so superior.

"I'm a believer in *real* courage," Ida said. "My great-grandmother saw her sister scalped; she did not lose courage; she stayed right where she was, hidden in the woodpile; she didn't let out a peep."

Momma tried this: "Do you think the world is getting better? Maybe it used to be worse. Or is it the same old thing? My mother thinks it's still bad and going down—she had to hide in a cellar under rags while the cossacks killed her father. And five brothers. But she peeked. I can't tell the story: some words put the smell of things right up my nose and I get sick. Those cossacks, they put Momma's father and the five brothers in the ground up to their necks. Wait a moment:

I have to catch my breath." Momma gasps faintly. "They bury the legs and arms so the men can't move; the beards are in the dirt. Then the cossacks make their horses gallop. She watched the horses' feet kick them in the head. The brains would run out. Momma said their eyes fell out onto the ground."

Ida is listening to the anecdote with an intelligent look—idle but taut and ready to respond although not by making the first move by declaring her interest, or degree of it, to Momma.

Lila says without transition but softly, vulnerably, "Are you always a careful talker? When the sky's the limit? When the highfliers are around?" Then: "If there are any."

Ida says—slowly—her voice has curlicues of *clear* inflection—"I'm a careful speaker. It's an old habit. I don't know that I'm so special." Meaning that she *was,* since she was modest, meaning also Momma's wit, of its sort, has made a point (of its sort).

Lila never understood the point of modesty for women. She said, pushily but melodiously, "If I talked like you, what would you think? Do you think I ought to talk like you? Would you like it if I did? You think we ought to talk alike?"

Momma mixed fineness with naïveté—a social brew—and *took* the lead.

Rather than be a mentor to Momma or ask for a twin or say no directly, Ida, electric, luminous, says, "In the matter of how people talk in this country, we need to be called to order."

Momma smiles modestly, daringly: "I suppose I'm daring, I'm over people's heads. I like to take a chance."

The rainlight grows yellower, as if it were on its way to clarity, but the rain persists windlessly, moderating itself almost not at all in the sudden light.

"I mean in general," Ida says, veiling her eyes.

Lila says, "In general, I do what I have to do; I prefer to look like a winner. I'm not someone who pleads her case."

Ida peers at Lila and then quickly stops peering. She is richer, freer, and "smarter" than Lila—she is in command. She is someone who knows what it is to be *top of the heap*: for her, for both women, winning is equivalent to guiltlessness; victory represents virtue, blamelessness.

Regal and modest, as if simple and self-defined, Ida *makes a move* (Ma's phrase). Ida smiles—her smiles tend to be fixed, grammatical—but her eyes shift from interest and bullying (or manipulation) into beauty.

And Ida says, "Lila—" with each syllable cut short and with a smile for each syllable, a differing smile, and a downward flash of the eyes for each syllable and a pause between. And then a still-facedness, almost a smile. It is very intelligent, perhaps it is rehearsed. (*You can't hang someone for how they say your name. . . .*)

Momma sat very still, and then—making the situation mysterious—she said, in a largely unreadable *tone,* "Ida," with a very long dwindle of breath.

The degree of irony—knowledge of the world as an activity concerned with self-protection—in Ida's face altered into friendliness; and she said, "Lila, you *are* adorable, you know I adore you, I hope you know it—you *do* know it—Lila—you know I'm someone you can count on—lifelong—Lila—"

Because it had a rehearsed quality—Ida's speech—Momma thinks she sees the symptoms of the local thing of having-a-go-round with Lila. Ma is ruthless but subject to being *ashamed* (her term).

Momma sits in a subdued and pale and cautious way, denying the sexual. She wants romance and feeling—Ida on a string. Besides, the movements of feeling between her and Ida have only irony and subtlety and powers of mind in them, only those—Ida has this effect on people often, and so she thinks the world lacks sexuality altogether.

Lila says, "Oh, lifelong isn't necessary: twenty-four hours is enough for me. Where people are concerned, I'm not demanding."

Ida says, with a certain twisted loftiness and down-to-earth whine or complaint, "Friendship is usually taken by serious people, Lila, to be something one can rely on."

Lila says, "I'm someone who takes chances, but I'm a big frog in a little pond. If I ask someone seriously, 'What are you doing?,' people don't ever listen even to the question; I fall flat on my face. I bet that doesn't ever happen to you. I didn't finish college, I was too wild, but actually I know a thing or two, even if I don't get much credit for it. Well, take the cash and let the credit go—isn't that how you expect *a Jewish woman—a Jewess*—to talk?"

Ida—knowingly, lyrically—says, "If Ida Nicholson were Lila Silenowicz, she would say here, 'I have to catch my breath . . .' " She did an imitation of Lila's voice—one of Lila's voices—she captured Lila's mocking politeness.

Lila smiled a soft, plumy smile—dovelike. Then she said, "Ida, I wouldn't say that: I would say, *Ida, you may be too much for me.*"

"I'm still an amateur at being Lila Silenowicz," Ida says with an air of modesty, of wit that isn't modest: it's suffocating in its confidence—its confident pleading.

Momma doesn't want to be darling; she says darkly, restlessly, "I think I probably am a streetwalker at *heart.*"

"Lila!" Ida waits.

"Look at us—drinking and smoking. Wouldn't your mother say we were like prostitutes?"

Ida is genuinely puzzled, but she is also genuinely combative—not easily put off. What she sees, though, is someone who passed from initial invitation to some depth or other of guilt. Lila doesn't seem to Ida to have any moral sophistication (Lila feels that way about Ida). Ida doesn't know whether to keep matters "social" or not. She says with contemptuous readiness of *wit* (a further mistake sensually), "Oh, Lila, you? The way you change, it's like the life of a tadpole."

Lila feels it's tomboy seduction that Ida offers—Lila was never a tomboy. She doesn't speak—she waits to see what will happen (to see what her *power* is here).

Ida lifts her head and sort of moves it in a nursery way, of pride and mental energy, a brightness of thought. She is convinced of her own sexuality as a matter of argument, no matter what others think.

Lila is self-willed and illiterate, cruel and unstable. She is full of rivalry and caprice now.

"Oh, Lila, you are impossible, you are so brilliant, you are adorable," Ida says. "Isn't she adorable?" she asks the rainy air. She is bringing Momma to heel. She is aware Momma is jealous of her.

"My momma has always admired *you*," Momma says. "She thinks you probably have tastes in common; Momma thinks men are awful—all except S.L. My husband. You never can remember his name."

"Initials," Ida corrected her.

Ida wants Momma to admit Ida's authority.

Momma wants to be the authority.

"Samuel Lewis—S.L." Momma thinks she has the authority here.

Ida makes a face. The look on Lila's face is teasing, and not pierced and corrected by Ida's power. Ida is inclined to think that the supposed intelligence of Jews is a mistake.

Ida raises her eyebrows and slowly expels cigarette smoke. Her nose and cheekbones are chic. She's pigeon-chested but handsome-bodied all the same, clean, unwhorish—ungainly. *She's too proud to be pretty.*

The damp gives Lila's skin and her lips and lipstick and her eyes a luster. She sits and judges the silence. Then she puckers her mouth, too—to get a grip on what Ida is feeling. Lila says, "Oh, I'm not adorable; you're being nice; you're being too nice; you're being way, way, way too nice to me." Momma has pleasure and power shoved inside a-wildness-at-the-moment: "I'll be honest, I'm out to be fancy today, so if you feel like that, that's my reward. I like a kind word or three; I'm easy to satisfy; but everybody has their conceit; I certainly have mine; now you know everything: I suppose it's more than you want to know."

Momma bends her head down defeatedly—*adorably.* Momma is as brave as a brave child. She is determined—energetic. With her head down, she pushes her skirt lower on her fine legs. *The world isn't a hard place to have a good time in if you use your head. Play with fire and see what happens.*

When she looks up, she has a freed, soft, hot-eyed face. She feels that she is throwing herself on a blade—she is wounded—inwardly startled. Seductive Momma. Momma's *tempestuous* assault on the other woman: "I'm what you call reasonable if you decide to reevaluate; I'm a *reasonable* woman, but I won't hold you to it, although I'm someone who likes loyalty."

"Me, too," Ida said in a giddy winning-an-argument way. Then, as if she'd thought, *She's not good-looking enough to ask this much of me* (the defense of the sadistic mind): "I don't think anyone thinks you're reasonable, Lilly. Do you think so, that people do? Do you think people think that's your type, the reasonable type?" She's drolly shrewd—it's what Lila calls *Ida's dry way.* "*I'm* reasonable," Ida says in humble summing up. A sad and modest Victory. *Her mind is very quick but she never did anything with it except be quick.*

"I don't know," Momma says. Momma aims her head, a complicated gun, at Ida: "I'm popular. You know what they say—I have papers, I have the papers to show it; you know what the statistics are. I'm reasonable enough. I shouldn't be the one to say so, but I'll take that risk: don't let on I was the one to tell you, don't let anyone know I was a fool wanting to make a good impression on you."

"Fearless! Fearless!" Ida maybe girlishly shrieks.

A sudden, swift look crosses Momma's face: *You can never tell the truth to anyone to their face or ask it, either.* Momma would like to belong to Ida, *body and soul—up to a point: let's wait and see.* "Yes? Well, who knows which way the cat will jump tomorrow?" My mother is in deep. She is where the lions and the tigers walk. Perhaps what she is saying is clearer than I understand it to be.

Ida's fondness for women attracted women. Women saw her as an impressive friend humbled by caring for them. She knows this. Ida says, in a highly good-natured voice that is ironically *moral,* "Lila, I adore you." She grins, openly foolish, as if declaring a truce on meaning. "And it's lifelong." She means it only in a way. She is suggesting laws of affection which she means to enforce.

Momma says, "I know everyone backbites." She doesn't mean *backbites:* she picked something Ida doesn't do. She means backslides. She means people disappoint you. "I put a sweet face on it, but it hurts me.

If you want to hate me, hate me for that, that I'm someone who puts being serious at the head of the list." She wants to set up what the laws are and what the punishments are. "I'm silly, I know, but who knows how much time anyone has? I haven't time to waste on getting hurt."

Ida looks droll but firm: she knows Momma wants her to love her: Ida thinks, *Well, this is war, this is war,* and *I'm a guest.* She says in mostly a droll and clowning and smartly foolish way—richly superior, that is: *I'm the one who is the lawgiver here*—"Well, I don't know how I feel about that. I'm *always* a loyal one."

Momma feels Ida is lying *all the time.* Momma is drunk with consciousness. And purpose. "I'm a seeker, I don't think I'm a finder. You know what they say? Still waters cut deep. But I'm telling you too much about myself. It's a *free-for-all.* I'm going to ask you to be nicer to me. It won't hurt you to be nice: you're a first-family woman and I know I'm not, but there are still things for you to learn."

"This is my nicest, Lilly. I am never nicer than this—"

"That's all there is? There isn't any more? Then you're boring—if you have limits like that." Momma says it with unfocused eyes. She thinks, *I don't care.*

Ida says, "The jig's up." She sits straight, a narrow-backed, nervously elegant woman, cigaretted, alert—plain. "Well, this is—regrettable," she says. Her eyes are shy and weird, then abruptly bold and fixed.

Momma flinches because she envies Ida her being able to use a word like *regrettable* without self-consciousness. Nerves pull at Momma's face, at her eyebrows, at her eyes—her eyes have a startled focus. *There's no inertia in me, there's nothing inert, and there's no peace: I always take the High Road.* She says, "Well, maybe it's time I said I had a headache."

Ida's face is a shallow egg—with features scattered on it. A potent ugliness. Now she formally sees how proud Lila is, just how *fiery* (Ida's word), and Ida's heart breaks. She is suffused with sudden pain—sympathy—a feeling of grace—emptiness is dissolved—but she substitutes sympathy for herself instead of for *women* or for Momma, since she is more alone than Momma is; so the emptiness returns but it's not entirely empty: it has a burning drama in it. Momma is in agony from the work of her performance and of creating feelings in Ida, but Ida is in *pain*, which is worse, but they are *both enjoying it in an awful way*, as Ida might describe it in a semi-grownup way.

"It's raining too hard for me to go home just now, Lilly," Ida says with a kind of gentle grandeur. Then, for the first time sharing her wit with Lila, taking Lila in as a partner in certain enterprises, Ida repeats from earlier, "What do you think of the rain, Lila?" And she gives a hasty smile and casts her eyes down to the porch floor, awake inwardly with the nervous unexpectedness of her own generosity and feeling it as love of a kind.

Momma wets her lips and says in a haphazard voice, "You know, some religious people take rain as a hint, but you try to have a good time anyway—and give a good time—did it wash away Sodom and Gomorrah, do you remember? Of course you remember, you like *The Bible*. I have no memory for those things. You know what they say, people and their sins ought to get a little time off for good behavior. I don't think I know what good behavior is. Well, that's enough: I'm not good at being silly: I don't want to be silly in front of *you*."

"Silly is as silly does," Ida says—perched.

Momma says, "It's not raining violets today—it's more cats and dogs. The rain—well, the rain—you know these old houses is like arks. Are. All the animals two by two—I have a houseload of people coming in an hour."

The central active meaning of Mom's life is that in her, when everything is taut on an occasion that matters to her, self-approval *when the evidence is in* becomes pervasive in her, lunatic, a moonlight, a flattery of the world, as summer moonlight is. Her pleasure in herself becomes a conscious sexual power—the reflexive self-knowledge of a woman who attracts. For the moment, Momma has a rich willingness to be somewhat agreeable in her sexuality.

For Ida, Momma is *the real thing*—as if famous and European, of that order but in its own category: self-exhibiting, in some ways discreet; but talkative. Momma can give an impression—breasts and clothes and face—of supple strength and a crouching will and endless laughter and mind and martyrdom: a 1920s thing, from the movies. The drugged catlike weave of shadows on Momma's belly, her being the extremely fragile and supple huntress—Ida sees this as extreme prettiness and a will to dissipate the megrims, boredom, and ennui, the kind that kill you.

Ida is here for a lot of reasons. Ida is a nervous collector and judge, but she is in Momma's shoes when she is in Paris: there *she* has to perform for the women she admires. She feels she attracts as many people there as Lila does—Ida will compete with anyone.

That's a high value to set on yourself, Ma thinks. Ida seems to Momma to be beautiful in her holding back—women's beauties and abilities seem fearsome and of prior interest to Momma.

The sight and presence of Ida's *"beauty"* (will and courage and freedom) excite Momma, who makes a mad offering of a devoted glance— Ma, who is painfully, flyingly awake with hope, and cynicism.

Ida has gooseflesh.

Ma says, "I'll be frank; I'll be brutally frank: I'm nervous, I'm nervous about you. You're intelligent, you like books, but watch, I don't have a yellow streak. If I make a fool of myself, I expect you to know you have only yourself to blame; you know where you stand in this town, you have genuine *stature* around here. It's more than that: What you say counts. So, if I get tense, blame yourself . . . blame your own . . . *stature.* Will you do that for me?" She is being *Brave Like Ida.*

"Lila, are you someone who might be a good friend? I see that you might be that. Oh, it is unbearable."

"I am a good friend. Don't let the way I look fool you. I have the soul of a good friend."

"You're a darling!"

But the world is unbearable: a chill goes through Momma: in Ida's voice is a quality of unyielding announcement on the matter. *Ida is someone who has to run things—I wasn't good enough for her to hold back and let me speak, too.* I think what Momma sees is that her seeing Ida as hav-

ing a realer "beauty" is not triumph enough for Ida—Ida wants to
hurt Momma, so that Ida can know more satisfactorily than in
Momma's being merely temporarily agreeable that she, Ida, is splendid, is the more splendid creature. You can't call Momma "darling"
unless you do it with a note of defeat, or conspiracy, without causing
trouble with her. To Ma, what Ida does seems romantically naïve.

This is what I think Momma saw: *Ida owns everyone in sight.*
Momma is sexed *angrily and ignorantly* and is sexually fired by curiosity. And she did not marry for money. Ida sometimes to Momma
seems only to have the shine and edginess and sharpness of calculation
of money, and to be hardly flesh and blood at all. Momma feels that
Ida is like her, like Momma, but is less well educated in love, that she
is at an earlier and more dangerous stage: Ida is sexed ungenerously,
like a schoolgirl.

Momma's romantic standing is not a *"safe"* thing for her. *A woman
like me finds out love is a different kettle of fish—I should have been a prosti-
tute.* This stuff boils in Momma; it is her sexual temper—it supplies
the vivacity in Ma's sultry, wanting-vengeance prettiness. Tempestu-
ousness and mind—Ma suspects everyone of cheapness when it comes
to love—*except S.L.,* her husband. Lila romanticizes his emotional
extravagance, his carelessness—perhaps he is romantic.

She is alive and reckless and glowing now and does not seem
devoted to remaining at home and being respectable—but she has
been that so far in her life; and she feels clever in her choices. I think
she is as morally illiterate as Ida, and as unscathed so far: this is what
she claims by being so willful—that she is usually right, unpunished.
This is what her destructiveness comes from.

Both women feel that women draw you in and are grotesquely
lonely and grotesquely powerful in intimacies. Ida has a coarse look.
What it is is that Ida has to be the star. Ida's courage is self-denial and
self-indulgence mixed.

Momma's performance is ill-mounted, since it rests on Ida's *having
a heart.* Ma has risen from the void of dailiness and nobodyhood to
flutter in the midst of her whitish fire, but she flutters burningly in a

void of *heartlessness: it is worthless to be a pretty woman, but everything else is worse.*

Ida governs herself shrewdly.

Momma is excited-looking: conscious-looking, alive, symmetrical—alight.

Ida "loves" Lila's temporary *brilliance*—perhaps only as a distraction. But Ida looks, and probably is, *happy for the moment*—but in a grim way: *This is where the party is.* Ida is game. She says, "Oh, Lila, I am happy to be here, deluge and all. Isn't it nice that we are *neighbors?* What would life be without neighbors? A desert? A *bad* Sahara?" She smiles nervously—boldly. A kind of sweat breaks out on her upper lip; she doesn't care.

Lila, being so pretty, has lived with this kind of drama since early childhood and she has a peculiar air of being at home in it: Momma's eyes and eyelids consider the speech, the praise. Momma looks *selfish* rather than surrendering—that means she's not pleased as she studies Ida's offer, its number of caveats. What it was was Ida is being *careful.* She should have spoken extravagantly, but she is too sure that Momma can be bought *reasonably.* Ma is a marvel of disobedience and a mistress of local manners carefully learned and fully felt. Her face is a somewhat contemptuous wound: comprehension and expressiveness tear her face when she *catches on* that Ida is smitten but impervious, *made of steel,* when that shows. It shows that *Ida has more class than I do; that's where the battle lines get drawn, although I will say this for myself: I give credit where credit is due.* That's a lie, often. Often she is destructive and fights the worth in other people. *This is a democracy, and who's to stop me from doing what I think is best for me?*

Ida is enamored and is *immune* to her, *superior, la-di-da and all.*

Lila arranges her voice: "I'm glad you came to see me." It's not her being a femme fatale or whatever, or being amusing anymore—she is holding back. She sounds a little like Ida.

Ida raises her head, blinks, puffs on her cigarette—looks at Ma, level-eyed, looks away.

This is interwoven with Ma shifting her legs, then her torso, and its burden of breasts on the slender ribs.

Both women are controlled—and full of signals—so many that I don't see how they can keep track of what they are doing in the world, what with all their speed and knowledge and feelings and all the breaths they have to take.

They avoid each other's eyes, except passingly, for more than a minute—it is as intense as speech. Then they are still. Both have small smiles. *This is where the lions and the tigers walk.*

Momma has a dark light coming from her. She is a nervous star that gives a dreamer's light *even at this late date.*

She says, "Did you come over in the rain to see me for a purpose? You wanted to see me all dressed up for a party, when I was nervous? A ready-made fool? All dressed up and no place to go."

Ida says at once, "Oh, Lila, no—no lovey-dovey."

She tramples on Lila's music—that request for *sympathy.* "I hate lovey-dovey—*lovey-dovey* is brutal. It's *terrible.*" A love speech, bossy, intent, deep-feelinged: Ida's sort of deep feelings.

Momma is perplexed by so much intensity, so much *style,* and all that energy, with none coming toward her—except maybe nibblingly, condescendingly—but directed at Ma's flirtatious mockery. It was a love speech asking for rough play.

Ida's personal fires are alight and skeletal. They are not like the expansive whirlwinds and fires in which Momma is trapped and consumed; Ida's have focus and great style. Momma feels Ida's unforgivingness as character and strength, but it's directed toward what Lila is—a beauty of a certain kind, a flirt and willful, a Jew—and that is unforgivable. But that's how things are. *You have to take love as you find it.*

Ma's tolerance and acquisitiveness and Ida's nervousness—and her courage—are the paramount social factors, the strong movers in the board game, in the scene: both women tacitly agree on that. The *soft surrenders* (Lila's phrase) that go with *love when it works* are what Ida was forbidding in her love speech.

Momma thinks of *two bones kissing* and sees how what is painful in emotion might be adjudged banal—or tedious—as *clattering—and you can get away with it,* loving and calling love boring. She isn't really sure. She is a lively fire of spirit and mood, intention and will, and she can't really do that herself, take love lightly.

Lila knows *how to keep up a social air when things are tough.* It is not a new experience for her that there is *tragic* hatred in the moment; i.e., infatuation, and rivalry, a lot of failure—*love of a kind, of all kinds* . . . women deal in love. Momma's Theory of the Ego (*that everyone and her mother thinks she is the Queen of the Earth*) now holds, in this flying moment, that Ida cannot bear not being the prime example of *beauty* in the room, in the world: *She only chases me so she can be better than someone like me: she has to be the star; her husband, Ben, is the same way, but he kowtows to her because she has the money and he bullies everyone else.*

Momma calls a moment like this, this-kind-of-thing, *We're getting in deep.* It is her form of mountain-climbing: exhaustion, danger, despair. The fires of mind and of physical courage in her are a working heat for *her getting her own way*—according to her Theory of the Ego—but in such an extravagantly putting-on-a-show fashion that it does not seem to her to be of the same family as Ida's putting on a show, which is more measured, purposeful, meanly hammerlike, tap, tap, tap . . . *She's like a machine. She has a position to keep up—there are demands on her all day long—she can't give her all to any one thing*—that's Lila being *fair* . . . *But she's a fake:* that's Lila being Lila.

Physical desire in Ida is the trembling of nerves in a strong woman's frequently disowned body. Ida is warm—or hot—but without *dignity* in physical negotiation, *a rich woman.* She maintains her value against Lila's more and more immodest-seeming glamour: why is this woman still shining at the age she is? (Daddy would say Ma was on a rampage.) A wild pathos and self-pity invest Ida with an air of threat in her desirousness—she feels she *deserves* erotic reward. Ida's class, her being superior to Momma in self-control and focus, her sexual abnegation *at times,* her hardness about defeat and the hurt of others oppress Momma as signs of *not* being infatuated with her is what I think. Whereas Ida feels love is one substance throughout eternity—that it shouldn't matter what deformities that will and privilege and folly have forced on the softer tissues of the self in the course of your living the way you live if someone loves you.

Momma feels that love is invented daily and that each person does it differently. Momma, in some wordless way, *trusts* herself in these matters. She is at home here.

Neither woman intends to be a fool—being a fool is something only men do.

Of course, if you contemplate these attitudes and consider the feelings they have, it is clear that at the moment Ida hates Momma, and Momma hates Ida. But they get along.

Lila thinks of it this way, that Ida puts *a quick kibosh on anything she can't run.* Ida does not know just how two-sided the thing of sex is—or how improvised it is. Momma feels that Ida is being "cute," attractive in her way, even gorgeous—but not in the romantic vein. Momma often says, *A truth about me is that I fight back.* Momma is a brute. She would like to break Ida's bones.

To put a cast of reason on Ma's brutality, she wants to hurt Ida in order to frighten her, *so that Ida won't eat me up alive.*

Ma says, "I'm always lovey-dovey. I think I was born that way. Laugh, they say, and the world laughs with you, but sometimes when you laugh alone it gets very dark. Look how dark it's getting—it's turning into a thunderstorm."

The rain *is* getting stronger, brackish and threatening; and wind flings the dampness around.

It genuinely hurt Ida to be cornered—to be straightforward—to admit to having feelings. Her hurt is *coldly* stormy at the moment.

But she looks Ma in the face and smiles one of her top-grade, friendly, large-area smiles and says in a tragically rebuking manner, "You're wearing your diamond bracelets—I suppose that means you mean business today."

Momma says stubbornly, "Did you get wet? Did you ruin your shoes? Coming through the rain to see me? Did you do that for me?"

Ida says, "You don't show any damage from the rain—you show no damage yet, at all—Lila."

Ma's radiance is skittery in this light. *I can keep it up until the cows come home.* But that's not true. Some centrally human element gets worn out in these skirmishes. Why does Ida *lie*—i.e., *avoid things?* Does Ida *know things* (about the world) *that I don't know?* So Ma gets depressed about herself. The effect of Ida's will and style on her. When this sort of thing happens to Momma, she becomes ill. She dies. She becomes stern. *Perhaps everything will be all right, I can handle this, I'm not nineteen.*

Ida is relentlessly enthralled and ruthless still, and makes no promises, even with her eyes; her escape will be part of Lila's come-uppance.

And this: the beauty Ida feels (and shows) has subsided and is more memory than immediate fact, and that imprisons Ida, who can't hold back from agonized nostalgia about her own great moments in the same way that Momma can from hers. For a moment, Ida can't act at all. Ida is not exhausted but she is *slain: You have killed me, Lila.*

In exhaustion, Momma is partly set free from her own radiance. Momma doesn't *care at all about anything at all,* and Ida is stilled in some ways but is nevertheless a restless spirit and unsoftened and is trapped. So the smart and powerful one has become the stupid and powerless one.

Opposites flitter and dance *in the fairy light:* women's enchant-ments are eerie. The story is in their eyelids and in the obscure or clear glances they send to each other. Also, they breathe meaningfully. It seems that Ida will not let *someone without much education and breeding, who is wild and careless,* run things at the moment. Skinny Ida has a *don't-tread-on-me* wonderfulness of carriage, plus Very Good Manners and a Christian cheerfulness. A Christian sense of secular silliness, ten-der just now but hard-souled, too.

Lila thinks, *Ida hasn't beaten me down. My luck is good. Ida is really very approachable—of course, you have to approach her on your hands and knees.*

The two women continue to breathe meaningfully in each other's company—this is more or less at a level of happiness, but *you can never tell* (Lila's phrase).

Ida says, "The rain—it's all water over the dam." She has a creaturely tension, *like a thoroughbred.* She means, *Let's forgive ourselves.*

Lila is close enough to sexual giddiness that she blushes spectrally. "It is spilt milk," Momma says. "Ha, ha, well, well, well, said the hole in the ground—" Momma does a very small version of what she thinks a rich Gentile woman's intellectual madness coming out as nonsensical talk and a laugh is like.

Mindlessness seems well bred to Ida, but, of course, not in Momma—Ida does, *deliciously,* voluptuously, hate Momma. Hatred is *elegant* in Ida.

Momma *feels ruthless right back.* Momma feels apprehension inside, but she doesn't show it.

The two women laugh, complicitously.

Lila says, "And more well, well, well—you know me, Ida, I'm a wife and a mother and a devil, a Jewish devil!"

Ida says, "Yes, yes. Don't be hard on yourself, Lilly. It's hard enough as it is. We don't need trouble—isn't that right!"

Momma says, "Yes, that's right! That's just right!"

Ida, a little drunk, says to herself, *Lila is a black torch of a woman.* Out loud, she says, "You were always *pretty . . .*" By her rules—of ego and selfishness and loyalty—never to give Momma an intense compliment is a sign of *love.* It is keeping things balanced. Ida lives deeply inside her own biography.

But Ma feels she doesn't have enough money or standing and that she doesn't have enough power with Ida to be satisfied with that. Momma is *"infatuated"* but cross; she is drunk—mostly with the ease of being with someone quick-minded, not male. She wants to show Ida how to be magnetic in courtship: "Oh, believe me, I'll go on record as saying you're better-looking than I am, in the ways that count. In the ways that really count, you have the kind of looks I admire most. I count you as the best-looking."

Ida takes that as her due. She doesn't see that Ma is enraged and being exemplary. She says primly, "You're interesting-looking, Lila." Ida thinks that is a witty way to be romantic. Lila feels Ida continues to be *not romantic, not a squanderer.* She is reading Ida's mind: she thinks she sees that Ida thinks it an extravagance to care for Momma in the first place, *a penniless no one.*

This kind of *selfish shenanigans* dries Momma up physically, but she likes it on the whole. Momma laughs musically, yet she is disgusted. She says, in a mad way, "I have to laugh: What did you think the excitement was all about? What did you come to see *me* for?" Ma thinks it's bad taste of Ida not to be more honest—*heartfelt.* Momma is called by some people The Prettiest Woman in Central Illinois. Ma is lighting up again, but it's temper, a squall of will. In a frightened and careless and disobedient way (and in a hysterical and cold and experienced way), Momma knows that in a battle for personal power Ida is the local champion; Momma feels the tournament quality of Ida. Momma says again—odd, mocking, and tender, too, "I'll go on record—you're better-looking than I am in the ways that count. I wish I looked more like you."

She means it, but she's saying it's better, it's safer not to have real looks.

She's praising Ida and saying Ida is trash.

I don't shut my eyes and give up; I'm not a goody-goody two-shoes.

Ida half understands the category she's being put in and she thinks: *She owes me one for that.* She leans down and touches, with one finger, Momma's shoe, Momma's foot. Then she sits back.

Momma's face, brownish, ill-looking, with lines of nervousness on it, now, in her sensitivity, her speed, her strangeness and as a soul in the cosmos and in her strength—and maybe in wickedness and charity—smooths out.

Ida is big-eyed, calm-faced—but sweaty—full of her own fund of fidgety and fanatic self-approval. She crosses her legs—*coarsely*—in front of Ma's now obtuse face. She would argue, *I don't deserve this, I have done nothing to deserve this.*

Momma's eyes go from Ida's eyes to Ida's wrists (fine-boned) and Ida's nails (bitten). The trick for Momma as she smiles a little inside her attractiveness at the moment is to show she is really clear about what Ida is *worth* as a person. "I have a good time now and then," Momma says, unable to be innocent and awed. She says this with her head tilted.

The force in Ida's soul makes her surface twitch a little with puffs of waitfulness. "We deserve a good time," Ida says, not looking at Momma and then looking her full in the face. Ida sinks down in her chair. Then she sits upright. *Like a countess*—that took strength of will.

Momma says, in a presumptuous and urgent tone, "Around here you're supposed to go to special cities to have a good time. I'm from the provinces. But I'm having a good time right now—it's because of you."

Ida sighs narrowly and says, "You're not very Jewish; you're not like Hamlet."

Not mild? Not moderate?

Ma is determined to tack down a triumph. She says, "I'm always interested when we talk, I'm always interested in the things you have to say." Mild. Moderate.

Ida looks at her, aslant, smiling—it really is a grin; it would be a grimace if Ida were less clever.

Ma, looking sideways at Ida, says, knowing it will upset Ida, "You'd be surprised what I think of you, you'd be surprised what I say when I'm not afraid of how I sound, what I say behind your back—I don't think you can imagine it."

Ida, victimized, girlish—i.e., girlish if victimized—says girlishly, "Tell me what you say about me. What do you say behind my back? I have to know. I have to know things like that—that's so interesting. It's important to me. Tell me, you must tell me, it's not fair what you're doing—I *have* to know."

Ida's style here is girls'-school stuff from a social class Ma is not in. Ma flinches, because she usually assumes people of that class will hurt her as much as they can, as much as they dare (she's pretty)—she expects *pain* from that quarter.

Ma is evasive: "I let people know that you make me think about things in a new way: you have real power over me—I talk about that all the time . . . Then I have to think whether I want that or not, whether I want you to be such an influence or not, whether I can afford it—a lot of the time, I don't know. You make me think, but I feel like crying. It's too hard to say it now. I'll tell you one thing: I'm not one of your critics—no, I'm not one of your critics *at all*—"

"Lila, you're just impossible—you frighten me—" Then: "Tell me what you say about me. Tell me in the same words . . ."

"Oh, I quote you a lot—you're *interesting* . . ."

"Lila, tell me *what you say.*"

"I don't twist what you say. I listen to you carefully. I feel I understand you. I feel you understand me."

"I feel that, too," Ida said decisively. She's decided Momma boasts about knowing her. Ida decides to accept that. But her glance and manner shift everything from privacy to the Whole World, where she is the richer woman and Lila is the weaker of the two. *It is always her deciding it—especially if I was looking good*—in the interplay between them. Ma believes Ida doesn't *know how to take turns.*

Ma says, "I'm sophisticated in many, many ways, amn't I?"

Ida directs at Ma a large, cajoling, swiftly childlike (pleading) smile: it's intent, it is ironic and *sincere* and clever—it seems to mean Ida does *sincerely* love Ma in *some* way even if she's in control of herself and of the whole thing all-in-all despite Momma's hard-won upper hand at moments. At this moment, Ma flinches. It makes her feel things, that smile. So Ma is raw, exacerbated, strained—alive—resistant; thinking well of herself is what usually seduces Ma—and she felt proud of herself for having elicited that smile; but she is not yet seduced. She is in control, too—for the moment.

Momma loves women's responses. Men's lives don't interest her— they are out of reach, obscure, obtuse, slow, and wooden.

Momma breathes and resettles her breasts, and her face glimmers and is shiny and knowing—a weird thing. I suppose this is a moment of experienced affection for the two women. Momma hasn't yet said to many people but perhaps feels, *I'm thirteen years past the high-water mark of my looks, when I was the party and that was that; but I'm still going.* My mother's heartbeat was a constant lyric exclamation of ignorance and blasphemy, excitement and exacerbation, beauty and amusement of a kind. Ma "knows, as a matter of common sense," that Ida believes that on *the highest level only a Christian mind can matter.*

To Ida seriously, Momma is like a dumb animal, without truth, but an enjoyable woman, fiery and a marvel—coarsely spiritual and naïve—a Jew. Momma, teased and tormented by life, is fascinated in a number of dark ways by being defined in this manner.

Ida is prompted to take charge firmly and openly of the seductive drama in Lila's shifting glowingness. She jumps up, crosses to Lila in French-schoolgirl style—self-consciously wry—and sits beside her on the squealing glider. Ida is a big-city person, and can't live in the moments the way Lila can. She abruptly kisses Lila on the temple, then rapidly adds a second kiss to the first, pulls back, looks at Momma's profile, then sits straight and utters a watchful, shepherding laugh. The style is nervously a woman's lawlessness that excuses itself as tenderness. A delicate joke. *How can you mind it?*

The risk and nihilism of stylishness jolts Momma with a sense of pleasure and of the abyss. I mean Ma's life rests on contracts among women, sacraments between women, and everything Ida does is an example of freedom from that. Ida admits to no such freedom. Ma feels herself fall toward an abyss for what is merely a lied-about romp.

With weird perversity, in a slow voice, very melodic and undramatic, and not moving her body, but softening a little but not enough to be a real welcome, Ma says, "You're being so nice to me, I feel like the farmer's daughter . . ."

"Darling Lila," Ida says, insulted but still puckered for another kiss: "Me, a traveling salesman?"

The elegance impresses Lila, who, like Ida, then calls on her inner resources—i.e., mostly temper—"Well, you do just breeze in and

out—between trips." But such sympathy is in Momma's temper, as is
not there when she speaks to men, and I cannot doubt that women are
real, are vivid to Momma as no man is. Momma's nerves and mind and
experiences comprehend what a woman does, the sounds and tics and
implications—the meanings. "Who lives like you?" Momma says.
"You pack up and go when you want to go. Some people would kill to
have your kind of life."

It is curious how Ida comes into flower: the slow, cautious, shrewd
small-town thing of her background shows first in her opened face,
then the boarding-school-mannered thing of being mannerly shows
next, and then comes Ida's rebellion and *good, sharp mind* (her terms),
and then these in a parade with the sophistications of *New York and
Europe* (Ma's terms) as part of a moment of stillness, of her looking
inward while outwardly her appearance glistens and glows with her
nervous parade in this manner.

But she is quick to be apologetic (to stifle envy): "It's empty, Lila.
Such emptiness . . ."

Ma said—crassly in the face of the fatuously self-regarding ego in
so automatic a response—"That's what they all say to me." I.e., *They
all come to me to ease their emptiness.*

Ida flinches, sits tautly; then Momma, looking Ida pretty much in
the eye, touches Ida's arm, in a way possible only to someone who is
physically passionate: inside an intense doctrine of carefulness that
implies all the machineries and aches and jealousies and spent bleak-
nesses of response—and it is pretentious in its way, perhaps self-
conscious, like Ida's elegance, that touch.

Then Momma puts her hand back in her own lap and stares
straight ahead and not at Ida. "Look at us, sitting like those pictures
of farmers getting married." A countryside wedding-photograph.

Lila is sort of saying that the two of them are not lovers but are
faintly married to one another by means of an American codification
of women as neighbors—the idea of neighbors came to her from Ida
earlier but she does not remember that. She feels a sacrament was in

the nervous subtlety of minor touch that had in it a sincerity of person, the mark of individual sensuality, and that identified it as sacrilege—not a woman's touch, or a daughter's touch, or a lover's touch: rather, it was *Lila's-touch-under-the-circumstances.*

Ida is too tempo-ridden, too impatient to do more than guess at that, to do more than come to a summing-up: she knows there is little of ancient virtue or of chastity in Lila or in Lila's touch—the touch is too minor a thing for her, although she recognizes the pride and knowledge and she saw that it stayed within certain ideal limits of the self. Momma wants Ida to be sincere and victimizable by touch to the extent that Momma is. What Momma senses as Ida's summing-up is *She would like me to be a fiery idiot.* Ida wants Momma to be swifter and more allusive—*I wish she were smarter.*

Ida literally cannot deal with a real moment but runs across it on swift ideas of things: conclusions. She detects the illegal or bandit sacrament Lila offers, and it breaks Ida's heart—so to speak—but she can't pause or deal with it. She would say *I can't manage otherwise.*

Lila feels at home only among women, but it is always for her as if she were in an earthen pit with them. Lila's responsive mind and heat and Ida's intelligence enlarge the space—the pit and its freedoms—with mutual sympathy but with rivalry and a kind of peace that was not the absence of pain or of striving but its being in a feminine dimension and made up of feminine meanings.

(The talk between women on which I eavesdrop is meanly hidden from me except for the musics in their voices and their gestures. I may have everything wrong.)

The rain seems to fall inside my head curtainingly. One must imagine the reality of Momma's wet hips after a bath, breasts released from brassiere, unpinned masses of hair—this is hinted at: "Sit here by me, do you want to?" Ma says that to the woman who is already sitting there. Ma promises the thing that has already been done. It's not a trick except in the sense that it makes things smooth, it suggests peace. She says this to the woman who can't manage otherwise than to think Ma is *a fiery idiot*. Ma is not patient this way even with me.

Momma wants *the ideal thing* to be two women being together. "It's like school and money to be two women," Momma says in her most musical voice—the music means she is being *deep*.

Momma means the world of men, the surface of the planet, the topographies of violence and political sashaying around and quarreling are put aside, and one is as in a classroom with an admired teacher, or one is like a rich girl with a nice-mooded housekeeper or with a well-intentioned and intelligent aunt.

Ida, with her tigerish mind (Ma's image: *She has a mind like a tiger*), seizes what Lila says (and does); what Ida thinks—in her summing-up way—is that Lila likes her.

Momma is familiar with not being listened to. And if her head droops while Ida now deposits a slew of quick, but sexually unquickened, kisses, *safe* kisses, boarding-school kisses, temporary, not those of love forever, love for all time, it is not in sadness but in temper and perversity.

"You don't listen to someone like me," Ma says despairingly—but like a joke, a parody of something or other—and she pushes Ida but with the side of her arm. Even that blunt touch makes Ma vibrate. Ma does not want kiddie kisses from a woman older than she is.

Ida is used to being *punished*—her word—for her *virtues*—her swiftness of mind, her boldness, her money, her social standing. Girlishly, victimized, her frizzed hair frizzier with personal heat now, Ida stiffens but persists boldly with her kisses.

Ma's lips are twitching as she submits—to *Ida's boldness*—as she holds her head where Ida can kiss her cheek, her temple, her brow, her eye.

Ida plants rhythmic, tiny, baby-syllable kisses—like stitches in good sewing in a schoolroom—a sexual baby talk, a parable of innocence, sanitary and commanding kisses. The kisses move toward Momma's mouth.

Ma feels that the innocence is a bribe; it has to do with money-and-position, with false claims: this is a romance; and it draws Momma in a sad way to be plundered by Ida, who has *real money-and-position* (which Ma doesn't have and enviously wants).

The skittery approach to her lips elicits anger sexually because it is not phrased seriously, physically. It is an assault—blind-beggar stuff—childish fiddling. Ma hates being touched if it is not expert—and, furthermore, if it is not an ultimate matter: life and death.

Or if it were innocent *and reliable* Ma could bear it. But she suspects—in a fundamental way, in her belly—that Ida wants to rip up and demean the actual; the evidence is the compression, the schooled conclusions in Ida, who clearly feels that *a kiss is a kiss,* when physically, of course, that is not true. Ma is grateful but irritated—and Ida seems absolutely evil to Ma, an evil child, blind, and contemptible— *the mean one of the brood.*

Ma has no frivolous abandonment in her. Her blasphemy and recklessness are not frivolous; they are costly and serious constructions. *Lifelong. . . .* She is tempted socially by Ida and her kisses, and she is repelled by the temporariness and by the sense of the world Ida shows in this kind of kiss at this moment.

Ida is full of temper. Her nakedness of affection has the temper of assault: sweet raping. But rape. Her nerves, her money, her wit back her in this.

Momma writhes and shifts with inner shouts—the seeds of temper, her own—and thinks of turning her mouth over to Ida. But then she can't do it. She says, "Oh, you are chic. You are someone who travels. I have to catch my breath—"

Ida pants slightly—*comically.*

Momma, in her small-town privacies inside her, is horrified but resigned. She has never known anyone sexually who was not an astonishment—and in some ways a depressing oddity—animal-like, childish, nurseryish—and she sees in the panting that kind of overt animal mockery of the moment of intimacy. That is to say, she sees *how Ida ends her stories:* dissatisfaction and the decapitation of the favorite.

Ida wants to steal Ma—abduct her—win her from rivals, own her attention—but not only Ma—I mean Ida has a general theory of doing this—so the moment has a *publicly* romantic odor to Ma.

Ma looks pleadingly, sweetly, *virginally,* at Ida, beside her on the glider. Ma can claim sisterliness if she wants: "In some ways, we're almost twins."

"Oh, yes," says Ida, as if delighted. "Twins, certainly." She grasps Lila's hand. Such will, such fine-boned will is in Ida that Momma smiles—inside her other moods she feels she is in a schoolyard again, a girl.

Ida's sense of romance progresses by delicacies of parody—i.e., it is always two steps from the real—toward the heartier implications: commands, exploitations, secrets, alliances, bondages, rages: a display of self, an outbreak of darkness; she wants to bloom as a flower, a woman, a girl, a boy, a man. (Momma wants to bloom like that, too.) Ida names herself parodistically: "I kiss like John Gilbert, don't I? Don't you think so?"

Ma ought to say, *Oh, yes,* and lean back, and so on.

But Momma is not tamed, she is masochistic and flexible, and ashamed of that in relation to men, and crazy and vengeful as a result. Momma is crazy and vengeful freshly at every occasion of wrong. She is doing a thing: she is *blooming* as someone who cannot be tamed by sweat-mustached Ida.

She can fake being ladylike and distant from things and she can fake being commanding—she can imitate Ida. Her denial, her fakery are comic in her style. She sits facing forward, and she refuses to alter her posture.

A passionate woman being unmoved is funny.

Ida titters.

Momma dislikes comedy because of her sensibility—disgust and inner temper: a heat: distrust—these don't turn into bearable jokes for her without contempt—for herself, for everyone—and she has too much physical merit still, although less surely, to hold herself, or romance, or the possibilities of a courtship moment, in contempt.

Momma's outrageous and inwardly wretched comedy taunts Ida, who, childlike, then tugs at Ma's shoulder.

But the tug is elegant—and startling. How startling Ida tends to be. Self-loving rather than making a gesture that actually included Momma: Ida needs to be loved as the good child whose every move embodies innocence and prettiness rather than as the active doer she is.

Momma resists all force applied to herself. "No," Momma says. "Absolutely no." She is not breathing at all. Then she is breathing lightly. Then heavily. She says, gently scathing, "Eeeny, meeny, miney, mo, *I caught a Lila by the toe*—oh, Ida . . ." Then, leaning, straight-backed, at a slant away from Ida, a summing-up: "No one can count on you."

Ida, in her momentum, makes flirtatious offers of obedience: "Everyone can count on me. I am your slave—Lilly—you know that." Then, owlishly: "You know you can count on me lifelong." Then: "Ly—fff(i)ff—longgg—" The length she drew the word to was roughly the span of attention before one blinks mentally and registers what is said—it was the equivalent of five or six syllables. Her voice is not torn by love and desire—i.e., by folly. Nothing is implied of any state of feeling other than a sophisticated one—i.e., one in which it is known that *attachments come and go.* Her promise is a parody of promises, it has no human ordinariness. It has intelligence and cruelty, though, and longing.

Momma straightens her head and does this and that, and then it emerges, as in a charade, that she is *listening* in an ordinary human way: she *listens* to the promise—now a memory in the air. She is smiling dimly, unreadably, beautifully.

In the haze of illusions and realisms, female lawlessness and its codes, and female parodies, and female truths give way apparently, and Momma turns her head and smilingly, tacitly listens with the calm maternal-innocent set of her face, which then alters into a lover's wicked stare—accusing and reckless. This hint at the humiliation of the mother by the lying boarding-school seducer, Ida, is a parody, too; but her being a lover and challenging Ida, that part, is not parody, so it's all different now: it's physical and remorseless, like some affairs that kids have in high school.

That makes her *vulgar*—i.e., blunt and obvious—and sexual. This is rebellion on a giant scale, to be so local with Ida. Ma is claiming to be a more serious person than Ida by bringing in this real stuff in this championship way.

Ida is jocular about rebellion. Ida treats all claims to leadership as childish, even her own. Ida puts a small kiss—shyly—on Momma's jaw.

A gust of feeling whirls Ma around. But she is not a mother, not a child—those are not sexual beings. In this assignation, Momma's sense of what is to be done is real; Ida's taste, and sense of things, prefers the *symbolic:* the summing-up.

Ma feels that if she is *honest with herself,* she is, as a person (a sexual body and a quick mind), very little better off, if at all, with Ida's understanding than she is with S.L.'s.

Ma tugs at the tail of her bandanna. "S.L. may be in the house," she says, with almost rabid sorrow: she holds up that hoop for Ida to go through.

Ida grimaces—it's a snarl: that was stylish back then, for a stylish woman to mimic a gangster or something. See, Ma is punishing Ida by invoking "a law" that makes Ida behave. Ida grabs Lila by the elbows and says, "You Garbo!" Elusive woman. Garbo isn't married. It is *Garbo-minus,* so to speak, that Momma is. This is in Ida's face as she moves back to her chair, thwarted, probably enraged.

Lila feels somewhat lower-class, however. Momma says, "I never paid attention in school, so I'm easy to know." She says, "You want another drink? You want another sandwich?"

Ida says, "Does S.L. drink?"

"He'll be sober—when he comes around the mountain." It is truly jolting when Momma breaks her own style open and imitates Daddy with all the depth of knowledge she has of him physically.

Ida stares at her.

Lila says, "I can read your mind. I know what you're thinking." She swings her foot.

"What am I thinking?"

"That's for me to know and you to find out." Momma says it seriously, in a musical voice. Ma does not know how small-town this is, but then—with gooseflesh and a sinking in her stomach and a light beading of sweat along her back—she can tell what a mistaken device it is in Ida's opinion.

It is Homeric and not Tantric, the way the erotic and the spiritual merge in Ma; but if you use school ideas of things, the erotic is a matter of grasp and idea—that is, a demystification of feelings for the sake of excitement—and it is not spiritual at all: it is merely modern, then. Feelings reside in art and in sex but not in school, unless perceptions and illusions are counted as feelings, which is what Ida does and Ma wants to do—things coming out even, correct answers, being perfect: Ida wants those and the sense of those and the appetite for those to be counted as feelings. Ma is another *type,* but she has schoolish yearnings.

The reason school is the way it is is that in a classroom there is only one teacher, one power: a tyranny . . .

In life, there are always at least two people, or you can't call it life.

"If I said now Ida is my friend, you'd agree, but if I acted on it, woe is me, and that's where the trouble starts." Ma says this hastily, as if S.L. might walk in any moment, but then she slows down and finishes saying it in a stately, melodious way. But her mouth and eyes are sultry—are gusty with feeling; she is so complicated now that no scientific theory can be as hard to unravel as her mood is. She is epically grownup in this way.

Ida, with a curious thwacking gesture of her knees against each other, matches Momma in complexity: she may now be the most grownup person in the world. "Let's not go into what's wrong. I don't believe in diagrams," Ida says. Lightly.

Ma says, "If we were a friend to one another, I could take you for granted and you wouldn't put up with that for one second."

Ida does not dawdle when she thinks. She takes the hurdle. "That's brilliant. Your seeing that. Listen: You *can* take me for granted."

"Now?" *Now that I am brilliant.* Ma thinks Ida ought to, and will, love her *better* after today.

Ida already "loves" her—that's all been settled. Ida says in a dignified, faintly disgusted way, "I *am* your friend."

Momma says, "Then I have no say in it—" Now she sees the trap clearly.

"Lilly—"

"I say someone is my friend when I say so. If you mean one word of it, tell me—you went to Switzerland with Colleen Butterson—that was the word that went out—what was that all about? Tell me if we're good friends now."

"Lilly—" Ida says, in a whole other voice. *Don't be silly. Don't break the law* (of discretion).

Ma bursts into an angry laugh—angry because she doesn't want to be *sidestepped.* "You want me to sign a blank check. We have rules around here—and no one makes them up." *She* makes them up, is what that means.

Ma knows *from experience* that the truth now between her and Ida (the atmosphere of *rich* equality) is that Momma is a fool for trying to impose her own sense of truth on a woman as firm-hearted as Ida.

Ida says, in an intelligently threatening (and wanly disillusioned) voice, "We don't give pledges, Lilly. We trust each other." A different law. A notion of law different from Lila's. Then: "Are we mad?" Ida says, summing up and taking over. "No. Yes." A witty joke. A party atmosphere. It is clear that in some ways Ida is a nicer person than Lila is. Than my mother.

Momma laughs. "*I like* the rain," she says naughtily—it's an intentionally clumsy imitation of Ida.

Ida doesn't laugh right away. Momma starts to breathe *defiantly;* and she says meaningfully (her way), "It makes my pioneer hair frizzy."

"Oh, Lila," Ida says, relieved. Then she laughs.

Lila's self-satisfaction begins to glow again. "I can't keep up with you," she complains. A touch of wit, maybe.

Neither has the sought-for command of the erotic at this juncture, but that works out in Ma's favor, since Ma can live in erotic chaos and Ida can't.

Momma's momentum carries her along: "I've lived my life in small towns. You have Paris and St. Louis."

Ida stares for a small second, locating what is meant, getting the point. Ida says, "What is wanting in Alton is naughtiness—madness—but there's not much more in St. Louis. You'd find it dull, Lila."

Lila thinks of Ida's excitements and naughtiness as being open to her now as soon as she *learns the passwords If I bother.* Momma smiles faintly—maternally. Ma pants: *It is an effort to keep up with Ida—she's a real flier.* "I'm not a dreamer," Momma says aloud, almost idly, commenting on the contest.

Ida says, "It must be terrible to be without daydreams. We would die in this town without our—don't repeat this—*wickedness.*"

Momma suddenly blows Ida a kiss. Everyone knows that Ida always gets even. Then Momma rises: a swirl of heat—the thin, finely curved legs, the pale, night-framed face, the paled, used lipstick (from drinking and smoking), the extreme prettiness of the woman—gusts around the porch. Ma hears a thump like that of a car door—she lifts her head toward the porch roof—then she swiftly bends over and kisses Ida on the mouth: light, quick, and real. A real kiss which can break the heart of the one who receives it and of anyone who sees it. "You are a hero, Lila," Ida says.

With a swish of her skirt, Ma turns and walks back to the glider and sits down. She says, "Well, there, I don't feel inferior now, no matter how smart you are, Ida."

Ida moistens her lips for the first time. She smiles dimly—her eyes are filmed or curtained.

"You look Jewish like that," Ma says.

Ida smiles more widely, complicatedly. Her eyes are in focus.

Ma says, "Let's wait and see if the house shakes." She means from S.L.'s footsteps on the wooden floors. She finds the noises men make menacing: they twang at her nerves.

The rain falls weightily.

Ma says, "We have another minute or two to be friends in."

SPRING FUGUE

The first orchestral realization that something is up: Playing Vivaldi's "The Four Seasons" on a spavined CD player. It was a gray day in early February and the sun came out; and I was thinking, "The Dry Cleaners, The Dry Cleaners, The Dry Cleaners, The Dry Cleaners."

The first crocus: The Sunflower Market, Thai Vegetables and Seeds, 2809 Broadway, February 14th. Spindly and snow-flecked.

First cold, March 19th–April 2nd. My wife and I are on our way to our accountant's. On the way I see two drunks fighting in front of the OTB on Broadway at Ninety-first; April is the duelists' month. Tacitly flirting with my wife, I carry two small packets of Kleenex in my pockets—one for her, because of her allergies: she makes a small nifty nasal piccolo announcement of the annual change in her life. I make the second really bad pun of the season: We sound like Bruce Springsteen and accompanist doing Bach's "The Cold Bug Variations."

First episode of spring nosiness not having to do with allergies or nose-blowing: I don't know why the soul's primary mechanics should

consider spying or snooping a natural attribute of renewed life, but in
the office icebox I see a small gold-colored can, shaped like a shoe-
polish can, of caviar, and I wonder, jealously, who is so happy and so
bent on celebration (or self-indulgence), but when I open it, it is
empty, and written on the bottom of the can, in pencil, is the phrase
Hard Cheese.

First philosophical guess: My guess is that spring is a natural way of
suggesting adolescence as something one should start to go through
again: genetic duty and genetic activity *are* romance. Hmm. . . .
Nature is as tricky as any politician.

The thought of George Bush leads to The First Depression of the
Season.

First emotional detail: More light on the windowsill.

First piece of strange advice to one's self: *Lighten up.*

First symptom of intellectual confusion (on waking after dreams of
fair women and of various unspeakable acts with them; memory, those
astonishing chambers of lost realities, becomes overactive, leaving a
broad sensation of gambling. . . . Roué-lette): The enumeration of the
bedroom furnishings—a nightstand, one-night stand, two-night
stands, three-night stands. . . .

No, no.

In the bathroom, first session practicing smile.

First impulse of active love: A sloppy kiss while my wife is putting on
her shoes.

She gazes at me. "Oh, it's spring," she says.

Shopping list for first three-day weekend in the country to rent a house
for the summer: Contac, Kleenex, Beatles tape, citronella candles (to
leave in the rented house if we find it), jump rope (for losing weight),

walking shoes, jeans one size too small (to force oneself to diet), a handful of short-lived cut lilac to carry in the car as an *aide-mémoire*. . . .

First equinoctial death shudder and racial memory of human sacrifice for the sake of warmth and the return of summer: A roadkill on 32A outside of Saugerties—a no longer hibernating but probably still torpid, thin woodchuck.

Second such event after returning home: Cutting my thumb while using a new, Belgian, serrated-edge slicing knife that slipped on a small Israeli tomato, while I was thinking about Super Tuesday two years ago and whistling Dixie.

Am I unconsciously Angry?

First hysterical delusion: Advertised medicines that come to mind when seeing in a moment of stress spring flowers in the mind—Nuprin-yellow jonquils, tetracycline-colored tulips (red-and-yellow ones). Tylenol-colored clouds (Tylenol is Lonely T spelled backward). Advil-colored dirt. Theragran-M-colored drying blood.

With my hand betoweled and my soul a little mad with pessimism about the current ways we live, and with gaiety, heroism, and the spring wound, I phone my wife at her office. She makes more money than I do.

Advice, sympathy, *information* from my wife's assistant while I am waiting for my wife to end a meeting. It is possible that even the assistant makes more money than I do. (I am a schoolteacher.) She says that in the stores is a helping-the-blood-clot-and-disinfectant-and-anesthetic spray; and there are clutch bandages. But: "Beware," she says, "the spray depletes the ozone layer, and the clutch bandage harms circulation." The finger may turn Nuprin-yellow, crocus-yellow, coward's yellow.

The conversation with my wife is out of a melodramatic domestic novel, except that at work she is Nietzschean. I refer to her being possessed by the will-to-power.

My wife says, "How deep is the cut?"

"I think I see the bone."

She says, "Do you see any white?"

"Yes."

"That's the tendon. Bones aren't white while you're still alive. They're not white until you clean them after you rob them from a grave. You may have cut the tendon. Can you move it?"

"No. Yes. It looks like a bone."

"It isn't the bone. But there are nerves in there—"

"Is that true? That's not just hypochondria?"

"You should be able to see only one nerve, unless it's a really big cut—do you see it?"

"See the nerve?"

"It's a thing, it's visible."

"What does it look like?"

"A thread. Does it make you sick to look at the wound?"

"No. What makes you think that?"

"Well, take a look and tell me what you see."

There is a silence and then she calls out, "Hey, hey, hey."

"I fainted a little. I'm sort of on my knees here. Hold on, let me get up. Whoo, that was stupid. What I saw was gray-white; there's quite a lot of gray-white. I suppose I saw blood but it looked gray-white and blood isn't gray-white, it's bluish, I remember, I—"

"You're in shock. Is there anyone with you?"

"I was cutting a tomato."

"Yes?"

"Someone is coming over—someone will be here soon. You. But you can't come home. You're at work. Should I go get a clotting spray?"

"Go to the emergency room at the hospital. You did this call?"

"I don't remember," I say miserably.

"You cut your thumb?"

"Yes. I guess so. Unless this is all a dream," I say hopefully.

"Did you dial with your left hand?"

"I wrapped my hand in a towel and I squeezed the towel with the

other hand. I dialed with my little finger. It's touch-tone, the phone
is. . . . I think."

"I forget if there are large numbers on the touch-tone phone or
small ones."

"Tiny, really."

"Are they stubborn or easy?"

"Stubborn."

"Then if you dialed and didn't bleed all over the phone you're
probably O.K."

"Would you say you were showing sympathy?"

"You may quiver with madness and shock at my saying this, but I
promise that if you stay overnight at the hospital I will bring you volumes of Kundera, Solzhenitsyn, Havel, so you can see what horror and
suffering truly are."

"Shit."

"On the other hand, our Maltese doorman's sister-in-law died of
sepsis after a knife cut in her hand which she got chopping beets when
she was visiting her mother-in-law in Valletta. Wait for me. I'm coming home."

My wife is a Spring Goddess. A Nietzschean Nightingale (Florence).
"Here," she says. "Let me look. . . . A kiss won't make that well. Let's
go." A kiss or two later, as we pass a homeless guy who at first I think
is me in the third person hailing a taxi, and as my shock begins to lift,
I say to her, sadly, "When I was a child, I had a Swiss barometer with
a wooden house on it. The house had two doors. Out of one came a boy
in shorts and with a Tyrolean hat on, and I think a girl in a dirndl
came out of the other. They went inside if it was going to rain."
Nowadays I suppose you might have a homeless person carved in
wood and sleeping on a subway grating to indicate good weather and
going into an arcade or a subway to indicate rain.

Some prose written after the third kiss from her (and after the doctor
took three stitches in my thumb). I sit at her desk in her office look-

ing out her large window: Give me the huge actual clouds of the
Republic and not the meager udders of water vapor painted on the old
backdrops the Republic Studios used in John Wayne's day. We like
the actual big baggy clouds of a New York spring. One doesn't want
to flog a transiting cloud to death, but if we are to have sentimental
light, let us have it at least in its obvious local form—dry, white, sere,
and, I guess, provincial. The spiritual splendor of our drizzly and
slaphappy spring weather, our streets jammed with sneezing pedestri-
ans, our skies loony with bluster are our local equivalents of lilac
hedges and meadows.

Blustery, raw, and rare—and more wind-of-the-sea-scoured than
half-melted St. Petersburg. Yuck to cities that have an immersed-in-
swamp-and-lagoon moist-air light. They are for watercolorists.
Where water laps at the edges of the stones and bricks of somewhat
wavery real estate is not home. Home is New York, stony and tall: its
real estate is real.

So is its spring.

WHAT I DO FOR MONEY

At dawn, in the suffusion of light and return of visibility, in the woods where I camped out on my red-and-blue air mattress in a nylon shed-tent, open in front and partly at the sides and with a now luminous rooflet tied overhead to two guardian trees, I woke. The light and mist among the tree trunks, the near silence of the birds, the biological, organic clutter around me on the ground softened my mood.

I have a streak of biological piety. These are my woods, set high in the northern Catskill Mountains, not very high mountains. They are not very old woods, any more than are the woods in the adjacent state park. All this territory was lumbered over twice in the last two hundred years. In this glade, only two trees are particularly large, and one is a sycamore planted a hundred years ago and one is a pine about the same age.

The light makes the blue nylon a holy color, like a tone in a Bellini painting, like the color of a cloak of the Madonna; it is a glowing, Bellini blue, and it fills me with awe. The side of the mountain that descends, that falls, is on my right. Behind the descending columns of trunks of trees—saplings, and older, bigger trees—is a vast space of now luminous, as-if-new air. . . . In a harsh world, this silent, glowing beauty, this ordinary, momentary prettiness, is, as I said, a speechless, pagan piety.

Suddenly fully wakeful, straightening my clothes, lighting my spirit stove, I contemplate my situation. I light a cigarette; I am a dying man. I have an inoperable brain tumor. The process of finding this out took nearly two months. And I am being let go at work, in a harsh process—the company has been sold and is losing money or not making enough; the errors have been those of top management, some of whom are being let go as well. I am one step down from top management, and my work on this level has been successful—in the general debacle this has aroused jealousy, rage really, even hatred. I may have been too distracted by the headaches I was having to handle things well. Was I arrogant? No. I was rather meek and apologetic. But I went on being right, and lo, a vicious war.

I am thirty-five years old, divorced, not estranged from my children, but they are turning into people very like my wife, whom I don't miss. It is a kind of programmatic, thought-out, mind-filled selfishness, a self-willed sort, not shallow, not stupid, not even cold: more like an intelligent Episcopalian tantrum among theories of selflessness and God knows what all. I mean it is this in my ex-wife and children that isolates me.

I don't know how bad any of this makes me feel. I have a brain tumor. I have sliding films of headache and sporadic interferences with vision. I suppose I have despised my bosses for a long time now, thought them amateur and self-loving, hardly honest in relation to the work of running a large company. I suppose I have despised—and forgiven—my ex-wife for as long. I don't think I have been disloyal to any of them, not very much, not very often. But I'm not on the whole a careful man, and I become frantic inwardly—it is a moral uproar—when I am, I suppose, conceitedly convinced that I can see the wastage, the extent of the bad decisions, the crude wrecking of lives and possibilities in others—which they are egoistically, obstinately set on causing . . . that corporate and *suburban* selfishness.

I am said to be lucky, but the work I do—product design, but at the point where such design is redone to become industrially and commercially practicable—and its quality, the things I'm after, are insulting to some people. . . . Or perhaps it's just competition. I have been aware of this, told about this since college. And in college. And long before that, in grade school. I have been able to adjust and to protect myself to some extent until now, but last year I began to slip. The tumor. Destiny melting my mind, maybe. Probably.

Anyway, I am being treated shabbily, filthily by former allies and colleagues. They sweat and tremble, but they say, "We want you to leave. . . . We don't think this last idea of yours is any good." Then they take it back and say, "It's good, but you'll have to work with Martin. . . ." I have never worked with Martin Jones: he's an ambitious little madman, a cheap thief—of ideas, of office supplies, of money, when he can manage it. He's the keeper of the little escort book—he's the upper-echelon pimp. With the bribes he offers and the inside information he gets and his tirelessness and the pity he purposefully arouses—he is always either ill or suffering a domestic tragedy—he is irresistible on a certain level. He is pudgy and pretentious, clever and whiny, repulsive, even loathsome. But he makes even that work in his favor. He himself boasts that he is tirelessly rotten—violent. . . . That's his way of saying: *Fear me.* Everyone in the office does fear him except for the two operating officers at the top. Martin became obsessed with me just before the collapse of profits. He is determined to gain control of my working life—this is the man I have to deal with now. Surely they know this is forcing me out. Does everyone eat shit who earns a salary? Does everyone who eats shit insist that everyone else eat more shit?

Little Phil Moore, the short one, the coked-up one, at one time a friend—I brought him to these woods—he is working with Martin, the horror Pimp, co-opted or willingly. He came to my office and said, "You worked us over. . . . You're putting us through hoops. . . . You don't like us: you want to leave." Claiming innocence for him and

Martin. He's just doing his job. And he's working out his ego in putting the squeeze on me. Well, he's partly right. I *want* to leave. But I didn't initiate my leaving. They have to give me severance.

They are half afraid of me—of the stink I might cause. I am half enraged. Tired. But they are not afraid enough of me, and the negotiation over severance pay has been difficult verging on nightmare. Martin, the horror Pimp, has no fear of lying; he lies to any extent. He farts and talks stupidly and calls me at four in the morning to say he has a discarded memo of mine speaking of my resignation. He speaks in a false voice. He uses being disgusting—and silly—to drive someone like me out of a fight. I lose my will to fight Mr. Protozoan Slime. It is not like tussling with Achilles; there is no honor anywhere in the moments of such a struggle. And he is proud of himself.

He has asked me to give in because we are both Presbyterian. He's said, "We stick together, don't we, we white men?" The issue is whether I'll take less money and vamoose and let him win. Or try to work with him in the time I have left. Or I can sell these woods and hire a severance negotiator. But I don't want to sell these woods, these moments of light. Ah, Christ.

I actually feel a little rested, refreshed, prepared physically for the day, for anything that happens, for everything that is existent, including death. I feel I understand the violence of the world. *Egos are involved . . .* what a dread phrase *. . . in the procedures of unreason.* I've lived a long time in relation to the weird unreason of others. But this moment is colored by the softness of the morning air, wilderness air, and mountain light, and the odor of trees and rock. I have the energy to be *serious* or *unserious . . . savagely indignant* or *mordant. . . .* The energy, the clearheadedness . . . In the office, as in any sport, I have to be like *them,* the opponents, in order to do battle or to deal with them, in order to come up with useful tactics and the requisite language noises.

God, office politics. They have eaten up my life. My chief strength in the world (such as it has been until now) is to be snotty and airy toward ugliness, is to skate right by it. It is treacherous toward democracy for me to be snotty and airy about it in relation to my colleagues, although it is patriotic to find America beautiful after all, or before all. Treacherous to my colleagues, whom I despise. I don't give a fuck about anything they give a fuck about. Except perhaps money.

I am between marriages. I suppose I should think about my two children. I come to the woods in order not to think about them. I don't know how much of my death I want to share with my children. I don't like to hide things from them. But I do cold-bloodedly think of and warm-bloodedly feel the massive, tantrum-y selfishness my ex-wife has encouraged in them. Actually, she told me she would do that if I did not return to her. *What do I care about them? You know how selfish I am, Hank,* she said. Do you suppose she would want me now, on the skids and tumorous? I don't want to die with her. I can teach charitably or I can charitably empty bedpans for the short rest of my life, if I get enough money from the firm. The life I have left will be better if I accept the need to be sly steadily, with daily regularity: *Dearest, tell me, do I look blankly friendly? Can you tell me if I give off a hint of menacing slyness? Do I appear to be a good citizen?* My life would go better, but I would sicken and die even faster than I am sickening and dying now, and doesn't dying free you from the need to accept the world any longer?

I went to a country wedding once—a Methodist minister's son married a pretty girl in an agonizingly pretentious stone chapel upstate. Built on the shore of a lake in a grove of birches, the chapel was pretty in a horrendously striving, American way—self-consciously Christian, trying for tradition. It had some architectural quality but not a quality of spiritual exercise and no aura from generations of belief. It was not pure with the hope of God, like the wooden churches visible across the lake from it. The morning had been rainy. The rain stopped just as we settled ourselves in church; the sun came out; the turn-of-the-century stained-glass windows began to glow effulgently in a kind of harsh American glory of light.

The first bridesmaid down the aisle had a two-year-old child who would not leave her or let her march without him, and so the woman marched carrying a bouquet in one hand with a child balanced on her hip and held by her other hand—a different bouquet. She marched with a curiously mild, unassertive, consciously lovely, almost sated-but-frantic air down the aisle in the overwhelming light.

Is it a fate to have been happy?

Here is another definition of a life I have not lived. At a night club upstate that wedding weekend, an oldish and overweight, gray-haired woman with an obvious paunch and a white violin and a back-up band sang and fiddled a song that she had written. She sang and chanted that she could get everyone to dance: "I'll make you wild. . . ." She sang and chanted it. She had set her amplifiers at some high register and every-thing she did was loudly amplified, a bit thunderous and a bit shrill with electronic treble, electronic tremble. She was loud, hypnotic, gifted, and her insistence was inspired in its way, that she could make us wild. . . . Dionysiac. And people did begin to dance. The woman became more and more suggestive, dirty, and commanding, in a some-how Scotch-Irish way that was *gypsylike* and irresistible. It was also part of the American backwoods, the camp meetings, the harvest festivals.

Everyone in the audience, in the crowd, who was not crippled or arthritic—the drunken midlifers and the eighty-year-olds and the stoned younger ones, countryside working class—danced stiffly wildly. We were whitely and self-consciously orgiastic. In a somewhat consciously traditional way and as rebels as well. The sexual self-revelations, such as they were, suited the room and the lake. And explained the privacy of clubs and summer places. Explained my par-ents' summertime snobbery, explained night clubs and lakeside resorts in a new and somewhat comic way, a touching way, with a sense of kinship. All the things I have not lived were present. I never was Dionysian.

Bad news, broken heart, absurd tension. Still, the light among the trees and the fragments of sky, pale, glowing blue like the nylon over my head with the light in it, say it will be a pretty day. *Je m'en fout-isme*—I-don't-give-a-damn-ism: is that the note I whistle? From the time I was old enough and strong enough to have my own way at least partly, even as a boy, I have insisted on living part of each day, a moment or two, without suffering. And without cold willfulness. A civilized moment or two of freedom and of emotion.

I bought this land last year, five acres; four are wooded and steep and set among gray, lichenous rocks and closed in by a forty-foot rock face and a lower, sloping meadow—small, less than an acre, and ringed with hemlocks—and in the woods between the meadow and these rocks a small, green, wooden, three-room house with three porches and a steep, wood-shingled roof and summer-camp shutters.

I would like to do a tree census—find out how many trees I own, how many branches, how many twigs and leaves. And bugs. A quarter of a million leaves. A million leaves . . . I am a millionaire of rustling leaves . . . of grass blades. Of molecules of air . . . I own the air I breathe at this minute. Cubic yards of air, invisible stones of a luminous temple.

What are the statistics? Seventy-five maples, eighty beeches, seventeen oaks, seven junior oaks, seven hemlocks including one, uh, picturesque giant. And so on. But I am inventing that. Sitting now on a log, drinking coffee, having a death-time cigarette, sitting on my red-and-blue air mattress, I look around at the uneven ground and nearby cliff, the trees that grew against the rock and that are fastened to the rock, leafy pilasters. The scattered and decaying leaves on the ground. The trees I own are not quite singular for me; they are *trees,* a generalized mass: *my trees.* Do you suppose God is this way about souls? I haven't named any of my trees. In the morning light, I look around— *the leaner, the life-is-a-beech, the straight-up maple near the boundary line to the east, the birch society, a crooked copse.* . . . Those aren't names of long-term affection. The feelings I have toward them are half-baked, inchoate, are unlike any feeling I have had toward animals or people or things . . . the patient, fluttering trees . . . A wind is springing up, stirs my semi-named, half-nameless trees. . . . A blur of vegetation,

branches thickened to the eye by their motion, the cinder roses of
shadow move on the ground. . . . The terms come from a Spanish
poem: the smear of vegetation . . . cinder roses. . . . Thought stops.
The great invisible chain links of mountain wind lash at my woods. I
listen with abrupt, incredible simplicity to the sound of that wind,
the forceful and shifting exercise of the morning wind. All around me
spread shivering whorls of tethered shadows, an infinity of motions of
a million twigs. The world is active and stirs eccentrically and
rustlingly, stirs differently in the blond, sunlit upper air and in the
more constrained greenish lower air. Nature has said, *I will make the
tethered trees wild.*

Dionysiac release? I suppose so. A rehearsal for the release of seeds.
An invisible embrace. The motion of the mountainside.

Clouds, too, are a smear, they move so rapidly in the wind. Capi-
talism has a spiritual side—a pagan spiritual side and a Christian
one, one of self-examination and of values, of truths beyond truths.
And it has a civilly spiritual side: a keep-your-house-pretty side, a
wear-the-right-clothes side. The responsibility for the condition of
the immediate world is clearly placed, whether the community uses
its knowledge of such identifiable responsibility with intelligence or
not. These trees will outlive me unless I become thoroughly a capi-
talist or a destructive dying man, rampantly assertive, and have them
lumbered.

I control the fate of the trees rustling in a morning wind, in the
shudder of the air. The cinder roses of the skidding and fluttering and
whirling shadows are sometimes like the splashed gray letters of a
restless alphabet slipping over rocks and dead branches on the ground,
over wild grass in the meadow, grass stained reddish here and there by
reddish seed heads, with yellow and white wildflowers visible among
the grasses. A dry stream, over moss, sedum, tansy, goutweed, bluets,
wild mustard, and wild phlox, rockets in openings among the trees.
Shadows and leaves in their vegetable and aerial life move over me in
a profound sweetening of the moment.

My life is a mess; yet I am fairly happy. Perhaps unfairly. I can't say I understand happiness. In my case it always has an uncaring, what-the-hell element and is a form of dizzied satisfaction that is unfeeling at its center, freed from feeling, almost a cry of *enough*. The sense of completion is like a satisfaction with its spine of shameful triumph . . . of peace and escape. It is shallow of me and in my blood—an old traditional thing—and it is the deepest and most savage emotion I ever have, it is the deepest part of me, to be happy. It is based on my ignoring an important number of things, but I have a rebellious nature of this sort. In a pagan sense it is a serious business to be happy.

This is absurd, this sequence of thoughts. How far would I go morally, toward death, how far did I go, to own my so far unnamed, not deeply known trees? If I want money now, I have to think harder about how to negotiate, how to handle *cleverly* the situations that will establish the amount of money I will have while I die. I have to figure out how to put the fear of God into the pimp-Jones and the rat-Moore.

I will probably do what is necessary—what part of my soul do I want to save at this point? What do I care about? When I was a child, no one told me what life was actually like. . . . I wish I had been told. Now I am waiting while the wind mumbles and stammers, twitches, as if it were alive and standing still, an immense, transparent ruminant-acrobat, a glass creature resting from its stampede of a moment ago. I wait for it to return, the large, invisible, active, somersaulting mountain wind among the trees in my wood. The brief, embracing wind.

Death? Ugliness? Who gives a goddamn fuck? Who gives a good goddamn fuck? Here it comes, the first transparent steps—and leaps—of the wind among the trees.

RELIGION

In the end I guess at him. I use a-sense-of-things. In a kind of clouded gray space inside my head, I guess at him. I probably can't do this, guess at him and be right.

We are silent, one day, Jass and I, after doing dares—daring each other to *shinny* up the pipe-frame of the row of swings in Jackson Park, riding the swing up and over the bar. Then I stood on the ground and held Jass on my shoulders while he threw the swings back over the bars. He was agreeable to us covering our tracks.

We lay sprawled on the itchy grass in that park. It seems too intense to mention the odors of the ground, of the season. Such sensory reality was part of being that age, being boys. Jass's unreliable comradeship, today's fate of the world, the fate of the world so far, and us, him and me, lying on the grass and the odors of the grass are mixed together, unalterably.

Intense rivalry is infatuation of a kind, a sensitivity to the whole *shebang* of the other person because you want to win. I never started conversations or said things without being asked. He seems more bold.

He as if moves in a field or meadow or big schoolyard of such holding back in me. He asks, "Are you scared to think about being dead?"

"I don't know."

"Come on. Imagine yourself buried."

After a moment: "Naw. I don't want to."

I'm not always aware of color. If I relax, I feel a creeping suffusion of color into the day: blue sky, white clouds, oddly various, changeable greens—as if color itself were nervous and changeable—and greenish shadows on largely pinkish-white-beige-ocher Jass, the topography of the boy's face. I *like* the existence of language, but aural color is different from visual color. It smacks of magic, and real color is just the world.

I asked Jass, "Are you frightened of being hurt—in the body?"

I had an adolescent voice: an infatuation and uncertainty toward issues of courage.

Then I hear him. First, the sound. Then the hidden mathematician-thinker-spy called memory deals with what he says and makes it orderly.

He said, "I don't know. I don't mind it."

"You don't get frightened?"

"I'm not afraid *of being hurt.*"

I recognized that he had a manner of insensitivity and dry boldness, but it was only a manner, and it seemed sensitive and cagey in its way.

It frightened me back then, that he—and other kids—knew what they thought. I had to think a long time to know what I thought.

I said, shielding my eyes, "I'm not *frightened* about dying."

I get up. I stand on the sloping and somewhat faintly spinning disk-like floor of park grass, tree roots.

"I have to go home."

In a more clearly sequential movement than mine, he got up. He has a tensed, wry, small smile—nice—*friendly-for-the-moment*. In real life, if someone wants to talk or walk or whatever with you, it can be very moving.

We walk maybe twenty yards, and then he starts taking giant steps as in Simple Simon. I start to walk with large Boy Scout hiking strides. Then, after a little while, he starts to hop; he hops up a slope in the small park and onto a six-lane boulevard, Delmar. I speed up and push him into the rear of a passing bus, and I hurry on, not worrying if he is hurt or not. I am deep inside my innocence. I hop past stone walls and up a steeply sloping macadam-and-pebble street in front of a stone church in a neighborhood of large houses. Then he passes me. Then we're running, racing. He's the faster sprinter. He sprints and slows, sprints and slows. I can outlast him in a mile, but he suddenly sprints far ahead, and I give up and start to walk. He's ten, fifteen yards ahead of me. He waits for me to draw near him. He's not breathing hard. I am. We're near the intersection of two winding, tree-lined, lawn-skirted, large-house-lined suburban streets, a perspectival crucifix, empty of movement. When we cross the street, the scene assumes a faintly wheeling spoked motion. I am partly still out of breath.

Jass holds his arms out in the attitude of the crucifixion. He says, "Do you dislike Jesus?"

I start to count out loud, "Wuhin, tooo(eee), three-uh, foerrrr, fi-i-i(ve)—"

"Whu-it ehr-are yuh-oo dooooinbn Wo/ih/hileeee?" Wiley, my name. It is odd, what actual voices, unidealized, are like in the real air of a real day.

"I'm counting—if I count to seventeen, I get to see God."

"No shit? *Honest to-ooo Gohw-idd—aw-er yew gointa see Gawh-dddd(uh) now?*"

"It's not a swindle, asshole. I'm not asking you for anything."

Jass believes the world is tricky. "Are you going to see God here—right now—in University City? On Melbourne?" The name of the street.

"Nahuhhhhhhh. I won't see God if you're here. Wait: *now, there He is . . .*"

"You masturbate too much," Jass says, and hits me on the arm, the side of the shoulder, hard. This is a very quiet neighborhood. The intersection is silent, is empty. He looks at me from a distance. "Admit it," he says.

He is notorious for talking dirty in the locker room and for doing dirty things and getting everyone else to do them. I shake my head.

He says abruptly, addressing my (comparative) *purity:* "You—and Winston Churchill . . ." Noble and unnecessarily ambitiously disciplined.

Then he jumps me and we are wrestling. He is further into exerting himself to win than I expected—the strained, wrestlingly moving, tensed-and-taut physical weight and will are a shock, are dismaying—he is right on me, right on top, like an animal, his braced haunches and physical mass, the fleshiness, wriggling *tautly* with wild, would-be-victorious purpose.

I hammer him in the face, saying, "Don't you *ever* think about *ideals?*"

He is forcing my arms down. He looms over me. He demands with a surprising amount of breath and only a little breathlessness, "What are you thinking about now? Are you looking for God?"

I frighteningly turn and twist. We're leery of the ways we each think the other is a nut. We're as if dressed in spikes to keep feelings off us. They leap bodilessly on us all the time anyway, feelings that seem like cat-family moods, dog moods, horse moods.

"I have Christian ideals," he says, still breathless, sitting on me, suffocating me.

I am startled when people are themselves and are not my thoughts of them.

I find fighting with someone shocking, dispurifying: it dirties the very air, the very envelope of the world. I half expect birds to fall from the sky, poisoned.

"Shit, get off me," I said, close to madness. He and I both know I am dangerous despite all my precautions.

He had me pinioned. He watched me in a peculiar way—with a haughtiness-of-a-sort. "It's all bullshit," he says. And he gets up.

I see as if down a hallway and through a partway-open door; I see something-or-other in him and me: some of what I see becomes words, although not entirely or clearly. We used to wonder if we would find it easy to kill, to lead others, to be commanders. He said that that was bullshit but he asked, too, if it was bullshit, but he wasn't asking *me*.

He was willing to accept the distance between souls. I don't think he knew yet if such isolation as he felt was incurable. He's asking for company—companionship—something. But he doesn't trust me, and he wants to be the winner. Having released me, he stands, and I see the sunlight on his forehead and nose, a subtle armor protecting him from nothing.

"Maybe it is all bullshit, *cocksucker*," I say.

I admired Jass. I was pretty sure he would be admired anywhere in the world he went—admired and pitied . . . *the beautiful sand-colored one.*

I drew on my studies and I said, in order to be nice—a degree of clement attention: "If I combine *original* and *primary* . . . I get *originary*. Do you know, does the originary *real* world *matter?*"

He shrugged. No one at school ever gave away what he or she really felt (truly thought) to anyone, not really. Or the details of what he or she *knew*. Jass maybe wanted to play at *serious talk* or *intelligent talk* (the latter was the term used by somewhat better-bred kids).

The sport, the actual dimensions of the game here, has to do with power, real power in real sunlight. He wants to know which levers control fear and death and being amused in the world. He wanted to be like me but not completely like me, not a Jew—not haunted. This is a moment of my education that mattered, this knowing myself head-on from him and also from inside me, two ways at the same time, glaringly and with a blur so that I squinted.

His actual face in sunlight—and then the air and light at yet another intersection, at the high point of this enclave of houses, yet another perspectival drooping and curving crucifix lined with well-tended palaces—are part of a moment raw with limited and eccentric friendliness. It wasn't perfect.

He said, "Do you believe in Heaven?"

"No. Do you?"

"Yes."

"Why?"

"Why not?" Silence. He said, "I think *Heaven* is a great thought."

"Are you serious?" It was good to be tactful if someone was serious about some pious matter or other.

"I'm serious," he said with his eyelids half shut—that meant he was lying, but not entirely. So did him having his eyes wide, wide open and fixed directly on you, which he did next.

I asked, "Are you being sarcastic?"

"You're the one who's sarcastic."

"You are! You're being sarcastic!"

"You're looking at yourself."

"No, I'm not." I started to laugh exasperatedly. He didn't really know how to talk about a subject.

"What's so funny?" he said.

"Your Adam's apple is funny," I said.

The present-tense eyes of the Protestant boy have a quality of well-practiced, frigidly hot attentiveness. His is the best attention I know at this point in school. He takes athletic, picayune, little breaths; he listens with no real movements of his eyes. They have a quality of male will—sort of. Focused, his eyes have, when they look at you, a mocking, American love letter thing—upper middle class, suburban Protestant, deadpan and intelligent.

In the hovering fatedness of any exchange, he says, "Kiss my ass."

I say to him, "Boy, what crap you hand out."

Did you ever feel betrothed in your youth to the heat of your present-tense reality, to the slippery and sliding *focus* on *trying to talk*—something like that? At yet another intersection, I had a sense of falling, of losing mental control, and my eyes blurred in the all-ways-dimensional now, the mind's and the world's great sea, the afternoon light. Real eyes are really real. It is impossible to *think* your way through moments spent with someone else.

In eight years, Jass will be killed in aerial combat in Korea, because his Sabre jet hadn't yet been fitted with an afterburner—it was something of a scandal. He had sent me a postcard a month or so before: *Dear Smart Guy: Guess what? Now I'm as smart as you . . .*

What do you feel and think when you lose out in an aerial combat for real, when it is going to kill you—is it chagrin you feel? Do you have a sudden knowledge of yourself?

Jass breathes with athletic artfulness. His powers of physical improvisation were really considerable. "Shit," he says. Then: "Shut up."

"Sure," I said, uncertain-eyed, but haughty. I know he likes to hurt people. *He likes to play around.*

He says, "The way you talk is stupid. Are you an honest person?"

I can't untangle the mockery, or figure out the seriousness.

Syllables in their purposes alight—like geese in a dimly lit yard with a masked whisper and rush, caught air, materialized, aerial—*what-he-says*—what he said never amounted to much. Interplay blows you this way and that. Meanings, obscene, nonsensical. Incomplete. *I can't handle him.*

His rough, mocking gaze drags across my cheeks and eyes. He jumps on me again. We are arguing this way—about beliefs. We are studying affection. This was not particularly intelligent. "Let's have a truce," I say. The moment, the smells when he throws me down, the smells of dirt and of grass, have a hotly defeated, presence-of-another-will quality of defeat. Warm, rough, dirty . . .

He moves off me. And we stand up, and arrange our clothes, and he says: "You're so fancy. *Jews* are always so fancy."

"Cut it out," I say.

"Scissors, scissors," he says, nonsensically.

It is all nonsensical. No part of it was ever final enough to make sense.

WAKING

When I was a child, at a certain moment, I woke in a different house made of wood. The slow movement of my eyelids, whispering and scraping, in tiny lurchings, tickled me. A sense of the disorder of the wicked vaudeville, the foul inventiveness of pain kept me uneasy, so that I was as if crouched. I have been ill.

It is almost light. The child is in pain; he lies half in, half out of an abominable breath-bag. The ill child watches in a feverishly illiterate way the slow oozing of the increase in light. Inside the delicacy of the uneducated stare, soft, opened, lightly fluttering, the pallor of consciousness, tampered with by pain, observes, anyway, the shimmer of the advance of the light.

After a while, cool and flighty, mindless cousinhood to sense breaks out—the first time in weeks, but then after a while it passes into spasms of sweaty apprehension, of waiting for the pain—of madness—in its criminal mysteriousness to return and blind me. This continues and doesn't worsen: that it doesn't worsen puts a weird and private jollity on his face. The recognized thump and rattle of a window frame, a dull, tremulous bass, and the rapid soprano twitterings of the glass panes in the mullions make the child twitch; then the noise takes on a weight of the familiar; it is beautiful with monotony; it persists.

Then pale-gray and yellow and pink fragments of light appear and slowly unbud, until I am embiered by rose after rose of unlikely light in a room filled with morning. The light is palpably warm. It warms and regulates my soul ungeometric with madness. The child gags and stutters in his breathing. My hand, a childish hand, burns and aches; it has a wind inside it, under it; it moves; it unfurls. The child stiffens in uneasy dominion over this phenomenon of his unfamiliar body. See, he has been ill a long while. The hesitations of thin, unstable, brown-papery, rustling minutes are a matter of steep consciousness for him. Mother-shoulders of air hold pinkish and silvery dabs of light aloft— prismatic dust—and the child persists in his truancy from grief. In the blurred flourish of mind in naming this light as light, as if it were the light in the other house, the child unmovingly romps, dizzied with illness, in a marvelous fluster of intellectual will. Consciousness does not dare call the roll of who is living and who is dead, because the disorganized child-life behind the blindly seeing spy holes of my face is so shaky.

My dead mother was fond of me. Which one of us is lost now? Lila, my adoptive mother, will someday say to me, *I used to wonder what was wrong with you; you didn't die when she did.* The penalties are in place whether I die or not. Exhaustion in any act of extended will becomes panic and grief: *Many, many times, I've thought something was wrong with you, you lived when you shouldn't. No one thought you would live after she died. When she was alive, she kept you with her every minute; she said, "Why should he be sad? He likes to be with me. I'm strong, I can do two things at once." You wouldn't let anyone touch you but her. No one could see her without seeing you hanging on her like a monkey. You was a pair, let me tell you: anything in you that's good, it comes from her. If there's a mind in you, you got it from her. It's sad she died, but that's how things are. What can you do about it, I ask you.*

The lion breath of grief stinks. The infant is a co-traveler of the light, mad and swift, glancing and unrooted. *Is your life grotesque? Are you a grotesque creature, Aaron?*

Wiley?

I can't insist that I am human, that I am licensed. The stale and cruel stench of vomit. I lay stinking and half mad in excrement, in vomit and in tired, perhaps secretly tireless grief and rage . . . peeking at life but still lost in vileness.

The room, my room, my shell, my outer identity (I did not name it "room"), it ticked and creaked, hummed and tinkled in the wind.

In the bed, constrained by taut sheets and tucked blankets and by chairs set around the bed, I wait. The people here have not yet invested in a crib. Somber conceit: the nearly silent sweeps of sight, the slower blotting up, the sending out on expeditions of sight, the brushing past the sides of sight by things, things in their rays, things brush against or flutter or scurry tickingly by the sides of sight, sight is an imaginary finger or nose: palpings, hesitations: a set of physical hypotheses ranging through the room; things press back, insectlike, itchy, ghostly, real. For a while, any shadow is a wall. That it is my bed . . .

The woman came to the door of the room, to the edge of the shallows of breath and stink and harsh light and sickness where I am. The confusion of light and the window sounds and wind noises held her and me in the invalid's observation. The Lost Woman now was shorter and had different eyes. I assumed her prettiness was kindness. I felt the clenching and the whirring of the possibility of the return of madness, because this woman (I thought) had let me suffer and go mad, a single second's flicker of (mistaken) fact on a tiny fulcrum of a lunatic child's absurdly clear reasoning. The child was not careful. He said inwardly, *Momma.* The small boy was rigid and racked with the pulse of diarrhea then.

Lila Silenowicz said, "Oh, my God, you're worse than a pigeon."
She made a joke *for her own amusement.*

The woman does not look at the child closely. Around her is a
space, a blankness, of *coolness,* the border where the too difficult heat of
shape and identity in someone stops and outline takes over.

Lila has an air of submission to tragedy—this has a domestic tone,
scary and alert. I am not exactly visible. I am a sick child. Lila's tragic
and clear-eyed air has a blustery, softish heat, and an immeasurable
quality—an absence of boundaries except for her outline—this is part
of what identifies her to me as my mother.

My body's feelings of recall, my body's interpretations of people
are shudderings that seem like magical nonsense to the mind, but
they have a profound quality of unarguable sense. Her presence is
heavy with heat like real sunlight; my mind manages my body's
uproar by narrowing itself—it is the mind squinting.

Lila sniffed at the shit-odor, pursed her lips, and, holding her
breath, came near and looked at me from the other side of the chairs—
over the wall of chairs—a sultry and yet airy scrutiny, flirtatious, self-
conscious, proddingly clever. . . . She is sadder than anyone else who
tends me. She leans forward, one hand on a chair arm, and she pulls
the sheet that's over me away from me and takes a towel, one of several, set out on one of the chairs around the bed, "I'm not good at
this," she says.

That remark silences me with its absolute strangeness. She earlier
(the other woman) and other women—my nurse now (a fat woman),
and Lila's twelve-year-old daughter—were (are) proud: they boast and
dance-in-a-way (when they hold me, when they touch me). Lila's apol-
ogy startles the child with its illegality: it is illicit and part of her heartless awareness. I might be incurable. There had been no limit to her
absence and none to my dying—well, some suspicion had slowed the
process of my dying. Being placed openly first by someone, being close
to someone in certain ways, and being lawless when you are alone with
someone—these are roughly equivalent for the child as life-giving.

The child: there are no words for how blackly thorny he is.

Lila has a quality of being indomitably *obscene,* guilty, blameworthy, unrepentant. She stares at you and does what she likes.

I could not successfully blackmail either of my mothers. Neither was merciful. All that worked with either of them was me being secretive.

Lila, cleaning up some of the mess with the towel, watches her own clumsiness. *I play to myself in the balcony* is a remark of hers. She is nosy and yet, this morning, she is dream-stained, quilted or padded or tufted with night heats. Her odor, her dark eyes, the rhythms and manner of movements of her hands gave the child the un-Euclidean turmoil of doubt. Nothing matches from before. She ostentatiously holds her breath, she disgustedly mops at the bed, she throws the towel into an open hamper—its lid is off; it is a woven, basketlike thing—and she takes another towel from the chair seat and wraps me in it. She plays her eyes on me, self-reflexively; she is contemplating the dangers before she lifts me: "Don't throw up now," she says.

Her eyelids blink rapidly. This softens her stare, makes her very pretty—greatly pretty. Lila says, getting ready—she is very hesitant—"I can't let it simmer on my back burners all day. I'm the last of the red-hot mommas. My motto is 'strike while the iron is hot and get things done.' I'm the executive type." She moistens her lips, squints blindly, pushes her hair behind her ears. She stands flat-footed. She sets her breasts with her left hand. Her breasts have a powdery largeness. A constant nervousness is worsened if she has to touch someone. She bends near; her shadow is an imported dusk; her arms are around me; she lifts me, the giant woman, owl-fluffy *Momma* and her large, owl-soft breasts. And then, over that, the nearness to her is a moonish glare that tugs tidally at my breath and at my mind.

"Phew, you stink, pretty baby," she says.

Her voice is troubled, vaguely storm-lit, spotted with lurid light: she has an innate melodrama.

She ferries us past the obstreperous transparency of the windows—mostly a curious shine but still knowable as part of the outer, widening morning.

"Well, another day, and you're still sick, don't you know it? Don't you always know it?"

She is sad; she is out of breath; charmingly, conceitedly, she is drudgery-minded. She picks on me: "Hold your head up; don't let your head do that; straighten it; stop looking like an idiot: I warn you, I'm not good with idiots—once you lose my sympathy, you lose *me*. . . . Listen, I'll tell the world: I'm not a nursemaid; that's not what I'm good at." Heavy-fleshed, small-town Lila walks, and I shake with the rhythms of her body. Her movements are interfered with by me— my weight and looseness and indiscipline of posture.

In the bathroom, she sits me lankly on the sink. My feet are in the white basin; she props me with her shoulder and unwraps the outer towel, shifting me, and slipping it out and throwing it on the floor. And then she unpins the other towel, the one that I slept in, the dia- per towel: "What a mess: don't look innocent; you do it, you're the mess: you're worse than a horse. You're lucky you don't get thrown out with the diaper. You could learn to handle your bowels: it wouldn't kill you. I hope you're listening. Cooperation, they say, is the mark of a leader. Don't make me wear myself out." Her fingers are clumsy but neat, shy then bold—she has a glidy, pinchy, nervous touch. It is a touch that seemingly can easily be frightened off, like a fly. My eyes have grown flimsy with nerves—an obscure physical crowdedness of sensation in skin and mind.

"Are you looking at me? I can't tell what you're up to; you're one of the crazy ones; you're a crazy little *meshuggener,* a *meshuggener* sheikh. Are you getting better? I think you're improving. My guess is you're sitting there and you know what I'm saying: tell me if I'm right."

She's bluffing, partly bluffing, mostly bluffing. As she speaks, she stops believing herself, because my eyelids are so unblinkingly dulled—I am masked in lostness in the vividly glaring bathroom light. She has turned on the lights, a bulb overhead, and bulbs along- side the mirror so that reflected everywhere on the white walls are melted foil, blurred gilding, moonish flares. The mirror shines outward, and morning light bulges in at the window. Against my back are her breasts, sleeping, stirring animals, slick lambs vaguely furry with sensations; and, as in a dream, like masses of very pale pigeons or piles of silent whitish leaves.

Her large, moonish female face, with lines and vistas focused with her curiosity about my illness, about me, has a foreign meaning, like paths in a strange garden. She unpins and strips me down below.

I am a half-lifeless drowsiness and limp and boneless, but I am an inward mass of tense amazement. Moving my head, my chin into my chest, I cannot understand what I see down below—myself or her hands.

I am too ignorant, too embarrassed. Sightless with embarrassment, perhaps with rage among unreadable meanings. Although I don't move, the woman says, "Hold still . . ." Life and consciousness are hard to bear.

The terrible preliminary sensations of nakedness, tickling birdlike glitter of the nerves, cut the moment into strange shapes and spaces; Momma's eyes are as large as a sparrow, the sparrow being at an unreadable distance from me in meaning if not in real inches. Fluttering bird breath. Eyelid-bird-wings. A thin fabric shimmer-noose followed by a tube rises over my face and wraps my head—it is smelly; and light pierces the web that, as it ascends, hauls at my eyelids, blocks my nose, and opens my mouth so that I breathe a forced indraft of air—silvery, silent, shiny, bathroom air.

Naked. My amazement and dullness are aflame. I am all hurting pleasure and nauseating pain. My no-longer puritan mother, a lawless sensibility, neat-handed and oppressively new, says, "Are you playing tricks? You're hiding something from me—believe me, boys playing tricks are not news to me." This one has a dark-and-light face, a fanatic's fervor: a form of nervousness: she quivers with distinct but distant shamelessness—like a bird. This is especially distant from me, and is as if holy and wrapped in light, in speculative mercy, this thing of sharing a moment of life. . . . The only meaning one knows lies in the distinctions between mercy and the limitlessness of mad, veering pain. She is electric and unbridled and she is acuity and an impatient will-toward-mercy, a fanatic of uncertain persuasion.

She is tentatively and then recklessly fearless: she has a fearless prettiness. She is being a disciplined other self—other from her usual self—maternal: of course, a challenge. I do not recognize it, but I can hear the ticking of her waiting for me to recognize her. I have never been seduced before.

My mind moves into and out of thickets of shadow—the changing complexions of liking and not liking are sickly in the motions of the moment: this woman bristled with prettiness; her thin and mobile wrists, the lacquered fingernails, the shaped lines of eyebrows plucked in a very round curve jabbed like love before there was love: I spied on her; I could not look; at moments I did not even spy. I submitted and was angry and mocking and interested, but perhaps only another child would have known that I was interested. I mean, the dictionary had been torn, and while all the words remained, nothing was attached in the same way to anything else, up and down, Momma or me. Meaning was a sharp and even a tearing issue.

The child starts to tremble. The sudden life in his ears, and in his mind, as well as the crawling and swarming creature-thing—things, sensations—on his skin (the porcelain beneath his feet, the shift, geometrical, not fractured, of glare in the mirror when he shifts his head), makes him pale and shuddery—he is a tense shuddering and a fixed pallor. . . .

"I know you're sick. See, I'm being careful. I know I'm not real careful: you make me nervous, I admit it: I do things too hard. I pulled your shirt too hard, didn't I? See, I know what I'm doing—you can trust me. I admire good nursing. You don't know me, but charity is my middle name. I know some very, very good nurses. They say that with some people you have to treat them like being sick is an honor. I know you're in the right, but I want you to know I'm not a good nurse first thing in the morning. I just want to know on my own hook, *Are you lying to me?* Listen, I like your looks—you're a Baby Sheikh. You're pretty. If you ask me, it's a shame what happened to you. I'm all ears—

I'm sympathy itself, on a monument. . . . Tell me, are you snapping out of it or not? I know you're better. I know you're a little better."

The child didn't know what she meant; he didn't know her intentions. He sagged immediately; he meant to hide in his illness.

"Be a nice child—don't play tricks on me," she said. "Are you back in the land of the living? Tell me. Let me know if you are. Are you going to throw up? You look like it. You better give me some warning. I'm not good about people throwing up. Listen, I'm starting a fuss with you: don't throw up."

But she says this in a voice of such intense melody, so supple and enticing, that the child is torn open . . . He has no formal means for knowing anything about her. His mouth opens wide—it is distorted. No ease controls his reactions. He is as if pushed and yet caught—a small madman in a new galaxy.

"If you throw up, I will, too—" her voice is large and echoey in the bathroom but it curls down into smallness and music, hooks him and then, as an aftereffect, yanks him. His ears hum—his skull shivers. Little packets of skin on his chest vibrate. Bits of his mind explode daintily—he is close to convulsions.

She stops. Blank-faced, this mother, here, has some fear: a sense of shame, calculations about scandal, the aroma of female apocalypse. The garish light and suffering, in the child, the sheer final violence of his disorder in the white, cubelike room, with its chill and pallors and half heats, are convulsed; only his illness-weakened body's shyness halts the progress of the convulsions. Shyness saves him.

"You look like you're going to run amok," she says, getting it wrong. "I'm not good at boys; I hope you're not too wild." She used to be, earlier, someone of almost unshadowed strength of opinion. Now she is evasive and blown about, uncertain, subject to fate, playful. Embarrassed.

"Listen: Be smart. Learn to be nice. I don't use big words, but I like brains. I like it when people are honest with me. I'm heartless, you know, that's what they all say. The way to my heart is to look, listen, and be nice to me. I have a nice side. I'm not one of those women who make a big thing out of sugar and spice and everything nice; everything doesn't have to be nice; I do what I do, take me or leave me. I know something's going on in you. Tell me what's on your mind, why don't you?" She asks this in a melodious voice out of keeping with the words but not as much out of keeping when you heard her as when you remembered and puzzled over what you thought she said. This one likes to fool people.

To the child the sweetness of her voice is like a bunch of robins pulling worms from him as from a lawn after a rain. She poisons my ears with sweetness. The wind inside and under my hands lifts and moves them; they shift like leaves—it is an odd, manual half-smile. And the skin on his tiny, rash-fiery chest stirs and wrinkles . . . He guesses that her intention is to amuse and to stir hopes and half-hopes, and the child half blindly looks at her. Her voice when it is being particularly pretty is like an odd kiss on the mind under the bone under the hair of my head and on what is in my chest.

"Look at you—you're shaking—what's the big idea, will you tell me, please?" She is looking at my body more than at my face, perhaps at the way the bones show. If she sees in his face the loony shifts of lit and slopping and breaking and melting and burning lights which are his mind holding for the moment his sense of her, she avoids it as too difficult to know about and to answer to. She is someone who hates to be mistaken. By looking at my body, she makes us into two people: one is an odd citizen and the other is a liar. "You want me to go 'Rock-a-bye-baby in the tree-top'! Will you come down? I don't know what you're doing and I can't tell if you're crazy or not."

This making a deal is new to me; it is not like before at all. It is racking. Meaninglessness and trickery seem sweet—honeyed.

I wanted to tear her open, I wanted to dive into her and scatter her as one does leaves from a pile of leaves. As one breaks a toy. This came and went in blinks.

"I've read that baths are calming, hot baths—they do it a lot in Hollywood. And," she said half under her breath, "in loony bins. I'll give you a bath; you'll like that. Maybe I should give you a bath.

You'll have to cooperate." She cheated when she negotiated; it was not a joke. Propping the child with one hand, she went ahead. She says, "Hold still," and she moves toward the tub, an arm's distance, and finds her arm is not long enough; and she glances at the trembling child, maybe incurably deranged, and she remarks, "You have a speaking face. Hold still." And she takes her hand, her face, her eyes, the gorgeous bird consciousness in each of them, away—I am a mass of audiences, distant and near audiences. "I think you know what I'm saying. Now stay still; don't fall. I'm turning on the water."

I predicted to myself the sound of water coming from a faucet— part of the continuous sequences, now perhaps partially restored, of the world. An incomplete and strange restoration. My home for a long time now has been—madness. Catatonia. Autism. The movement is open at one end—inconceivably open. Memory hides it that the three walls of consciousness in a present moment have a fourth side open: perhaps I will die now. In memory, I am a child at the door of that room, with the figures in the room mostly stilled.

But in the real moment the child was sitting on the sink and staring unfocusedly at the ghostly distance between the back of her head and my eyes. The pain (of madness) was close and granular; a suffocating delirium. It compressed part of my consciousness so that the distance between sleeping and waking was no distance at all. My mother does not smell of the real belonging of before. Her breath is not one of the decisive terms of companionship in my language. I breathe in a rhythm that I share with no one. Any gamble I made may end in my return to madness: it is part of what gambling is, it is part of the stakes. Madness is at the open edge of the moment. My childhood sense of farce was not a joke but rested on the utter faithlessness of spirit in the flatness of madness and farce: a happy ending of a terrible kind. Vile. But to accept this woman means the absolute has rejected me. I have two mothers. . . .

Now I suddenly focus and see her, the softened volumes of Lila's body busying itself with the tub.

I remembered the smell of linoleum and words such as "hot *wasser.*" This present version of my mother in a white room did not smell like the other one in a brown room. These walls did not smell like the walls in a country house at the edge of fields of mud and snow. The woman's hair and arms—the softness behind the shoulders (where my hands rest when I am bathed in a sink in some kind of cloth-lined basin: this is from long before) are not the same.

The rhythm of illness and shock and the truth of death are the original terms of my life, and they make a faery music. The glamour and finely made tunefulness of so much oddity line the inside of my eyelids and the inside of my ears and the inside of my mouth with an unfamiliar sensation of newness as home, as the familiar thing now. The sound of water in the tub has, then, its own infinity for me which this woman notices.

"You like water, do you? Are you an Arab in the desert, are you a little sheikh?" The faithless and farcical little gambler stares—and listens.

I did not speak, because speech refers to absent things, and I could not tolerate absence: whatever is real is here, near me. Words are a category of extreme failure in these kidnaper-rooms, chambers of time unexpectedly askew. I was astounded to feel that any pardon extended by me toward the wrong woman caused a certain amount of cure. A state of pardon is unlike a state of illness. But I knew it was blasphemy . . . I *knew* it was violently wrong.

The paradoxes of observation heartbreakingly start with dissimilarities. I am wrenched into observing things; this woman is not the same as before. Something has killed me but I am not entirely dead: I have a seed of life in me. The mind's limits are very clear in childhood. Madness and my mother are perched and gorgeous; one is a horrible bird outside the window and in the mirror about to fly redly in the room. And the other is a strange woman pretending to be the most familiar part of the world for me—this is farce, this is the farcical underpinning of my reality—my reality, such as it is.

Splashingly enormous, the water noise transports me. The sound in the earlier house was never like this. I begin to topple from the sink.

She is not looking at me; she is saying, "See how calm I'm being; some people would say that's a miracle." Then she looks and she cries out, "Whoa! Hold your horses!" She half rises and reaches; she restores my balance; when her hand touches me, the mood of prettiness from before makes her touch incandescent. The complications of her identity unlock me, and my openly thumping heartbeat authenticates the circumstance as interesting to me.

She glances at me, and she shoves me—settling a doll in place on a couch. "Now, let's have a little hot water on the subject. Watch my dust . . . as they say. Listen, I think you're just too cunning for words; now it's your turn to flatter me and be nice and just keep your balance, Mr. Rag Doll," she says as she tests and alters the proportions of hot to cold in the water.

The noise of the water is louder and steadier than anything I had ever heard; it makes me heave with excited vomit. "You don't have to throw up; count to ten; put your head down." But I don't know what she means.

Still, her voice has ten thousand times the power of my sleep and of my blinking and of my thoughts to think and see and to change things. I listen to her *before* I think, if you know what I mean. "I have no talent as a nurse, I'm no good with plants, either." I simply stare at her. And the heaves stop. Her voice is a mixture of brilliant little tones; it is bruisedly soft. "But I'm a real lifesaver, many have said so, and I tend to agree; I don't mind tooting my own horn: I'm not the worst person to have in your corner."

I'm a child: I don't know very much. I can have very odd forms of truth.

No will in her exists to lift me into any abrupt buoyancy of childhood based on knowledge. I am a foreign lump in her life. But her will does draw me into contemplation of her shameless incandescence like the bathroom light, and which I imagine as being in her and as being passed into me, like milk. In her will is some intention toward my being a living child, but not a childish or a moody one. Her will is meant by her, consciously, to illuminate the world. She thinks herself a *genius*—a *wicked* genius . . .

"I think you're watching me," she says. "Believe me, first thing in the morning is not my best time. I'm not eighteen. They tell me I'm not bad to look at. You think I'm O.K. to look at? Maybe I should have put on my diamonds for you. That usually gets the men going, I don't know why. Maybe it means I know a thing or two. Now, sit up. I get tired of having to hold you up every two minutes. Smile and be pretty. You look like something the cat dragged in. I guess you don't smile. Well, I can't do it alone. You have to help me . . . *pupik.*"

Pupik!

"If you're too cute for me, I can get rough; I'm not a sweetheart in those ways: listen to me. A word to the wise, *pupik.*"

Pupik?

"I had two sons." They died as infants. "They're gone: it ruined my life, *pupik.* . . . I don't know if I like you. . . . When they died it ruined my life, but I don't give up easily."

I was fascinated by her strong-willed cleverness, her harsh dreams, her purposes, her self's mix of charity, deathliness, and shameless *calculation.*

On my skin is partly wiped-off salve. I have a rash that burns. She stands up and takes a handful of toilet paper, and she energetically but haphazardly sets to work, wiping me here and there. The rash, when I look down, resembles the heads of kitchen matches.

"Are you looking at yourself?" She moves her head forward, and she is looking directly into my eyes from halfway to one side, and I explode again inside myself: my mouth opens as if to vomit, and I gag and shudder. My eyes, at first all right, go blank, and perhaps they roll.

She is gone. Her breath, her nearness have pulled away. Her hands still hold me. She has no tenderness of a nurse's sort: she is sexual and intelligent and cold. She is my fate.

When I don't throw up, when I calm down, she becomes suddenly gasping-breathed and intent, and she uses handful after handful of toilet paper on my skimpy buttocks and my thighs. She rinses me off with her wet hand first, and that isolates me in a blind state of screechlike response. Then she uses a washcloth—she wants to keep the washrag clean.

As she does these things, she talks: "You're worse than a dog. Of course, I wouldn't know. I'm allergic to dogs; they don't like me." Bubbles of breath move in me. What she's doing is physically interesting to me—*comfort* is a word that is part of being sane. Sanity seems riskier, colder, harsher, a more excited state than madness. It resembles her. . . .

"This isn't comfortable for me, either, kiddo-kiddoo, but we have to get a few things accomplished. You're filthy, believe me. And I get things done. I'm a doer—"

My life is now a dream about meanings even when I am awake.

She says, "This is making me sick, *pupik*. I'm not a softy, but sometimes I'm not at my best. I can do it. Just watch my smoke, boop-boop-a-doop. My God, my God, I bet you think I don't have a mind—well, I'm not *a little woman;* I'm not a stay-at-home. A word to the wise. I'm the I-Don't-Care Girl. When I get going, I'm a house afire." Then: "I set the house afire . . ."

Generally, it was like madness having my mother speak with another voice, in another vocabulary. In some form, it happens to everyone; a woman's life changes, and so does her voice and vocabulary; or you hear her differently. But probably not as completely as this. The word *Momma* is now shorter and paler than it was, and it does not utter any of the old words of endearment—*Liebe, bubeleh, Aaron.* . . . Where have my earlier names gone to, the first ones?

Puzzles and something tentative, and a tinge of mutual animosity form a large-scale abstract error. Mother is murderous and adorable. Momma's infinite unlawfulness is what killed me. The vastness of her absence had its own absolute character, erasing all law. You might find your missing mother in a drawer, or the sky might release her from a haze of blue light—that has happened; she has appeared in that way before: in two places at once—in the odors of a drawer and from inside a closet where she was placing things.

The ill body is formal, taut and wary with etiquette, with limitations. The worst parts of the past are forgiven if I am soothed.
She talked to be *nice*—a form of illicit intention. "A short life but a
busy one. What do you think? Tell me honestly—ha, ha; that will
be the day. . . ."

I stared and stared at the illustrations and definitions of my
mother now.

"Did you have bad dreams? I had bad dreams last night, I'm a poor
sleeper: that's bad for the skin."

The pain of trusting her threatens me and then becomes a fall, a
collapsing floor, a shrieking matter—that short-lived—comic—in a
lyric vein. At any rate, it ends that way. "Here's to you; mud in your
eye; up we go, a short life and a *happy* one," she says. She gasps: she
lifts me. Of the people I heard speak after my mother died, Lila was
the easiest for me to hear.

One can love a woman for the terrific clarity of purpose in her talk.
The lies are life. My degree of error was painful for me. Old knowl-
edges that I have now grew from her presence, but she never believed
that—she believed she seduced me with the reality of her breasts.
That was all. But my consciousness is alight with her. The light in the
grained, opaque window, frosted in a pattern like overlapping gingko
leaves, means that morning is within reach, that I might be able to
walk as far as its milk edge. A lurking boy inside his consciousness, I
feel I am actually inside the sleep-ship, in its hold, where the cargoes
are, its freight of replicas, real, but I am awake even though my real
mother is dead . . . She says, "You're dirtier than dirt. You're going to
stain the water. You're worse than Lady Macbeth."

She stands erect; and she pants . . . I feel the ends of her hair as ting-
ling sharpnesses that poke and move tinglingly on my shocked skin.
Her weighty real self makes my reality that of a leafless twig. My vulnerability becomes a high whisper, obscene and continuous, not happiness but good enough.

The slumped, bare-buttocked, emotionally palsied, and intent kid
and Lila are not much like a Madonna and Child. She holds me while

water noisily and mistily pours into the tub. She's no athlete; she mutters under her breath at my weight and smell. "I'm going to pull my back if I'm not careful."

She lowers me; she holds me by the shoulders and turns me and lowers me—she is going to stand me and prop me on the edge of the tub—and it is as if her arms were slow, straining wings, my wings. And her breath stiffens into a caw. I descend at the end of my featherless wings; the obscene high whisper extends. My feet slide on the curved white porcelain rim of the tub; she stoops and folds me into her side, me facing outward; and she leans over and reaches toward the splashing water; and as she does this the child's eyes pinch the volumes of Lila's back into morsels of reality; the ghostly and ambitious fingers of a child's sight do this.

I have to half dream things if I am to see them. I blink and half know—or half remember—what they are but nothing is dated or fixed; it is felt and arranged freshly, confusingly. Her flow of movements is preeny and gentle, artificial, true. She says, "Is there someone at home in you now? Do you know what's going on, *pupik*?"

Her emanations of heat and breath, the life in her, are sudden and nutty and shrewd, and oblique and practical and distant and so swift I would love her for that alone, for no other reason. But I have other reasons. The side of her neck and her mouth have each a different accomplice-fleshiness—and dimension. We were, she and I, astounded by each other off and on. The heat, the hardly comprehended shapes of us, to my eye the flight of her back and arm are an unrolled, unrolling, unstill, stilled Truth, hot, thunderous, and portentous with the water, liquid and noisy in the hollow of the tub. Comprehension, incomprehension have a cackling, trees-full-of-birds cast to them. The cold and the heat and the steam, the tile—and heat from Momma's ribs—I am groggy and agog in the moist air. The comprehensions and curiosity and ignorance cackle and stir: the flier's perch: small, frail bones and some foreign kind of flesh: but they are ideas of things: and they fly away again and they disappear in the glare of the whiteness of the room, whiteness: as ominous and tempting as paper, an omen. And all the twitters and flutters of childhood shrink into an intensity of the wish to bear the pain of sensation and of emotion. I cannot tell you how the child yearned for such—carpentries.

My hiccupping and gagging and throbbing diaphragm reflect my painfully stretched and enlarged childish consciousness. Suffering the pressure of generality, of naming this woman as the *same* mother, I take the bathroom light as the light of consciousness itself. At the distance of mind at which I move from the broken early root and specific love into being awake now, I become a swollen, a painfully distended, and contingent theater, subdued toward its own body and excited toward the imposture that is meant to occur from here on in. The present reality is a form of possession by spirits of strained logic. . . . My mother is real, she is alive, her presence is real. But the dead might return and upend everything. Mostly, pain and absence are upended here now.

She lets the water run a moment longer. She sits up and I stare at her, but as if at nothing. She says, "What's the matter? Have you seen a ghost? I look terrible; I slept badly; I look like a ghost."

Her voice and the earth and its movements, and the ideas in my head, and the realities of things, my history cause me to swoon. And surely the total of strangeness might be expected to lead to disorder. In my swoon, I organize the odors of her presence and the hollow volumes of memory and doubt in me, and delight and absence then and in this instant. Movements of souls flirt their way in me toward the white light in the room, a startled and batlike or owl-like acute childhood watchfulness, love or infatuation, a posture of optimistic attention, childish, provisional, passionate, gigantically peaceful *provisionally*—it is perhaps the same for everyone. I remember the bill-like clicks and hisses in my breath as a child, the outward sound of the muffled cackles inside me of ideas roosting in regard to this particular woman despite insistently recurring nausea and profound inanition and the rooted habits of despair. . . . A form of consciousness.

It is a stupendously ill-defined moment. I cannot hold each moment accountable for every other of my life but I do just that. I put my useless hand on top of her hand, which is clenched in a curve on my curved ribs; and she freezes. How clever she must be not to cry out at the strangeness of us. Perhaps she has different senses and does not come to her senses as if to doors—various doors—as I do, but fluffs up like pillows and wet pigeons instead. It is possible that she is very stupid about me and that she knows it and is clever in the lesser way of the admitted darkness of her being who she is. And it is possible that she suspects that this moment might become too special for me and that I will splinter all up and down myself and be unable to enter the next moment except in insane uncontrol, not so uncommon a childhood thing, but I might become too uncontrolled ever to be capable of control again. She knows of people, she has known people who have become mad, who were destroyed, she has known people who became tubercular, and some who were suicidal directly, she has known many who died. She knew my earlier mother. A willingness to live is an uncertain thing; she will talk about this later to me, when I am older; it is her central premise: you do it for people, give them a reason to live, or you remove it; she called it *killing someone.* "Doctors and nurses are too expensive. . . . Come to me: I'll get things fixed. Trust me." It is an idea she and my adoptive father, S.L., shared. When either of them says of something, *It bored me to death,* they mean it. S.L. says often, *People who bore you are killing you,* and Lila says, *S.L., don't exaggerate: there's something to it, but that's not the whole story. I know many, many interesting people who would just as soon see someone dead as not.* She cannot know everything, she is imperfect and real, but she knows things about excitement and crazedness, the willingness to live, and she knows about boredom. She is efficacy itself, up to a point. . . . Ah, Momma, I want to live . . .

I make my way into the next moment through a hedge of being battered inside, outside by feelings—and the hedge is on fire. Lila moves her arm; I am in its crook; she looks at me. The inverted bone-

saucer of her forehead, pored and tinted, and the widow's-peaked dark
hair in profusion around it, my presumed mother's hair, is a kind of
toy black bonfire. It really burns me, as if I were tied to a stake and set
on fire, or as if I had been pushed into the oven of a lit stove. I feel the
passage of seconds as like being in a burning thing on wheels.

She refits me in her arms, so that I face inward and am pressed
against her breast, the front of me. I recognize this woman to be a
fierce clown and soldier and fireman in the forces and blazing electricities, the slapsticks and complex comedies of being-at-home-in-
the-world among corrections and lies, feathered and metaled,
stabbing and comically wounding and always in the shadow of death.

"You're a liar, aren't you?" she said. "You're a real liar. You're like
me. Well, that's one for the books, isn't it?"

She looked at me some more.

Far from continuous time, and beside it in my mind, pleatedly
adjacent, if I might say that, is a fountain, a collection of lost
moments—one, two, seven, a million of them. And they all felt as one
thing, a possibly dreamed and super-real thing of *knowing* something:
this woman before was like the huge halls of some giant structure that
seems to define what is rational in the mad way of the colossal; and
some of that remains with me even today. I suppose it is a poetry, the
ruins of what was giant in one moment, small and yet powerful in a
razed way inside another moment: and she is intimate on another
scale, the scale of tragedy and hurt, or woundedness—without quite
meaning it; she cheats on it. I am somehow a far-off example of the
immediate and tragic for her; I am pathetic and dispensable, a child
who can be seen as a ruse or lie, and as a religion, and then as a fraud
or scheme of jealousy and love. Who knows? For a child, judging her
then among his physical responses to her, her tones broke the child's
heart over and over again. But it is almost happiness, such broken-
heartedness. The suffering is immense at the difference in the maternal love now, but so many disparate factors enter into real-life
kindness that one's childish sense of it, masculine and hurt, comes to
a familiarity of being at home in it in a certain suspicious and ill-

intentioned manner. I was amused by her more than I was by death. I was also easily attached to love, but not so easily either. I think she fell in love with me, not completely, perhaps only temporarily, but enough. Boredom and amusement, life and death, these are the two separate aspects of consciousness of my mind.

In the continuous reality of the moments, my future, the consequences here, her future, her life under the burden of my company, lie within a frame of music, the music of that woman's character and my own: "No one around here is good at love . . . except your mother. No point in your looking at me like that: my mother is what you'd call a real bitch; and I'm not the sweetest girl in town, I'll tell you. I'll tell you the truth: you look to me like a fool: you look like a cupid, all ready to love, all set up and raring to go; it's no good doing this to me with these goo-goo-googly eyes of yours—you have to do it to S.L. and Momma: they have the money. And they're not used to anything good. S.L. is stuck up, and Momma thinks she's the only real Jew who ever lived. They can't live without me, and I can't stand them. . . . I hope you're good at liking people, *pupik*—it would help out around a lot. And you have to be sweet to Nonie." Nonie was her nearly thirteen-year-old daughter. "I like you; you won me over; I liked you when your mother was alive—I offered good money for you; she thought I was joking; but I knew what I was doing. Let me tell you what kind of world it is: you don't want to know—that's what kind of world it is. You think my eyes are pretty? You think I have a nice mouth? Let that be what kind of world it is. O.K., *pupik,* is that a bargain? My God, if your mother—if Ceil—saw you now, she'd kill a few people, let me tell you, but God knows I'm doing my best."

An inherent unsteadiness of the physical basis of love afflicts her. And me. Nothing, nothing now in the real moment is physically true in a lasting way, although it quite clearly is true now, odors and love, orders and categories, phyla and genera of flirtation. . . . The child—inwardly—smiles as at a manifestation of *art*—at any play with logic and continuous time, at truth in spite of everything—as in this woman's touch. He smiles inwardly a grin of explanation that is only half explanation and which is also a childish acceptance of *the joke.* Reality, polyphonic, polychromatic, radiant, is very funny as error. I can't help it. The pressure of the puzzle, of the reality of the woman's presence, becomes that inner, maybe languorous smile of brotherhood and sisterhood in all the jokes and with the outwardly hooded eyes of the suspicion necessary for childish self-government in regard to what he knows.

His distrust of this woman becomes a form of obsessive amusement attached to her, so easily that it is a form of love as well as a convalescent surrender to the majesty of what is here—it is not logical; it is *logical-anyway.* So he laughs—glumly or gloomily or stupidly—but silently. His no-doubt thin face and loony eyes, his small, nervous mouth show some dreadful kind of lunatic ridicule of her and shocked amusement of a puny kind. The identities of everyone here are wicked mixtures of histories and energies appreciably hungry for an affection that, to be blunt, was attached to, and meant for, someone else. But what are we to do?

She says, "That's some sad smile, let me tell you. Well, it's nice to have a little love, a nice lover like you. What's wrong with a little yes before breakfast . . . ?

That is just something she says . . . She knows how to say it . . . She doesn't mean it every moment—look, the mind and the real climb in darkness here. Grief is a pulsation of one's breath. The mind's power to reconstitute itself in another mood is among physical responses which overturn and darken and ignite and illuminate and excite the self which clings to its ennui as a bed of rest and of thought, as the other scientific, skeptical, unloved, self-bound consciousness. The mind persists in its faiths and its ennui as a form of wit. The still hurtling and seething waters of the tub are not credible, either. Nothing real has immediate reason. Only bits of reason itself have immediate reason. One waits years for the elements of reason to gather and to elect one another to good sense. It is both sweet and strong to have a sense of reason in one's mind toward one's life.

Childhood, in its farcical intellectuality, and its promiscuity of attachments, is part awe, part an about-to-ignore-the-awe pride—or conceit. If this woman had been the Empress of Egypt (if there had been an Empress of Egypt), everything then, like everything in the bathroom would have been intense and real *and foreign* in a general way; one has to see that the general is real, one has to have a strong grasp of the nature of abstraction and of the nature of law and of the laws of things in this other way, this other house—this happened to Moses, didn't it?

It is a logical and curative dream and a test of the soul, it is abstract and physical, and it is real. I am a child lunatic, but I am not a discarded child lunatic. And this is ordinary childish sanity, I think. The child is more silent than Moses stuttering as an Egyptian. The child will stutter when he does speak. It is really no wonder that ancient Moses stuttered: he stumbled over what his words meant in his experience, in his mind, over the unshareability of it.

Moses calmly oversaw the slaughter of many. The walls of Jericho came down. The profundity of Wiley's moment has to do with charity and self-love on one side of the equation and with an unreasonable degree of meaning on the other. I mean, it is one order of profound meaning if it is the same woman, and it is another phylum of meaning if it is not the same woman because the two different parts of the mind, two different parts of waking consciousness, the self and the judge, or conscience if you like, or immediacy and thought are differently arranged: the interpretation becomes the basis of faith in the livability of the flow of actual continuous time. Memory and truth have changed and become ghost things—it is a particular thing that happened. It cannot be diagnosed. It is me. To the extent I matter to Lila, it is *us*.

But in *me* the terms are general and have to be. The child's feelings curve in a singular universe of pain and comfort-of-a-kind, and his feelings are far and near, are both roof and floor, are truth with this vast, central error in it. He must be intelligent in order to live. And the child is in ambush, hiding everything, like an explorer on a

strange planet looking at the inhabitants from his hiding place, trying
to learn. The awful, seriously unblessed, but perhaps meaning-ridden
clown in his life, the child, his life just was there in these ways. Silence
was inevitable. Lila said, "It's pretty that you don't speak."

The nature of truth is extraordinary and unresting. I managed to
be mentally amazed and ill. The child managed the discipline of
accepting her gaze. And of hiding my reason and unreason. That
woman and I will never have the same reasons for anything. How
unreasonable my life seemed moment by moment as I lived it: it was
just one puzzle after another. I stare at each moment and wonder what
it can mean. It is exhilarating and intoxicating to be the ill child, to
be cruelly blasé, cruelly deadened, greatly punishing, while accepting
her gaze as only a dead and logically unsatisfied child can accept being
gazed at by the hunting wit in a clever woman's eyes.

Her sight softens and moves like water and sharpens and tickles.
The child stirs. He almost writhes. The giant woman says, "Just hold
your horses—do you know what I'm saying?" She says, "You know
what? You and I are a pretty pair—you know that? You can have a
good time with that puss of yours if you get well. So you get well and
make a lot of people suffer is what I'm telling you. Does that sound all
right to you? Does that sound good to you, *pupik?*"

She is a theater of prediction, but she will shape the chronicle plays
along the lines she lays out here. In her stare is the weight and pene-
tration of her mind—it is her intelligence about me that distends me
with breathlessness. And amusement. And that is, in part, an ignorance of me. I remember no ignorance of me in her before. But this is
real; she does not know me. Poor woman. Truths and lies, monuments
of loss and actualities of the recurrence of love, proofs beyond doubting of disloyalty which indicate loyalty, it is happening again, it is
hard, it is slippery, but I move in this medium of the politics, the policies of love and wakefulness with an ease of fins and tail (or of wings
or of sturdy legs). "I will say this: You had the right mother, in some
ways. I can see you struggling to live. Me, my mother is death itself.

I wake up every morning wondering why I bother." Everything means something here. I have to learn what it is.

I broadcast a version of what was inexplicable, a smudged, half-incomprehensible portrait, unendurable and exciting, onto the extreme and mysterious and loosened beauty of Lila Silenowicz. Her beauty, archangelic and ghostly, is of the order of a body—nothing as real and human as a familiar face.

Lila and I are villainously deformed in our predicaments. Ha-ha. We like that. The woman's gloomy odor, her manner, tense and flirtatious, the reality of her will—of Lila's daydreams made real: she dreams while she's awake—the child feels it as he used to feel the onset of variations of voice at twilight when the other stopped working. Mothering me is a thought this one has: she wakes from it, and her breathing, her atmosphere change; and she returns to it—see: this woman's *mind* is motherhood. I exist because of her mind, not her body. I live and breathe in this tumultuous and shattering noise because of her mind.

This false-and-true interpretation of things is how my life was given to me the second time.

She says, "Now is everything apologized for? Do you think we can get on with our business now?"

My heartbeat is such that I am in a burrow of thuds. The wing-beats of the mother-violence—of her freedom—in part, they are the motions my history makes bearing me rapidly aloft, along. The child's stomach zigzags abruptly into spasms; and I vomited.

Lila swept him up toward the basin. "Not in your bathwater: that's the limit, I don't want to draw the water again!"

The clutch of illness, volcanic with spasmodic, bilious force: a wracked and scalded mouth.

"Well, get it over; it won't kill you; you're the type nothing can kill. You'll be there at the end—do you hear me, *pupik*? It's only vomit. It's not the end of the world."

As he finishes, he chokes.

Lila wipes his face. "Hold still; I'll clean this up; I'll clean this up, *too*. I don't think you're better. But I don't know. This isn't a lot of vomit." She is working hastily. "Are you better? I can't tell. You know what? I'm not good at this, *pupik:* I'm thirty-three years old—that's not for publication. I can't afford to jump to conclusions. My God, my God, S.L. blames me for everything. I'd never hear the end of it about you. People like me don't get a chance to be wrong. I'm not a sweet little stay-at-home do-nothing. Everybody knows that about me, but a lot of people like me anyway. A lot of people don't like me—I'm an outstanding person and I have rivals; I have rivals coming and going; they're coming out of my ears, *pupik*. You don't know what that's like. You make me look ignorant, and I'll have to pay through the nose and I'll have to keep on paying. They all suspect me where you're concerned, as it is. So my advice to you is to pitch right in. All this vomiting you do is not going to win you friends and influence people."

Her dead children and my dead mother haunt her. It is hard to think of her as real in that way, as maybe a fantastically hurt woman, fantastically willful.

She tossed the smelly washcloth she had used on me onto the floor near the dirty towels. She groaned. She didn't call out for my nurse or for S.L. to come and give an opinion whether I was awake and "sane." She straightened her large breasts with shy touches of her quick, slender hands.

Willful, moody, and charitable for the moment, sighing and clever, she lifts me and turns toward the tub. She stands a moment: "That's too much water—well, maybe you won't drown. And maybe you will." And, holding me under one arm and pushing my knees onto the rim of the tub as she stoops, she turns off the water, an effort that makes her grunt and which takes a hundred years, the struggle with the faucet.

Then, eyeing herself in the dulled, filmy reflection on the white wall, or my reflection, she says, "Let me catch my breath." She catches her breath inside her mouth, and she tucks it into the sacks inside her breasts, I think. "Don't vomit in the bathwater," she says.

I cannot talk; speech is too explosive a matter. I am too wounded. "Peekaboo," she says.

But she says it with finality to someone she knows is crippled and ordinary, is less than ordinary.

I heard the metal sounds of the water echoing in memory. I looked at Lila. My eyes catch at the bluish dust the shadows are, and then the irregular stippling of ashen shadow of her face. It is hers, not secretly mine. She said, "Will you vomit or not? No one's looking—you can tell me. We're two of a kind; trust me; I'm not a snitch." A locally notable woman, she is wrapped in a manner that is startled and rich with references to conspiracies. "Do you love me? I'm a charmer. I've ruined one or two nights' sleep in my time."

Her large face gleams in the driftingly warm bathroom air; her face is heart-shaped and pale.

I twitched. It was as if flies strutted on my forehead.

She turned away from me, bent, and tested the water. She stirred it, the water. Noises tinkled then, and the water circled, thin and tin-like, rippling, planeless.

She is in some odd posture, half squatting by the tub, one knee up near her shoulder, the other down on a blue bathroom rug. I'm forcedly kneeling on the rim, held. Shifting her hands, she holds me tight and moves me out over the water. She swings me out; her hands cup my ribs; the water shivers beneath me, close to me: my feet are still back at the rim. I look down into a seesawing dim mirror that vaguely reflects her and me. She lifts me higher, until my feet are drawn from their loose white anchorage. Vague heat curlingly half tickles the sole of my spindly feet. I draw my feet up, only a little. I am not capable of much movement. My mother's hands are fragilely intelligent now, rather than strong, as they were. They are just barely firm enough. They are large in relation to me. The hair on her head touches my hair: our heads are near to each other; her hair lies on my hair as if it grew from my skull. She lowers me, and pale steam, lazy arcs of vapor, rise to touch me in private places. Warm, grainy water closes its lips around my anguishedly tickled feet. That sensation echoingly ran in me, destroying me as if it were a wheeled, rattling thing and I was glass and waxed paper.

It breaks everything and crushes me into silent cries, twitches: the cries do not emerge from me, but stay inside and move restlessly and with obliterating anguish inside my shoulders which hunch as if to shield my head from this sensational catastrophe—my head is the major porch of sensation and it is flooded, too, but perhaps not for very long, not all the way to its top. The water moves mouthlike up my ankles and legs. The mouth closely, claspingly swallows more and more of me. Then my waist is in the water. Water encircles my belly in a collar of ambiguous sensation. The water is not smooth; I am smoother than it is. My sensations burn and scream and tickle, they are themselves a spasm of wild intentness, clenched or locked, unbearable. The water is amazing—formal, formidable, submissive, dangerous. It fits me closely and relentlessly on its inside, but it is full and oval and is itself on its outside. My feet slide uneasily at the end of my straightening legs along the grit-speckled bottom of the tub. I am moistly in the middle of a soft, splashy clanging of the water. I do not understand water, this water, its degree of subservience and of danger-to-me.

I lean forward, and my chest ruffles and pushes at it, the water; and it, the water, goes down and then pushes up alongside my ribs like a balloon or pillow. It affects me echoingly in each of its shifts. Lila pulls me so that I sit upright; the water returns complacently, sweet liar, trickster, to its earlier shape. Lila starts in on my face with a washcloth. "Let's get you clean," she says. My face becomes a fingertip poking up into the washcloth. I am violently aware of the washcloth. Lila, who seems large to me, is, by grown-up measurements, delicately built, so she is inclined to overdo things when she is physical, when she wants to indicate she is as strong and useful as other stronger, hard-working people are—as *everyone else,* she might say. The sensation of tinily gritty porcelain teases my doubled-up and untrusting and strenuously rest-less rump. The sensation of air is on my neck and shoulders. The breath of the surface of the water rises around my face and touches my lips. A film of rinsed soapiness, abrasive stuff, is on my face. Damp prickles of steam are in my mouth, on my gums and teeth. The odor of water sti-fles me. My breathing is comical and repellent to me. The watery echo of it is unpleasing. My breathing is amateurish. I start to gasp; and that worries Momma, who says, "Stop that!"

I don't quite stop. Momma breathes to show me how. It seems the water and Momma and I share muted, somber, imitative breaths. She scrubs my hands; she goes between the fingers. What are intrinsically giggles are tarted up into the indignity of being scrubbed, which is like being clawed by a tiger—discomfort that is a tearing pleasure. She and I both avert ourselves from conscious attention to this moment. But we are very attentive to it. Dreamily, the water puffs heat at the underside of my chin. And onto my weakly bowing neck. I feel the pillowy water around my unpracticed hands, the woman's-breast, dog-stomach water.

Lila slowed in what she did. I lower my head tentatively to look at gray bits of whatever it is in the water: swirls of film that turn rain-bowish in the light.

This local reality half shared—that is to say, judged and fixed as something other than private hallucination by my *mother's* being here—becomes strangely blank, elegant in a way, stripped of particu-larities, and close to a proud madness of making things into a theater of meaning. *Bathwater.* You take the reality of cleanliness and foist it on the reality of the water so that *dirt* and *impure water* do not exist. Lila as a presence is hardened like a bean, smoothed into firmness like carved soap or tile, so that she becomes a marble portrait set up as my *mother.* A mixture of purposes have made her into my *mother* whether I am the sculptor or not.

But what a peculiar nature it is that the actual felt nature of pres-ence, of love is in the unwise, pagan moment. The future becomes a home. The past is instructively dire. The present is the moment of

love but it is only a bath—sensation becomes faith. The delicate and
then rude acrobatics of *love* have an elegantly half-calmed (and still
acrobatic) hysteria. I forget that Lila is anyone other than my
mother. . . . I find this difficult to describe but commonplace to
remember.

Here, at one end of this moment, is the curious wavering and
gravid faith that has to do with truth and with puzzles or lies—lies
and threats: it is hard to say. The distances in the mind are almost
other realms of actuality, but in all of them I am lost in contexts of
intellectual urgency about what my life means. Or what this and that
in my life mean. This is new water; I have seen water before but not
like this. How many rules have been changed! I lower my face
through actualities, through visible and tangible plumes of steam,
motionful but nearly bodiless, but visible to the child, just as the
rumblings of the house, the furnace, the wind outside, the house keeping its footing on an earth rushing through the oddly white reeds and
weedy edges of morning are audible to the child. And Lila's feelings
are present like dark space itself. Certain distortions are squeezed from
night's existence and from nightmares' melodramas and become water
in the damp center of my eyeblinks. My face is in the water; the water
cups, masks, fits itself to the porchlike face; I choke in a pink hall; I
swallow, I cough; I nakedly surrender to the death, almost jolly, that
chokingly waits, unhallowed, impious, in coughed suffocation here. I
return to some of the distances of before when my real mother was
alive; I want to be saved. Here in the flamingly clenched garden of
suffocation I find the eternal return of rescue—everything rushes forward, and is wrenched and knotted, clenched in a cough. The whitely
echoing tile, the room, the steam and breath and the presence of Lila.
She slaps my back, after a pause. Lila has, in her, great hounds that
tear her. She says, "Come on. . . . Be well. Do me proud and I will
keep the murderers away from you. . . ." She has had two sons that
died as infants from suffocation, or something like it. She was blamed
as heartless. Why does her heart not stop at this moment? She does

not like to be near children, but she is here, near me. She wants to be
perhaps only the mother-of-record. Lila can open the present moment
in a romantic sense as in giving a party. She cannot ever save me—
except in this way—not when *her* children are dead. It is a code of
honor, of what comes first, and what comes second. I did not ever
really trust her. Her sense of things is of present moments, chances, in
which nothing is fixed, nothing is predestined; and if it is she does not
care, she is free, even if only for a moment.

In her freedom, she saves me, although she cannot ever save
me. . . . She says so, "I can't save anyone. . . . God helps those who
help themselves. . . ." Her pride, her blasphemies, her sultriness of
temper are those of the first free person—that is how she acts. But
that freedom hardens year by year with the statistics of event. In an
insistent uneducatedness, in her insistence on not having to study
anything as she goes along, she advances like a river—and like a river
scow—in a tormenting roiling of crosscurrents. The bow wave is a
whitening of her face, a hysteria. The toughness that carries her is not
any ordinary faith or soft maternity, it is just a hard refusal to be
shamed. She pulls the child up largely by his neck. She pounds on his
back. She says in a tensely musical voice, *"Don't do that. Don't be a fool.
Don't do that to yourself."*

Then she says in a heartless tone—but it is partly a joke, a tactic—
"You'll live." She says it again, in a different tone, more musically,
with a thread of ridicule in it—she is ridiculing me—or herself:
"You'll live." Then a third time, thoughtfully, with her hand on my
head, "You'll live," while she stares into space.

Then a fourth time, having removed her hand, she says it as
poetry, ironic and pessimistic, acknowledging that I am laughing at
her (I breathed before she rescued me), she says in a melancholy tone:
"You'll live."

She moves me so that I ache for her: I don't want her humiliated.
Embedded in water, I feel my heart race bumpily at the vital sweetness of my being a dishonest trademark for her view of herself.

Lila says, "Don't give me a scare like that: my heart! My God, you want to kill me? I don't like that kind of thing. Are you listening to me? I don't want it; don't do it to me."

The distant term *my mother* proceeds among the summarizing sense of other women's faults and virtues. Echoes throb and tinkle among the tile walls and the glass of the mirror and of the window. Her hair has grown lank, partly disarranged in the damp; I remember that *from before*. Her eyes are intent, emotional, deranged and passionate, deranged with passion, with flickers of lawfulness. Her eyelids flutter; they are shiny in the steamy bathroom. Her shoulders are a curious brown, almost a twig color—probably a shadow caused by the way she is sitting. The true potency, though, is the infinite white seduction, the persuasiveness, of her smell of fear and hurt and anger, softened for me, laid aside for me. The gentleness such as it was seemed to be focused in her soft breasts, the facelike nipples peering through her nightgown.

That is not all the child saw: he saw the momentary strengthlessness of her throat. I felt no larger than her knee. I could feel my having a face. And that the expression on it turned her mood but could not control it, her mood. It is infinitely sophisticated, childhood, being a child.

She sees ill health and the child being doubting, and she refuses to identify with her pain and reproach—or hatred even. The expressionless, or kneelike, face the child has at the moment is not innocent. It is partly malicious, and comic, if it is seen, if she sees the malice. His will is separate from hers.

The movements of the water in the white tub, the recent suffocation hurts still and induces a particular round-eyed memory of pain. Perhaps it is a form of the presence of pain; it rends the child; perhaps the boy is mad. There is some quality of space about my mother now: she does not want me dead; she does not want me to be company for her; she is ignorant and closed-off; she does not want me to suffer; she wants me to have a good time; she wants me and my life to make sense—it is odd how much that meant, that wish in *this woman, my mother, my mother now.*

The moment consists of an un-ideal reality of being *loved* by some-one who cannot love but within limits, in sheer unadulterated moder-ation, in common sense woundedness. The moment failed to be intense, although it was much too intense; the woman here, combined with my errors and my true perceptions about her, is far odder as sub-stance than water is: my mother is odder than water. An intense, quasi-lyrical laughter fills me. I hadn't known the water had sections to it such as surface and inside; and that the inside could leak if you licked it; that it could crawl into you in a dully willed way.

She has no idea who I am. But she knows she does not know, and that is hugely different from before, and it is a great relief; this one knows how bad I am; it is soothing not to be claimed and forgiven. I mean the way water enters you is by a law of some kind but not a law having to do with sin and ultimacies of wrath and anathema. And Lila's love was effective enough, according to laws of a frolicking but dangerous sort, more dangerous in the surfaces and interiors, less sta-ble, more overt, with no grounding in hidden laws—only in difficult, real ones of the actual moment.

The water is toothed and grabby. It slaps your hand and smashes your breath. It is a crushing and uncrushing weight on my legs. I can manage. My emotions are toothed and grabby, too, and shy, very shy. They are frolicsome, too, perhaps obtuse—and devious. The medium of personal attachment slows my heart and seems almost to crush it.

I'm staring, appalled and fascinated at the woman who is odder than water. The woman, in a watery, watchful way, watches me while she moves and leans forward and, with inordinate skill, kisses my head and says again, "You'll live, *pupik,* won't you? It's true, isn't it?"

I look at her. I don't want to hide it that I am awake. Are you sure of what you're doing, Momma? No. Of course not. She does it *anyway.* She says, "Do you know the philosophy of *anyway?* People told me, *Don't do it,* but I did it *anyway,* and that's my philosophy." She says with a little snort or whistle (the tiles make the sounds sharper; I'm amazed at the sharpness of the sound in my head and throat at the back of my mouth), "Let's be friends. Lean forward and I'll scrub your back." She says, "I bet you're the one who kills me. . . ."

I don't turn and look at the disarranged and startling woman. She jerkily and energetically rubs my back with a washcloth; her movements with the cloth splash into the water at one end and rise wetly along the bumps of my spine; the pressure of her strokes forces me near the water that choked me so that the water throws splayed paws on my face. The cloth moves down into depths of water, and into the cleft in my buttocks, which suddenly exist in my mind as dulled spaces around a glaring light moving around rubblingly down there.

Momma's breath is like a cap over my round skull—such purposeful breath—the washcloth moves into the hole and tenderly cleans it; and then, shifting her finger, she touches the tiny beans—the future testicles—then the penis that feels like a fine glinting blankness, a hint of how the soul might try to draw its own image in a rowdy future.

No part of me is forbidden this woman. Her breath, my being a test of her merit, the peculiar home feeling of this, fills me—my chest and skull—just as my damp hair and her breath cover my skull rufflingly. Her touch explodes in me as nauseated and then quickly denied pleasure, verging on extreme delight, which induces passivity and yet a violence of feeling and of light in me. I hate the sensation and yet I collect it and ponder it and hold myself in readiness to receive it again. Imbecile child. Sense has departed from the present moment in order to exist in the burning thickets of the touch sensorily.

A pressure in him grows; it pushes and tugs at his mouth, at his eyes. And at his behind, which squirms. He closes his eyes in fright. The present is warm and immediate, burning and sexual, filled with presentiment, with the possibility that this is humiliation; one breathes suspiciously at the cold edge of the large dark of futurity. An exhilarated terror. One likes it. The jumble of illness and grief, delight and horror, and moderated grief—I am furrowed and implanted—I am a cornfield already partly grown or stubbled, itchy and streaming with light. I am clenched, with light hustling in me without reason or caution—it is not exactly my will. Her face is like an eye opening and closing when I look up at her; it discloses and sharpens itself, fish-faced moon goddess, monumental, absurd. I see her split and faded rose-mouth. Her smart and ignorant meddling touch moves over my rash-bitten, half-starved, meager, frightened body. I put my wet hand up in the air; it is clearly a willed movement. I think I pulled her forward, or I gestured and she came forward; or she didn't move at all; and it didn't matter. But with my other hand, with poor sick-child clumsiness, I splash the water; sickness makes the motion thin and shy; still, the water rises; it has the extraordinary broken beauty of glass and whispers and of an outcry; but the child is silent, and it is only the noise and then the echo of water being splashed that one hears.

And irrational tracks and arcs appear on her nightgown—small trails. Some appear on her face. The child stares and stares. The climax is in seeing the defacement, the rain or tears, or spit, the water of the future, the mark of the rock in a tide branding an enormous liner sailing by—no: halted there. The marks look like handprints, or twig prints on snow or sand or mud, or red marks on skin. Her steam-pale face and one breast and its nipple, the latter through wet fabric, peer at me. I gaze at the drying and elemental painting I have made.

She says, "I see that Meanness is going to be your middle name."

Oh, I hate her. I also loved being named.

My head went so far back in my looking up at her that I fell backward, infantlike, against the curved porcelain of the back of the tub. I did not cry. Lila observed that silence of the child. She says, "Well, gentlemen are quiet about things—it's a useful trait." Then, in a peculiarly distant voice: "I can see that Too Much Mischief is going to be your middle name, *too.*"

Rage and mindliness and interest in each other (at times) and flirtation and seduction—and death, death, of course, numberless deaths—she says, that madwoman to that mad child, "Am I your first love? Or are you just willing to play with me?"

. . .

Not very lovingly but with a great amount of complicitous duty or
alliance, or teasing amusement, she helps bring the child upright in
the water again, to a sitting position, and she says, "Here. I'll kiss it
and make it well."

I am unfenced. Scramblingly, I faint a little. I misplace my senses.
She can feel it and observe it: "You're quite the Beau Brummell," she
says. "I think I can like you. Maybe you'll do. We'll have to wait and
see. Here, it's time to get dry; let me give you a hand; I like someone
who knows how to cooperate; here we go," and, dropping the washcloth in the water, she puts both her arms around my chest and she
wetly lifts me. She says, "Hold still! What are you doing? Be careful;
don't be a fool; you always were a fool—I bet." She hauls and tugs and
lifts and succeeds; she is in command of epic force; she might as well
be a goddess or an angel, as far as I can see.

I drip with water onto her. My wet, meager chest lies against the
nightgown over her far from meager chest. "Being affectionate, that's
always a plus in this world," she said.

I have wild reasons and mystical ones for the ways I'm a fool. Many
of hers are planned and have to do with complications springing from
her friendliness and from what friendliness was for her. She shudders,
but only a little. I like when she blinks inwardly and physically, when
the darkness in her is in place, and she and I seem to be dreaming
simultaneously, when our dreams seem to grow out of each other and
then to be entangled again and then to be halves of the same thought.
In certain neural corridors in me, her touch ignites a pink-fiery sense
of cleanliness and a sense of secrets as well. I burn in the darkness in
me with being cleaned. I am wet between my legs and on my tight
scrotum and dick and on my buttocks and spine and between my
shoulder blades. This is among the rubbles of fear and the pressure of
unease.

She is like a wooden board that I sat on and that hit me in the head
somehow and smashed the soft, fluid textures of the mind and soul

and the more heated affections. Nothing between us is complete or
settled; but since everything in her is brilliant or is deep and dark, like
a pit, the dangerousness and the comfort form a reality of mothering
that the child accepts. I grip her weakly, which is to say gently; but in
me is a male rage of affixing myself to her. Much of that rage is a
melancholy languor—she half-understands this sort of thing.

I say now that she had a sense of infuriated tragedy, and of bitter-
ness and irony; and this was *affectionate;* and the child knew it. It is not
very different from before. Maybe it is Jewish. In her is also a deep
infuriated tic of harshness and ridicule toward what-is-not-her-child.
That is swathed in flirtation now. And I despise the change in her and
her lust for change. But I am not angry and never will be again.

For each of us, the woodenness, the horror of affection—dead
mother, dead sons—makes an area where we perch and watch and also
perform in this odd way of ours, muscleless and without music but
intimately and with fatality.

She and I share a peculiarly full and not very joyous and yet happy
enough (or savory) nakedness. The window and the mirror are glazed
with steam. Holding me, Momma takes a towel and wipes the window and the mirror and throws that towel on the floor, too. And she
takes yet another towel—she is showing off: this is many more towels
than the other house had. "Get hold of the mirror, here; hold on to the
mirror while I dry you," she says in a cranky mean voice. She wants me
to stand in the sink and hold on to the upper edge of the small mirror,
but I can't stand up very well. She pronounced the word *mirror* as
"meer"—breath—"uh." It used to be glottal and dark and less airy:
"mirrr—errrrr." Halfway between the sounds is the streaked mirror, is
the pupil of a ghost's eye in front of me.

Momma rubs my wet, shivering shoulders. Momma and her will.
Silently, as I hang from the *meer-uh,* propped by Ma's hands, the wordless, and illegal, attachment—not a sacrament—proceeds. Nothing in
it is a *hidden* fatality. We always knew we were merely human.
Nothing is or was ideal. Nothing. And I don't care. She holds me with

one hand and towels my hair and my rump, my trembling self, the thinness of my skull. She likes power. I am accustomed to death. I can feel it in her—how she likes running things.

She says, "Handsome is as handsome does; I'm telling you, *pupik,* you're not fooling anybody. Don't make me laugh."

Twice an infant, pale with unvoiced utterance, the child slides back and forth to her movements in a sacrament only of the puzzled and the puzzling.

She says, "I didn't think you were like this."

The child does not speak. His mother is cynical, not sentimental and not appalled, and so he is not, either. He and she are nonplussed and knowing: mother and son. He has entered her life, which is populated by people who preceded him. Where am I in that web of jealousy? (What detectives we have to be.)

She is patting me. I leaned finally, heavily against her shoulder. Her shoulder pushed me erect. She says aloud, "Ha, ha." The distances in her mind and mine are unalike; the differences are amusing to us. We are matter-of-fact, she and I, and we are hysterical and astounded, and we are antagonists, independent of each other and full of mutual mistrust and blame and amusement.

She is a tremendous egoist. "You like me enough, you think I'm so wonderful you're ready now to meet the world? You look like hell to me, you know that? You'll depress S.L. I know it. I'm too conceited to do a botched job, I'm the best there is, I'm the Queen of the May, still, I can't say I've done too good a job on you. We'll have to wait; we'll give it a day or two; I'll make a date with you: we'll try it again to see if you can cheer up and put on a little weight. I want you to be a credit to me. I have a position in the world. The truth is the truth, *pupik.* I like you too much to lie to you. You're not ready for anything but a funeral home. Well, time heals all wounds. At least we've made a start. Isn't that a step in the right direction? I think it is, and I'm the boss here, I'm the Queen of the May. Do you mind or do you think you can put up with the way we do things around here?"

She looks at me in the mirror—I am a bruised, meager, naked child. She wraps a towel around my weak body. She moves my hand to hold the towel; she folds my hand around the towel. At first, I can't do it; then I won't. Then at last I do it. "We'll try again tomorrow, *pupik*. I like you. I have faith in you. Is that all right with you?"

When Lila looked at me, a movement of feeling in me was a speech of sorts; she read my face and posture: I gripped, like a small Roman, my towel. A rough translation of that as speech would be a reply to her of *I don't mind.*

CAR BUYING

Momma pretty often displayed me naked to visitors. Even when I was four years old, she would still dress me in front of people who were strangers to me or she would let them do it under her supervising eye. I was, the child was—well, the term back then was *cupid*—I was part cupid, a dohickey meant to excite, sweetly erotic, gently obscene, gently compared to some things: but people breathed hard sometimes, there was a lot of genteel fiddling, a lot of sentiment and affection had a kind of nostalgia that was strictly nerve-caressing to it. Hands were on me all the time. The child was a creature who was useful in giving pleasure in this way; this may be out of style now; but then it was a social use he had.

So, my mother's daughter, Nonie, eleven years older than the child and a little backward in school, and often upset, often *hurt*—lonely and embattled on a level of immense suffering and anger in the way some women have who seem gifted early in life with sexual rage— Nonie offers me clothed or naked to girls or boys if they will play with her. Here she is enticing three children, two girls and a boy, with a life-size and reasonably intelligent but mute thing with a human anatomy and "a sweet smile, a million dollar smile"—so Momma used to say. But come to think about it, she got the terms from her husband: he said it first.

The child can be dressed and undressed for use in various games, medical or adventuresome, sentimental, impassioned or cooing, intent or giggly. The child would do it. I would do it. I did it. This stuff was not really secret so I guess it was accepted but it was discreet so I guess it wasn't really shameless. It was only partly shameless. I remember doing it mostly on porches, front and back and side porches—sometimes in garages and even in the cars in the garage—but sometimes behind shrubs and in basements and in girls' bedrooms on the far side of the bed, unseeable from the doorway.

It was taken as innocent. It was taken as innocent in that stubborn way that means real trouble if any part of the situation is tampered with. The child didn't speak. He was mute until he was four and a half years old. This stuff was ignored in part or was permitted as a temporary and minor local corruption although I cannot imagine why that was so, why the neighborhood was sophisticated rather than puritan unless it was that it was, for the locality, a rich neighborhood and not church-ridden.

Anyway, when I began to speak, Nonie, who by then was fifteen, but admitting to people only to being thirteen and a half (this was sometimes even done with family), was confronted by speech in what had been a dumb (mute) child, dumber than she, certainly. She has the loss of her pleasures and of the use of the child's body with other children and the loss of love, the end of a love affair to contend with. She does not know what to do.

I was no longer a cupid: I had become a ghost. What I know and remember and will do has some of the effect for her of ghostliness, a haunting by someone, by something of insubstantial reality, of unreal body. A child. A boy child.

Until now she has been the chief authority on my wishes: *I know what he wants, he wants thus-and-thus.* I usually acceded to that—out of curiosity and politics (she knew better what one could get by asking than I did)—but no longer do accede; she is not sure the situation is irreversible—she will imagine until she dies that the child is enclosed in silence and obedience to her hurt, her will.

She is thirteen. She takes me outside on a day when the enormous vanes of our famous wind turn and creak. My nurse watches for a while from the kitchen window. We look at a snail, at a grasshopper. We go around to the far side of the house, and there we make our way through the branches of the yews to the trellis that hides the square brick-and-mortar columns that support the porch on this side of the house, and there, inside the furry and itching wall of those conifers, we come to a place where the trellis is broken, where the broken edges of the diagonally nailed lathes are pale, sharp, silent guardian flames that bite you if you are incautious at the gate to darkness.

She knees me forward, she pushes me with the side of her leg as if in memory of the first time, a long time ago, and I half-understand with her that if she plays with me, I have to be younger than I am, and I don't protest.

One crawls through and gets pricked by splinters, and one comes to the windlessness of *here-under-the-house.* The house stretches above, wood-walled, monstrous, echoing above us. A plaid automobile rug, a dented kettle, a mop handle without the mop, tin spoons and two tin knives, a dirtied doll are here, near a hole eight or nine inches deep; dust whispers, slides, falls into it, blown when we move and create a stifled force of air in the windlessness here. Children play here. She gives the plan of the story, she gives orders, some description, threats, blandishments. With a twig of yew, she dusts my lips—"You are a little girl-baby—I am making you pretty. . . ." She says, "Now stand up—I will make you pretty some more." Resting her face against my ribs, she unbuttons my pants, she removes them and has me lie on her lap. Face up. She pokes at my belly with the twig: "You have appendicitis—"

She inserts the twig into my mouth—I turn my head away; she grabs my nose, presses the nostils together. I open my mouth. The twig, its bark, its smell of dust, its needles enter my mouth, scratch on my palate—I gag and wiggle and then convulse: Nonie slaps down my struggling arms and legs. "Do what I tell you, you have to do what I tell you—this is a game—we're playing a *game!*" A moral value in a world of children. She pours dirt on my lips: "This is food—you have to eat it—" Intent with interest, she digs with the twig, a fake stethoscope, into the soft flesh between my legs behind my balls. I roll over on her leg and push at her with both my hands. She sits on the blanket, a fat-thighed girl, she says consoling and argumentative things, she makes promises, she turns me away from her and lies me sort of across her lap, her folded legs, her plump thighs. My bared bottom seems to develop vision, to look up in a way at the air. She says, "You've been bad—I have to spank you." I behave as if I still don't speak. I shake my head no. She has never hurt me before—not very much—not so that I am certain of malice.

The first blow was soft: time continued. The second, sharper blow disordered me as if I had a covering of dust that now each particle ticklingly and stingingly glowed and disposed of feeling in me. *"Too hard,"* I said indignantly. It was not within the range of things we did when we played, my being hurt except in casual ways, the sideways brutalities as of the splinters coming through the trellis to this windless darkness.

She hits me again.

"No—I don't want to do this!"

Partly undressed, I now feel for the first time that embarrassment, or even chagrin, that will enter my dreams, of having been lured or having gotten myself further into the role of baby than was sensible. The third blow perhaps surprises her, too, it has no meaning as part of a game as I have known games until now.

I turn an angry face toward her—she looks triumphant and studious. She presses her knees against my sides and squeezes so that I vibrate.

In a singular unity of self, the child wriggles and kicks. Nonie says, "You're just a baby—you have to do what I say." She wants to enjoy me as her parents do. She is curious about why I am loved the way I am. She pushes my head back—my neck—her having more strength than I do turns me into a creature of animus such that I grunt and let loose my urine. I pee on her leg. She yells, *"What have you done! Did you dare do that? I'll teach you a lesson!"* She holds my wrist while I wriggle and kick at her in a rage that I am here under the porch, in this dusty place with her, this cave of games.

I pry at her fingers and I succeed in loosening one finger. She lets me go. I turn. She scoots on the blanket and gruntingly she gets her fleshy, round legs around me from behind, she corrals me and turns with her legs and knees and feet, I am captured by the giant woman squid or titan.

My ignorance, my not knowing what is coming next, has that special taste it has in one's childhood. I scowl into her face. The inability to hurt someone locks you into hysteria, into being an audience—a kind of farce-prison.

I stoop and scrabble at the loose blowy dust; I throw it at her. The thrown dust moves in the air with a weak delicacy and Nonie waves it off, blows at it. It is terrible; none of it stains her. She leans back on her arms and kicks at me, she says, *"Don't fight with me!"* Her plump leg knocks me in the chest and then squeezes me: a knot of wood forms there, then that place becomes rough-edged, and as if discolored it feels blurry and bilious, it blocks my breathing. Nonie kicks me in the stomach: *"You shouldn't throw dirt at me!"*

I sit down in a bubble of asphyxiation. You can see her think and decide to laugh. Although I can't breathe, I throw myself at her. She grabs the mop handle, she holds it with both her hands and pushes me back with it, she pushes with it against my rucked shirt, my chest. I am naked below. She pushes in such a way that it is like a blow—the problem of her power in the world, of its limits is hard: she cannot make its elements coincide with her notions about *good sense* and what is practical and *what-is-bearable* as far as she is concerned.

She says, "You're spoiled; you were bothering me—oh, ha-ha, you're just a pest." My feeling dishonored is what she wants: she is convinced I ought not be a source of pain or hurt for her at all. She is

morally self-assured—a form of moral hysteria since moral questions
are painful, all of them, steadily.

The child says, *"You stop this!"*

She hits me with the mop handle to correct my facial expression
and to make my state of mind acceptable to her.

Then she keeps hitting me rapidly so that the yell she sees I am
about to make, I can't utter—my yell is halted mid-throat: and this,
too, interests her. I am penned in and netted by her ability, her reflexes
and her harshness.

Her face, her eyes wince and are averted; and I stare at her. My pain
echoes in her pleasurably. I begin to be piled with sensations as with
rocks piled in a heavy, smelly, stained canvas sack. It feels *dirty.* I want
to be clean. Inside me it stinks of shaken bile. My eyes jerk and bug
out to see tiny, barely comprehensible areas of the visible. Momma
will tell me one day that women hope to kill you by means of what
they make you feel—it is normal, she insists.

Now I am phosphorescent and wounded; I am a dully gleaming
unseemliness. My heart shambles, jostles. Pain usurps my attention,
and I can't remember now what painlessness actually was like. I am in
the pain continuum. This pain is partly a lapse of intelligence: it is a
silly, grinning, leering idiot who looks at Nonie. Pain sets me free
from my usual curatorships of sense and bounding companionships to
things. Memories that are impossible when one is happy gather and
make a continuum going back to the beginning, dog-headed presences, old thumpings, prickings, abominable and noisome. Nonie has
a look of scrubbing away at a *foulness.* My back bristles and wrinkles. I
stare at her from within the pain continuum that is contiguous to the
one she is in; she has been in pain and had stared at me from within
her pain continuum and I had not noticed it. The hate I feel is odd, is
tilted and complicitous. When she hits me on the side of the head
with the pole, the bone of the skull vibrates, and my head and eyes
and mouth are invaded by, they gorge on, skinny sensations, shiny,
cold. The sensations spin and ring like coins on marble or glass but
almost at once they grow thick and wadded and vile—now specific

and disordering pain overwhelms the sense of dishonor and gifts me with more enmity than I had yet known—not love and adoration: Nonie has made a psychological error by not pretending sufficiently well to *Purity* of *Motive;* but she is following out the line of her desires, her mood; and she does not feel this as an error yet.

Why pain knocks love into you is that strong feeling has to be something, and if hate is too dangerous, or is unknown—if it isn't contagious as hers was for me—then one collapses into love, into eagerness—eagerness to please.

Nonie's face was a roughened blur for me, an erasure where the paper grows furry and a yellowish oval becomes a hole where the light shows through. The fingers, polar and smelly, of my pain and the smell of Nonie's hair and the sound of her voice coil around me: she says, "I'm the good one, you're the bad one." *Look and fear me.* Under the porch, in the half-light.

I establish an I-hate-you posture: this is because of my nurse, Annemarie, I think; she has taught me different stuff from this; I have a *this-is-bad, I won't feel anything, I won't cry, I'll wait until it's over* posture.

This breaks the connection between me and my tormentor, between my state and her will. Everything my tormentor knows is part of a pointless bludgeoning, a blundering. To leave someone alone, alone and crazed and charged with guilt and without your complicity, this changes things so that she feels bad (goaded and restless); an irregular gasping enters her breath, she is half-laughing, *corrosively.* She jabs with the stick in front of my eyes. The pains inside me now are like a glare and a noise and some like a night outdoors. I do not have to fear her, I dislike her so. When pain really matters, it stops being tragedy—or comedy: It becomes melodrama.

I felt a baby's disbelief in pain, and the conviction that Nonie was wrong and would be punished for this.

She saw that in my manner. The stick approached, the skin winced, the stick entered the eyesocket, the shallow, childish cup of bone around the soft eye. My scream shoved a scream out of Nonie: hers was, *"You made me do it! You walked into it! You did it on purpose!"*

When I screamed, I lifted my head—the jabbing stick jerked downward to my nose, to the nostril; the stick disarranged the center of my face—a squishing-squashing sensation.

I expected this not to have happened, to be untrue, this lightless exile, this unbearable, endless, greasy slide in private time. I see out my eyes in flickers. In my gullet, the air drags. Gasping, swollen-faced, airless, I feel my fear. I am still on my feet. A wordless sense of animals in a ring, of pain, that's what I feel, and an unforgivingness.

It is true that she is, in a number of ways, more the victim now than I am, if I don't slobber into lover.

One gags everywhere inside oneself. The distance from here to painlessness is a matter of an astronomy of human goodness not fully to be calculated ever. I am aware of Nonie's disgust, her triumph, and her *staring*. On my hand, after I touch my face, are gouts and trickles, wormy runnels of blood—they hop and twitch like some kind of hot grasshoppers or warm, flustered, giggling worms. Assaulted and chilled, I tried to walk but the blood came too fast and I was too sickened, too ashamed and angry and faint. The wind moved outside this place, in the air and yews, and the sky was a clear blue far away with dim clouds in it, blue-stained white filmy things—this sky entered my dreams.

Everything in the world was in one dimension with everything else but this place wasn't as real as the place was that had colors in it somewhere. I even saw the blood on my hand when I took it away from my face as gray—it was a serious world, the one with gray blood in it. I didn't know a great deal. I squatted, my knees came up alongside my chest. I had no vocabulary for some things: *I don't like this; this is bad.* The presence of something like rough-textured brick or rough-skinned concrete, the pressure of something that could tear your skin jutting from a field in which everything was in the pallid light of shock and faintness, tore you in such a way that the tear could not be sewn again. I thought maybe it was final; I didn't know.

Nonie utters a birdlike shriek. She passes out.

After a while, I crawled out through the trellis and went, a human child in search of help.

Lila, my mother, refused to "suffer"—she had enough "trouble" as it was—and S.L. was summoned from his work: *you wanted a son.*

He drove me over the bridge to St. Louis, to the hospital there. Then began the medical sequence—the doctors cleaned and probed, then sutured. Now one lives with sewn skin, sickly self-horror and the stomach-turning shock of memory and doctors' clumsiness (no matter how skilled they are) and the present moment in which one aches. One's own smells are medical, the antiseptic smells, so do the bandages.

We drove back over the bridge. For several minutes we were among the sunstruck girders; they combed the windy, eddying air that then thumped the car. The air transparently duplicated the muddy swirls of the Mississippi which seemed distant and tiny below us.

S.L. drove with his arm around me. He said he wasn't going to punish Nonie—she was upset and hysterical, grief-stricken, she was "worse off" than I was, he expected me to forgive her. When we got home, he insisted I go to her as I had in the past: we both now recollected a history of pain. He was carrying me and I made him put me down. He tried to draw me by the hand, but I grabbed and clung to the newel post.

Annemarie, my nurse, came and rescued me; she took me upstairs and I tried to get her to lock my door against Daddy and Nonie and she did but Daddy protested. For forty-eight hours, Annemarie had to stay with me because otherwise I became violent and my soul's obstinacy led to recklessness such that it threatened to tear the stitches.

Nonie, whose face did not look sad, came to the door of my room—and did not seem to be much aware of me at all while she supposedly tried to make peace. This was the first occasion of her violence toward me. Over the next two years, there would be seven more serious occasions including one with a knife and one with boiling

water. Twice she pushed me from heights. I have eighteen scars, most
of them small, on me from her attempts. Her sadness now is that of
her trying to handle a dark and amazing and very difficult *happiness.*
It is a success that she's had, this event. Nonie did not apologize or
confess, and she was not punished, but was helped to "recover." So
the child, me, would not touch S.L. or eat. The child languished, and
S.L. had no choice but to languish for a while. He had to do without
being comforted. He was doubly kind to Nonie who he thought was
suffering as he did day by day—he thought she suffered over me, and
he picked on Ma.

Ma's nerves under pressure got weird. She grew more devil-may-
care than ever and she wrecked her car. Nonie had become frenzied
and strange in her guilt and happiness—a terrible combination—and
she suffered a weird gnawing pain because Ma had wrecked her car
and Daddy languished; she began to have something like hysterics
very often. The nicer Dad was to her, the worse she got. And she got
into fights with other kids at school. In a sense guilt proceeds in a
demonic fashion always to infect and wreck. And one builds props and
stays. But, meanwhile, everyone in our house is unconsoled. We are an
ordinary household now. An unhappy child is a grave punishment.

On a warm, airless afternoon, I woke from a nap, S.L. was waking
me—that gloom-smitten, urgent, politeness-needled man—God,
how he wanted to be fine and sensitive, a gentleman. I resisted him at
first, but the heat and the way I felt made me sick, and I grew limp in
his arms and let him lift me and dress me. And besides he kept saying
he knew something that would make me feel better.

He said he was going to fix everything.

He was dressed in business clothes—a yellowish suit, vest, hat; he
wore spats. He dressed me in short pants (yellow ones), a white shirt,
high white shoes. A cane over his wrist, an unlit cigar in his mouth,
he carried me in my bandages, my silence, my loud breathing—a
groan, a sigh, small sobbing breaths, sorts of tiny, inadvertent screams
of doubt about being with Dad—downstairs, then outside abruptly
among the terrible straw brooms of hot light. He moved heavily in

the heat, suffering too; he said, "I suffer when you suffer, this is no picnic for me. But soon we'll be all happy, it will all be right as pie—apple pie with cheese on it—you'll like that, won't you?"

Over the worn and slightly shaking boards of the porch (gray but worn pinkish in places) from which a bitter heat rises and pinches us, over noisy and shifting gravel, over soft lawn, over sidewalk pavement, we go.

His sweaty discomfort, his loud breathing and mine match each other: "We're a duet, we're a groaners' duet."

On the far edge of the bluff overlooking Portsmouth where a short row of small wooden houses stands, ugly unlike the other houses on the bluff, we enter one that has all its blinds drawn—we enter without calling out or ringing a doorbell. S.L. opened a screen door with one hand: that door, frail, wooden and with old wire netting bent in places, rattled and slammed; and he pushed open *the regular door,* and we were in a dark hallway that smelled of cooking and dust, not of soap and the straw summer rugs as our house did.

A woman in a red sundress and white shoes hurried out of a shadowy room smiling in an intense way that turned her face into a mirror reflecting our arrival.

At some moments, her body seemed to be like a goldfish—some yards up here had goldfish ponds in them where bright fish swam with soft flutters of gauzy fins and with curvatures of fat-muscled torsos. Her teeth stuck forward.

"Cheery Cherry," Daddy said.

She is in a state of contingent *amusement*—she is beyond law, she is ready to *laugh* in a bandit way: this was what made Daddy call her Cheery Cherry.

In her nervous pleasure, she touches him and his pulse strengthens noisily.

"Lookit your suit, here, let me dampen it and straighten the lapel, you're all sweaty from carreeuhn theuh chee-iiilld (uh)—I swear to God, you must be the kindest man alive. . . ."

"I sweat to God," Daddy said.

"Do you want a glass of water? How about sody pop? Poor thayng, look at all the bayenduhges—kitchykoo—I gayiss it's too hot, he don't want to smile none, do he, sweet little thang—"

Her hand moves on Daddy's sleeve, the muscle of his arm—then his hip—briefly, his neck.

A hill woman, a drunk: she was good to men, but she was a mean drunk; she came from harsh people; she thought S.L. was a godsend; I don't blame her; I don't blame either one of them: I'll be honest, I didn't like her, and Lila was hurt, Lila didn't care but she was in pain because of that woman anyway but she never let him know it.

Cherry is harsh and grating in rhythm, in force, she is soft and repetitive, clumsy and muscular in nature.

She always, *always,* waits for violence, expects it, awaits it—attends on it.

She was a whore at one time, and she went back to it when times were hard. She had a crazed husband, Ken, who lived on her but he wasn't happy about it, he wasn't happy about anything.

"It's like a griddle out there, and I'm the pancake, ha-ha," says S.L.

"Oh, honey, you're something so spay-she-ull I cayen't stand it—"

She was focused with the will to make him understand it.

S.L. has an exhibitionist's stance, an exhibitionist's kindness, *he puts on a show,* he smells openly of money and of "love"—*high-falutin'* attachments to *a crippled child,* to "poor" Cherry, to manners, too, a code of politeness.

(Where she comes from, there was a lot of killing: women didn't count for much, I'll tell you her good point, she was appreciative.)

Dad has a fleshy and engorged look. He aches with his secrets. His pulse ticks with his physical response to her. He pulsates with a kind of horror and amusement that Cherry has called out in him. This is what makes him a glorious lecher. He blooms and parades; then he is sacrificed—he calls this being *a gentleman, a trooper, a white man even if it kills you.* So, sexually long-suffering, phallically edgy, he sinks into the well, the circumstances, of arousal. Her *amusement* grows. She is interested in life when she can feel her sexual life as the axis of the actual, breathing moment.

Her sense of his *goodness,* his worthiness rests on his responses to her—on his cheapness and his chivalry, his self-invented, unreliable grace: *she liked him a lot; as men go, he wasn't bad.*

Like some big-pricked men, he tends to be operatic about his own responsiveness, he is urged on to further arousal.

He says to Cherry, "What am I supposed to do with this?" and he sticks out the astonishing topography of his erection in his pants, and his hot, flushed face, like his eyes, blinks and blinks with his breath.

Twice in his life that he spoke of, he "performed" in whorehouses. He went with men he knew, they took him because of his reputation; he let himself be used; he submitted to being Living Pornography, instruction: he went to it, he worked away on a whore, naked, pink-pricked, both of them intent, with maybe four men sitting near the bed and drinking scotch and beer, and watching.

He is anguishedly shy and bold now. His sense of the heat-noise outside makes him blink faster when Cheery Cherry moves herself against him—she's all a-sweat at once; her eyes grin. She has an odd smile. Pulling away from her, settling and resettling his buttocks, this susceptible man excites himself—but it's as if she is doing it, her will, her will-lessness, whichever.

He has a landscape of choice. He dresses to impose law on all this, he tries to guide how he is admired and chosen by his clothes. He chooses what he will do—he does it with mixed pain and chagrin, pride and a snaking torrent of pleasure. He does it in front of an audience—the pleasure and pain and anger of others—this small-town exhibitionist.

"I like to know what I'm doing, I don't know what I'm doing, you gotta leave me a little space to breathe, hon," he says.

He is again in a state of sexual riot, great consciousness of muscle and of heavy genitalia. Casanova feels his nipples shine among blond hairs. He makes the choice to be excited but he suffers in that state—

he prefers that pain, though, to other kinds of pain. He holds me against his chest and bites his lip and shakes his head at Cherry. "Peace—and plenty," he says, "peace and plenty." He runs his hand over a tabletop and feels the startling silk of its high finish and the shaved stubble of grit in it. His hands are as if alive. He feels abstention as a choking pain but he smiles, blinkingly—"I'm not made of wood." He pushes himself against the table to rearrange his pants— his crotch—and Cherry grabs him—his thigh—and says, "Don't do that, you'll hurt it, I'll do it."

"How do you know what I'm doing?"

"You want to straighten the big fella, I know you," she says in her twang.

He has a heavy defiance, a deep, deep secrecy. He resettles his weight differently: "The little one here—he don't feel good—" Daddy speaks in her kind of Ruralese. "It sure is getting me down, we got to go, we got to get a move on, I got to get him fixed up or I'll have me a stroke—a stroke." He strokes the underside of my skimpy thigh and he moves his abdomen, first into, then away from Cherry's helpful grasp.

He tastes the air he breathes. "I'll talk to you this afternoon," he says to Cherry.

The lightless hall, the sundots and revolving and widening spears of light—the false twilight—Dad is a haze and field of sensational *weightiness, longness,* and a kind of strong fatness—and she is *stroking* him and he is moistening his lips. His eyes are plumped out in ribaldry and praise—he got her to be like this—*he gave her money.* He rests his sight on a kind of sight of her breasts: "The tidbits, they ain't watermelons—" He bumps against her hips, her haunches—strong, ungainly, serious flesh: "You'll be the death of me, you have the flesh of fate."

Cherry says, "I love it when you talk to me liyuk thayat."

His taste for sexual and romantic drama is greatly pleased here. Never fully abstemious, he is a blurred poet of Eden and the consequent despair of such frequent and inevitable exiles—romanticized death.

Cherry's body has an exaggerated willfulness, a flitter in it, a quality of presence: she is largely naked inside her thin, summery red dress. Cherry knows this is familiar ground for S.L., being chased by a woman—Lila never saw S.L. properly in this light; she knew women pursued him but she never understood what it was like for him.

She wanted to be the only one who was pursued.

Cherry has an urgency, a drunkenness, about him, about herself and him. She says, "You want to fuck, you want to talk about fucking?"

(Lila said, *I could never want to compete with a woman like that.*)

His heart booms like a big wooden sloop banging against a dock.

But I feel him loving me better than her. *The terrible idea of the inside slot of her, the soft grease*—a man with a big prick tends to find cunt incurably desirable, amazing—*it's the woman who has it who's hard to take: they got to get even with you for every little thing. You can't always tell if they like you or not, because if they like you, they hate you so much. I got treated well at moments, I never got treated well as a general rule. Now I'll tell you something, I was something they liked, and sometimes, just sometimes, they was nice to me; and a woman's who's nice to you doesn't lose you, do you take my meaning, or do I have to draw you a diagram?*

"Later this afternoon," he says. "Yes."

They distribute rampant breaths and odd foot movements in the hallway, and he moves slightly upreared in the chest, carrying me.

Cherry has a shocked look, "Wayell shooor, hunn—"

She grabs him around the neck, holds him—she says, emotionally, but slyly, "I love your big balls, they got that shiny skee-in like Christmas tree thangs."

That she wants him more than he wants her—this is what excites him, although sometimes it sickens him in people and in her, too. But it is essential to him: *I don't know why it is you have to play hard-to-get with S.L. and chase him at the same time; he wants you to be a whore but hard-to-get: you figure it out, I can't.*

"Now let me go, hon; I'll see you this afternoon—count on me," but no one can count on his sense of time or him keeping an appointment.

Dramatically, Dad turns and we go through a door leaving her behind, we clatter down some dark stairs, and through a doorway, opening and closing a thin wooden door that slams inside the nausea and blackened-and-glaring headache the child has. Daddy is much renewed, a little disheveled; he is kind of feeling good now. Also, lousy.

The garage. The sting of the smell of gas. The thick, queasy—hellish—smell of oil.

"How are you, Ken?" Daddy says in a very loud voice to a man with a reddish, sunken face. A tic of muscle beats fast in Dad's throat.

The reddish, sunken man says loudly, "Not too bad, sir—yayuss suhrr"—a low, crazy-angry countryman's voice—"En theyattttt-sssuhhhh thhuh tree-oooth—"

And that's the truth.

He opens the car door for us—it's a black Dodge. We drive out of the garage into the sunstruck world below its dome of heat, and the damp air in the car from the garage gives way and becomes an acrid bitter presence when we are in the light. We drive past houses sparking with hidden and then showy flares of white fire. Dad fearful, large, and handsome in Ken's car, S.L.'s fear—the world seems uncertain—on the road into town—steep, narrow, open on one side to an abrupt fall through space. Ken, red-faced, gaunt, squealingly fishtails the car on the absurdly tight curves of the road.

Daddy says, "The child, now Ken—be good to *the child*—"

"Isn't that the truth? Isn't that the goddamn truth?"

Ken says that.

Daddy sets his face, turns it into concrete or plaster colored with patience: "Isn't Ken a real good driver, honey?" Daddy asks me. His arm is around me.

Ken bends over the wheel, hunched and sour. *(He was a pimp for her and she was a whore—that's the truth of it.)*

The car skids and rocks. The outside world jiggles and flows. The spreading hollow flows upward and things in it get larger in the leaping and sliding views from here. The glassy sparking and hot whirl.

"Daddy, I don't feel good."

"Hold on, we got to be nice, we're getting a nice ride, *noblesse oblige*—even if it kills you."

"Daddy—"

"Ken, we got a child here vomits easy—"

"Ain't it the truth, ain't it always the truth."

"Stick your head out the car window, get a little air," Daddy said to me and fairly gently pushed my head out into the dirty burning air. Around the last turn and onto the flats—the child is in the silenced, ringing, bell jar just before sickness. Then the child gags and convulses. "Woodsman, spare my suit," Daddy says.

The car stops.

"You're a master with the brakes, you've got the magic foot."

"Well, here we are," Ken said, modestly—maybe angrily—ignoring what Dad said.

"You shoulda been a racing car driver or a fireman, and we say thank you, thank you, kind sir."

Ken sat, both hands hung on the black steering wheel, his elbows were down, his shoulders forward; his face, angled like a bird's, stared forward; he is uselessly shrewd, uselessly cautious, uselessly angry.

"Thank you *again,* kind sir," Dad said. "You're O.K. in my book, Ken."

S.L. was afraid all the time.

"It's the little accidents of life, it's the little kindnesses that get to you, they're the honey in the cake, they're what make life worth living, people just plain are *nicer* in small towns, that's what it comes to, there's a truth for you; children are the meaning of life; here's the meaning of life, have to be nice to the meaning of life, don't we, Ken? A smart man's got no choice."

Dad means it and he's ironic—he has a kind of grace of implication.

Ken said, darkly, "Ain't it the truth?" A low restless voice.

I'm lifted out into the palely beautiful and obtrusive light.

Reddish Ken is coquettish in a rural, fixed way.

"Who knows what it's all about, life is just a bowl of cherries is what
I say. Well, get a move on now, Ken, and let me know about Sam."

Ken and Sam, a tenant farmer, work for Dad.

My dad owns two asparagus farms and other things.

Ken nodded with what was his business look—shame and glee.
He turned on the car motor and worked it into a low, subtle, steady
mutter, a kind of poetry: "Wayell—hev uh guhdd dahay—" he said.
The motor noise and the heat and the car walls and windows twisted
and cut the sounds his voice laid on the air—and the car drove off.

"Good riddance to garbage," Daddy says.

Lila was sophisticated about *S.L.'s playing around,* she said she wanted
him to *leave me alone sometimes and I'll pay what's required,* but she was
jealous at times, she was immensely jealous as a person, and she did
not ever seem to want him to leave her entirely; she wasn't sure, she
wasn't sure what knowing him as a husband, knowing him carnally,
what it cost her. *Her* life was what occupied her. She didn't want to be
jealous or *humiliated;* she didn't want to feel strongly about S.L.; she
told me this—to be forced to feel *more than I can bear* by S.L. Or not
him, by her *marriage,* by the pressure of ideas, by aspects of herself: *I'm
the party, I'm everyone's party, S.L.'s my prop—my setting.*

But he felt the same way.

The deeper stuff between them was steadily lied about, was known
and then not known, *forgotten* that's called, but it was too elaborate
and too real to be excavated; it wasn't forgotten, it was felt every day.
They lived and died together, in relation to each other. The lecher, the
anthology of amorous surprise, the calculator, I hear his breath snuffling and roaring in my ear: *Grow up and set me free from that bitch, your
mother.* He said that.

But he represents the world to me, not meaning at a distance from
the world as Lila does. He embodies endurance and style in the middle of the world—and ruse and cowardice—and having a good time—
and being a realist up and down the scale among real events—but I
didn't think he was good at any of it.

Momma was meaning and song and Dad was the world in which meaning was a male secret that women commented on.

You can never have meaning and the world at the same time.

She brought me back alive to this burg, he said to guests, it was part of his social routine to say that; he and Lila had *started out in Fort Worth but my mother was too hard on everyone, so we loaded our furniture on a train and shipped it to New Orleans and then we had it put on a barge and we watched it sail up the Mississippi: I never had a lot of gumption, I didn't want to go north, I was scared, I admit it, but I liked seeing our furniture on that barge, it was a funny sight, and people here weren't so bad, they were trash, but I got used to them; we were in Memphis for a few days and heard some real good music and met some nice people, gangsters, but they knew how to party, we had a good time with each other in those days, your mother and I, it sure was funny going north on the Mississippi; the three c's, cotton and cows and corn, I'm just a country boy.*

He sweats lightly, a nervous whore, he's also armored, sure of himself, *a smart-aleck.*

Whenever he's away from her during the day or for longer than that, he moves at the edge of scandal, but when he's with her he's suddenly within the bounds of propriety: *without me, he goes crazy, he'll never admit it, but it's true.*

Lila is his sanity.

A man's life is a scandal—nature and war, it's all shit. His life was filled with scandal. Lila said, *Men get into trouble but it depends on their wives what happens to them because of that.*

On their social rank—and on being a Jew. Maybe it depends on their being political about their lives as well as on their qualities of the phallic and of violence. Daddy rode a cock horse whether or not it was thought of as scandalous or O.K. or ordinary for *a man like him* to do that. S.L. said to me, *I had a famous prick—now come on, let's see yours, kiddo.*

He was held captive, captivated—she felt she'd outwitted him and gained control *but he got even, he wasn't good to me; he was good to me sometimes but he got even, let me tell you. I didn't think he could be such a good fighter as that.*

She said to me once, *He proposed to me the first time we met, it was at a dance: my mother was taking me to visit other towns to get me away from the man—Bert Sorenstein—who was the love of my life. But Bert had no job, he was a gambler, and I was at this dance in Dallas, I was a sensation, I say it who shouldn't, it's not smart to toot your own horn, but I will say it, and this blond man, I asked him if he was a Jew, and he said he was whatever I liked best, whatever would make me smile: you know I never had a really good smile: my best feature was my being serious. So I wouldn't smile and he got frantic, so I knew he liked me, I could tell he was mad about me. Not just the you-know-what* (an erection). *No one ever looked at me like that but Bert but Bert was cool, he was a gambler in everything. S.L. had a breathlessness that moved me; he really didn't care about a thing but me; he told me right away it was the war had ruined him, he didn't care about nothing; did I say he was in uniform? A summer uniform? He was so gorgeous you wouldn't believe it, you couldn't believe it. I shouldn't have believed it and I didn't but I didn't want an ugly man, they spend all their time getting even. That first night was a night I can't forget, I still think about it, everybody was staring, we were scandalous, they knew what was going to happen. Of course, I'm dark and he's fair, so some of it was coloring. But he was so set on me, well, the first time we danced for about ten seconds, I was a very, very good dancer; and he danced for a while and then he said, "Will you marry me?" That's how it started. I made him let me dance with someone else but he came right back so fast it was funny, I can't laugh now but I laughed then. I guess I have to laugh now, too, we were so dumb, but who else was there for us? He wasn't a bad dancer; he knew a lot, and I could make him look good even when he was in that mood. Momma almost died because of his uniform: it was like her daughter was dancing with the Czar. I knew S.L. was no good but Momma wanted him, and if she wanted to throw my life away, I was willing: does that sound crazy? Well, she was crazy but she wanted me to have what she never had: my father wasn't a good-looking man. I figured I'd have a good time, I'd make my bed and I'd lie in it.*

He said something very similar: *I thought she was something, I knew she was trouble, but I thought I could teach her, and if I couldn't, well, I'd make my bed and I'd lie in it.*

Lila said, *Really the truth is, Momma chose him, he courted Momma and she liked him, but I had to live with him. She was quick to think he was rich. I thought she always kept her nerve and knew what was going on and I could relax and trust her, so I believed her. Every few minutes, from right off the bat, he would ask me to marry him. He didn't put a price on anything, you don't know what that's like. It's like a breath of fresh air; he was maybe the fiftieth proposal I had, but it was never fun at that stage before, we got along fine, and that was a surprise to me, he didn't torture me, so we decided to get married. I'll tell you the truth, he thought I was rich and I thought he was rich, and we liked each other's looks; so, we both got fooled, but we stuck it out.*

They made their bed and they lay in it.

I wanted a man who couldn't boss me and tell me what to do and he wanted a woman who would tell him what to do, not that he likes to listen.

He said to me, *I thought she was real smart, I like brains in a woman, no one ever excited me like that. It was all worth it for a while but in the end, nothing's worth it, that's the trouble, nothing in the whole goddamn world is worth it including you my goddamned fine feathered friend.*

Then he grabbed me and whispered, *I love you, Wileykins.*

He said, *I like the devil better than the other one: the devil's a gentleman and gives you a contract. When you're a kid, you're sweet, but I don't think kids are happy, they don't know anything about anything that counts, you have to have money and you have to have your balls before you can know what's good and what's bad. With good balls and a pocketful of money, the world is yours if you want it, if you can stand the ashes and the discontent. Wiley, I won't lie to you: everything turns to ashes. You put an apple in your mouth and you start to chew and it turns to ashes. There's no such thing as a lucky man, there's no point envying any man, they're all lying, everyone's sad.*

Samuel Lewis Silenowicz—self-willed, powerful, a male loose in the universe: he told me when I was older that *I wanted to be near women, I wanted a little happiness, is that so bad? It must be, it must be, because you sure do get yourself punished if that's what you enjoy in this world. There's not a woman alive who can be nice to you if she likes you. They have to despise you or you can't get the time of day from them. They like to pretend they*

*worship you. I don't understand it. I do understand it. I hate it. I hate them.
You're the one for me.*

After he and Lila were dead, I was told something that she never
had told me: *He was much too broken and unstable a man to be able to manage anything, he was a sweet man but he'd been in the war, and Lila and her
mother knew it, someone always had to take care of him.*

*The adoption people said he was too unstable to be allowed to adopt a child;
a lot of people felt very guilty toward you for keeping their mouths shut about this.*

That was an opinion. It was true after the fact. It was partly true
before—Lila never admitted to that but others had spoken of it to me,
his doctors chiefly: *We aren't sure,* they said. We weren't sure.

You have your real mother's mind and you don't have S.L.'s craziness in you.
But I do.

Other people said he was *a good-natured but bad-tempered man . . . a
climber and a little wild . . . a man who liked to make trouble.*

Sometimes at home in the bedroom, in Portsmouth, the biggest
room in the house—it had a sleeping porch and a dressing room and
a really big bathroom—he would walk around, naked or dressed in a
towel, when he was young. His vanity—and his style—changed
somewhat when he was thirty-six or so, and he got heavier, and his
face bulked out and *he got a small-town face, not pretty anymore, but people
still looked at him plenty on the street sometimes.* He still had a look of
voluptuous vanity then, and a kind of openness and snobbery, I think,
and sensual presence, sexual power that was arresting and strange. He
would walk around singing, *I can live without my wife, I get a lot of news
of my wife—isn't it a stupid life?*

He would say, *I never wanted to be a rich man, I just wanted to be a good
man for a party.*

On the downtown street in Portsmouth, in the bright light, Daddy
and the bandaged child could be registered as pain. Certainly, they are
not happy men. Daddy pushes open a swing door, and we enter an
automobile showroom. Maybe eight, maybe ten polished and bulky
Buicks and Oldsmobiles are in it. My bandages show white in the

mirror at the back of the showroom. The patch of white in the mirror that runs along the whole back wall marks where I am in that Italianate mural, a prince's mural.

The cars have a great novelty of outline—they wear a distress of mirrorings, thin flowers of reflection, parti-colored. Some are as gray and as pale as water. The floor is highly polished and has reflections as well.

Daddy calls out, "We're here, live customers, live bait, where are the sharks?"

Three salesmen are materializing among the reflections: I doubt they are happy men, but I don't know.

"Hi, there."

"Hello, hello."

"Hi, hi, y'all."

In the eerie indoor light, their reflections hover and drift in the back mirror and on the waxed and shiny floor and on the waxed metal skins of the cars.

They are male presences attending to us.

Contradictory beams of light from the front windows and the overhead fixtures and small streaks of reflected light make us all as if airborne but solid, too. Thin hints of reality persist and make it grander that the men and Daddy are marvels, men who are flowering bushes of images and reflections—it is a near miracle.

At the same time, I know better. They are men: they smell; their smells are foreign smells, foreign to my life. The fabric of their clothes and the soap they use—the food they eat—makes their smells distant and strange to me. One of them is wearing a vest—and one is in shirt-sleeves—and one is in a morning coat—and spats.

Daddy, silver-framed with shadows flying everywhere around him when he moves his head, says more or less in my ear (he is carrying me), "I'm a regular P. T. Barnum, did you know that? You like it here?"

This stuff, the room, gripped the child's heart at once through the walls and veils of illness and unhappiness—through the pain—faintly at first but unyieldingly; and although he resisted, still his squeezed heart, his little boy self slowly bent inwardly as if he were hugged by what is here and his presence in it.

"This place is jolly like a jelly," Daddy said.

His hand is on my shoulder. Without entire conviction, I shrugged it off; and then, in further childhood politics, the child closed his eyes against this awesome, joyous, *earnest* place.

"Go ahead, pick out a car," S.L. said. He said, "That's what we're here for. I'm gonna let you buy a car for your mother." I stared at him and then alongside him, alongside his face in the white light. "Won't she like that? I bet you she will, you'll like it—" I didn't understand; I didn't believe what he was really saying—that I was to choose the car, the colossus, and I couldn't understand him, if you follow me. He whispered—his harsh breath flowing over me—"A Jew, Raskob, he runs General Motors for those bastard DuPonts—he's the brains—go ahead and buy and don't worry about the politics, the politics are good enough, O.K.?" He smiled past me at the salesmen. In a kind of nervous exuberance, he said, "I have to hand it to G.M., their engineers are on their G.D. toes; they know their goddamn chrome from a hole in the ground. Ignore the two Oldses over there, Olds is a pile of tin. The Buicks are good solid cars. They stand up to punishment, and people are impressed when you drive up in one of them. It's time a fine, bright boy like you started to learn how to spend money, and no nickel-and-dime stuff, man-sized money, the little shaver's got man-sized money to spend, now pay attention, you nice men hear me? Howdy . . . howdy," S.L. said to them in Ruralese. He has a grand overarching look in his face in this moment of *shopping*.

He likes shopping. It interests Daddy *a whole hell of a lot:* it is part of what has led *him* from his father's way of doing things. Still, he's an outsider at it, still.

The men's breath and voices—"Well, yessir, yessirree, yessirree bob," and "Who-ho-ha-ho—" and "Hot ain't it? Whew." "Hot enough—hot ain't no word for it, I don't think even *boiling* will cover it, what do you think of that?"—one of the salesmen, a skinny man, did a riff like that.

Daddy said at some point, "S. L. Silenowicz here—and son, Wiley—"

Everyone's being *friendly-but*—i.e., watchful, coy, dignified, sly— breath and voices honk with life and *foreignness*—foreign to us—an obvious foreignness of manias, habits, maybe even principles—and laws. Certainly, incomes.

One salesman has a face made of dishes and cups of flesh like pink sand. One is *silly* with pomaded hair with very tight waves in it very neatly combed and an insanely pleasant half-smile and eyes with no focus.

And one is thin as if made of wires and blue veins and white skin. He is inspired by some kind of male spirit that is entirely new to me. It is not like Daddy's in any conceivable way. This man is big- mouthed and taut—even a little jumpy; he has big eyes set in narrow sockets: he is really present.

The fat one has a fat man's specialized *buried-a-private-treasure* van- ity and *one guy there who thought he was a snappy dresser but he was a very simple guy, and there was one live wire; McIntyre always keeps one live wire on the payroll but he doesn't keep them long; McIntyre only uses fools.*

The thin one is the live wire—that means like the tungsten fila- ment in a lightbulb: *he's turned on, he's a bulb,* i.e., shrewd and clever— adventurous, bribable, not worn down, maybe tireless. His physical vanity is pungent. *He's got a smile that knocks you right over, you got to grab your wallet and hang on to it. It's funny, too, he's a funny-looking man.*

Daddy was fascinated by other men sometimes—some other men.

The salesman has a restless smile—S.L. has no real smile: S.L. is darkly humorous; *he's a humorous guy.* The thin man is so tightly expressive and self-promising and restless that he makes the room ache, it's a kind of danger he radiates, there's a steady butting at you, a sense of precipice.

I stare at them head-on. Part of me is private and dark and oblique here.

Dad said, "Well, now, we all love children, they got such good hearts, and this little fella's real nice. And I'm the king of the hill, I'm the cock of the walk, and I'm gonna teach him how to spend money, I'm gonna see to it that this fella's a big spender, he's going to buy a car for his mom, she didn't take care of the oil level, and she tore hell out of the engine block, and the car acted up, and she ran it into a bridge girder—now how about that? But she didn't end up in the Mississippi, we ended up here, ain't that nice, and everybody loves kids and everybody loves a mother, and he certainly does love his mother, 'cause he's a scholar and gentleman, he's an officer of the palace guard, he's going to buy a car for his mom—ain't that nice? Let's make it nice for him, what do you say? You wouldn't insult motherhood, would you? You wouldn't insult a little kid with big money to spend, would you? Say hello to him, his name is Wiley. He wants the best that money can buy for his lady-mom."

Their day's labor is to be placed at my disposal.

Dad's eyes are humid, sentimental, innocent, partly withdrawn, gentle . . . Dishonest. His meanness showed. His nobility, too. *He sweeps the feet right out from under you.* Two of the salesmen looked blank—the thin one caught on and looked ironic at Dad's wish to be peaceably, sacredly important in this way. Not that he, either, knew what game this was. But he was in the world in a way different from the way S.L. was—the thin guy was poised watchfully, tautly, but he tried not to show that: he was sort of very cold-tempered, sort of *hot-bodied like a hair-trigger—a hick, a redneck:* that's S.L. describing him.

Daddy sighed patiently because people were dumb and didn't understand what he said, didn't understand his projects, his enterprises, didn't understand the king's metaphysics or concern for his subjects' happiness. Daddy said, "Now lookee here—" and he reached into his pants pocket sadly. The sadness is his politeness, his rural etiquette; he has a rural mournfulness at men's being difficult and making life difficult; it's not ghetto lament, it's the real thing but a crazy version—the thin man's eyes are really sane; they're like carpenters' levels with green liquid in them; but his intensity is kind of nuts the way the filament in a lightbulb that buzzes and burns white can seem nuts. Blond Daddy, with false naïveté on his face, and some of the real, and them with their

versions of male false naïveté mixed with the real thing, *we were all hicks,*
that much cash money turns people into hicks, believe me, Daddy slowly, in
great luscious hammy pantomime, took a wad of bills from his pocket:
"I won't say this is big enough to choke a horse, less'n you gotta horse
nearby we can try it on and see if he chokes. Now I'm telling you fellas,
this kiddy here wants a car, and he has cash, he has *this* cash, fifteen hundred dollars, gentlemen—gentlemen, I believe we have here fifteen
hundred dollars—that can buy any car in this place, right?"

"Right," the thin one said, shaking very faintly and grinning as if
Daddy was bait for a shark—it was kind of an invitation, and very
knowing, I didn't understand it at the time.

The other salesmen said little things, like "Aw" and "Ahhhh" and
"Uh."

Dad said later, *They looked greedy as sin. They work on commission. If*
they split it, that's maybe fifty dollars each, enough to buy a used car, a Model-
A or to have a real good time in Chicago, a binge for a couple of weeks, whores,
whiskey, the works, or to buy a couch and a washing machine and other little
things for the little woman.

Dad counted the corners of the bills, new bills, fifteen of them:
they were stiff.

He put them folded, they crackled, into my shirt pocket.

"Now, I know you guys are ace number one crackerjack salesmen,
I want you to give the kid real good service—" To me he said, "Now,
here you go; now you have a little money to spend. You go buy the car
you want, you go pick a machine to give your mother."

I am to be like a full-grown man, it seems, and command the
attention of these men.

I can remember my eyes getting *funny,* hard and round like fists.
My despair is wobbling like a ball between my legs in water when I
try to sit on that ball. It's going to escape me. Dad is inhibited and
respectful and interested and he is liberal-hearted and an exhibitionist. "We're holding little services, services for feeling *good.* O.K.,
sweetheart, now I want a little cooperation from you, I want to see *you*
feeling better."

The presence of that much cash is like the gleam of naked skin. I bite my lip with surprise and suspicion. I feel sick—the moment is profound for me, vertiginous.

Daddy said, "This little king here, our Valentino, be nice to him. My brother-in-law the mayor, my friend and brother-in-law the fire chief, we all want you to be nice to our friend, extend him *every courtesy* 'cause you know he's got the cash and he can do what he wants with it; we want one and all to be happy in this town; you can trust us."

Two of the salesmen are smiling uncertainly as if they are willing to be happy at his say-so. I am powerful in a way, I have real power for the moment at Daddy's say-so.

The fat salesman and the empty one are eager: they somewhat laboriously assume an atmosphere of jolly truce, a broad pleasure dealing *idealistically* with a kid in this grown-up place, hot weather, the Great Depression, and all. I am numb and brutal with rank and secretive delight. I'm a little the way Nonie was when she hit me, in the few, cold minutes in which she hurt me. I thought harm was near now and real in them, too, and that Daddy should be careful and guard us. Him and me.

Daddy said, standing straight and noble, "I'll tell you nice fellas something, money doesn't matter but kindness surely does—" His voice buzzed, beelike but big, summery and *large.* My chest hollowed out behind the money in my pocket.

I felt the rancorous envy of the skinny man, his pride and dislike and contempt for Daddy and the rigmarole.

It's not just judgment, though—it's a kind of wrestling for eminence.

I felt S.L.'s strength-in-the-world, his mind as power; its *stupidity*—his intelligence had a bend in it, a dud quality: *he was no better than a child sometimes.* A potent child, however.

Fathers are singular men behind the name *Father.*

I felt I had money for a face. I saw myself in the slightly darkened chamber inside the mirror; I saw an altered face.

Things stir in me and suffocate me internally. I am truly equal now to a good dog or horse, that agile, that strong, that marvelous, I have the rippling silver-and-green paper at my disposal—even if only as a joke.

I loved money so. I looked up at Daddy and he squatted to be nearer me; I leaned toward him but I kept my face turned away.

With his lecher's sensitivity, he knew what I was feeling, sort of. He reached his large fingers into my shirt pocket, he pulled the money out. I sighed abruptly. He said, "See that." He took one bill, "It says, one hundred, it's a hunderd dollars—" I leaned against him and I sighed really deeply; he said, "This isn't just ordinary money, Wiley, ordinary money's mean, this is *money* that's got heart's blood in it, this is for you to be happy. When you're king, you can put your face on it and make the whole world happy." He took his cigar out of his mouth. "Or when I'm king, I'll do that for you. Hows about you giving me onesy-twosy little kisses?" I shook my head no. "Be mean, it's all right. Here, crinkle it up." The hundred-dollar bill. He closed my fist around the wad. The peculiar paper felt more like cloth to me than paper. "It's all yours, honey—"

I stared at him. Slowly he straightened the bill, put it with the others, folded them, put them in my hand, he guides my hand so that the money is in my pocket, over my heart. He aimed my hand, he had to loosen my fingers one by one, the money is my pocket.

We look at each other, he and I. I turned away from him—slowly—I put one foot in front of the other. The crazed and intense and unfocused affection I felt for money, for automobiles, displaces the unslaked disgust I still feel at a world of wounds and pain, Nonie's too, and Daddy's, and strangers who smell of food unlike the food I eat and know and of different kinds of clothes from those I know now.

I feel *real happiness* (of a kind).

Daddy: "We're just a pair of no goods, we're putting on the Ritz, we're putting on the dog—"

Electric fans push air like setters' tongues over me.

. . .

Daddy's voice at the other end of the showroom says, "That fucker Hoover's done us in."

He's talking to the skinny man, as I expected.

The skinny man's voice has baritone depth, and a will to be rapid, but its depth of near bass makes it sluggish with an urging-on breath in it.

He says, "That fuck, Hoover."

The fat salesman says in a weird tone, piously but murderous: "It ain't right, letting people starve; death's too good for some of them bastards."

Daddy said, with a sigh, "That's right. But I'll tell you gentlemen something, you spend your life fightin' the bastards, you got no life left at all."

The skinny man asks pointedly, "Is that a fact? I guess that's fact: you want to win, you got to be meaner than they are."

Daddy said, "Everyone wants a hero to be mean for them—"

The skinny salesman said, "Heh-heh, well, yeah, Mean Jesus with a Sword for president; go get things done for me, J.C."

Daddy said, "Well, we're all clowns and cocksuckers in the end, I'm telling you men the truth."

"I'll say amen to that," the fat one said.

Daddy said, "I'll tell you what, lookit there—" Dad turns his head. On the other side of the big plate glass window, a blowsy big-boned woman is swaying past in the heat—sashaying. The salesmen follow his lead. Dad said, "That's ripe. Listen, you like movies? Make your life like the movies and devil take the hindmost. Live nice, that's my motto, I'm a good-hearted man."

One of the salesmen says, "How about that? You want I should go give the tot a hand?"

"Naw, naw, let him have his day; it ain't no fun to be a child: let him be a man, a *little* man."

The skinny salesman has an odd look. He leans against a car trunk.

Daddy says to him, "You're a devil of a fella. I'm right, wouldn't you say I was right?"

"Why, sure—hell, a man buys Buicks is right."

Daddy and the other man speak with what seems both love and hate in their voices.

"No, no," Daddy insists, "in your heart, you know I'm right, you know kids are O.K. and this other stuff is filth. Filth."

"If you say so—hell, you're the boss; you want me to shoot anyone for you, I'm your man—" His large eyes refer to Daddy's cash by being jocular and impious.

Daddy admires the feral facial style, the dexterity of the other man's face. Then he says (his breath is fast), "If I say so, hell, that's what you say, listen: you like good times, you like sweet people— what's wrong with being simple? Don't tell me you don't like what's clear and simple."

The skinny salesman says: "What I am saying—sir—is that a man's got to—"

"To have *balls,* I know *that*—"

"Sure, a man's got to have balls, a man's got balls—unless he don't— What I'm saying here, what I'm announcing, is, a man's got things he's got to do, you know what I'm sayin, I cain't *give* you no Buick, you got to pay for it: your kid there, he takes out his little wee-wee and does number one on one of the Buicks, I got to step over and stop the little twinkler. It ain't like he's bad, you know—it ain't like you trust me none, I didn't see you put the money none in *my* pocket, I don't recall I heard you say to me, 'Here, I'm buying a car, pick one out for me'— Hell, man, I'm being as friendly as your average ten-cent whore—"

"I won't give you an argument on that."

Dad's friendly mood is like an ass the salesman has to kiss.

Powered by the radiance in my pocket, I drift in an alley of Buicks. With every step I take, the bills bite at me, like a chicken pecking through my shirt at my skin.

I touch the large headlight on a black sedan. I see my sore, thin self in the vertical pond world of the mirror, in that spread of scene, cars, potted palms, men, and bandaged child.

My pleasure is thick and like wool and like grass, too, at night. My heart is a small wooden hammer that beats on my ribs: this rattles me. I stoop to look under the cars. I hear the sounds of the men talking clattering along the floor. The salesmen and I believe Daddy will decide which car if any we buy. My conceit about the money in my pocket has the slow wings of river gulls—large white birds reflecting the blue of the sky.

I stand up and look at the mural again. Past coupe, roadster, sedan with special tonneau, *maroon* and black coach, in the flattened ungeometry of the mirror, a cigared man smiles. The scene, impalpable, drowning, holds movements. Everything has coronas of shine. Two of the salesmen peer toward the bandaged child over hoods and around grilles. The child stands on tiptoe and myriad white-bandaged things stir in mirror, fenders, grilles, and bumpers, speechless phantoms in the hallucinatory room.

Dad says to the salesmen, "I'm nothing but a smart-aleck whore myself. . . . But I got a good heart and I know how to have a good time and that's worth more than you might think—it's worth a lot more. I'll tell you my honest-to-God theory: I don't think salesmanship can pull us out of the Depression but you men are doing real well. But people got to stop being mean. Still, you never can tell: this is a whore's civilization."

The skinny salesman has a mysterious look of satisfaction that curves into a threatening ecstasy of conviction, maybe of being able to manage Daddy. I open the door of a blue Buick. The car light goes on. I pause, and behind me I hear foosteps. It's the skinny salesman—he's abandoned Daddy, and he is coming swiftly toward me. I start to climb into the car. "Hey there, now, little man, lemme give you a hand." He comes close and lifts me. I have one knee on the car seat and I am panting a little.

His hands, his touch, his odor are thoroughly foreign. This is translated into a violence of heartbeat. My thin ribs, my thin sheet-

Car Buying   139

ing of skin and small muscle slide and squirm inside the salesman's grip, in a kind of outrage. He can see me come to harm and not die himself with sympathy or sadness: he's not a woman where I'm concerned. I sigh—a babyish showing-off; he is ogling me. I hated and held in contempt all men but S.L. whether I really did or not: that's what loyalty is. I'm a good son, I'm his sweetheart provided I *hated* the people I liked. The child smiles past the skinny salesman's thin shoulder at S.L.—I love S.L. best. He often asks me if I do. Putting S.L. first was the chief duty I had while I lived with the Silenowiczes.

The salesman wants my admiration, my inferiority, S.L.'s: this is a foreign sort of love.

Then, aware that I have the money, I look at him, I stare at him with my disbelief in the worth of everything that is not S.L. I stare without compromise.

He said in a weird accent, "Yes, that's a gorgeous child—" *Yayuhs, they-it's uh guh-gar-jus chi-i-le.*

The orphan emotions. The bandages.

He showed me the windshield-wiper knob and the ashtray. He pulled it partway out and flicked it with his thumbnail to make a rapid drumming sound. I stared with unremitting attention. I was walling emotions off with floating walls of refusal that were like the sides of a ship. The man near me, his giant hands, his voice, his purposes, I am entangled in bad things.

The other salesmen and Daddy gather near me and ask: "That the one you want?"

"He's got a real deadpan there, don't he, he's just not nice, he's not himself, would it hurt you to smile? Maybe it would, maybe his chin is too sore—"

I am excused from any outward confession of feeling—my deadened face has its electricities behind it.

I hold my arms out to S.L., blond, solidly set, juicy. He doesn't *love* as I do. His emotions are very full—very frequent; they stop and start, they frequently go dead. And his terrors are not like mine; like a lot of male terrors, they are the grounds of bluff, masquerade and wit, non-sense, pretense.

S.L. is lonely and without meaning without me; and meaning is consolation. His sense and knowledge of the world is dark, is unconsoled and meaningless. He is afraid in ways that the child is not afraid. His cowardice, as absolute as passionate love, reaches a hand toward me, flutters and is pale in that air. I knew this as a child—how large the feelings are in my father. *It's an effort to live every day.* I take his hand and feel in him the horror, the rage, the sense of the world's filth. The child's casualness, his fearlessness torment this poseur and hand-some man who tried to re-create the child's terror as a terror of the child's not loving S.L. *enough.*

He is *a genius* at creating a mean nerviness in people, a sensitive and far-fetched devotion and storminess toward him. For a while.

This man has in his head, a thousand times, a dozen times a day, recollections of the war he served in. I adore him—literally, but I can't trust him to defend our religion, which is Him. He likes to escape from me. He forgets *all* our arrangements. He deals in odd emotional currencies that include my "sense of humor," my willingness to "forgive" him.

Our power makes me want to be bad.

The child spits on the grille of the coupe.

"That's not nice," S.L. says. He's a little bored now with this stuff, this shopping.

Intently, sensually, the child rubs the spit off with his hand.

S.L. mutters, "Pretty world, pretty world."

He imagines pornographic scenes. He told me once, *Men want everyone else's prick cut off—it's a special favor if they make an exception of you.* He sees shoals of *whorish* women swimming, their buttocks break the surface of the water. His breathing quickens. He shifts his posture. He bestirs himself. "Get to work, Wileykins, pick a car for Momma."

The child regards him from down the aisle of cars. S.L. stares vaguely—benevolently—childward, but not really at me: the smiles hive in the shadows at the corners of his lips.

He has a half-erection.

The child's *sweet* youth and fragility cheer S.L. who says, "You have to do it by yourself, I'm not going to interfere one bit, not one little bittle bit."

S.L. feels sane, justified at the moment, effectual: his daily gamble is *goodness is known to me.*

The child leans forward, then to the right, to the left—his retinue of reflected selves kowtows and sways everywhere. The white bandages are everywhere—small albino birds. S.L. watches obliquely the return of pleasure to the cautious child. He sees these things with his lecher's clever and experienced and deadened eyes—he sees things I see dimly through my sense of him.

"How's the big shot doing?" My father looks handsome and furtive, my other self.

The ways the child knows him are unjust.

Do You Remember the Time I Gave You Fifteen Hundred Dollars to Buy a Car? For Your Mother? There Was No Cheating. I Meant It. I Did It. The Money Was Real. It Was Cash. It Was an Interesting Thing to Do— That I Did—Do You Remember?

"Daddy?"

"Yes? Have you picked a car?"

"Which car do you want me to pick, Daddy?"

"*Macher,* it's your day, whatever you pick is fine, you got the moolah, just pay for it like an officer and a gentleman."

"Daddy?"

"I'm here. You decided yet? You have your hand over your pocket? You think the money will fly away? Well, you know something, maybe you're right, you're a hell of a fella, I can learn from you."

I thought Daddy was wrong to have aroused so much enmity as he had in the salesmen when he was so *weak* (so good-natured). I couldn't help him here. His pleasure now is of the *Who cares? Who gives a fuck?* variety. And I *was much happier than that.* Our cantankerous—and blissful—little comedy, Dad's and mine, is Dad and me *us versus everybody.*

"The blue one, Daddy, I want the blue one."

"Speak up, Skipper: what you want, you shall have: that *I promise you.*"

I shouted, "I WANT THE BLUE ONE!"

"O.K." To the salesmen, he said, "Write it up, the little feller's bought his mother a car."

A story is a brighter substance when it isn't finished, when it is still partly hints and guesses, a family matter like a child's face. Because I loved my father, his lies and will and money, I went over and put my head against his legs; I said to his haunch: "I want the car now, Daddy, let's take the car now and go home now in it."

He said that was a good idea; and I climbed into the interior cavity of The Great Machine Selected by Me and Now Owned by My Dad while a mechanic fussed over it. I had to hand the money to the skinny salesman: his moneyless beauty was no longer electric for me but had become vague.

The car had a lot of smell in it, plush and rubber floor mat and varnish on the wood steering wheel.

A mechanic, bony and with expressionless eyes and with dark swabs of grease on his coveralls—he looked incompetent—said, "We just put it on the floor this morning; ain't no one yet test drove it; but it looks okeydokey."

The engine noise is like a lot of metal legs, nickel and tin, clinking and clanking and melting and hissing. Or like little guns banging on and on. Or a really big, rushingly ablaze bonfire of leaves, maybe. Daddy is revving it up and letting it quiet down: he's a better driver even than Ken.

"Let's go, Daddy."

"I'm waiting for you to say, *Home, James:* that's what a gentleman says to a chauffeur, to the man who drives the car for him. You own it, I drive it, I have to wait for you to say, Home, James—ho-oh-m Jaymes. It's your car—until we give it, you give it to your mother."

I whispered, "Houhmmm Jaymes . . ."

"Louder!"

I shouted it.

A part of the wall is pulled open by six men, three to a side, and we drive down a ramp—a moveable and clattering wooden ramp that three more men put in place—we bounce onto the cobblestones of the street into the host of yellows, the burst of whites and heat of the day.

On the new car's plumpish slidings, the subtle broilings and bubblings of its motor, with wayward bits of shine erratically pulled back and forth and whipped around and made to vanish from the dashboard, and then others, flitting, wobbling, dancing, to appear on it, in the hot light, we drove past parked cars and a car parts store and the hollow shadow of a repair garage with its wide doors open on the men within and a venetian blinds depot, with our progress (the car's portrait) in plate glass windows floating several feet above the sidewalk in eerie beauty and madness.

Thumpingly over the cobblestones that shone like the cheeks of little angels and along trolley tracks that glittered with light in starry parallels, along a commercial route, we drove into a quieter area, not far away, and past three towering and silent warehouses, we came, in a quiet and empty part of town, to where the road up to where we lived was cut into the side of whitish rock and scrub growth and lined with a low wall of concrete—an ascent with problems and privileges that made Dad clench his jaw and grit his teeth and also smile and nod (because we were going to the good part of town). Almost as quickly as a trained fighter with a sword, Daddy shifts down with victorious, fast skill, and the car boils upward on its surprised torque and in all its grand weight against what might seem a phalanx of the air or a guardian row of elephants that push their light-struck brows against our advance. The loud and echoing sound of the car motor and the wind-tumult and the whiteness of the cliff glittering like a headache or a mood of madness—the shifting heights and drops are a kind of childish madness itself. The hood, the radiator cap seem to haul us at the slant some seesaws have, we are dragged up, the world is blown backwards like a cape.

Daddy's face is almost at a forty-five degree angle to the dash-board, a sign that he is intent: this has something to do with his eye-sight, something to do with the mystery of having a face.

His open and fleshily vulnerable features, his blond beard stubble, shine with sweat and light. He means to have a deadpan look but his face is theatrically naked, blurred, oscillant: I have taken and keep most of these things, these qualities of his face. S.L. has a look of soft, other-minded insolence—and irony—when he drives: it looks funny on the kid. It looks funny on me now.

S.L. was a genius at some things: *You think people would under-stand, a car is not a horse, you think people would understand what's going on, it's like you're wearing seven league boots, it's not like with horses, you haven't got no time to think, I drove horse wagons, when I was a kid I knew about horses, I had good hands, but you got to have a special kind of mind for a car, you got to let the world go and you got to admit that when science comes in, then what you thought was common sense goes out the window because it ain't common sense no more; I ain't talking like a professor because I want to make a point here and I can't do that when I use my dress up lan-guage. Listen to me: once you got a machine of any kind what you thought before was common sense is crazy now. I can give you a good example: with a horse, it's all rhythm, you get your butt into it, you get your pulse into it; but a car ain't no animal, it ain't got no rhythm, it's got steadiness or unsteadi-ness, pardon my country English, I'm talking like a mechanic, one of the ones who knows what he's doing, a car ain't got any of that kind of rhythm, it ain't like a horse, it's like a clock: it's like a clock but when the hands go 'round, you're in a different place, you're passing a different tree: now this is crazy, and you got to be crazy to do it, you got to understand you're crazy to get into the car in the first place. Would you climb into a clock to spend an hour or two? You got to understand the clock ain't got nothing to do with you sitting there, except you're the reason, but the car seat don't matter, the axles matter, the flywheel matters, what's going on in the cylinders matters. Wheels don't sit on the ground like feet do, and horses don't have gears. Horses get set and pull, a lot of times they balk, like a woman, but in a car, it's all clock stuff, you can't change the speed on this kind of clock, it's rolling along, and you change the way it rolls, and it keeps ticking just as fast, and it's got to fly straight up: well, not straight up, it depends on the hill, it depends on what you got in the backseat, how fat your mother-in-law is, that settles a lot of questions about how it rolls or how it climbs; you got to realize that when it's standing still, it's in a hole, and it's got to get up and get out of the hole: standing still for any kind of clock is a hole, but every single minute it's on, it's got to tick. People think cars and watches is pure convenience, they're crazy, they got their feet on the ground all right, but they're not in that car if they think that they just can get in and go, they think they can just wind and wind a watch, they're butchers, they got no feel, that's how come they get killed; these wonderful machines is wasted on them; you have to do it by feel and knowledge, you have to be smart, I drive by the seat of my pants and I tick off the miles, it takes brain, it takes brain power, real brain power, you have to know how to hold your horses, ha-ha, you have to fit yourself to what's there, I know whereof I speak.*

(S.L. ought to teach a class in it, Lila said, I know a lot of men who don't know as much as he does about these things. People don't like to listen to him any more than they like to listen to a pretty woman but he knows whereof he speaks. He's done some thinking.)

Out the windows, now, the roofs of the town appear even with us. The tops of trees, like the sky edge of fountains, or eruptions from water mains, are balls of points or of a bubbling and rounded glare. The leaves with their summer skins, that shiny skin on them, glare as much almost as glass does. A minute passes and now the roofs form a broken rug and the silent sky flows into the basins of the windows.

We climb into a more and more simplified air almost as if we are climbing the tightly wound stairs inside a church steeple that is largely open to the light.

"This road tests a driver; I don't know how your bitch mother manages it; how does she manage to get home, the way she drives?"

By nerve and speeding.

The road heads into the west at an upward slant, into an afternoon's real sunlight spread at this altitude through larger and clearer and yet clearer volumes of space.

I don't understand how this road is attached to the town behind (and below) us or how the car fits itself to it, but I already know more about how this moment fits with others than Daddy does although he would deny it—he would stake his life, his sanity, such as it is, his soul, too on his being right about these connections.

But he is mad—foolish—and he finds the best transitions to be mad ones, as if the world, like the moment, was newborn; he closes and slams the books on moments in a kind of applause. Those points of actuality—sex and a kind of wit in some events and kinds of courage and kinds of cowardice and his knowledge of cars and his powers of theory apart from books and set in specialized tones and languages—are points where this flying and hurdling man, a horse-bird-plane-motor-and-lecher of a creature, touches down on sanity and is reorganized: one might say he is held together by the glances he exchanges with someone twice a day—anyone—and by certain things having to do with material objects, cars, asparagus plants and asparagus farms (in sandy river bottom soil). When I am not there, he has no compass reading for goodness. When I am there, I am a compass set up as a knower or indicator of true worth. These are my dad's secret terms, his private rhetoric that he uses only with men: he says now, "Level and true, lower a plumb line, and you are there." A measure of the vertical? The perpendicular, like a steeple? An indicator of other meanings? His voice has a certain loud, inflected humming that I, the child, have to translate down into a thin sound, shrinking the symphonic tones to a solo piping, thinly inflected: "Daddy, I like this car."

I hold his hand.

"Lower a plumb line and you are there—"

He is in motion, Dad and the wheels and gearings of his mental states, as well as the outer revolutions of the wheel of fate, and I am the axis, the still point for him—and this is suffocating: I feel it as a gift I give him, as a duty.

I felt myself being absorbed into his physical existence, creeks and plowed fields and nearby Mississippi (heart and big emotions), and into the lights and flows of force and of electricity of the amusement park, the roller coaster and dodgem and racing cars, gloom and joy, madness and specialness, *a park* of *his mind*—his mind thinking, handling things, in and out of the light, taking up and dropping subjects.

He shifts me half onto his lap. "You drive, I may want a chauffeur one of these days." His hands cover mine. His breath riffles the hair on the top of my head. His large thigh pushes against my buttocks.

The growing extent of daylight moved around us. Dad said, "Well, it's hot but it's not such a bad day after all, you got yourself all cheered up, you're not such a bad driver, here, sit on the seat right here, and practice your smile, I want a new chapter, we soldiers got to stick together, we got to smile, we got to earn our keep, where do you keep your smiles, show me the drawer you keep them in, I'll show you the one to wear, where is it, where is the smile you owe me, you want me to give you a good tickle, you need that kind of boost to do a decent job in the world."

He stroked—with his large hand—his giant hand—my side, my ribs; he made me wriggle once or twice, convulse really, that kind of agony, do you know it? The idea, the model of smiling—even of laughing—was invoked: a dark smile flew through my inner dark toward my nose and eyes as much as toward my mouth: I snorted and my eyes watered; then my mouth tasted some of the white water, enamel and warm ice and sky quality of a kind of smile.

I touched his sleeve so that he turned to look and saw me smiling in that fashion.

While I crawled up and over the back of the seat, my father said, "I knew I could cheer you up like you never been cheered up before."

He said, "I want you to remember this: it was no ordinary whatsis; this was special, and I did it for you, boogiekins. Now we're turning over a new leaf—you ain't never going to be sad again: I hear the wind telling me, I hear the birds saying it, it's a rule, it's a rule of nature. The bad stuff's over—what do you think of that, *pisherkins?*"

"That's fine."

Daddy shifted up, the car noise lessened. Our neighborhood, which began at Cherry's house, unscrolled out the windows, houses,

and park, until we came to the driveway of our house. How complicated our degree of wealth is: see the poorly tended gravel and the row
of ratty azaleas—but the driveway is gravel. Daddy was the first
unghettoed man in his family and he knew precious little about lawns
and flowers. He had taste, though. But he was sloppy and forgetful so
the house looks like *a slum farmhouse,* Momma said, which is to say, a
little overgrown and natural, and not citylike. I remember it as
strange and lovely—beautiful and big: but that's probably just me.

The history of the house covers a lot of different matters.

The front porch rides on its trellised substructure—brick columns
and a hidden, dirty shade where lozenges of light from the trellis lay
on strange, lighter-than-ordinary (almost indoor) dust.

"Honk the horn, let's get your mother out here to see what we've
got for her." He whispered and nuzzled me and said, "You got a great
big car for her."

The horn was a trio of long silvery trumpets on the fender that
blasted out Apocalypse—they were so loud and so tuned and toned
that I heard the noises shoot off the wooden wall of our house and then
off the wall of the clapboard house nearest us and the strange clarion
notes were doubled and quadrupled and overlapping: birds flew up,
leaves stirred. "That's enough," Daddy said.

He opened the door, the car door—the lecher is aware in part of
him of my physical restlessness, its range—he lowers me casually by
one arm: that is he holds my wrist and I twist and descend. My foot
hits the edge of the running board, and I prop it there and lean out as
if to be upside down or merely parallel, bandaged head risked like
that. I jump and am held midair and am lowered finally to the gravel.

"Enough!" he said. A house window opened, and from behind the
screen, Nonie said, "What is it?"

I grew still at once—a pale fox of a child in the shadow of a copper
beech.

Daddy moved his big head to a funny angle so that he could look
out the car window and up toward the house window. He said, "Come

see what we've got for you, darling. Nonie, go get your mother and come outside, Wiley has a present for you. And your mother."

"No," I said, but to him. "No!" I turned and then I turned back because I heard him getting out the car. I ran to him and he picked me up and I yanked at his shirt—I pulled myself partway up, I pulled two childish handsful of his shirt—he didn't notice. He said, "We like everybody and everybody likes us. Ah, home sweet home, it's good up here, this is a good place to live, Wileykins."

He was putting me in my place, he was using his child-hand, he was getting his money's worth and his applause, so to speak; and maybe, chiefly, he was getting his sense of a happy home back, the atmosphere of charity and loyalty we had had in the house—he had brought it back, bought it; now he was enjoying it—which is to say, he was enforcing it; or rather, that he had made a mad leap, and in no natural way, but only in his way, to the new moment. And tone. I stared into his face with terrible reproach that was hardly final because he would not look at me and much of what was on my face was the request, *Look at me.* He ducked his head and avoided me and said, to the house, to vanished Nonie, "Hurry up, get your mother and come outside—hurry up—it's time to be happy."

"Daddy—"

"Be still, be nice, pussycatkins."

"It's not for Nonie— No. No!"

"What's the matter, you going to be selfish now? Haven't you had a good time? Didn't you like the automobile place?"

"I liked it, Daddy. Nonie hurt me."

"It was an accident."

"It was not."

"Stop this, Wileykins, as a favor to God and a summer day—" he said that in his role as great poet. Then he said, in his harassed and fleeing self, man attacked by Furies daily, their dark wings and stink covering us, "Let her have a little pleasure, too. Be good. I'm good to you: you be good to me. Have pity on a working man. Be a scholar and a gentleman, like you really are. Are you a son who rises and sets or are you a pain in the neck? Show your good side, Little Sunshine."

Dad is breasting the moments—his and the world's that are focused here—and everything is surrounded by terror and light for him. He said almost dreamily, panting a little with pain in abeyance, he spoke without judgment, "I surely do like to live well— This is a nice moment, Wileykins—take my word for it—"

S.L.—Sam Lewis—is panting slightly. He is a study in teeth and fabrics—he has studied in magazines, observed men in restaurants in St. Louis and Chicago. In bad dreams, the schools he went to, and then the army training, appear most often as mixtures of animals and machines—grunting cows and hippos among whirling knives—but sometimes as sharks, huge ones: *Everyone takes a bite out of you, everyone cuts his cut.*

The enormous car and its fantastically styled sweep of metal is something historically new. The mind boggles at this extent of invention, it mimics no natural thing: it is pure will, pure wish, married by means of history and accident to that sense of time and distance that money is—so many inches, so many minutes at your disposal. Buy it. Buy it. Another kind of bite. S.L. who talked in his sleep had a recurring subject at night: *The Indians are coming.* He said it now, "Hey, kiddykins, you think the Indians are coming back to get their land?" The only children's toys he liked were Indian warbonnets and bows and arrows. I can feel his pulse jump with stage fright and nervousness about the women and with pride and daring and girlish-and-grown-up-male stubbornness about this inventory of success—of pleasures, this lawn even if weedy, this neighborhood, these trees, *this safety,* this bold and absurd and unimaginable car.

Pulse and eyes, posture, the set of his lips, the glare of his eyes— the happy hunter with his trophy shows *his SIMPLE pleasure* when the outcry of the slammed screen door makes him say, makes him whisper, "Here they come, won't they laugh and smile now, to see you bought—what you wrought—"

Lila's wife-voice from somewhere invisible to me on the porch says sharply, "Nonie! Don't!" *Don't slam the screen door.*

Lila's voice has that exposed nerve of physical pain and moral hurt that made her such a registrar of things.

A tiny breeze flicks here and there, a brief nervous pulse of wind, warm and steeply scented, as if Dad's pulse and *SIMPLE happiness* had turned itself into breeze.

The sounds of rapid footsteps on the unsteady boards of the front porch are a rapid tattoo of drama for me. Swiftly gliding shadows race out from the women and fly over the gravel like the wings of goddesses and join the shadows under the tree. I see the New Car in its splendor of chrome, paint, and wax, radiator ornament and spare tire in its slick bisected case and chrome fastening, and the set of horns as a guarantee of pleasure.

But Momma's face—the female reality—and Nonie's shouts, "What is it, what did you buy? Oh not blue, not ugh-ugh *blue!*" suddenly hurl out lines of order and scale that change everything.

Both women have small, fine skulls; and Lila wore something with a floppy collar: she is hip-shot and glamorous, she has on a sort of turban, she is being both *cute* and sexual just now because she had intended to reward S.L., to show Sam Lewis she appreciates the car he got her—she's sorry she racked up the other one, chewed up the engine block and so on.

Of course, this guilt-ridden and obstinate woman, good-looking and sexual, fine-nerved, open-nerved, as exposed as an almost lidless eye, she has the gleam and delicacy of an eyeball become a person—a woman—and in the round hole, the pupil at the center, perches a moody bird-goddess so to speak, patron of rationality, and thoroughly mad.

I mean, for me and Dad, sometimes, she is our talker, our dictionary—who else can we trust as much? But hers is a mad voice, she wants freedom, too; this jealous and willful eye can transmute itself into the cow-goddess Juno, with her great flanks and ill-temper, but the eyes still dominate that creation. She is less mad indoors—she seems unsuitable and frail out of doors on this unwalled lawn. She often says, *I know nothing about men—except a little bit about how to be romantic now and then.* But she's bold and doesn't hide because of her ladyish helplessness, although she is quick often to sadness because it's useful to her to be pitied—she's beside herself with amazement: with a kind of dangerous madness.

"That's not the kind of car I wanted, S.L."

Daddy knows her, knows her power over him: he breathes asthmatically with shock and then so quickly with a kind of hatred that you wonder about him and her: they are madnesses in a whirl, each startled by the other's reality of madness: it is the most acute pain imaginable.

Nonie was supposed to be suffering over my anger with her and my being in bandages and she did look out of sorts, temperamental: but remorse didn't show. The naked way she held her face into the air was pretty. She was bold, and she was playing dumb, and she looked rubbery and outdoorsy, practical, not a luxury like Momma. Her childlike prettiness had the effect of promising she would be pleasant. She was domestically available, not partyish like Momma but isolated.

An orbit of a third madness—leashed and bounded somewhat.

Sunlight lies in bands among the stripes of shadow on the steps to the porch where Momma and Nonie stand *en tableau,* with Momma's fine, exposed face (under her turban) showing a faint softening of age compared to Nonie, to Nonie's startling freshness. Nonie is a step or two lower. Momma's face rides in the air above the shifty masses of her breasts. Her face seems to rise propelled by spirit and meaning into a higher reach of air above her contrary and downward body in the style for women's flesh that she affected that month—small-town, her version, this small town, and the local availability of stuff, or in St. Louis, and so on, and influenced by the movies, the downward-flowing weight of breasts and thighs and then the fineness of ankle and wrist, the languorous whatever, the moody reality of primarily sexual flesh.

Lila's face was made up to represent sweet, naked, fragile welcome—for Daddy who was bringing her her new car. Now her face was puckered and marred. She was very pretty but she was grotesque and absurd, overcostumed and witchlike, thoroughly crazy about what was going on, about what words could do, and will, and what men felt.

Between her body and Daddy's ran innumerable strings—or even chains—of attachment, and awareness of each other's character.

She said in a half-and-half voice (half pleading, half exasperated and threatening) and with a smile that jaggedly frowned instead of being a smile: "What kind of car is *that,* S.L.?"

He, his good humor already marred, even half-collapsed, but struggling on—*like a chicken with its head cut off*—said like a salesman and not exactly addressing Momma, or her tone (they never could talk to each other in public), he said pompously but without conviction and almost as if begging for corroboration: "That's the Buick eight cylinder deluxe sport sedan."

"S.L., that's not the kind of car I asked for." Of course, she wasn't sure of that but she wasn't "reasonable"—I mean she wasn't *prepared to listen to him*—she had her hurt, her disappointment to deal with here. In a very mysterious and quite mad way, she demanded, "S.L., what is *that?*"

Still smiling, still salesmanlike but off at an angle, so to speak, into a now *Christian* and humiliated, thoroughly humiliated purity of offering himself and the car to her, he said: "That's for you."

"I want a small car." Momma closed her mouth and twitched and twittered a little, moving toward being jocular, witty, *a fascinating Jewess*—some such role, I think—but it came out very young and vulnerable: "I told you I wanted a *small* car—" Then suddenly she manages to be *charming:* "I'm deluxe but I'm not up to a sedan, I'm not a playboy, S.L." She paused, ran her hands over her hips to permit laughter, to encourage it—she was hardly a boy. Then seductively, mildly, she said, "Why did you get that one? It's so big, it's too big." Then in a woman's tone, flattering him but with a lot of creeping, flowing anger underneath, "It's much too big for me."

Is she going to burst into tears? Is she going to scream?

The child might: he had not, after all, imagined the possibility of *unhappiness* here.

Lila's brightly red lipsticked mouth is half-threatening but flirtatious. Her breasts are like mad faces. Nonie's voice is a bird-shriek: "I don't like that color, Daddy!"

"How can I steer a car like that, Sam Lewis?" Momma asked. In those days, cars had no power devices and steering took strength.

The air trembled with possible further realities.

Suddenly Daddy said as if with a broken heart: *"Don't be a bitch, sweetheart—your son Wiley picked it out."*

I.e., you have no manners, no heart.

Then he said it: "Don't you have any manners, don't you have a heart—I guess you don't—you don't have manners and you don't have heart, *sweetheart.*

I can't remember him ever calling her by her name, Lila, ever.

Her body now displayed a trembling that he was attacking her right to be considered an irresistibly attractive and knowing woman who was sensitive and rarely wrong, and so on.

"What do you mean? What are you saying to me?" Her hand flew to her breast: "Wiley picked it out?"

Daddy says now, "What do you think I mean? Are you getting so old, you don't speak English anymore? Do you belong in a ghetto with your ugly mother? I'm telling you, he bought the car, I gave him the money, and he picked out the car he liked for his mother—he was an unhappy child, sweetypie, you bitch, and if you weren't so self-centered, you might just have taken a look and seen for yourself that your son had a smile on his face which you have ruined again—look, sweetheart, he *was* happy—"

"I don't want a child picking out a car for me, S.L.!"

I was staring at them. Momma looked at me. Daddy did too. Daddy blinked, grew tired at once, cautious and slack: "It's a bargain—it's cheap at the price, this year—it's a special model, it's a real good buy. So we bought it—they'll really see you coming in this one."

"They'll hang me! There's a Depression on—where's your common sense, S.L.?"

"Bitch, don't ask me about my common sense, where's your heart, what common sense do you have, you're all meanness." Then as if in a bored attempt to make Lila generous, after all: "Wiley presents, with his compliments, a new car he bought with his very own money for his lady mother whom he's unfortunate enough to think is a lady who cares about nice things."

"S.L.! What are you saying! You let a child pick out a car for me! A car that's too big for me to steer! People will laugh at me in that thing!"

"Goddamn it, pussycatkins, that's a good car!"

"Good! Maybe it's good. But that's not a small car! I have to have a small car, I told you I had to have a small car."

"Be nice—you look good in a big car!"

"I can't steer it. I can't handle a big car. A car is a practical thing, you can't make jokes about a car. I'm through with showing off for you, I don't want a car because it tickles you, I have things to do, I have to live, too."

We are in the air-and-light by the corner of our house, in shadow, at the edge of reaches of outspread, burning, and sparkling air.

"Darling—"

"I have to have a small car! I'm not good at parking. I get all *upset*—I told *you*."

Momma's breast heaves. Her breath catches in her throat, in her mouth. The swift excitement of her dealing with the event is like a large fire in dry grass, hot and sucking out the air in her. She might die then and there. Her sun-and-shadow masked face was broken and reckless—practiced and complex—and airless and suffocated. Because of him. Her having been pretty has gone on for a long time. Her being something of a girl still and "adorable" and "redoubtable" gave her an unfair degree of fascination. The shadows under her eyebrows, in her mouth, under her chin made her a soft bandit, helmeted—turbaned. Sunlight sizzled on the gravel of the driveway. She is squeezed by the

perpetually recurring injustice of not being listened to—but she has
never listened to Daddy except with her body. She isn't listening now.
Her behavior is crazed, considering her desires. In her posture is a
hint, a set of signs showing her as not to be taken as *sweet* as well as
signs saying *I'm not meek:* it's unpleasant; it rends you, that such a fragile and exposed system believes itself capable of things it is not capable of.

Daddy stiffened. Anyone's anger, anyone's hurt is an attack on
him, her upset especially.

I blinked. I saw less well. I breathed noisily because I couldn't
really breathe at all if Momma couldn't. I had no depth in me to
accompany the disappointment in S.L. I have no compartments in me
that open onto depths: I am a child. I reflected them—I am a satellite.

In the sunny and shaded Midwestern air, among the fat trees, I
began to jerk with an explosion of pre-hilarity. The near and looming
white clapboarded wall of the house jumps up into the air and the
stippled hills and gullies of the graveled driveway leap out toward the
shining street as my head jerks with the onset of nausea or madness or
laughter.

The hot air touched my bandages. Ignorance, hurt, extreme pleasure, extreme sophistication in a way and blankness had like electricities rushing in me drawn into existence an abundance of currents that
now grabbed at one another and caused something like an epileptic
seizure. Or an electrical and magnetic storm, a child's lunatic seizure.
Momma's nostrils—the light goes through them so that they're
orange, and tiny droplets of sweat mark the edge of her lipstick which
is almost without color in the sun so that she has a beading of spherical glares around a burned, a blackened mouth. A special radiance is
in the fine hairs along her temples. The grass of the carefully mown
but clovered and crabbed lawn spreads on a kind of whirring bladelike
plane. White, small stones and gnawed restless shadows of the driveway and me gasping and yelling with childish laughter—is it hysteria?—near the new, large, blue, reflection-spotted car. The dreadful
silver simplicity in me exploded everywhere in me; I am holding a

making-a-white-party, a braying party. The ragged light, this grief-stricken hilarity, my black astonishment ate my face. "What does he think is so funny?" Momma asked. "I'm glad someone is enjoying himself; I suppose it's nice to be a child, after all."

I started to cough—Daddy hit me on the back. A breeze disturbed the casual wall of leaves so that the ragged shadow fluttered to match my breath. A purple finch on the weigela canceled its whistle and waited in summer idleness for the laughter to be still.

Nonie said, "He's a dope."

Momma said, "Is he all right? I wonder if he's all there, that child." She's *always* quick to defend herself. Then, remembering I was theirs, she said, "He thinks we're entertaining."

I began to convulse.

I was about to throw up.

It stopped. Now everyone ignored it that I had laughed.

Momma stood righteously pretty, sultry, and she scowled sadly and angrily, too, at Daddy.

Daddy said, "It's a good car, Lila, it has power to burn; it's a bargain; people will know you're coming. It's what the doctor ordered for the woman who's too busy to stay at home."

"S.L., the world's not a fairy tale! I can't appear anywhere in *that.* What does a child know? I don't care what horsepower it has, why do you insult me like this? Why do you play silly games about what I want when I know what I want? Why don't you ever listen to me? I think before I speak, I speak English, I have a mind."

But it is hard for him to listen directly, it is forbidden to him to hear her directly.

Daddy said, "You look like an old crow when you get ugly, you get ugly just like your mother, you don't know what you look like; I wish you could see how ugly you look, you ought to get hold of your temper before it ruins everything; you will, if you know what's good for you. Watch out. Watch yourself. You're no chicken anymore."

Momma said, "It's not a joke, it's not a joke when I talk, I say things that mean something; I'm not a dummy: why don't you listen to *me*? What have you *done*? We're not children anymore, S.L. I don't want *my car* picked out by *a child*. I don't think you are ever in your right mind. What kind of trouble are we in now, S.L.? I'll tell you this: I don't want that car."

She was working on the death and threat in her voice, on the serious reaches of not being nice—of wanting to hurt someone.

The hysteria and comedy start up again in the child.

Lila casts a heated glance of wonder at me.

I didn't like her at the moment but I thought she was right.

Daddy's face under the brim of his hat was pink and patient and contemptuous, almost sweet—a tactic. He clearly looked as if he wouldn't ever hear her so long as she was stubborn, so that I wanted to shout, DADDY, *LISTEN!* S.L.'s flushed and rosy obstinacy, his boyish, brave downcastness was a way of registering that his *grown-up* view of her was that she was *a termagant*.

She was aware of the ferocity and stupidity of his temper and she liked baiting him and feeling that he was a frightening man and that she was a lion tamer. She could astound him by her being fearless—and so careless. She was stubborn in a dirty way. She put a dirty look on her face. He couldn't make her show fear without being rougher than he would be able to excuse unless he went closer to being mad than he wanted since that would flatter her and show her she had power.

And then she would laugh at him and keep a record of it.

Near me, the finch launched itself, it flew suddenly. Its wing-strokes enlarged it. It flew straight and then curved upward and made the air strange and then it was gone.

She said scaldingly, "I'm sorry if it upsets your pride but my life is a serious matter: I don't play with everything the way you do. I mean what I say." She retreated suddenly to a somehow threatening, angry politeness. "It makes me laugh, you say you're a gentleman. And you think a child can pick out *my* car."

I blinked but the giggles, the laughter in my mouth, the hot and cold *fish* swimming there made me splurt out loud again.

How come Daddy hadn't thought about that, about a child picking out *Momma's* car?

Or the salesmen's pride?

Some things don't matter, and some things do, and a man has to pick and choose.

Dad had a sarcastically reproachful look. His shoulders in his coat were lumpy with muscle. He puts a sterner look on his face. "Bitch. You are a real bitch. You really, truly are, Mrs. Silenowicz. I am ashamed that you are Mrs. Silenowicz." Plea and warning and contempt. Then, "My wi-i-ife."

"You make me say things over and over, all that machine is good for is to cart politicians to an Irish funeral." She was being *glamorous* and quick and valuable: *fascinating, funny.* She was stealing the world. I began to laugh in strangled snorts. Momma said, "I'm not that charitable a woman, as you know, S.L.—I don't even like Jewish funerals. Irish ones give me pimples."

"Don't you *like* your son, Madame *Mother?* He chose the car for *you—*"

"What does that mean? That I'm stuck with it? You put the idea in his head. You made the trouble. He knows enough to know what's going on. You're the silly one, you get so silly, you make me a crazy woman! Do you know you talk so crazily, it makes you ugly? You're getting so ugly, I don't know what you're going to do, you don't like *anyone,* you're just a middle-aged, ugly, crazy man."

She looks as though she might explode with madness.

Daddy made a face at her, a you're-an-ugly-woman accusation: "Can't you ever appreciate what's going on here? What's wrong with you, haven't you any *love* in you?"

"S.L., it's a car, it's not a valentine. I *want* a car. How much of what's stupid do I have to live through? This is making me crazy."

"I can't stand this ugliness. You're destroying me."

Nonie said suddenly, staring bulging-eyed at Daddy, she said in a high voice, "I don't like that car, Daddy, I don't like that color."

She loves him—she is mad with the urge to have him care for her the most.

Momma said, "Wiley, if I had your eyes, I'd like that color, too. Your father should have given you the right advice, I don't blame you, don't you blame me; blame him."

"Christ and hell on a crutch, you bitch—why ruin what that kid had today! You ruin everything every chance you get! No one can be happy around you! Why do people have to put up with witches like you!"

"I can't stand this! I don't want that car! I'm dying of aggravation! Don't talk to me about love, and who I love and what I ruin. This has nothing to do with *love*! So don't start on that, not with me, not today, I've tied the rag on."

She doesn't have that smell or the anguished and long-necked frightened-bold carriage she gets, so that's a tactic—her degree of sanity and hurt seems to slide around, often, so that you can't tell with her.

Nonie started to open the rear door of the car, I don't know why, and when the door swung open, as it moved on its own weight, when it was perpendicular to the car, it began to wobble outward away from the car toward Nonie, who had taken her hand from the handle.

Then—I think—she touched the door to fix it, to put it back, and to fend it off: she was very quick and athletic.

The door turned sideways so that its inner side faced upward, toward the tree branches. While Nonie's hand was on its edge. She held the door—it looked like that—the inside handles shone in the clear air. Nonie jerked her hand free and made a wheeing scream. She has both her arms near her body and the door is sailing in its lateral posture and is seesawing a little toward her while she screams and pulls in her stomach and dodges a little. She was staring and at a certain point she began to scream—it was a grown-up, a real end-of-the-world scream. This is really true. You can guess what I did. I began to heave with laughter and to snort with childish bellows and wheezes, a truly stupid sound.

And Nonie screamed on: *What is this?* and *I didn't do anything!*

Her fine hooked nose was white with disbelief, with horror at so painful and expensive a humiliation.

The unattached and sailing and slowly falling door teetered, skimming lower and lower—Nonie's eyes are twisted like snails—I have both hands over my mouth, then at my temples—the door floats and falls toward the gravel. A breeze rippled the leaves above us. Momma's eyes are blinking. The door skidded onto the gravel, it crunched and slid for several inches. The grinding and tearing noises were serious sounds, strange, rough, long-drawn, convincing. Then it was over. The door had ground and scraped its way along and crunched itself to a stop. Daddy was bent forward as if to listen—there was something helpless in the posture of his hands. He was horrified.

He leaps toward the now stilled door—he looks dextrous.

Momma is saying, "Oh my God, oh my God, what is that, S.L.?"

The door lay, upholstery side up, on white gravel.

I was laughing with true wildness. A blue jay began to make anxious jarring sounds at my noise: it jars, jar-jar-jar—is it jeering at us? I think it's nervous.

Momma said, "My God, S.L., will they take the car back now or are we going to be stuck with it because of what Nonie did to that door?"

Daddy said, "I'll be damned, I'll be goddamned." I don't think he was listening to Momma.

Nonie said, "I didn't do anything, YOU BITCH!" to Momma.

Momma ignored her.

Nonie said in an odd—mad—voice, "I don't like that car, Daddy."

Lila said quasi-philosophically—a little like a detective, as well: "Why did the door do that? What do you call a thing like that, when something like that happens—to a new car? To a door like that?"

"Leave me alone for a minute," he said. "Let me figure this out."

I was still laughing.

He was red in the face, puzzled, upset, angry. Dad's luck. His day was odd inside him. He thought and then, red-faced, he turned to Nonie and said, "What did you do to *that door?*"

Nonie shouted, "I DIDN'T DO IT, WILEY DID IT! I DIDN'T TOUCH THE DOOR, HE MUST'VE DONE IT."

If she was upset enough—if she put enough upset in her voice—if she was near to being destroyed, he had to be concerned about her.

He hadn't the energy to say, *You touched the door, you opened it, I saw you; just tell me what happened,* or to be logical about her or hinges of the door (the pins hadn't been inserted in the hinges on that door). Partly because she never could tell a straight story—it was embarrassing usually to watch her try—and then settle for lies and dull things and self-praise.

The sunlit reaches of the air, the stretched linen of the sunstruck Portsmouth air, the sunwarmed wall of the house, the baked and slightly smelly old paint, the not very dark shade beneath the copper beech, enclosed the enormities and obliquity of our lives.

Her defense of herself was not intended to be harmless for me, and Daddy didn't want to fight with her. He'd consoled me and worn himself out, I guess. It's the end of the afternoon, *the shank*—he took Nonie's "facts" and her lies in ways that I did not, as truths about her soul and its sadness. Partly I am his other self—if he hurts me, he punishes himself. S.L. strode toward me, his trouser legs flapping in the hot air, he grabbed my shoulder—he didn't want to deal with Nonie and look at her just then—he grabbed the little laugher, I was nutty with laughter. He had a huge look of hatred—engorged and passionate—his big face was puffy with it, with true hatred because I hadn't protected him or his gesture or made his life worthwhile since I'd been consoled and I wasn't consoling him. I felt his emotion boiling near the small kettle of hilarity that was me. Then his emotion boiled in me and raced back at him. I used to pretend to myself I didn't know what he felt. But that was a lie. We knew that the larger one of us two was enraged with hurt. So much had gone wrong today and no one took care of him. I hadn't held his hand when the scene started, I hadn't cried or taken his part. At this very moment I don't look at him with the love the car buying had left in me. I am not loyal—or obsessed with him. It's better to hate *me* than the others since I'm the one he likes and I'm not as good at hurting him as they are. At this stage of almost any afternoon or evening he has no interest in justice, only in lessening his pain, his solitude. The heated air in the torn blue-green baize of the shadow of the copper beech has the effect of desert distances. In my dreams, Daddy and I often are Arab chieftains alone in a desert. The pain inside his ribs, Christ, near his heart—I feel it, I felt it then. I see the angry look in his poor, staring roan-colored eyes often in my dreams still. I did nothing nice for him that day. Nothing. His face came so close to me, it entered my comprehension and remains in me as part of the shape of my own. I can still smell in the present tense his sour breath. He shouted at me, "WILEY, WHAT DID YOU DO TO THAT DOOR?"

He meant *What are you doing to me?*

I was already laughing—with mad hysteria, antagonism, contempt. And I laughed some more—at him—and groaned—and sent him rays of huge reproach—huger than his since he could not at that moment really look at me. He could read my feelings, too: *Daddy, stop being so stupid. It's hurting me.* He could read that in me.

"You damned brat!" He said it with a kind of agony. Sometimes I think foolishness might be the greatest human value. I think it's really asinine to write *Poor Wiley, poor S.L.*—still, I write it here.

I said, "Daddy," while I laughed, while I pulled back, away from him.

He slapped me.

Not hard.

Hard enough.

I blacked out. It's one of the things I can't live with—a gesture like that. *You always were a prima donna about people's feelings, you were finicky, everything had to be just so with you—you never cared if you broke anyone's heart or not.*

Momma's voice caught us: "S.L., DON'T BE SUCH A FOOL! HE WAS STANDING HERE THE WHOLE TIME. YOU SAW HIM. HE DIDN'T TOUCH THE DOOR. WHY DOES NONIE MAKE YOU ACT SO CRAZY?"

She was a fool, too—she was jealous of Nonie. She said later, to me, *You broke his heart from the very beginning.* I said to her, *So what.*

She made it worse that day. She said, "YOU DON'T LOVE HER AND YOU LOVE HIM, IS THAT IT?"

God. Oh my God.

He is in pain—he is maddened—he is desperate. The pain and horror in him scalds me. Having consoled me with his strength and folly, Daddy now wants me to share *his* pain and folly, and the blame, too. Ma "knows"—she wants his attention for herself—she does know, she is laughing now in a bitter way—"Oh my God," she says, "oh my God, I have to catch my breath, if anyone could see us, what would they say? We would look so dumb I don't how we are to live."

She means all the wrong choices and all the mistakes, I think.

Nonie says, "HE DID IT, DADDY!"

Momma says, "Uhhhh, ohhhh." Then, "Ahhhhh."

That means we look so stupid to her that she's giving up.

Daddy wheels, he makes almost a full circle, then he finishes the circle and stares at me, he says, "Oh my Gawdd—" It's anguish. He says, he shakes me and says, "You're really selfish, you really have a cold heart. . . ."

I feel the madness in him still.

Momma said, "You hit the child, and he still has his bandages on."

Now she's ahead of him in the shame and redemption stakes.

How pretty and strange we all look in the shade and bits of sunlight alongside our house.

S.L. pushed his hat back. I saw myself in his glasses as he looked down at me. "You're bad," he said, "but oh my God, I don't want you to be sad anymore," and he knelt in front of me. His hands held my arms. He kissed me with his humid lips all over my face, especially where he'd hit me, he kissed my wounded chin—then my lips.

The hot air around us vibrates.

He said, "Forget I hit you. It was a mistake. Listen, my fine feathered friend, you're my sunshine, don't you ever forget that, don't you ever ever *worry* about that 'cause it's as sure as God made little green apples."

Momma's standing over *there* and Nonie's on the grass eyeing the fallen door, and Daddy and I are here at the middle of the whirling scene.

I don't know.

He pressed his stubbled cheek harshly against my face: "Tell me you love me. Tell me it's O.K."

"You're not nice to me, Daddy."

"Leave him alone for five minutes, S.L. Stop torturing him every few minutes. He'll come around."

I pushed him away.

He held me anyway, rubbed my face with the raw junkyard of his, the rattling sounds coming from it of breath and eyelids clicking.

"Say you love me a little."

I nodded.

I did love him a little.

He looked at me and moved his hat back still farther on his head.

Then it fell. He turned and picked it up—then he stood up, and he walked toward the car door. "No pins in the hinges," he says now, unashamed. "I'm not surprised: no one remembers anything, no one gives a man any credit; well, we're all fools and clowns, it's all ingratitude, we have to make the best of a bad business, I guess."

They betrayed him at the car place, he means. Betrayed us.

He will protect us.

He is vaguely suicidal, undone—he is sailing down the chute of his despair—it's not like Momma's being in the land of lament; the weight and thunder of him carries him more swiftly down and down and *down* in mood and not maneuverably—he has to be a saint to bear it. To pass it off as not too important, his despair just now.

He turned to his daughter and said, "Nonie, give me a hand."

Lila can't lift things; she's fragile.

Nonie started to complain, but he said, "Come on and I'll buy you an ice cream cone tonight, Miss Ice Cream Lover."

"O.K., Daddy," she said in a kind of businesslike and yet arch way.

Grunting and clumsy, Nonie and Daddy got the door onto the backseat of the car.

Momma and I—and the blue jay—watched.

Daddy climbed into the wounded Buick. Embarrassed sunlight flowed unevenly around him.

He said, ladling out blame and with a fixed and angry—and embarrassed—face, even when his tone changed in the middle of his speech, "They don't know their business at that goddamned car place, I'll go light a fire under them, I'll find out what this is all about; they're good joes, they won't steer me wrong, they'll treat me right."

I held Momma's hand.

The noise of the car motor running overcame and then faded behind the noises of sunlight and leaves and Momma's breath as Daddy, looking businesslike and resolute, backed the quarter-undoored Buick down the gravel driveway and out into the street in the white light we used to have on the top of that bluff.

LILA AND S.L.

Lila stands in the doorway of the upstairs sleeping porch.

"S.L., are you looking at my legs, I have good legs, do you like my legs? I think they're still good, S.L." Then: "We're alone in the house. We're alone here. On the sleeping porch. In the rain."

His wicker chair creaks. She's sweetly sourly ignominious, fretful with considerable delicacy, in her manner of invitation and sensual grace.

S.L.'s face takes on an incautious look, the effect is almost of love, but he closes his eyes and thins his lips and looks blank.

"Tell me, S.L.—I wonder what you think you know about me—" She addresses him, his blank look, his having-rejected-her face. Then: "Let's be human," she says. "I like a little romance on Sundays." She has a fragile odor of risk and good humor and of imminent self-abandonment.

She shows she knows that if she can inspire a recklessness in S.L., she'll feel herself to be *still in luck,* that is, a major force as far as matters of personal powers of attraction and fucking. And she shows some disguises and arrogance toward S.L., and recklessness—she uses the charity stuff and denies it—shrewdly and as if she had no choice, and also she can turn around and show she doesn't care, she can manage.

S.L.'s face takes on an incautious look, and the effect is almost of *love*. He says, "This rain—does it put you in the mood—*honey?*" The *honey* is interestingly curled, a little sarcastic, tentative in regard to affection—this is a tone he uses at times. He's often afraid of Lila—he considers his fear to be a reproach to her. "Lila, you're too much," he says—it might be that he's angry and sarcastic and not drawn by her anymore. And his voice, his posture are insulting—to a surprising but not final extent. He doesn't use the hard, don't-touch-me sarcasm that is one of his forms of anger.

Lila sits loosely and moves her knees back and forth a little—S.L.'s got a disturbed face—he's susceptible to her; he's got maybe three-quarters of an erection.

"You ought to try to understand me, S.L.—it wouldn't hurt you. . . . No one would think you were a sissy if we had a little romance."

Some of her systems are primitive. She's eyeing him—as if unfrightened; the imminence of a fuck can't make her shy—she's a grownup: that's rough in a way, that's roughhousing in a ladyish way—silken and *loose*.

She has a slight grin of blinded sophistication. She staringly waits for the outcome of what she's doing.

S.L. grabs at and then drops and eludes memories of her and him at the flopping and shoving of a fuck, of fucks at the center of what they've done at times with each other in bed.

Daddy says, "Well, what the shit?" He breathed, in and out, in and out. "Honey, why not? Hey isn't that the hell of it? A good time? Why not?"

Lila doesn't like men *who are like locomotives*. She likes to leash and control. Or she has to. She said, as if he had said something else, as if he had asked her, as if he had initiated this stuff, "I wouldn't mind a small part." She's boldly crooked. She spreads her legs a little wider in case he's pissed at her. Her body has an amusedly sexual stance.

S.L.'s disturbed by the hint of a *subtlety* in her; he doesn't want to have to react to or be obtuse or be nagged by its actions: "I'm just a truck driver at heart, honey," he said. "I don't know nothin' 'bout parties 'round here."

A good many people's daydreams, including her own and his, have entered into what Lila's like now, except for the threats in her manner: those are real, not daydreamy. She's absorbed many sexual details and *methods* in her time—she's a fairly large piece of the world, all in all.

S.L. tries to figure out Lila's motives: Lila's competing with other women for him—that interests her. And he's a convenience; they've been together thirteen years. He feels shocked by sexual desire, vulnerable, achy.

Lila would like to have S.L.'s sexual moods explained to her. His neck is rigid; he shifts his legs; his hands are on his thigh, near his crotch. The heat he feels draws his belly up, as if into his chest and throat, and he is crowded with it, the barnyard heat, which holds his outer and middling and inner attention. He feels a slight tenderness toward the sensory—he's shocked by each of his heartbeats—for several moments. A moist, heated emptiness lunges upward in him and waits for sensation, is hungry for it; and a "contrary" leadenness moves down in him until it joins in the general area of his thighs with a sullen impetus of self-erasure, a vaguely genital impulse, perhaps toward pain. It is a large part of his mind; then it becomes background; then it returns and is imperative and central.

He laughs, his face and eyes are swollen at once when he does, a personal oddity of appearance, to go with the particular sounds of that laugh, which expresses concupiscence and contains an announcement of sexual style and a recklessness about women and some toughness and considerable ignorance.

"You feel like being nice to me—" Lila asks. Again she spreads her legs; she offers a whorey smile.

He says, "Keep talking to me, keep talking. You ever hear of talking too much, honey . . ." His eyes are heavier yet, they glare romantically and then lighten: "I'm not a talker, I'm a fucker, and you know

it." But he looks a little pouting, childish, cupidlike—it's a passionate physical joke that he looks that way. People who know S.L. and
Lila talk about which one is the suitor of the other: which one is the
most loved is what it comes to.

"Oh I know it, I'm aggressive—I'm the Veteran of Foreign Wars."
S.L. says, tasting his feelings, "You're something to write home
about—"

His attention rests on her like a bright light, as if she were in a
prison cell and was being kept awake. Lila has a sort of air of drama like
that, as if her mood matches that one note of his excitement. She sits
almost somberly and then finds it in herself to produce one of her
"good" smiles, but it is not aimed but is as if she were alone in a cell
with an invisible watcher; and she moves her head invitingly but not
so openly, placating him as an invisible watcher, as if she admits that
placating him is something she does habitually or is due him from her,
or that she really is in a prison of sexual (or social) dependence on him.

S.L. carries himself pretty much as someone whose body and face
are *young still*. His face is cagey, however. His "youthfulness" is worth
something: I mean he makes use of it: he's a businessman. He looks
sad, sadly honest—as if to say he's not on the make. But he is on the
make in being a *young* man: this is part of his real-world esthetic and
is a complex thing: he says to her, "I'm just a real-life hero from first-
to-last."

She says, "You're a real man—I'll say that for you."

Although his face and posture have not moved a lot, his mood has:
he's now this handsome man who's amiable, who's sensitive, who's *jus-
tifiably* moody and knows his own value and who's angry the world is
what it is—he's someone who wants to be comforted sexually for this.

His displays of mood are a species of temperament, so that when
he's sufficiently self-regarding to be *a hero* like Achilles or someone in
a movie, he would like to shout and whimper and discuss his worries—show himself nakedly, like showing his prick. If he and Lila
were drunk and Lila encouraged him, he would crazily (in a nonsense
form) or seriously do just that. But it would be taking a chance to try

that here because Lila might start a fight or twist the moment—she is pretty largely untamed.

Lila brightens her face to rule his sadness and moods and dramas and to show that they are out of bounds sexually. Or some of them are. Or all of them except at her say-so. Or unless he explodes . . .

"It's all hunky-dory," he says and shakes himself. He has a cloudy look of forgetfulness and a look of a willingness to be male—although he looks sad and although she is *difficult.* He's got a good face, *romantic* eyes and mouth—he does look young—he's *really pretty,* and at the moment somber.

Lila has a funny sort of almost youthful self-congratulation, a late adolescent conceit on her face, but calculation like a meanness of spirit or sign of age appears and flickers and is almost sly—she grants herself some *honesty* of expression. There is a loss of style involved. She grants herself some well-marked desire, and she intends to protect herself and to be treated well no matter what she seems to risk: "I'm an honest woman who feels a little crazy, S.L."

She looks at him hopefully, then twenty-year-oldishly—which is a sweet joke—then sort of as her own age: perhaps she is wild—it is really hard to say. S.L. has his head bent forward; his eyes travel upward and he looks at Lila while he holds himself with one hand. He sighs. He stands. He will go to her. She has a sly look. S.L.'s fuck-stuff with her is not very codified. When he stands, his hand holding the bulge of his pants, his face takes on a crude, startled look: he wants to fuck, he wants to fuck Lila (maybe). He says with complicity, "Are there any more at home like you?"

Lila's sad, knowing little smile is very pretty; she "knows" he is meeting her halfway to the best of his understanding. But she's sad. "I'm home for you," she says; it is a dirty remark. "You're a handsome Sam—" Sam is his name. "You're a handsome Sammy-sam . . ."

"Sammy-sam-sam," he says.

She can't think of which nursery rhyme he means to refer to—or what song from an operetta or from vaudeville. His eyes indicate he's referring to something sweet. He feels a need for simplicity: an unheedingness surrounds his attentiveness and makes it blind—and sexual. It is always a little sexual.

His nursery rhyme: "Blow the house down," he says.

It's raining; the summer rain makes the porch private. He's day-dreamy about a fuck and a blow job; he has a *let's-be-ladies-and-gentlemen-air* that he gets when he's after something that doesn't blackmail her so much that she despairs or blows up. She has gotten smart over the years. He has a thick poetry of posture, a gross and vir-ile eloquence of posture, which she likes; it signals his own fuck-momentum; she might give in; he lets his breathing drift into a fuck rhythm—he's considered a good lay. The half-recollection, half-prediction of sensations violates, then empties his eyes.

Lila bats her eyelashes and burlesquely eyes his pants caught on his stiffened prick, and she strokes him there, a nice-wife-forward-woman-playful-naughty-sly-whore—a compromise. The troubled actuality of this contains a taunting heavy sweetness: a sense of the uncertainty of things, and premonitions and foretastes are clustered in her in an incomplete sentimentality about fucking, I think. Her bold ongoingness is a form of self-love: she owes it to herself.

He feels enough confidence in his physical reality—he is large-wristed, big-shouldered—that it becomes a conviction of his spiritual stature *as a man.* He's not a whiner or a pleader or a rapist (except to a point): he's S.L., king of the house, monarch of the truth, soul keeper (women and children don't have souls).

His assurance is in part about the weight and size of his perturbed genitals as it is about his imminent performance—but he is not so confident with Lila. He is aware she does not think him a bastard or liar or creep: when she dislikes him, it is because she finds him stupid. She has always refused to live anywhere except near her own family; S.L. cannot bully her. He calls her creepy and poisonous and things like that, and with the limitations of her life as a woman with (some) money, she takes his word that he knows what he says he knows. She doesn't disbelieve him enough. Or she believes him still: this gives a perceptible and eccentric *loveliness* hastily, and harshly, to his face.

I mean he lives up to it. The mutual role-playing here is meant to indulge each other and it is a sexual act as tangibly as self-display or dirty talk. Both S.L. and Lila shiver with taut nerves in regard to each other.

Then S.L. changes: his self-appraisal is realistic now since she agrees with it. He's sarcastic and moved because of his male *beauty* and knowledgeability as a grownup. She does this for him, has this power, I mean.

Momma's glancing up at him, at his face, now his eyes: she stares into his eyes boldly. I think his eyes seem to her to request and yet discredit what is about to occur. She doesn't know why. She is oddly loyal. His eyes anger her but not in an overall way but inside the sexual moment—she doesn't know how to purify him. She sits and is solemn and sexual for him—and is also a little angry.

Perhaps, too, he has fooled her and she has fooled herself in regard to him. She puts her hand back on his clothed crotch.

He says, "A little fucketty-fuck for the married people? All right?"

Lila smiles like a shopper who isn't sure of the salesman; she's too nervous and too angry to smile as a lecherous woman. She is brave and shows bravado toward his temper but she has a hard kernel of caution, perhaps a respect, for men: a vague, tormented mistiness enters her eyes. Nerves, stage fright, deep fright, fright beyond belief, but general, not specifically caused by the moment, hysteria—sort of pleasurably, dirtily vast.

She's not drunk; she makes herself unmorbid, insensitive, as if she were drunk—this is a discipline, a test of a Real Woman, not a wallflower, not someone on the sidelines. As a local beauty and a college beauty, she distrusts nature where she's concerned. And this event and S.L. make her a wife in courtship, but she is Lila-in-courtship: she feels blasphemous, daring, and crazed. She would be greatly hurt to discover she was naïve finally. If her mood were otherwise, she would smile in a certain sly way and tug at his pants, but she's not in that other mood.

He is not enough in love with her or with himself to be sexually romantic all the way through himself. He is sexually romantic as a form of politeness. Her uncertainties used to affect him, but nowadays he feels that these events wobble along and what he notices is unclear: he doesn't pay attention to what he notices. He sometimes says, *I am an old married man . . .* He doesn't say that now, but he thinks *so what?* meaning *don't pay attention . . .*

She stirs herself to improve the occasion; she has a notion about life that it is something she is good at: on her face is an obscure gaiety; and she smiles at him in a way that denies her opinion that this moment and the world itself rest on machines of a terrible ordinariness and that it's best not just to be amiable but to work at being romantic— her smile is romantic and particular and slinkily furtive—she's smiled like that and influenced men before, often. She is not quite willful.

S.L. bends toward the smile, lowers his face to hers and kisses and mouths the smile in a rush of ready intimacy. One's sense of him physically is his being packed tight, stuffed with fantasies and thoughts and warmths.

Lila—obligingly—kisses back with a grand lewdness and breadth of appetite. It is not clear what she feels. While the kiss continues, S.L. sits on the couch with a certain physical virtuosity, but the movement and his weight are also oxlike. *Nicely* his leg and hers press together. Kissing changes the scale of his sensations and rules them, as in sleep when an episode takes over and fills the head as if the episode were the world.

His style becomes S.L.-the-lewd. He holds Lila toughly and kisses her with amiable contempt and some seductive looseness. She likes this well enough, or she puts up with it; and she offers a flexible languor. She proceeds inwardly in a separate tonality from him.

S.L. kisses proudly and then in moderate suggestion of someone working class and then even with a jazz or black quality. His tongue's at work, so's hers, in a moderate uproar of sexual impetus.

Then her movements become bucking and exigent—and nervous—maybe false. S.L. writhes too: it is a bizarre tangle of implications and rhythms, baroque.

Patterns of rainy light move on them. S.L.'s intent and Lila appreciates that. Lila looks snotty; some anger flavors her sexual reality and makes it familiar and like childhood and suggests how curious and responsive, how rebellious and manipulative she was, and obstinate and blank and suggestible and restless: not steady and not interested in being steady.

S.L.'s attractiveness makes her want to see if he's attached to her strongly. "Kiss me some more on my *mouth*," she says, although he is kissing her on her mouth.

S.L. uses warm-hearted insults a lot for talk but also as sexual stuff. What he says aloud is, "You kiss like a wife—" He ends the kiss; he pulls away a bit and says into her mouth, "You fuck like a wife." He isn't insulting only because it's sexy for him. He means it; and he wants to be the boss here, the expert . . . It isn't simple.

Her legs stir. She responds physically to his ferocity but she hates him mentally; this frees her for the sexual voyage with its purpose, which is to snuff him between her thighs, frees her to enjoy the perils of a fuck voyage and to have her own thoughts; it works for her sexually. But it isn't simple. She won't nurse him—she's a proud matron. She bites his lip.

He says, "LILA!" He kisses her wetly and slaps her breast and she mutters, "uh" or "ow." Her mouth's spread wide for him while he strokes her trembling leg. He and she touch tongues, lick each other's lips and gums. A tense and as if victorious soul resides in Lila's lip-writhings and focuses the kiss—but she's not triumphant; I mean he's on top. Maybe it's a triumph of marital attachment. Her face has ripe eyelids, is warmly expressive, sensual-seeming—but it is cold and coldly calculating too, which is at odds with or is a flavoring as she leans back and is flooded with, who knows what, passivity? Attention of a peculiar sort? S.L. remembers sketchily the look of her lips while he presses on them, so hard he is aware of the small bones of her jaw and of her teeth. She says, as if contented, "You're eating me up . . ." Maybe she's proud that at her age and after so many years she can still *get him going*—a phrase of hers. She likes his *carryings on* but it isn't simple liking.

S.L. *feels* her eyes staring at him and he feels her not staring but, as it were, listening to the kiss: the idea of her staring makes the closed-ness of the present state more real to him. In erotic jocularity—he intends his saying this to be agreeable to her—he says, "Ah, a funny honeymoon . . ." That's a line from an Eddie Cantor song about mak-ing whoopee. He has his own quick tact and he switches to the faintly mocking but still somewhat more romantic, palping her breast, "Ah, a loaf of bread, honey, and thou under a tree, thou, oh thou . . ." He has a sincere look on his face along with the jocularity—he has a ten-dency to go in for thematic sprawl.

Lila's hair is askew. "Well, I'm a woman, S.L.," she says to him—that's poor territory for the boast she intends to make to distract him from her age. She speaks pantingly, with her eyes cast aloft as if to sig-nal she's off-balance now, "I'm not a know-nothing."

She wants a fuck that's more final than usual, one that might change things: *fuck me and change my life.* . . . She'll take more risks and different ones and do fuck-movements different from when she was younger, and she wants him to appreciate it although chiefly she just wants not to be reproached by a lapse of ardor in him. It is not clear if she wants him or wants a fuck at all so much as it seems she wants to make use of this territory. . . . She's thirty-five years old; he's thirty-two. That was older back then than it is now.

His hands are on the inside of her thighs on private curves—his memory has her sexual odor in it. . . . Sexual curiosity—fluffy, severe—widens her muscularly but focuses him. She's about to laugh and sigh with her lower belly. Splayed on the couch, she bestirs herself blinkingly and puts her fine arms around S.L.'s shoulders, her face fat-tened and careless. . . . She's trapped and abandoned in carelessness: some of which is response, some is signal. If she focuses it would be as if she were fighting with him, fencing with him. Her knowledge of the world is hinted at in the puffy secrecy and patience and careless-ness of her face. In a way it's as if she's been lured here; she will be—

eaten. She's partially eaten now: her legs are gone, for instance—it's sort of like that and not like that in that she is actually alert.

Her notion of fucking, the prime requisite in sexual style, is courage, she believes, real or bluffed: this is so for men and women. One of S.L.'s good-sized hands is rayed over her breast. He's busy and interested in various neural blossomings and heats, irregularities of himself when he acts with sexual intent. Active circuits of warm blindness become qualities of vision more important than the eyesight of not-fucking.

His horselike eyes say *this-is-real-life*. His lower body's, uh, *hot*. Lila starts to stroke his hair with movements unsynchronized with the slidings of her haunches and the tics of her face. He's becoming pretty much enraged by—passion. Another way to put it is that S.L. is somewhat pleased and partly released into fuck moodiness. Lila stands higher than in her own view since one kind of status for a woman is determined by how many times and how well she gets fucked. He notices that Lila's responses are older and blatantly efficient at fuck negotiations between him and her, and not actually generous. He holds in both hands Lila's right breast, her larger breast, which he has pulled free of her dress and has on his face a look of such seriousness of intent that Lila holds her head proudly.

"You're like a queen," S.L. says.

Her breasts are publicly discussed—they have been since she was young. Lila feels she's somewhat like a historical queen who was also dutiful toward her realm; I mean the queen-image was very powerful back then in America. And Lila is modern American, tormented-low-down-willful. . . . These are the ways she feels.

Her face has a look of puckered queenliness—her body, her moods are a gift she makes. Her breath makes a dark sound, a whispery, vaguely ghostlike clarinet noise on the porch. S.L. as a speculation in excitement lifts Lila's legs. He sits back and puts her legs in his lap. He is sweating in the humid air, and he smiles at Lila and he lets spittle glisten on his lips, an odd obscenity that pleases him. He strokes her tit. She chuffs, dark-mooded. His eyes have a softened presence.

He and Lila are enclosed in the limits of their attention. He strokes his hair with one hand. His breath is noisier than hers. He considers, shrewdly, pleasures that aren't here. Something uneasy hovers in the deplorably fine rainmist on the porch. The rain is iterant. Small rivers flush and gurgle on the wood and shingles of the house. S.L. stares at Lila's tit pouched in his hands. A sexual blurriness is inside and outside both of them. His hand cups, pumps, presses on her big breast . . . he's here with her. . . . "You're a woman," he says, idly commanding. She bends her head back. She is as if splayed on the couch. His intrusively able hands press and finger and make handfuls—he sweats with increasing heat, increasing cruelty. She bestirs herself and puts her own arms around her upper chest in an embrace. She is sweetly dramatically, sultrily stormily obedient—responsive, perhaps more to sex than to S.L. No word covers what she is. S.L. sees her sweet-sweaty flesh, white, he feels it, he feels her sweat like a sweet acid from dead leaves. Her distance, her unsubmissiveness, hidden but perhaps hinted at, is like snow mixed with a warm softness, rotted, corrupt: her age, her mind, her soul . . . It is so complex, the peasant queenliness, the aging boy and girl, the married pair. "I am of the earth earthy," she murmurs: persuading herself? As a form of musical accompaniment? A hint of what she wants the sex to be? And she is quite stupendously still so that it is odd to speak of her passive stillness as an energy of self-expression, which ignites S.L. in such a way that he becomes dimmed rather than illuminated, flexibly languorous, fatly passive or automatic in his actions, pouty and lunatic. What a strange landscape to be in.

They each have a lauding look; she's a peculiar self-idolater anyway, sweetly and temperamentally flattering. Lila often feels unsexual people don't appreciate how hard it is to have a sexual life when you're good-looking and have "position." She's never been certain how the laws of self-respect work in actual fucking. S.L., with a darkly pleased but mostly unclear look on his face, grips *himself,* his prick, through his pants. All at once he has a sore look—he's consoling a restless but somewhat amused wound. His face, his look grows semi-engorged,

heroically hurt, suffering but about to be—I don't know—eased. He
is also bland with distance, a form of sexual confidence mixed with
ignorance mixed with local experience: caution and temper make his
face and its expression fruit-on-a-bough-ish. He finds sex to be low
and *gorgeous*. He stares at Lila's ghostly and warped, interestingly sleek
and panting throat. He feels sex as a frog-wetness and grunting, as
frog-deformity, or worse, as bugs or barnyard animals. He and Lila are
a good-looking couple; bizarre stuff is O.K., is a sign of privilege, for
the frog-lovers. The insides of Lila's breasts are tremor-ridden, musical. She wanders among her sensations as in an empty house—she is
somewhat wanton in imagination. She snorts as if she were being passionate but she's thoughtful and drifty. S.L. has a grown-up, staring-
off-to-one-side look while he senses his appetites transgressing
provisos and forbiddings—a great many coerced obediences are
undone here, are undone for once and all. He starts to snort—in
deeper tones than Lila's, while he pats her stomach and somewhat
blindly rubs and then, in a more awake style, pinches or tweaks her
nipple. Now he takes on a carpenter's air of carefulness; he runs his
fingers around her breast and, bending over, leaves his tongue in her
ear while he skates his fingers libidinously and with little slaps and
pinches of ownership and of veto, a little amateurishly, up and down
the rucked-up cloth of her clothes.

The shuffling sequence of tongue-and-hand improprieties
switches now to a dapper style—as if with drumbeats, an intrusive
rhythm. He moves his midsection irregularly and expressively and
with some would-be sexual dapperness, diluting the truer effect of his
outspread temperament, his male berserkerhood.

He says, "It's always fair weather when true friends get
together . . ."

And so on . . .

JIBBER-JABBER IN LITTLE ROCK

When I was ten, a year after my older sister had left us because of the family disasters, my mother sent me away, too. Daddy was ill, and we had no money. "It's over," he said. "Leave me alone." Momma sent me to live with an uncle I barely knew, her oldest brother. He lived in Little Rock, Arkansas, far from his mother, my grandmother, whom he didn't like and hadn't spoken to in twenty years and would not speak to in the course of the rest of his life.

Momma had been having affairs ever since Daddy became ill, I think. Perhaps she had done that before but I'd only noticed since. I'd walked through the living room when she had company of that sort, visiting her or when she was setting things up on the phone. She and Dad really hated each other by then, as much as the Little Rock uncle hated his mother.

Mom said, "Nobody loves you when you're old and gray . . ." She was forty-two, admitting to forty. "Forgive me," she said. "People play for keeps. Little Piggy goes to market and knows it all." I might add that someone—a childless widower—had courted her because of me. She'd known him all her life and he had a Cadillac and a married daughter. When he told her he thought it would be *nice* for him to take over my education, for him to send me to private school and then to college, it had irked her sexual pride.

She had been modest but she had become shameless. She walked around the house in a peignoir and made snide remarks about her men and sad remarks about growing older. I realized that sometimes my existence caused things to happen. She would come into a room and say, "Leave me alone." And: "You and I are too close—not close enough . . . whichever." She was maybe a little drunk. She said, "I'm classy, if you ask me—I'm *still in the game.* Do you know what that means? I still have chances. *Pisher,* you have to get out of my way. Forgive me. Be patient. You'll get your turn. . . ." She sighed. "You don't know about the last minute yet. I want what I want—we'll see if it's too late or not. . . . Leave me alone," she said. "Let me live. Let me get on with things. Let me try to live for God's sake—if you don't mind . . . Get out of my way. I'm not giving up without one last fling on the flying trapeze. I'm the daring old woman on the flying trapeze, *pisher.* . . . Watch my smoke. . . . The truth comes from whoever has the last word," she said. "I'm going to try."

I did not mind leaving her. I wanted to leave. I tried to be polite about it.

"Don't pull a long face," she said ironically, gently bitterly. She took me to the train station. She was a lousy mother, really. Her peculiar poetries of address and seduction and destruction drove everyone away.

She said, "Say something to me, *pisher,* before you go."

"Good-bye," I said.

"Whatever you want," she said dryly, lighting a cigarette. "Kiss me," she said. I stretched up and kissed her. "That's right," she said. "Wish me luck. . . ." I was silent. "Oh you don't like me anymore—is that it? Wait and see what happens when you get old. We'll see what we will see. You're a child: you'll be all right. Well, I don't care. . . ." Her face held a vast emptiness. She smelled of Mommahood, Momminess, still, her perfumed powder, her clothes, her skin. She also smelled of acrid, nervous, passionate intelligence-without-point-to-it, a kind of madness. I mean she smelled familiarly of being a woman and then there was this ugly, burnt quality of odor such that I trembled dimly halfway-to-being-emotionally-through-with-her-and-finding-her-repulsive. She said, "I don't like how my life turned out but it wouldn't hurt you to be patient with me. Wish me luck."

Taking a deep breath, I said, "Good luck. And leave me alone from now on. Don't come after me this time. No more changing your mind. Let me *go.*"

In photographs that year, I was an ugly child twisted with tension and self-disdain. I was as shy as if I were covered with mud. I was pitiable, and that hurt me. I was squat, ill-proportioned, with long thighs and a neck so long that I had been called for a while *Giraffe.* Dismounting from the train in Little Rock is a troll of a child, squinting, twisted, with no freckles and nothing impish about him.

The actual moment slides in and out of focus. I remember how strange and unpromising my aunt and uncle looked, large aunt, bucktoothed, pompous-looking; small, grinning, monkeylike uncle: they looked like self-important, emotionally ignorant people with money and no sense. In childhood one sees this but can't say it. One can only say *I don't like them.* In childhood one is several steps away from the literacy of self-defense. Many boys rarely or never look in grown-up eyes.

I was relieved that these people could stand the sight of me. The sufferance I was on in general, I mean in life, not in a story as someone active in response and in play, a presence, the pity and concern, the doubts and jealousies I aroused weren't really part of Happiness-and-Normalcy Land or Adjustmentville. Aunt Charlotte was marginally less unattractive than Uncle Simon, and when she held out her arms, I returned her embrace in a version of my most honorable, sincere-child way. I don't know if regular children do that, lie and suck up to grownups for the sake of shelter or not, shelter and the rest of it.

You can tell a lot in a hug, the dry boringness, the degree of emotional ignorance. Aunt Charlotte was a childless woman, plain and with a difficult husband, a proud, bossy woman in ugly clothes. It registers. I sincerely sucked up to Aunt Charlotte who was self-righteous and hairy and had a large bust. Aunt Charlotte responds to the hug of the wild boy, the fierce but dry seductiveness, the request.

I was, when I was with other boys, the most foul-mouthed, a specialist in vile vocabulary. I did not actually know about sex but I suspected that it existed. There is an odd musty smell to Aunt Charlotte and a look of command in her eyes. Uncle Simon, ah, Uncle Simon was quick-talking, he had a high tenor voice; his talk was a quick jibber-jabber. He had a lot of wavy, grayed hair, and canceled, or collapsed cheeks, small jowls, an enlarged nose, and a thin but protruding mouth that wandered half the width of his face when he talked.

His aura was male-womanly, and he was entirely averted inwardly, turned away emotionally from me and the moment. His "Hello," his "Let's shake hands" were so devoid of emotional presence that one sensed that for him being liked was everything—not in a fool's version, but in his own neurotic version. His manner was one of cold charity. He had a funny sharp smell that lonely conceited men, subduedly homosexual, retired military men and priests and aging gangsters had, that bitter worship of the male and the disdain for it. And the lifelong experience of not being able to interest the men one did admire, the settling for a bureaucratized version of admiration for the nearest bearable male.

In Uncle Simon's case, it was one of the U.S. senators from Arkansas. Simon had taken into his house a series of boys related to the family. I was the third such boy. Ten-year-olds are not actually childish; they are semi-adult but sexless and savvy about childhood. *One of those,* as a caption in my mind, meant his hands were too forward and too stiff. *He smells bad,* I thought despairingly, governs the sense of the emotional emptiness of the man.

He said in his quick, treble jibber-jabber, "Train trip interesting? Did you meet interesting people? You're not a snob: you're someone who talks to people on the train, aren't you? Or are you a Northerner, a Northerner through and through—ha-ha." He was a quick-witted, political joker who had no humor.

I had a dying father and a mother going mad, and I was very hungry and tired, very frightened in a cold, fearless fashion: I was prepared to run away. I don't think I have ever in my life been greeted with such a marvelous sangfroid. Even grownups who don't like children give you a glance that takes in whether you're ill or scared or not.

Wooden marionettes in a sense but flesh-and-blood all right was how they struck me. Still and all, I was wearily grateful that Uncle Simon and Aunt Charlotte could bear me even if that acceptance was so wooden and contradictorily had an iodine-and-bandage quality— that quality of weary grief, that quality of hurt and of hurt memory when you've been bandaged, do you know?

Their car was a Nash, which was a make I didn't admire. They had only one car; Uncle Simon didn't, or wouldn't, drive. Little Rock in 1940 looked *very* small, not unpleasant at all, but not a place where people read anything. I know about this from neighborhoods and households in St. Louis and its suburbs. This was a hell of a scary step down in sophistication.

Uncle Simon's house was marvelous looking, real stone, the orange and gray kind, and stucco, with a green roof, and set among very tall sycamores. It was far and away the largest house in its near neighborhood with the largest lawn. The others were small, one- or two-family wooden houses. Uncle Simon said his house had sixteen rooms and an attic and was set on the highest hill in Little Rock. He said it had been a bargain when he bought it.

He said he didn't know his neighbors.

Let's see, what else did he inform me of in his treble jibber-jabber in those first days: that Jesse Owens was a great man, a great American, that I should try to imitate Jesse Owens. Owens was black, and Uncle Simon meant something on the order of I ought to be a great athlete, beautifully shaped, beautifully mannered, and that I—forgive me the term—should *play the nigger* as an orphan. (Aunt Charlotte said, "Your uncle is a very, very smart man: listen to him and grow wise." Aunt Charlotte had asked me, and I, as virginal and strange toward touch as any ten-year-old, obeyed, and as part of my fearful sucking up, I had curled up beside her on a small couch. Uncle Simon told me to come and sit on *his* lap.)

He told me my parents, my adoptive parents actually, were not smart or realistic, were not even real citizens of the U.S.; he meant they were not as American as he was—not as up-to-date about the real nature of "these United States at all." He spoke in his crackled treble; I would say his was a gravelly voice but that usually implies a baritone; and his treble did have baritone aspects, not tones but aspects. I mean it was a complete voice, not squeezed, a long-term voice, not a deformity of age. Cracker barrel—but Jewish and nervous.

He told me I would work in his big clothing store, and he would send my salary to Lila. I was used to being kept prisoner by being given no money, and I was not only a thief, I had my ways for getting rides from policemen and streetcar conductors.

Then he told me about the big thing in his life, his friendship with the senior United States senator from Arkansas, a big shot in Washington because of his Democratic longevity in Congress, and his intelligence and statesmanship, and his committee chairmanships. I've forgotten which ones. Simon did not mention any other friends. And the phone did not ring. He was not surrounded by good fellowship although he acted as if he was. I nodded in a cold, wry, sickened, defeatedly eager way, a way favorable to him, not deadpan, not disgusted and sarcastic in the usual ten-year-old, end-of-childhood, bitterly pre-pubic way I might have.

But he made me sick. I felt sick. I had thoughts of savaging the large room we sat in, the ugly furniture, breaking the windows. Simon wanted a substitute for a son, someone male and small, to deal with from time to time in order to see himself as he aged in the speeches he made to a helpless auditor. He had no family feeling in regard to himself—I don't know why. I suspect eldest child vanity. He had five younger siblings, and they all had virtues he didn't have. I also suspected that at one time he had been fastidious and truly quickwitted and had not wanted a Jewish family in which some of the members, including his mother, permitted themselves impermissible behavior in that outraged way of some people of that sort.

I think Uncle Simon had a dim relation to his younger self in something he saw in me. And I don't think he had another human tie he cared about, not to Aunt Charlotte, not to anyone. And I don't think he cared.

S.L. said of Simon to me before I left St. Louis, "That's a stupid man for you. His trolley is off the tracks. . . ."

He wasn't stupid. But he wasn't aware of you except for things like money and shelter and manners; those were the generalities he actually used for fitting in, those were the general areas in which he faced the world.

The grownups and I felt I was like a wartime refugee. Years later in Rome, a quite old Russian countess who had a limp and a stammer and a fine face, said the Russian Revolution had overturned her life: "We were spilled out on the map of Europe like pills spilled from a medicine bottle, and we did not much care where we ended up; it was all the same; where we rolled, there we stayed. . . ."

It was like that for me. Uncle Simon was anti-war, not wanting to be fooled again as he had been during the First World War by Allied propaganda. He did not believe Hitler was a monster. I said I did. And that I was pro-war. "Hush," Aunt Charlotte said.

But my sanity—literally—depends on there being a degree of truth in how I live. I'm a much traumatized person. I was a super-heavily traumatized kid. I had been abused. I had lost my real mother. I had been denied food. I had nearly died twice so far. But I can manage if I don't fantasize or lie to myself, and there is something good and edible, so to speak, in each day. Ideas are not negotiable for me. You can shut up about them but you can't lie about them. You have to respect them. To know the Germans were human was a good thing. Not to understand the war at all meant, in my view, that Uncle Simon was a near schizophrenic, dead from the neck up—and from the waist down. He had managed to ignore the commonsense evidence of his

eyes and ears; he was shut off from the world. This too was a matter of
age. He was about fifty-six.

He told me he had spent the First World War as an ordnance officer in the army in New Jersey boxing for his regiment as a light mid-
dleweight. So he was not naïve about the world. It was then he had
met the senator who was an officer in the Quartermaster Corps but
was determined to see battle and become a politician. I may have the
story mixed up by now. He had tied his life to the senator's but not in
the sense of being at his side. They'd been separated in the war, and
the senator was mostly in Washington, where Uncle Simon had, I
think, never been. Simon had helped run the senator's Arkansas campaigns and his office, had served as a de facto public relations officer—
at any rate he had dealt with newspapers in the state. "Those were
great days, great days, great, mmm, great," Uncle Simon said in his
quick, sopranoish jibber-jabber. He was not a lucid storyteller or he
was infinitely discreet but I never heard from him or Aunt Charlotte
what those days had been like, the election campaigns, the negotiations, not even a crude story. No one in the family, even Lila, was
really a storyteller.

Simon had left home after the war, in the early 1920s, when all the
world was topsy-turvy, when everything was changing, and moved to
the town where the ex-lieutenant who became the senator lived.
Maybe—I offer this tentatively—maybe Uncle Simon was both smart
and brain-damaged, first by his mother, then by his boxing, and he
was in love with the American electoral process. Why not? The
crowds, the inner meanings, the shifts of allegiance—seriously, why
not? The connections to the police, the whores, the demi-whores or
sluts or broads of the campaigns, the nice ladies. The swift panorama
of men—why not?

Or it was just cold ambition, a Jew wanting to get close to the core
of power in the new place, a brave kid, smart but almost illiterate
about the implied and the implicit in the new kingdom. A refugee
like me but much older, in his late twenties. He wouldn't have had

the childish, odd, numbed shyness and the blunt studying of every-thing and the uneasy taste of nervous spittle in the mouth at foreign sights and sounds like a child. He would be a conquering tourist, a colonizer.

Aunt Charlotte's aged parents, in their nineties, lived in a suite at the back of the second floor. Charlotte's father was angrily dignified in a German mode and her mother was chirpily sweet. I played dominoes with the old man and piquet with the old woman. They were very old and failing but courteous and oddly determined. Simon had a heart condition, they told me. The old people disliked Simon; they made little jokes about him, or not jokes, but their faces became tragically persecuted. The black cook disliked him too. A large, soft-voiced woman. It seems a male thing to be disliked somewhat. In St. Louis our servants had often disliked S.L.; some had disliked him quite a lot; some had liked him. What Grandpa Hartman said of Uncle Simon was, "Little Napoleon—huff, huff." And Grandma Hartman had laughed tinklingly.

And Simon was quite short and relentless in a slightly muffled I-am-not-a-peasant-or-a-gangster way. I forgot to mention how I was dressed, in a slack suit, in long pants and a shirt of the same fabric. I wore glasses and had grossly curly, asymmetrical, unpleasing hair. I did not like my clothes or my shoes, which were Buster Brown brogans.

One room on the first floor of the house, a sunporch, had a sunken floor, slate, and a wall of almost continuous windows, and books and a radio in it. The chairs weren't comfortable but who cared. Outside the row of windows was the mixed light and shadow of the lawn under the trees where it was hidden from the street by a rise in the land, in a scoop decorated by a changeably black-leaved and partially sunlit web on it and roofed by a wild ceiling of large and small leafed-out branches mostly up high, as high as the eaves of the roof of the house.

A few thousand dusty books in low shelves, best-sellers, clumsy books, no longer famous, out-of-date, queerly no good. "There's no point in reading those," the black cook said. I know it's a cliché but she was an educated woman.

Uncle Simon insisted that I become athletic. I was, a bit, already, but he meant athletic in the way he had been in his twenties. Every evening on the large, tree-shaded front lawn, in the marvelous light, he measured me, my thighs, ankles, and calves, with a yellow tape from the store. In the late southern sun, or twilight but a brighter one than in the north, Simon produced in his jibber-jabber, slowed a bit, rules, adages, aphorisms about men and what a man should be.

Totally absorbed in issues and thoughts and memories of masculinity, he sat in a metal folding bridge chair under the tall trees of his bargain lawn and with a stopwatch set me off to run, across the lawn to the street and down the street either on the flat summit past the small wooden houses which was embarrassing or down the hill which was mostly just road with a wooded ravine on one side. I was to run only a short distance out of his sight. If he wanted me to run farther, he would stand at the corner of the house. I would return hot and panting in the twilight, but I must admit I never once ran with my full heart, although I experimented with it. But this sort of running, you see, was like an abstraction—or was classical—and not like running in the woods or playing football. It lacked the characteristics of actuality as some Talmudic injunctions did or some mantras, to use a term from later.

Gasping from the exercise of the physical ideal, and with the smell of macadam and sycamore leaves and daylong heat and sweat in my nostrils, I stood in front of him while he felt my buttocks to see if the muscles there were tightening, and he poked and ran his hands over the calves of my legs to see if I had runner's muscles and runner's tendons yet, and then he palped my thighs, front and back, and poked at the sides, and my abdomen. I had been, I think, a phenomenally pretty child once, when I was little—that was how I came to be adopted—and I hated being touched.

I hated any sort of touch, but some kinds of physical closeness, just behind the shell, were pearl-like, were laughable and as if sweet—

nothing is really sweet when you're ten. It is a rather acid know-it-all age for most middle-class children. Simon's turtle-skinned hands produced a touch, a series of touches, that had a dry, semi-brutal, professional quality that wasn't bad at all; it happened and was forgettable, that touch; but sometimes he did a long stroking thing, and I would cough spittle into his face, or fall on the grass with a sudden cramp, mostly imaginary, or across his lap and then off it, saying, "I'm tired!" and I would shield my eyes with my hands and lie on the grass or roll back and forth or scoot backwards, sometimes stainingly, until I was several feet from him.

He said I was crazy—crazy and spoiled, a Northerner, ruined by Lila and S.L., their true son, a real example of a wasted life of a city kid. He spoke reasonably, he didn't yell, but with a promissory note in his voice: he was going to fix me.

Sometimes, before he examined me or after, he would insist I run more, that I run shorter distances, on the lawn mostly, while he barked orders in his treble jibber-jabber, "Knees higher! Keep your head up!" That sort of thing.

He slapped me in an athletic way on my shoulders and butt and on the top of my head. Once I turned and said in a way that is sometimes called a snarl, "Don't ever do that!" He put his hand on the top of my head and gave me a lecture on not talking back and hit me again on the head. I grabbed a stick, but I merely waved it at him—I had struck my father or anyone else who ever hit me on the head, including a first-grade woman teacher and later a priest; this was the most sycophantic in this matter I had ever been—and I ran into the house.

Oh what an uproar! Oh what politics—old people and cook, Aunt Charlotte and Uncle Simon. And me.

I was Shirley Temple sweet and conciliatory and Jackie Coogan pathetic and I was immovable: "If you're going to hit me on the head, I would rather go to an orphanage." Like many orphans my mind was my real family, was brother to me, and fostering sister, and nursing mother, and fierce father: I never told anyone this because it would give them too much power.

Simon said I was being silly, emotional, unmanly.

"Call the orphanage," I said. "I'm ready."

Then when Grandma Hartman and Aunt C. were sympathetic, I became pathetic. At any sign of relenting on anyone's part, I became sweet and humble and loving—I'm afraid, though, it had that ten-year-old's acid to it.

Uncle Simon knew and said something about my being like "Queen Elizabeth." He meant the first one; the second one was just a princess so far. He meant tricky all the time. He said to me once, "Tricky, tricky, tricky will never do it."

He stopped hitting me on the head. I did not have to go to the orphans' home; the line of the permissible was drawn in a way, the line that no one writes about, the treaties and no-man's-lands and actual negotiations between children and their elders year by year.

The athletic training continued. I remained more or less twisted and nervous and substantially hideous. But not quite. I was healthier. I slept better. My looks, such as they were, returned, albeit twisted, nervous, substantially hideous, but I looked like a boy—do you follow me?

And like Mary, Queen of Scots, I lost out again since once the border of the permissible was established, Uncle Simon, like an army N.C.O., set out to humiliate me within the law for what he thought were the best, masculine reasons. I don't know how to say what I'm going to say next. But, look, there's power and rank and the love they evoke, which Jews often call *respect,* and then there's the phallic element, and I don't know what that is, some element of force-and-knowledge, not necessarily worldly or unworldly, and involving the heart and the brain, and it's *phallic*—it's different from Queen Elizabeth I or what Momma did when she got her own way or ran things. It's not necessarily even powerful in the world, this phallic thing. My adoptive father, a failure people said, had it, and my real father, who was illiterate (I knew him; I saw him at times; I was adopted because my mother had died; I couldn't stay with him because he believed in actual beatings and wanted me to be a rabbi and not cut my sidelocks;

he was crazy on the subject) had it; some school figures had it but in moderated or other forms. Uncle Simon didn't have it.

And he wasn't going to have it in me. The senator, Uncle Simon's senator, was interested in the war readiness of Arkansas. This was 1941. But Uncle Simon dallied and did not explore the few factories in Arkansas or the tanneries or talk to the unions or to the newspapermen. Simon read the paper carefully and made one or two phone calls a day, and men dropped into his men's store. I don't know if he had a brilliant and well-functioning network or not. How would he know if he never checked on it? Almost all bureaucrats and functionaries, almost everyone is something of a fake. Simon studied nothing and read nothing anymore. He was satisfied or nervous or merely set in his ways (Lila had said that of him). "A lifetime's experience is what I have," he said in his treble jibber-jabber. It does something to the mind to be attached to a fake: there was Aunt Charlotte for example.

But Uncle Simon was unsarcastically devoted to the senator. It was just that he was nostalgically devoted even when he was on the phone with him. Passed over? Left behind? But then why did the senator call him? He didn't call very often, it's true.

Simon asked me questions about public affairs and history and about politics. I mean it was a ritual grilling or test, a mode of instruction. If I answered with any conviction and showed an opinion or a structure of fact rather than stammering and being embarrassed to be asked such questions, he jibber-jabbered at me, hectoring me about male behavior. Lila and others had hectored and advised me on politic behavior, on getting-along-with-people. I read a book a day, musty or stupid or not, and the newspaper, and any magazines that were around. I had no spending money. I often felt he might want to discuss something actually without the politics of who he was and how he felt about his life.

He didn't want me to answer his questions. He wanted me to be junior and subservient, receptive. He wanted to drill ideas that the senator no longer listened to into my life and mind. I tried to kiss ass. I really tried. But psychology is odd: whenever I let myself, inside my head, call him a *skinflint asshole* I could like him some. Or when the cook or Charlotte's old parents attacked him, I could say and feel and see and realize, *He's not so bad.* . . . Or in the moments when I was actually fighting with him or was on the edge of it like a Scottish border laird. But when I *had* to like him, the thing of producing the faked emotion minute after minute, if you didn't in the end accept this fake liking as real—as if under torture you had finally been broken and had given in, after which you invented some sort of rigid, fake macho to make up for the oozing nightmare of submission—you lost any sense of real air and light, and you became a creature of oppression, feral and full of hatred except for the awful sentimentality of liking him.

He didn't interest me even as a tyrant suffocating me, that was the truth. And the phallic thing re-arose mentally—physically I was hardly phallic yet—from its own ashes over and over. Music is a big help; if you don't use it as background music or as a source of hallucination, but if you listen, it is amazingly curative. Some of the musicians in Russia who appeared after the war were surprisingly free, and I never knew what to think of the musicians who had remained in Nazi Germany, but I couldn't hear the strains of sentimentality and hatred in their music.

So I was willing to settle for him feeling the damage might be impermanent.

But that was lying in bed or sitting in the branches of a tree or on the toilet. Face to face with him in his life, settling-for-him seemed like an a priori foul betrayal of him, although I did not twist his life in any way, and he did twist mine. But he could sense that other betrayal, that indescribable thing of no affection and what it meant. But if I gave it, it would have no power because it would be false, it would be like other affections, like Aunt Charlotte's, which did him no good. He had so little from me that it might be called the shell of a reality, but he could sense the animal spirit inside. I suppose it was like the shell game with a pea, with a prize.

It was painful but real, myself as Lila's sad and not-entirely-O.K. banished son, an absurd, musty aunt, a difficult and to-be-satirized uncle, a fool with power over me, dying people upstairs, and the commandingly provincial and actually important senator offstage, and a whole, large cast of characters several hundred miles to the north in St. Louis. My nutty uncle and his quick jib-jabbing patterns of speech, I had to let him shape the way I talked. I had to imitate him at his insistence. I had to *adopt* his conclusions, his systems. I had to use his sense of truth. I could have moods only if they were like his, if they were miniature versions. He tested me daily on my ability to mimic him adequately. If we had been more closely attached by blood instead of being first cousins once removed, this might have happened normally. Or perhaps for boys ordinary life is hellish and that is why they have testosterone and become such hellions. I don't know. The imitation of Uncle Simon by one visiting subfireman (kid) had to be inadequate, juvenile, leaving him room to correct me, to strut and preen because that was what his waking—and I bet his sleeping—lives largely were, 90 percent preening.

He used to ask me to tell him my day in detail even if I had spent it near him or with him. "And in *good English*," he would say, and the son of a bitch meant *his* English. In those days I still had the energy to be able to imitate radio announcers and politicians, imitate and rearrange—I fairly often did it for company in St. Louis when I was allowed to show off. I could imitate upper level middlebrow English from novels on the order of *The Good Earth.* I could do the supposedly Chinese dialogue. I did it to make the asshole laugh. I did it to broaden the moment—and his mind. I did it for the hell of it and because I was a brat. I did it because I was pre-phallic, pre-something he had never been.

He said, "No, no. English like mine. . . . Don't be a *stoopnagel.*" He said, "Always use good English, respectable English. Get some self-discipline; it will do you some good." He meant well, but how can you mean well if you're stupid and close-minded? Besides, it was often visible in the tension in him, in his neck and hands, and then in his eyes that he meant to clap me into a box. He knew, not in language like this, but in his own terms, he knew what he was doing and admired and forgave it. One time, having forced me to sit on his lap, he tried to kiss me on the mouth after such an interrogation as the above and without knowing I knew how to do this, I opened my lips so that our teeth met and clattered and rang. He had bridges and maybe dentures, and he grew rigid and seemed to be numbed. He raised his hand to his teeth, and I slipped off his lap.

Then he reached for me and whopped me. Aunt C., who was in the room said, "It makes him mad to hear people use English disreputably."

Hard as it is to bear, there is a rank in these matters. As nearly as I can judge after all these years, looking back, his talk was made up of school-English improved a bit by official army English, eased a bit by Little Rock journalistic English and minor league sports English— which is very different from major league sports English, being jokey and deprecatory and defensive, and not wild, not inflected so much by ambition and worldliness. I hate to say this but I had already published in grown-up newspapers, poems and accounts of school occasions, and one time a piece on Eleanor Roosevelt. And one poem in a local literary magazine.

The jibing at you, jabbing jibber-jabber of his talk formed at that point in his life a dead and papery speech with a noticeable absence of human connections in it. Pugnacity had once kept his language alive, political issues that he dealt with in campaigns, alive and perhaps dishonest or bland—I don't know; I wasn't there. He still was a small, ugly, combative man but that stuff was dead within him. I was as a mean ten-year-old boy still a language-smitten child—it was the only non-self-aggrandizing area you could play around in in the school I had gone to. My uncle's jokes and his unbearable eyes and the emptiness of his life and the omniscience he claimed and his trembly jibbering-jabbering voice and his temper and his will, his old guy's last-minute narcissism and ready contempt left over from his political heyday and his considerable courage still—God, it was hard. Kissing ass is always hard. Maybe it's harder in a democracy where it is improvised at the will and intelligence of each kissee, unlegislated by custom, unworked out, and so harder and harsher, much rougher, hairier than in Europe or Asia—part of why democracies seem savage and scare some foreigners so.

Uncle Simon had a Jew's interest in the power, deftness, and strength (of varied kinds) of men of power. Difficult as I was, he made me sit on his lap while he told me about his meetings with famous ballplayers—"just as human as you and me. And he knew the value of discipline. He had wrists as big as your knees." A pitcher, Cy Young maybe. At the time when I was his captive, I listened to Uncle Simon, but memory is likely to take on aspects of critical interpretation, and I see his mouth and his eyes and balk—actually my memory balks—at pulling his words and phrases out of silence: "A big-timer knows how to *be* a gent'man with the small fry. There is not a big man, a politician, a great leader, a financier, an industrialist in the world who does not know this. Wiley, you can tell who a man is by how he deals with *little* people. . . ."

No one's little, Uncle Simon, I might say. I might say, Lila has a system of who and what you have time for. But some people feed you and some people drain you. My dad, S.L., says it's all show and lies and you have to watch out for the rednecks. Momma says, First you have to get the say-so and then you can be nice. In books I've read what you're talking about, Uncle Simon, is called the common touch and none of the really great figures had it although some of them were popular with the public. Lincoln and Caesar never had it, or Napoleon. Hitler does. But Generalissimo Franco doesn't.

Simon talked a lot about Franklin Roosevelt and his methods, but he was interested only in Roosevelt's relation to Congress, and particularly to the Senate, and even then only with reference to the methods and systems of Huey Long in a neighboring poor Southern state—bribe and pay and payoff. Uncle Simon never spoke cynically or used a cynical vocabulary. He was never ironic like S.L. when he spoke of a Huey Long hospital making jobs and pleasing the poor and quieting the rich families with doctor sons.

Simon's courtship rested on him sharing his knowledge with me, so that I might base and center my life on what he knew and grow to be as successful as he was, grow to be someone like him with the same collapsed remainder of life in him. I was supposed to give a further meaning, further in time, to what he knew, I was to bear and propagate the elements of omniscience in him both willingly and as he trained me. He wanted me to acknowledge that what Simon said was the chief treasure the world had to offer.

Momma said to me a couple of times, "Everyone is religious—it makes me sick." Her *everyone* was always men; women she referred to as *women* and never lumped into everyone, only into *they* as in *you know what they say*. Children were always *little children*. Simon's everyone was journalistic, was whoever was gathered at the fire, or whoever had political clout in Little Rock, or was the philosophers' *all* or mankind but used journalistically with special reference to Little Rock and the surrounding counties.

I felt that Simon (in his way, in his style) was interested in me and what I felt. He cared what I felt. But it genuinely hurt, how he finagled obedience, how he trained me, how he played with what I felt. I missed Momma, not emotionally, but in terms of amusement. She had warned me, "They're very very dull, they are dull people. Charlotte is really dull, and Simon is—well, you can stay awake by starting a fight with Simon. How sad life is, *pisher*—it has so many details."

My own brand of American English, my dear Americanola (dear to me), irritated Simon uncontrollably: his nose twitched, his jowls waggled, his eyelids flapped, his lips involuntarily parted: "Roosevelt doesn't have to do big-shot manly things—he's a cripple. He gets to be clever—and smart: that's why he's so good. . . ." His obvious androgyny, his wide repertoire of responses, his flexibility of response.

Aunt C. slipped up and sent a pro-war poem I wrote to the Little Rock *Gazette,* and they published it. That made Simon angry. Then he was scornful and haughty in his dry, jibbering-jabbering, nonstop omniscient way. He really thought I was inarticulate and illiterate and unfortunate in terms of language, and he really thought he was the cat's meow—that's Lila, of course—the big cheese local panjandrum

Mahatma Gandhi: that's how my father S.L. sometimes talked—when it came to rhetoric and brains.

And if you keep the context small and neat and if you niftily trim the edges and omit sickness and emotions, he was smart. But if you include any of those things or even something as dumb as dogs or flowers, he was a stupid shit. The belief, the faith that Uncle Simon was the center of the universe, the faith that love and being a son or like a son should bring, the sense that universal truths were bound up in him—him not as an object of sarcasm—stinks, and the pain, the teasing agony of it is really outside the scope of these sentences. But one can lie in bed, an ugly, nervous, more-than-irritating ten-year-old and feel the soft busyness of the dark air as acceptable death.

I make Simon mad—but he is interested. Is this what girls find in the world? I see now looking back, my inner tone and outward actions toward him, my attitude toward his merits as a thinker, match, mimic, mirror in some humanly awful way of hopeless ass-kissing and violent, heartbroken sarcasm, mirror in a ten-year-old's scale his behavior toward me. The staleness of what that felt like was terrible! And my uncle *sensed* that but only as a private set of dog images, me as a dog and like a dog whose pelt has a stale smell. He sniffs at me, he grabs me in his arms as if in a set of jaws, drops me and draws back and comments on my appearance—ugly, bookish appearance, but changing in his house, I must admit.

At other times he rubs me against him in a doglike way—he is a man of language; I am a mere barker and sniffler. His life has attained an awful decency, thoroughly tainted, but not to be judged, his public sinlessness, his important cipherhood. He still deals with the real world but mostly in a dead way, an honorific way; he is careful not to be overstrained. He drags me around with him all day every day unless we are fighting. People are rarely rude to him, I notice, in the ways they are rude to Lila and S.L. It takes me a while but I see after a while: no one flirts with him. He kisses ass, he flirts with customers.

Aunt C. obeys him. He says, like Lila—they are brother and sister—
"I can get a thing or two done still. . . ."

Uncle Simon's perceptions and systems of thought and of public
action had created his and my shelter, our position. He knew about
male disrespect, male assertion—he knew about sexual pride. He
knew about the emotional singularity of the male showiness under the
surface manner of salesmen—he had that, or had had it, himself. He
knew about the escapee's pugnacity and he knew how the world
treated outsiders. He was primed to deal in humiliation and subservience: I saw it often, in his store, with customers, and he withdrew
it and treated some customers as rough equals, slightly lower than
himself, and some as dirt although they were clearly men of power;
and in some style or other, they took it. Very little was at stake except
rank, but the details of this ranking, man by man, were Uncle Simon's
laugh, literally: he laughed, blinked, joked, smoked cigars, leaned
back in his chair, stood, and walked back and forth.

But the game was absolute for him; it never lapped over into truce
or into real amusement or into really mattering. It was petty. It was a
case of splitting hairs but using a smart but not refined ax to do it. It
seemed an enormous, enormous, enormous waste, the dried out,
pointless, endlessly detailed struggle over precedence.

No wonder Lila had for years refused to visit him. She wouldn't
talk to him on the telephone more than once a year and then only if
she had a headache, had taken aspirin, and was spending the day in
bed, "doing her duty with the telephone."

"Here," he would say to me, "tie this man's shoelaces for him." Or:
"You got something on the cuff of your trousers, Jim—the boy here
will clean it."

I couldn't do it. The second time Uncle Simon said this, I said,
"No, he won't. The boy won't."

Ah, the scene, the scene. Aunt C. whispered in my ear, "Cry and
you won't have to be punished."

"Go to hell," the boy said to his uncle.

"*No dinner for you!*" Simon shouted.

But the ill, old people and the black cook sneaked me food. And even Charlotte showed up in my room with bread and jam and milk.

Simon confronted me in my room the next morning. In a serious tone he demanded to know if I intended to live without discipline.

"Why don't you shut up—or talk to me sensibly," I replied in the shimmery morning air.

"You want to end up in a home?" Uncle Simon had not lost his temper. He was handling me.

I blew up. *I* was the one who lost his temper. But it was not real temper; it simply pushed the dialogue toward reality. "I'll write the school system in St. Louis, the superintendent, in U. City. He'll come and get me. He's offered me a home."

"What are you talking about?"

"Mr. Baker will come get me. . . . He said he would."

"What are you talking about?"

"I'm not supposed to boast," I said glumly.

"What are you talking about?"

"Mom told me not to tell you. I'm a genius, Uncle Simon, and people will help—if I ask them to. I don't have to take your shit if I don't want to."

I represent a foreign "civilization" located in no particular place but only in certain people. I represent layers of other education, of a whole order of other permissions. I know about politeness extended to a child. In a different realism from his—or Momma's or S.L.'s—I have a position in the world. It's still the same world; mine is still a childish piece of the ordinary world, but the rules, the position are different. Playgrounds, yards, sports, even mere footraces, sunporches, all are different for me. It is not really a matter of "language potential" or "leadership" although it was said to be that. It might very well be delusory, valueless. One verifiable *fact* about it, though, was that it was not local.

"You're gonna get a good swift kick and a paddling if you don't watch out," Uncle Simon said with almost good-natured violence.

But he was steaming with rage, because of the hierarchy thing. Because he wouldn't know to dress or address me if I came into his store as a nineteen-year-old. Because his world was local, delusory, a piece of oblivion. Because the very terms were lunatic with their swift implication of another level of privilege and rationality, of realism, as I said, than any he knew of or was used to.

But he was omniscient, intelligent, a shrewd, well-informed Jew, a man of affairs.

I said, the ugly child, not as ugly as when he arrived, said a little wearily, "Might I use the telephone? May I use the telephone?"

He came at me then. He had instructed me to stand up when he came into the room on this occasion. He looked quite happy and furious—no, it was a rictus. He was stricken—by sudden truth . . . unwanted, somewhat European truth. I ran out of the room and grabbed the phone in the hall. "Long distance!" I said breathlessly to the operator. Operators oversaw all such calls then. "Get me the superintendent of schools in University City, Missouri—that's outside St. Louis. . . ." Uncle Simon had grabbed my arm but now he just watched and listened. But he started pulling at me. I told the operator, "I'm a child. Tell him Wiley Silenowicz, Wiley, is in trouble in Little Rock, tell him I'm here at this number. . . . Ow, ow . . . Simon Cohen's house."

Simon shook me and started to slap me but stopped when I said, "Don't."

The phone operator did it. Sam Baker telephoned within the hour, while Simon was shouting at Auntie C. I got to speak to him. Then he called the local school board in Little Rock to find out what kinds of force he could command. Uncle Simon was a figure well-enough known in town that Baker—with what pull or by what accident—reached the senator, who called the house, and, guess what, peace broke out at once.

The senator is a noisy and indirect-eyed but impressively present sort of man. He seems intelligently dishonest and at the same time to have a keel or underlying sense of both sentimental and actual honesty at times. But then he is not total in anything. Talking to a partial-selfed person is more like talking for him than like engaging in a dialogue. But he was a very astute listener. On the other hand, I was smart enough to know that a child's talk bores an adult, a busy or well-employed adult. They can't wait to get out of the house and be among adults. The senator always stayed with me longer, sitting or talking, or taking a longer walk, than I liked or than I thought was workable.

For a while Auntie C. pretty much spoke for Unc Simon, who was far from humbled. He was not even silenced. But he said he didn't understand this sort of nonsense, and he would stand there, in the door to the sunporch, while Auntie C. relayed to me "the marching orders" for the day and she asked me what I wanted to do, but Simon, Uncle Simon, spoke to me and did not respond to any nickname I proposed or to any new form of affection, only to the old form, and the old routine—running at twilight—but with a certain oddly worked-out freedom allowed and no more six summer days a week in the store.

I had said I would make no scandal if he stopped coercing me in everything, but he ignored any idea of scandal—he completely redefined it in his mind. He seemed to have been only slightly affected, but I was at the limit of my strength, and I became silly, or a bit crazy, childishly crazed: "He has to leave me alone if I say it three times," I said. This was taken seriously as a rule although things I had thought more carefully were ignored.

For a while, I stopped work in the store entirely and spent my days with the limping and fragile and dying old people. Then with the cook in the kitchen who liked me well enough but whose affection was limited. I never knew or came across a devoted Uncle Tom or Aunt Thomasina. Of course, Unc Simmy with his methods of authority in the house and store did. The cook represented a civilization obscure to me but present in her presence—she told me to stop trying to be cute and to remember that Simon was Simon and wasn't going to change: "Charlotte has a little give, not much, but a little, but he ain't got none." She spoke Southern and noticeably so. If we talked about books, she spoke a different English but one that wasn't entirely pure either: "I got too little time to read to bother with trash." When she talked religion, her English grew stiffer and so did her enunciation, but she was not a passionately religious woman, not a gospeler. I was interested in her, but I preferred to be outside. And she was a grownup.

In the ravine, I met a gang of white boys. I went there alone two days running, and some white boys who used it as their wilderness took to hunting me, a preamble to friendship or to harm. I cared and pretty much didn't care what happened. I was intent on holding on to my mind but I was tired of it too. I was not a hero. I got beaten up some, hit a lot, kicked. I came to know one of the boys, a sissified boy, the only talkative one. But I didn't love him or put him solidly in my life either. The gang of boys scared me and harmed me some but, at times, they made me their ex officio leader because of my precocity: I could read maps and explain things and talk to cops and find my way in the woods and get us water or soda in strange houses and adjudicate quarrels and tell stories. They asked me to lead them on an illegal trek along the stream in the ravine to wherever it joined the Arkansas River. The police knew me by then. They let us go on out on a mud shoal in the big river, dirty-legged boys.

Ah, it is too hard a story to tell, the evanescence of attachments, the greater importance always of something else, the specific form this takes in one's life. Simon had begun to respect me as someone who had power. He was not vengeful toward me but he expected to win out in the end, no matter what. He expected me to work in the store, to brush lint off the suits men tried on, to brush men's behinds and backs: I went blind with distaste. I worked with two black kids in the storeroom, but you can imagine what they needed and how little I could give. Twice, for a few minutes, I suffered hysterical blindness, nerves.

Simon breathes noisily in the small cove of air around him. I suffer nausea when I am near him. What failure means and the pains of increasing age and what male destiny is when it winds down are reflected distortedly in a privileged child and his powers and his lacks—and his tendency to collapse. I have no regrets about what happened. I think it's funny. I had decided to return to St. Louis and to live with the Bakers for a half year and then transfer to a private school— the scholarship had been arranged for—but Lila had called and said she knew Simon would bore the hell out of me, and she needed me, life was hell, S.L. wouldn't live with her anymore unless I was there, and so on: "You won't let me down, will you? And you *know* how S.L. feels about you. The sun rises and sets on your hind end. You may be ugly, but he likes you. Wiley, he doesn't like me at all anymore."

I didn't know if I was strong enough to tell her to fuck off. I didn't know if I would go home. It weighed on me. I hadn't inwardly signed off toward my dad as I had toward Lila. I didn't know anything.

Simon. The albatross spirit of that aging man mounts on a thermal of last-minute heat, a heat of the feeling of possibility of last-minute victory, a triumph with, over, through the luminously reputable child, "the bluebird of happiness to a dying man," thus, S. L. Silenowicz. I mean the albatross knew that, knew the terms on which I was summoned—well, asked or sought, even besought—by his sister, the quickest-witted one in the family, the one who'd had the most *fun,* if I can put it like that. Let us imagine the broad-beamed, big-faced senator on a visit, and the child tells the senator's fortune, and takes a walk with him around the yard, the senator's arm on his shoulder, the two discussing armament, the Spitfire versus the Messerschmidt. It is not a day when interest flags. The generation gap is bridged well enough. The senator leaves. Now I am sitting on Simon's lap, a rigid boy trying not to be rigid, ugly, you know, wearing glasses, with badly cut, ugly hair; the boy is wearing a slack suit and Buster Browns. It hardly matters though, since I was the child who was not a child, but who was, off and on, *a bright bird of a soul* (S.L.), now a blue jay, I might add, cawing and mischievous, now a cuckoo in some other child's nest, now a silent red cardinal, bright-bright-faced, now a dimly visible, recessive bluebird haunting the shadows, a paled sunburst on its breast and—if one thinks of everyone as bird-souled— then in an invisible aviary, undergoing one adventure after another,

the birds shrieking and cawing and darting from room to room
among the shadows and in the pallor of emotional light that is all that
these domestic adventures permit—if one sees the smaller bird in the
talons of the larger one—or escaped while the larger one is shot and is
dying, one might suggest the complicity and the complexity of the
chase-and-response.

But what it was felt as was, oh, imprisonment and brief horror.
Uncle Simmy wanted me to run for him, to show what I had learned,
to demonstrate how much stronger I was after visiting him. And so I
did, but I was in the slack suit and not in shorts. And I was unhappy
because of what lay ahead of me—I felt the melancholia of wanting
things to be O.K. with him even while loathing him for not knowing
what to do, for being so Christly stupid. I didn't really dislike him.
The plunge and whir of the child's mind and Uncle Simon's deadish
fixity, the procession of imageries a greedy and unhappy child's opinions are, the history of abductions, the smiles of the late light among
the leaves, the half-wish in the child for death. . . . Oh I remember.
Oh how I remember. And then the dog showed up, a dog I knew from
when I was with the gang of boys, a neurotic terrier that we, the boys,
knew bit erratically.

Be careful, I said to Uncle Simon. Watch out. That dog bites.

No dog bites if it is carefully treated, Uncle Simon said, and he
stretched out his hand.

The dog bit him, and that, of course, is the end of the story.

THE WORLD IS THE HOME OF LOVE AND DEATH

S.L. and Wiley, Saturday, 8:10 A.M.,
April 1944

The time-ridden tickling of the air and the rustle of real moments: wakefulness. I open my eyes and light overprints me, the boy in that room, seen-from-years-further-on, visible from the corner of my eyes in the present tense of the memory and from far away now as I write. Then my consciousness in the room is like a ship placing its shadow on water as it goes along, the waters of the moments. On one bare shoulder, where the pajama top has fallen away, is a single gleaming epaulet of light. The lightly muscled boniness of the boy, the shy-looking skin, newish since puberty, are freakish. The mind moves secretively. If I begin when the story has gone on for a long time, then the characters should be known to be dependent on mostly unexamined memory. Such dependence is a flickering blindness alternating with sight.

The skull has boyish hair atop it. The skin registers light. Left-over, faded hallucinations from sleep and memories and distortions of the senses in the changes since puberty, the self is shadowy, undefined—I am rigged with the question *Is this me?* The sense of who *I* am was wrecked in my sleep, and this anguishing vulnerability is me, but I am foreign to myself. This is in a bedroom in University City, a suburb of St. Louis, in Missouri. It is 1944, the last year before people like us knew about the bomb and the camps. My father by adoption, S. L. Silenowicz, has risen from the other bed in the room, the twin to the one I am in, and he is sitting on my bed.

One story is that this is the sixth year of his invalidism. This is a month before his death but we don't know that. The story of his life and then the story of his invalidism and then the story of his tie to me during his illness are coming to an end; perhaps we did feel that but musically, as a sense of coherence in a form yet to be worked out. I am his adopted son: William *Wiley* Silenowicz. I was born Aaron Stein. He and I don't look alike, but I will look like him when I am old. I will look like both my fathers and like myself as well.

S.L. is ill with a bad heart and uncontrollably high blood pressure; killingly high blood pressure wasn't treatable yet in those years. And only some diseases were easily diagnosed, and his was one. I mean the one assigned to him. He has had four strokes so far. And been in a coma three times. We were told each time that if he did recover he would be a vegetable, but he never became a vegetable. He is forty-four years old.

Wrecked by sleep and dreams, my mind moves with a drowning hiss and thump (of the heart) of my being shipwrecked in the wreck of my father's life . . . the wreck of the ship *The Unbearable.* Life is unbearable. He has a flattedly musical voice, *gentlemanly* North Texas with a friendly overlay of jokingly lower class—you have to talk that way in America. He had Southern and Midwestern *rural* tones and he was folksy-incantatory, my invalid father. It was very male. He is telling me to wake up; it is not an emergency; he is using affectionate, coaxing tones, distant tones, those of a sick man.

He doesn't like people anymore. He is rude or silent with people. He plays with dialects and kinds of discourse in tones that are sometimes educated and openly socially complicated just as he did when he was well, but he does it mockingly—with people he doesn't like. His voice has grown smaller and paler with illness, but my father's voice is still the voice of a man who is large-chested. When he was well, he sometimes coaxed and wheedled and talked to bartenders or business partners and women and children and old people and animals—it was interesting to me, my father's voice and the ways he spoke that were formed in our flyaway democracy—but in a way he does only spiels and confessions, only those.

He is shaking my foot and saying—my head is turned away from him and he can't see my eyes—"Dead to the world? Can you hear me in there? Listen to me: we want you out here—" He has promised not to wake me. I'm a growing boy and under extreme strain, and my mother and father get scared at night and make scenes. S.L. says, "The world is waiting for you—wake up, Mr. Shakespeare—" I'm not a young poet or anything like that, but people think I have a big vocabulary. "Mr. Too Piss-elegant for Words. You're the *Black Prince of the Morning*—I admit it—time to get up so you can honor us with a sight of your bright and shiny eyes. You're a sight for sore eyes, this bright and shiny morning." He is kneading my thigh, patting the side of my thigh. "Talk to me, Sleeping Beauty. . . . Cat got your tongue?"

Loneliness in a voice is like small movements of water in a pool. I am not detached from him: what he does affects me physically. The sound is caught in my ear like the noise of a fly.

"You're the Cock of the Walk. . . . What a sleeping beauty. . . . I'm the Queen of the May. . . . *I want to see your eyes*. . . . Don't look at me like you're seeing a ghost . . . I'm not a ghost— You're asleep with your eyes open. . . . Why don't you join us for a while. . . ."

The ghost stuff of waking hardens.

Every surface in the room has a sheen in this light—the pillow near my eyes glows with whiteness. After the sly, scary changeability of identity I had in my dreams, I don't want to talk to him. There is a sense of papery masks and of staginess, lies and truths hidden by a mask of silence. Now he is touching my shoulder.

I am in the voice-house of him speaking. His voice, poolingly, lap-
pingly, moves in the dark flow of bedroom minutes. I am immersed in
connections to his voice. He says from his partly recumbent position
on the bed—rehearsingly, remindingly—"Get up: It's like tearing
down a stone wall with my bare hands to wake you. Wiley hates to
leave his sleep; Wiley loves his sleep . . . he's a dreamer. . . . Listen:
sleep is common as dirt: there are more sleepers than nice people: Get
up, sleepyhead. . . . Did you have nice dreams, are your handsies cold,
are your feetsies cold, are you cold? *Oh how I hate to get up in the morning*—is that what it is with you? Did you have bad dreams? Did you
get up on the wrong side of the bed this morning?"

I blink with my eyes unfocused, say, "I'm awake . . ."

The fullness of blood and erection—the potency there is in my
sleep (and not in his), this arousal at-the-edge of hallucination con-
verts it, his voice, into an ironic diabolism.

"Jesus . . . ," I mutter *nuttily,* a first-thing-on-waking response to
avoid saying something to hurt him, to avoid pushing him away from
me. One's consciousness moves from *thing* to *thing* in its acrobatics of
attention and decision, moves across what is called *a distance,* time and
bits of air and a sense of magic in the skull. After having been a child
so long I'm a pretty boy with *an erection* and trying to keep it away
from S.L.—I'm pretty big and he's a joker—and partly I am being
shameless: let him kill himself if he wants.

Attempting privacy is hopeless, me so skinny and my pajamas
gaping, and Dad being sick and *shameless,* nostalgically shameless,
twenty times as much as I am.

I try to cover myself. *He's* there . . .

"Boy, you're crazy—you're a crazy boy . . . I never saw anything as
crazy as you." He's looking down a chute of darkness at a white, very
young prick. His face is foreign in his doing that. When I was little,
I'd had finer hair and a little boy's chest. I find this change to be dizzying. I am blurred by it. He has an odor—this is like being in the odor
in a classroom the day of a really scary test. S.L. leans over my sleep-
heated body to kiss me. He is bigger and fleshier than me in his paja-

mas—not taller. We have had symbols and *symbolism* at school but I understand them as ways of saying *my father kisses me too much* without anyone knowing what you are saying. His real fingers touch my actual chest. I push his hand away—gently—I don't want to upset him, his *heart.* . . . The unwilled rationality of real time and real light, the elements of restless reality inside the room, my dad, with his arm partly over my skinny neck, is sloppily kissing the side of my head.

I endure his actual breath. He is big, sad, smelly with *loneliness* and a kind of sloppy cruelty. I have a thin blanket wadded in front of my cock. The smell of him is redolent of my exhaustion. In the six years he's been ill I haven't left him often.

The throbbing blindness-and-sight of memory is both statistical and esthetic; the flickers are like a lot of big leaves on an old tree when you are up on one of the higher branches in the tree. Old feelings are present—I know this man. I partly ache with life, a form of seamanship. I brace my legs, skinny legs and count the seconds. . . . LET IT KILL ME . . . BIG DEAL . . . WHAT THE FUCK . . . LET IT GO . . . *LET'S GO* . . . A madman-hero. I endure then I reproduce sarcastically silently his posture—tinkeringly. I make my stomach stick out. I purse my lips. Such physical sarcasm—or is it physical exploration?—is forbidden now but was permitted when I was little. He is saying, "Give me a nice kiss—do me a favor . . ." He is moving his face over my cheek—I bring my forearm to block him, and I go on imitating him. He has the gall to tug at my arm.

"Don't do that!" I mutter. *There's no point in daydreaming* that things are different—that gets too sexual, using him that way. You'd think when he got sick, he'd get sweet, but he was conceited to the end. . . . A sick man should be easy to be nice to but I'd swear he was as conceited as possible with the sexual pride of the devil . . . independent, wicked, male-sultry, with a male-sluttish potency, independent-unreachable, palely intent on kissing me.

For a year and a half now he has said this was a joke, a kind of a joke. As a mean joke, I raise my right leg and push against his ribs. I push him to the edge of the bed.

"Hey," he says.

I say as if I had not done anything (but I am slightly out of breath), "I'm not a little kid." Then I partly lose my equanimity: "I don't want you kissing me on the lips. I'm not a child anymore. . . . And please don't say childish things to me about my handsies and my feetsies . . ." I stand up. I'm six feet, two inches and a quarter tall. "That's not who I am . . ." I don't want to say I get *confused* about who I am and what, for instance, the actuality of my speaking out is—is it a hot, seary, scary thing, a warm-blooded assertion of what-I-can-do, my merit as other-than-a-son, a freight, a labyrinth of perhaps *intelligent* hallucination, a role that will become my second nature? This goes silently roaring in me as it does sometimes, tremendous and glittering like a huge loco-motive or like a huge figure on a stage or in a movie in a spotlight, a half-ruthless, half-asinine, *romantic* and personal light.

Daddy says with the occasional poetry that he has and which always astounds me: "Would you refuse a trip among the dead?" Then he says: "Don't be a bad sport . . ."

My mind flares like a sail on a moony sea in response to the power he has, his *clarity of will.* . . . My mother by adoption has said, *He talks you into things.* . . . Parents do that in your childhood to you. My father's ill; the spirit he has is different from anything he had when he was O.K. The voice-house of my father living holds my father's ghost . . . I can't help myself here. A white-lit wind of my own clarity of will pushes at me. . . . This is a matter of what is on my face and what is in my posture.

He says—in mock good humor, metallic and puncturing—"You're too snotty to be a pal . . ." He says, "I'm not exaggerating. You're not a good sport." He was being rhetorical and tricky, wasn't he? He says, "The worst thing you can do, Wiley, is not like some-one . . ." He gives a little laugh. "You play with fire when you don't like the people back who like you . . ." He speaks reminiscently with some sort of after-flavor of sophisticated threat. Imagine a kitchen match being struck, the abrupt-stinging glare, the *white-lit,* then yel-low- and orange-tipped stink: that is what the personal heat of his reality, his feelings and will were like—the moment was sensational in this manner, this gray-tinged, privately difficult, even somewhat hellish (for me) stuff, the *do-whatty* of his will and my own will, and the past, the sheer number of memories, ears and tongues and large and small creatures and events and some light, not daylight. The light of thought.

He says, "Don't be a fearful rabbit. Don't be a fierce wolf." I don't know what he is quoting or if he is. Wills in real time are different experiences from eulogy. Will and character are elements of sanity—God, the rhetorics of sanity. He says, "I mean, *be serious,* that's the test: if you can't be serious with someone who has feelings, then you aren't worth the powder it would take to shoot you. And my life isn't worth a hill of beans since you are my sunshine. Then you're crazy with having no heart."

He partly intends contradiction, and I have a kind of shuddery response as he gets *crazy.* I am being serious in a way but as boys do, guessingly. I faced it a long time ago: the world isn't what people say it is: but that's the way it is. Gauges flip back and forth and fail to control the back-and-forth billowing of maybe crazy obnoxiousness of feeling. One calms one's scorn by adopting a tone of self-address, the sort of tone in *It feels bad in the relentlessly proceeding light of the morning.* I can at best half-imagine what I looked like to him, a more or less delicate brute face, a tall fourteen-year-old . . . I can't read mirrors yet. A delicately browed, thin-boned, bookish and *brute* and girlish and shaped and prettyish face, cheekbones and thin, new eyebrows—not his son's face. I am only his adoptive son. I don't know if any facial patterns from my very early childhood survived, if the hints of manhood-to-come suggested my real family. I can't imagine the optical information he had, the periscope grammar in the third person of seeing *that boy,* the *he*—the dimensional and weighted volume of skinny mass and the dreamlikeness of recent size and of recently acknowledged wakefulness: it was like peeing in a hiding place, that sense of wakefulness. My dad says he can read me like a book but he doesn't mean *me*—he means something human and male—and similar to him which is only part of me. The faint lineny, nighttime-male-body-smells in the bedroom and the spring presentness and the sub-urban odors from outside through the open windows wrack me—do you remember when your senses and the mind identifying the sensory, when all that was new and in a new scale of height and early sexuality.

I say out loud to S.L.: "You be a good sport, not me. . . . Let me be the kid for a change—O.K.?" Because I am not a little kid.

Dad says, "You got no pity in you." He said, "You ever see a sick elephant die? I was a boy—I know about boys—I sneaked into a cir-cus, it wasn't a show: I never saw anything worse than an old elephant die . . . except battle. It was breathing its last . . . I've seen bad things—take a look at an elephant sometimes: their faces can be a les-son even to you. I tell you you stay the way you are, do what you want, I'm not a bad guy—go ahead, shoot me and get it over with—just don't make a circus out of everything, out of an old elephant. Some things aren't fit for a child to hear; I don't want to be stared at like a freak . . . Everyone blames *me* you're spoiled but what could *I* do: you were obstinate like an old elephant . . ."

A nellisfunt . . . A nold uh(n)nellisfunt . . .

The boy said back: "Well *I* spoil *you:* what can *I* do: *you're obstinate . . .*"

"Don't be a smart-aleck . . ."

He is speaking in a moment that moves; it is a hallway of sounds in which he moves and speaks. As he proceeds, he sees possibilities in his speech: in front of him, in back, possibilities in his words and in the listener's attention, a space-and-moments thing with a listener; maybe he thought or refelt things—or maybe he heard as a social per-son—or maybe he felt his hugeness of self in my mind as a giant and truthful man among liars. Without warning, he becomes angry; it was often said when he said angry things that it wasn't him—"*it is the sick-ness talking*"—but it was him: the temper was his. Mostly I think he was a man who was excited inside himself by his sarcasm and the indi-viduality and self-assertion and abuse of others in his rages. The drama of talking mattered to him but not as it would to a politician. Being sick and omnipotent—with sexual or erotic rage—meant that he was a capricious editor of his effect on the world.

He seemed to blow up and to be *huge* as he had been when I was a child. He remodeled his speech; the commanding officer, exasperated-exacerbated tone he used, the topic was how much he didn't like me, the topic was that I was an asshole compared to him and his illness and his magnitude: it was not a metaphor. He wanted something. My feelings zigzagged, hurt with a fed-upness, a rage at him, but my rage was unlike his. He says, "You don't care about anyone's feelings: you don't know the meaning of *cooperate. . . . Take that look off your face! Looking at people like that is what sends people like you straight to hell. . . .* Why can't you shut up? *Can you shut up?* You can do that, can't you? Jesus Christ, be your best self, be sweet. If you can't be human, say nothing—do you hear me—*KEEP YOUR MOUTH SHUT. . . .* Be a human being!"

It is like spilled battery acid when he shouts—it is scorchy and fumy. I cannot know everything about what is going on. Hatred directed at you, hatred displayed, has the flavor of the hater. It's Dad's hatred that is directed at me. It has that flavor—of my past with him. In the peculiar light of Dad's mood, I focus and clench. I have a sense of things-that-have-happened (in the past) sort of tumbling around silently in chambers of what is lost, of secrets in me. I don't have time now to know the ins and outs of the ghost blackness, the shadowy blankness of past things between him and me; and in the darkish-and-glaring cloud of such ignorance at the age I was, I know the conclusion: that I am not to hurt him back, I am not to laugh at him: he is sick.

In real life, attention is physical. My skin and muscles and eyes remember the times he has insulted me. *All of them.* I don't remember them one by one, only fragments to prove I am not making any of it up, the sense of him using this stuff and being aroused by it. The actuality of feelings, compound and time-riddled and onward-going as they are, is that they hold a cannibal echo of the past whether we like it or not: everything is reinterpreted all the time.

If I lose my deadpan, the knowledge of him-in-the-past becomes an illumination, a weight, a heat of light. That Daddy's rage diminished so rapidly means I did the face-stuff right and scared him a little. (One describes this to oneself as *my face showed nothing.*) He was looking. He and I keep count, but you can keep count only in a sense.

You can't be vengeful toward a sick man but sometimes I can't help myself. Along the corridors of the memories of the pain he caused, his role in *the pain continuum* of my life, his temper now stirs such summaries of pain and disgust and hurt: *I'm tired of it. . . . He's not really my father.*

The mind's electrical lawns and light and festivities, its aerial blacknesses, its angled fragments, its clouds and chutes of associations and opinions and present feelings become the electrical fulminations of excitement in actual moments, the reactive excitement of being with someone. He only half-knows this. He wants it not to be true. He cheats on it.

Dry or magically broad, the images and hypotheses, tentative insights as climate and light, as reality, are lit by *perhaps* and *maybe* and *let us suppose . . . let us suppose the people are morally limitless. . . .* The blindman's buff of mooded half-decision in him, his blind temperament and headlong mood make me feel he is stupid. And cowardly. I don't think he knows about people's minds and bodies remembering the past. Or he does know and goes into a rage. *He wants what he wants when he wants it.* Remembered bits fuel stuff; they mess things up too and block possibilities. I have an invisible force of temporary conclusion in a quickened mental light. Emotions here scratch and trigger things as if they were, in an electric sense, overloaded and unstable. They set off pale flames of emotional heat which burn jigglingly. I am hungry to bully him into silence toward my life. I hate his nervous examination of how much life (and youth) is in me.

He pursues the rage thing (he may think he knows what I am thinking); he says as if dismissively but watching me closely, "You're pitifully ugly."

He means physically and more-than-physically. And eerily he means I am not good enough for him which is fine with me. His tone is that he is disappointed in me, and that he is free-willed and determined and "goaded." The part of the insult that was just maneuvering and the part that was bluff and the part that was real hatred are elements of the giant humiliation and great elevation and as if great drama I felt talking to him, that day and other days, my dad, a full-grown male, a dying one. A lot of his mind and *opinions* are in that pantomimic, bulging-eyed stare.

Some of the new meaning now that I am grown swings definingly and blurrily. As a child, one had been a living consolatory factor and victim close to his heart, a measure of his life. The inner flush of attitude is unsayable but feelable hotly, like sweat; it has an aroused heartbeat.

A polite outer blindness takes over protectively. Dad and I are *wartime buddies* and to desert him would be a *serious* betrayal. *We have our ups and downs. . . . He can blow up if he wants to. . . . It's bad for him but I can take it.*

Ah, I am lying to myself. Actually I can't take it . . . not anymore. He has stupid methods: flattery and blackmail and then abuse. *He was always NO GOOD.* Well, *So what?* The next stab and opening-up-of-feeling in me has the regurgitant wildness and vileness of pride in that I know he won't stop. He's always right—he has to be right . . .

He says, "Are you a hyena feeding on carrion?" Then: "You like to eat the dead like a hyena does?"

His temper is shaped by his past, by things he's felt in the past, and by his defeat now. For him I'm *truly loathsome* now. An optimistic patience can be cowardice-and-courage strangely mixed. Or a mistake. Amusement—amusement-and-shame—are the most dangerous physically: they arouse even more of Dad's feelings of love-and-hatred, and he can become really stupid and murderous.

"This is a crazy day," he says disgustedly. With *real* disgust.

My sense of truth in opposition to his sense of truth is so intense that it is like being asleep and confronted by a mysterious dream while I am still wide-awake: I peer into a folded dream of his truth. . . .

"You're too deep in your thoughts to listen to me. You can't speak to me? You've lost all track of time," he says.

My future is in my stammering breath, *my* temper and its links to the past—postcards chopped into flashes of further breath—inward and outward blinks. I'm the last person left who will deal with him. When I leave him he will die. Or try to. He has no benefits to confer. My feelings toward him turn glidingly opalescent, translucent, a preening and unstilled plumage—a moral act, known to be one (people talk about it, my staying near him). But I can leave the room and never return. I can plunge at this moment into being through with him. Patterned flashes of adolescent privacy, the will-to-live as not-a-child, this isn't spark-speak stuff. I let it show on my face where it is pictorially epigrammatic—you know the ruses of adolescence?

I have the potency of strength and will and of erectile tissue . . . I-can-be-revenged . . . I am *real.*

He shouts at me, at what is on my face: "I DON'T LIKE YOU! I don't like you when you THINK. . . ."

One recognizes things a bit after they occur; this syncopation is part of the guess-hall of one's mind when something is happening, when you're trying to talk to your father, say. My strength is a form of my terror and is a form of terror to others . . . off-and-on. In the pornography of intelligence, my sense of his nearness to death and my closeness to hallucinatory-sexual elements that fill me lately are fed by everything that is *here.*

I say, "Leave me alone."

My *leave me alone* is a force of will in the room: this suddenly tinges and tints and tinctures Dad's rage in retrospect. It colors everything now. One feels oneself as a fire in the room, burning everything—including him.

Dad's temper and will are a really disastrous tsk-tsk locally: they *ruined* my childhood. . . . I wish I were well bred, lucky, well educated and with a superb father. But my family are only people.

My dad goes on with some disgust: "Keep your eye on the ball. . . . Pay attention to something *that's not just yourself.* . . . Would you mind doing me and the world and yourself that favor please?"

Why doesn't he shut up? His authority is how pitiable he is. Present tense actuality is all there ever is at a given moment but I feel indebted to him because I was a child once in his care, and he tried to amuse me. Essences, the essence of him, the essence of me don't exist in the moment. The surfaces of things contain *meanings,* skin and hair and light on the wall and the way each person is standing and breathing and the mood he's in and his emotion *today.* The grammar of tones and eyes, in the geography of the moments as they move, is the biggest element of how "Truth" changes in real life in the geography of the moments without becoming untrue. All the geographies: he's a sick man.

The "truths" I see I have to gamble on. If even a few people saw *correctly,* the history of the world wouldn't be what it is. You have to assume a universal degree of error and of *I don't give a fuck.* This leaves room for the other person, leaves you room *if-you-see-it-well-enough.*

Daddy is a man and is suffering. I'm a kid and I want to live.

We're father-and-son (sort of). We're not The Same Person. If you love him, he thinks you're a good sort, and that that means you are the same person he is, and that means that his mind and will are the same as yours—which is stupid but worldly.

"You're a smart kid, no two ways about it," Dad said sarcastically in a voice that meant he intended the opposite of the words, that I was dumb, *and* if I was smart in some ways, it was in ways that didn't matter. My dad is still carrying on with me; so it isn't certain he despises my mind.

Dad says, "A man can always hire someone to remember things for him." He has more systems for being in a present moment than

I do: those are the marks of age and of limited mind. It's part of the way he is someone-with-power. Of course, he's lost most of his power.

Dad says sarcastically, "Are you made of diamond?" But it's changed, the pitch or tone of intention, the meaning that's being thrown at me; now it's virulent *love* stuff—that sort of righteousness. He says, "Are you true blue and sharp as a diamond?" He's said that in ironic speech to me often, but, of course, the tone of irony changes and I am supposed to notice even if he uses the same words. He's calming down. Maybe. The nervous squinting and clenched eyes of my mind watch him and listen with blobs and jerks of comprehension, little detonations of which show—the guesswork and wildness, and the evasive pallors of temporizing in a young person, birdy flickings, flinchings, conceit and wrenching pain in the absence of personal favoritism in the other at the moment. Us and our nerves: a faint per- spiration on him; I am cooler and want to be really cool: I have a sweaty, nerve-slimed coolness.

The hope of grace—a mood-wrecked strain—tough, blank faces. You breathe in the tremendous restless weight of *time*—my mind is a dancing cemetery with a sort of waking order of revenant moments glimpsed; *I don't have to love this bastard* but I do in a way. . . . Ah, Christ, the fluidities of event. Do you want to be A Great Remem- berer? S.L., being ill and with a lot of time, perhaps, had become A Half-Great Rememberer.

He said, "Are you holding a grudge, Wileykins? You want to use your head and look around you and not use your heart? Well, listen, there's a catch; there's always a catch—fee-fi-fo-fum: I smell the blood of an Englishman: there's always a string attached—you want to be a whippersnapper? Do me a favor: don't be sensitive . . . is that O.K. with you, pooperkins?"

I think it takes serious bravery to talk to anyone.

He says, "Don't look so sour. Mr. Sour-grim. . . . The scene is over . . . I had my say. . . . Remember what I said—I meant every word of it."

It's likely you haven't the words for what you're feeling. I try to hold it uncaptioned, and time tugs it from the closed, imprisoning hands of my mind like a hawk pulling at and dismantling what the madman-hero—thrill-mad, resentful—has captured. Memory never shows things in sequence although you can ask it about the sequence.

Memory can't reproduce the real flavor of waiting in a real light or the reality of the pain then. I am sitting on the windowsill, my arms folded, my pajamas still falling off me, waiting for his peacemaking to finish. I think memory tends to romance, omitting the details and the suspense and the tired fear and anxiety and defiance, and a lot of the uncaringness. It omits the ordinariness and the scandal.

Sometimes conscious memory is so much sweeter than reality that compared to living I feel remembering like being gripped by an angel, the blinding brevity and the guidance.

I said to Dad, "I want to get dressed now . . ."

He said correctingly, "Go ahead—shower and shit and shampoo . . ." showing me how we talk, how men talk, how I should talk.

You can't remember the waiting or the mental oddity of thought while you shit. The cold water when I reach over to the sink and get some drops on my fingers from the leaky faucet and rub my eyes with the spottily, coldly wetted fingers and then palms while I'm sitting on the toilet, I remember some of the recent moments of the talk, in a dried out puzzled way.

I try to *rise above it*—a milk drinker. I have an idea of my innocence: it's very iffy and partial. Those who claim to be totally innocent are punished by stupidity. You can be moderately, limitedly innocent. You have to understand contemporary male innocence as it's practiced around you. And whatever else.

To be "moral"—which is to say kind to your dad and not horrified and not broken by him in his illness—is thrilling and dirty.

Dad comes walking into the bathroom—he often follows me in here—S.L. says, "You're like a monkey with a load of coconuts—be a good monkey, do me a favor, see no evil, do no evil, say no evil. . . . Be a little white-bottomed monkey—with a monkey face . . ."

I don't have a monkey face. He is seeing something else, the new-boned quality.

He pays no attention. "Not so little a monkey—do us all a *big* favor: see no evil, do no evil, say no evil . . ." He can't think of what else to say.

In the John

The opinions of a dreamer are set oddly in time. A daydream is a lying correction of waking life, of otherness and multiplicity and of the moment, in favor of one's dreams, of what one's head can picture. In real life you can prove you're O.K. and sane masculinely by hitting someone. Daddy patted me, my hair. *One,* I said to myself, *two.* Actuality is unconstrained by my ideas of it. But I am often constrained by ideas. Daddy is running the cold water. I think, approximately, *Oh whoop-de-doo, goddamn fucking MESS, snafu: it's all fucked up good—and proper—PERIOD.*

My hands remember things, my back does too; my feet remember this tile floor. My mind peers at nothingness: I am moving a turd out of me. Daddy is standing at the sink and I am on the toilet seat, hunched over my arms; my elbows on my knees, a yelled-at boy taking a shit—maybe patient, maybe loving, maybe malicious as hell: I don't know for sure. The familiarity of hiding my rage (and my boyish power) and shitting itself produce a gooey and oozy sensation, partly calcified, like my own tissues and bones and effluvia being squeezed in a football tackle or an embrace.

For a moment, I am blind-souled. Part of the drama of the legibility of my breathing is the drama of breath itself, a biological universal.

"Are you sent us from heaven? Don't make me laugh," Dad says. It's an old joke. I listen skimpily, with a pulsing heart, with no privacy except in lying and in deceiving him. Kinship, kiddyship . . . a clement attention toward him, as if he weren't in the room, me among the stuttering waves of sensation: is this an emotion? Is the immediate wish to leave, is the impetus to get out—is that choking and private impetus an *emotion?* Feelings run off like the sensibility, like images from a mirror into the air. . . . *We were happy; I was happy; make me happy some more.*

"Do you love me or not?" I mutter and ask. My mouth is in the crook of my elbow, and my head is down. I say it but really I am thinking it.

He says in a weird tone, "Now and then: it *depends* . . ." Then he says in a different tone, insiderly, perhaps also partly true and sad and cruel: "I can't love someone like you." It's all true, all of it, whatever he says, ha-ha. It's true if it's properly understood, but I am only the person who makes an effort to understand him now.

I would like him to apologize for the tirade. I don't want to be so quick to do it next time; he's not supposed to do tirade stuff at all because it strains his heart and sets off a climb in his blood pressure. But Dad hates shit that turns him into an obedient citizen; he controls his own uncontrol.

Time-riddled, lovely, slippery Dad. I would like real life to be as I dream it and as I plot it in my head, with rational clear meanings, ones that *I* know. Like I expect to hear the universe scream when I get an erection on the street in a dream. Or in real light. Or where my dad can see it. But real life is different from that stuff. An erection of mine amuses S.L. It's keepaway time. Ideals and dreams can be anything anyone says they are; they can't be measured . . . they laugh at real stuff—that's what they're for.

"Are you dead-to-the-world while you're wide awake?" he asks— he means am I daydreaming. He uses a kind of chivvying, half-baby-talk as in the past.

My posture hides my midsection as I sit on the john. But he knows what is going on . . . the longish, fluffed out thing. And I am dead-to-the-world while wide awake and close to sexual illusion. He was deep inside my privacy in the insobriety of the superminute which means all the minutes so far—in the really tippy thing of *two* people, the thing of not chickening out and leaving the refracted heat of the presence of the other soul for the comfort of one's own daydreams. A *clement attention* can feel hot in you—aroused, arousal is a lighted thing like an orange heat, the dance of it, in my pallor.

How much nerve do I have? A reluctance to see and judge veils my worded opinions as well as my sight of the slightly flabbed skin of my dad's neck and the gray beard stubble there. Dad is forty-four. How much am I willing to see? The opacities of bodies in real light is incomplete, the mooded dimensions which become calculation, a placement of the I in the steadying curve of the ribs. My visual registry of my dad includes my estimate of his health. It seduces him to be noticed. *He's worn me out.* I clean myself of shit carelessly: *He'll live to the afternoon.* . . .

I have special organs for intimately familiar registry—in a hug, for instance. I prefer the distances of speech: "Everything O.K. with you today?" I ask.

I hate asking this stuff. I hate my life. But to stay sane, about this stuff, and cool, and to have stamina, is male character. I used to regulate my own breathing toward a more masculine, a weightier effect by imitating the fashions of his breath, his style in the local light of the mad void of the arrival of each new moment. . . . The racing but tired sense of unadvisable risk and of beauty-of-a-familiar sort, the bathroom, the early morning, the tonality of things here (us with each other), afflicts me so that I *dislike* the two moles on Dad's wide, onetime muscular, now flaccid neck midway down the side of his throat and the stipplings of shadows on his strongly bearded chin. I am caught in the dimensionality of continuance. . . . This is different from mere time, everything unstatuelike, everything without stillness; it seems as ornate and striking as girls' breasts, the rhythm-beset continuance, the *logical* progression of *what-next* in the unstill, toppling moment, on top of the what-has-happened-so-far. Acts arise and fall: the axe: I find life too full of suspense.

Bones of skeletal light obliquely lie in odd reality on tiles and towel racks—shadows stretch from behind the towels at a slant toward the

tile floor and the white rug. Some future or other will not happen.
Some future will—incest and death. In me is a motionless and radiant
air with breath unrepresented: it is a dream of an eternity of attention
even while moments come without sound, without an ideological
whoosh. What do things mean if life keeps happening? Meaning
becomes a special project of ignorance, the soul's *as-if-sacred-seriousness.*

My prick bears a sporadic weight of hallucination. I am aware of a
dirty comic thing of cunt—real and fuzzy cunt, pinkish, reddish: its
grin of otherness. The sense of real cunt is obliterating. I remember
Daddy in his tirade hurting me in scattered fingertip-and-toe-itchy
ways. This comes back to *a sense of cunt.*

"Are you daydreaming, pooper?"

I nod.

He says, "You're young. . . ." Then he says, "You know enough,
you know too much, I'm just a big noise from Winnetka: you got
enough sense to *hee-year* a man with *good* sense?"

"What do you mean, Dad?" Pause. "Tell me what you *mean?*"

"I can't tell you everything, I can't give you every little thing on a
plate, I can't say it all—you have to know some things by your lone-
some. Don't be fresh—be fresh like a daisy, but don't be fresh."

It's hard to talk to grownups.

"Be like the thief of Baghdad . . ." he says. "He has a nice smile."
A movie, *The Thief of Baghdad,* had a star, Sabu, the elephant boy who
wore only a white thing over his dong and who had a thin, brown
chest and a *funny* friendly servile-mischievous, deep-spirited smile.

I say as if to his ghost while he's alive: "I'm fourteen: you're *forty-
four. . . . Be careful of me . . .*"

"What are you talking about *now?* I'm old. I'm ill. I get some
advantages . . ." He says, "David and Saul . . . David and Goliath . . ."

I don't get it.

He said dimly, nobly, distantly—like some old tall movie star—
"How many boys have *that* with their fathers?"

"What? David and Goliath?" I don't try to pretend he's my friend—he's a failed father who is ill and has some sort of fantasy about us being wartime friends.

Life is not entirely without its mercies; it is not entirely demonic or without limit. To notice the shape of Dad's breathing is like trying to hear a sentence; to hear a sentence is like following directions to find a gas station in a strange town. My awareness of his breath, partly medical, partly embarrassed is, in the end, as if I were in the presence of a male Medusa's face, a _merde_-oozer. He's not going to try to grab me when I stand up. I tend to try to be stonily male in Dad's presence, showing off.

Daddy, blond-haired, large-muscled, softening, partly rotted, laughs at something: "Ha-ha. Ha-ha . . ."

Part of the boy's somewhat meager collection of intimate facts is this brief, risky stage of a tie to S. L. Silenowicz. His arms, his _neck,_ his voice among the tiles (a stately baritone, jaded), the heat of his presence are part of the maybe after all truly half-sacred _dirty_ vocabularies of The Real.

My father's breath has become in these minutes a frightened snoring, a grossly skimming and scraping along sound: frightened spurts of uneven breath. He is faking it. He is awake to his power to affect me.

"You sound O.K. today . . ." I say and stand up.

He says, "Spare the bullshit and spoil me." I stick out my arm to keep him at a distance and move, in my pajamas to the shower. I will undress behind the purple shower curtain.

He says, "Wiley, I'm a young man and I'm sick and I have to die. How do you think that makes me feel? I'm done for. Well, you can kiss my ass, all of you. . . . Christ. Hell—I'm _scared_—I'm not ashamed of it," he says to the curtain which I am now behind. "I can't take care of anyone, I can't take care of _you,_ I'm sick. I'm sick of being sick. I wouldn't apologize to God Himself, do you hear me. Make God apologize to me—that's the ticket. What do you think of that? He would if he was a gentleman and not a devil. You ever been scared? Well, what I want to tell you, my advice to you is, you want to be a good guy, take me as I am. I don't want to be a hero no more, no more, no more . . ." *No more, no more, no more* was from a jazz song. "You don't know what it's like to be sick . . ."

"I've been sick . . ."

"You've *never* been sick. . . . You've never been sick like this. . . . No one knows. *It hurts all the time.* I'm scared all the goddamned time."

I know, you told me, I say silently.

"IT'S TERRIBLE EVERY SINGLE MINUTE EVERY SINGLE DAY, IT'S TERRIBLE DAY AND NIGHT—YOU WANT TO SEE THE SHOW? YOU WANT TO SEE ME DIE IN LITTLE PIECES? I'm dying, you think that's funny? You want to see the elephant die? I'm not playing anyone's game anymore, do you hear me?" I'd turned the water on in the shower. "You can go to hell—everyone can go to hell. It can all go to hell. I don't want any of this. . . . It's not living. My heart is *no good.* And the goddamned doctors're stupid—stupid and mean—they're killers. What do they know? They know how to send a bill. They don't feel anything. They don't feel any of it. . . . *I am dying like a dog.* . . . Every son-of-a-bitch and his cousin want me to go easy on *them.* . . . They tell me to act like a man. I'm not gonna do it. I live on charity. I hope every last one of those sons-of-bitches has to go through what I'm going through. They can kiss my ass. I got no time for their stupid filth."

For a moment, my mind's defenses are peeled back like a foreskin. I don't know what it means, the brutal excitement of being close to a man like him, to a guy who says that stuff. My eyes and mouth harden as in school when I stop listening, harden with darkness, with blindness, with sophisticated stupidity.

But then I change my mind and listen partly in retrospect: I figure Dad's speech is man stuff. I assume S.L. is realer even than my sense of him which is real too. My real, present-tense sensibility now today is closer to hearing him than when I was young; the veils over sounds, over intentions are torn . . . I see that he has secret shames— and conceit. Decorums, grammars, school correctness . . . of the sort there is among boys not in a classroom.

I remember when my body started to get sexual in the real way, balls dropping, the first unchildish hair, the first sizable boniness here and there. Then came the change in dreams and then my face changed, my skin and the size of my lips, and then my voice altering—and my new humors, *et cetera* . . . I remember how *unspeakable* in school that change was. I am interested in a know-it-all apprentice way: I'm one of those kids who sort of *personally* exist.

Childhood had seemed fantastic to me even when I was a child, the sweetness of things, the size—sometimes fantastic with disaster. Behind the curtain I have three-quarters of an erection; it is painful to me, the weird uncertainty of susceptible potency. I am a boy, an apprentice-man. Daddy said to me once, *The carrot, the carrot-dick stuff, that can k-k-kill you.* . . . He says now with a certain friendliness: "You have to jack off for both of us, that stuff can kill me."

Leave me alone. . . . His prying. He'd said this stuff before: nearly everything said between us has a history. *Intimacy* . . .

I turn the water up louder.

Dad was an exhibitionist. He winks at me (in memory). He still has a small-town style, a kind of out-of-date vanity as an old-fashioned man, a *gentleman*—nostalgia is a form of romance among men in the Midwest. Maybe it's always a style—sort of a *you know who I am . . . I am not a surprise.* . . . A form of seductiveness. He was in style still with rural people; this showed when he went into the VA hospital. Sometimes his sickness got worse when he was in a rage. He mostly slept in my room after I was ten years old, lived alongside me in actual days, actual nights. He lived with me, not Momma. He slept alongside my dreams at night.

Now he says, "You're like a weed. You grow like a weed." He doesn't know what tone to use. "We're a pair of Tarzans."

No, we're not.

We're in a third-floor apartment; treetops alongside the sidewalk stir outside. We're on *Kingsland Avenue* . . .

I had noticed the change in all my smells. He could bear to be near that—I was surprised and thought he was nuts. My ambitions as a child changed every few months when I started to grow, when I became *a growing boy.* My inner feelings were as if written on a sheaf of papers that were crumpled into a single black-and-white wad, flowers and *no-flowers* of odd heat, faintly cold and half-understood. Businesslike daily toughness, tough-nerved realism but the realism changed day to day as I did physically, a kind of flowering, partly dirty. Even in the cold water of the kinds of shower I took, I have hottish breath as if there were now a fire in my consciousness or a lot of fires: things burning without clear, or formal, outward reason; and the recurrent smoke of this stuff choked me even in the water. The odd, gulping atop the inner heat, atop the feverish heat at moments, the queer, private smoke that makes me comical, *a fool. . . .* Why would my ill father *want* to be near this smelly, incomplete, smoke-ridden, fever-brained person, this skinny, early man?

Dad on the other side of the curtain says, "Are you tired of being a saint? I guess your balls dropped—or didn't they?"

"I don't know . . ." I said from inside the water. I remembered my balls hung high and being little beans and now *there they are . . .* The delay or lags of the mind toward transformations . . . my balls had been throbbing for months.

"You got a lot to learn," Dad says on the other side of the curtain. I'm playing a bit with my whang-ee. He says: "I'm putting ideas in your head. You got too many there already—take some advice from me: don't be too important. Just be human. Don't let nothing get in the way of being *human.* Believe me, I know . . . I learned the hard way. Love and affection come first—you know about the bluebird of happiness? Well, that's the truth—the bluebird of happiness is right in your own backyard. So be human . . ."

The changing light of meaning inside a speech, the direct lying and hopeful swindling, and the hot air, and then in other phrases hopeful almost-sincerity, a hidden proposition and sincerity— *Be a fool and listen to me, let's be fools, love me, I love you, it's all a mug's game, stay close to me. . . .* Did he sound like this all along but I was too little to get it? I used to hear differently. Jealousy and temper, I experience them, but I mostly refuse to know about them. . . . *Am I girlish? Am I a saint?* He has said to me, *You save my life every night—you surely do.* . . . He experiences less terror if I am there. I was *protected* by the big ha-ha of art which defends such phrases as *fathers-and-sons;* but I have been aware for years that most of the fathers and sons I know are in a mess. My rank *as a boy* is high because my father's interest in me is so great. I am a star—like Sabu, in the movies.

"Elephant boy, *howdah-do, isn't it a fine howdah-do.* Wiley, the elephant boy? Is this a 'Sikh' joke?"

The water is in my face. The independence of others' wills is part of the loss of Eden; one understands Justice in the Universe differently. I am sometimes *interested* in the thing of his being interested in me and sometimes bored by it.

"Are you a rooster?" he says. "Are you crowing? Cock-a-doodle-ooo, not a cockadoodle-*dooodooo*—I bet the hens are laying eggs for you." His talk casts a sexual shadow. He has no money, he can't back up his bribes now; he can't bully anyone: he can't buy anyone. I don't know what he expects: S.L. was always a Big Expecter. I start to do what boys do, some boys anyway, jack off just out of range of the strange world. An act of espionage, of cleverness, of rebellion—behind the shower curtain. I am very quiet about it. An awful sweetness, an awfulness in general, a vertiginous pre-satisfaction sets in. Sensations are in as if winged motion in a gulf of simultaneous forgetfulness and omniscience. I am as if at an altitude above the multiplicity of wills in the prison house.

He is saying, "You're a growing boy—welcome to hell—well, I don't want to give you pause; I want to applaud you." He means everything, everything he says, one way or another. He says, "Be young and sweet: use your head. Remember I always said, use your head. You're a Jim Dandy, I'll tell the world." The surprised electricities of the self, dancing and mocking, raked by water noise, magnetically attract further naked electrical storms, response, in grasp and half-grasp in the speed of life. I feel Dad's voice as an electric touch, cruelly civilized in a burning way, this thing of the *air-raids* on you of an actual voice, that nervous actuality. . . . The delicate cliff of nests and its gates and the sore *and* smooth-electrical thorniness, that stuff and the soul dilating—*hurtfully*—the momentary collapse of *loneliness* and the onset of a rash availability, over and over, the rabbit heat and finch tones of sexual sensation enter me as a sort of rape. These windless transfers, mind to mind, man to man, the madly different inner labyrinths and dangers, it is like a dream although it is directly real.

Everything has significance as in a poem. Or as when you're in love. I'm sorry I lived in the ways I did live, but the different motions of parts of me went whirring and whirring among various electric reeds and in a biological light, meanings half-given to me, half-earned, half-stolen, the mathematics of mental things: the great stammerer speaks, *ah, ah,* what astounding feeling.

"Are you taking a cold shower? Are you getting rid of your feelings?"

Cleaning up I am coldly without feeling, and then suddenly wrenched by sensation and feeling. Who is *he* on the other side of the curtain? The soft-edged, masked-face manifestations of his importance to me shriek among the flusters of guessed-at meanings—the mind is listening: *all of it is real.* . . . A wild and stinking horde of ghosts hoots along my nerves and disorders my schoolboy calm. Freakishly compounded complexities of feeling in an interval-breathed self . . . in a moist pit of feeling, the agonies of pleasure and the dimensionalities of duration and recurrence. Specific memories in their changeable meaning, nanosecond by nanosecond, carom along lines of association, witnessy and radiant. . . . Unrepeatable singularity, the real geography of the moment, the vocal silence in the bathroom, calculation, sweet silence. . . . The mind is a sort of angel's egg of the universe and hatches stuff.

Daddy, back in our room, the two of us, Daddy sits himself in the too-small chair by the window. He is ill and listening to himself, sullen and distant. *He loved you. He always loved YOU.* "Maybe you should take a shower," I say, drying my hair. Some days he is afraid of bathing and of showers.

He says, "Spare me your opinions. I don't like smart-alecks. . . . Well, I guess we are in the land of broken hearts." What does he know? "Knowing you is like sitting in an electric chair," he says. Then he says, "Little Bird, you are my sunshine." *Sometimes an electric chair,* my mind adds.

The smart-aleck boy says aloud, "Sometimes an electric chair."

We go two-by-two in the flood. In my voice you hear my father's voice, Daddy's voice— What did you expect, that you could know anyone with impunity?

"Doncha kno-ohhh? Juh know *j'uhh {k}no{w}, know, know* better than to talk like a fool . . ." he says with a degree of grandeur.

Each flicker of mind is like a barn swallow circling, hunting, perching. I don't want to be graceless. The odd, true, jammed warehouse of a world and of an intimacy, the actual leaves in the slight wind at the window, agonized, temporary, interrupted tumbling, the skittery advance into the next moment, the thuds and rumbles and stolen strength of the heart, among the secrecies. A lost ecstatic real is part of the hortatory stillness: *dry your hair and dry between your toes and keep breathing. . . .* The real billows out in insistent kinship—the real does this in me, assigns me to itself. My parents came to me without footnotes.

My Dad says to me, "Pisher—" Then: "Little Pisser—" Then: "Macher Peepee—" Mockery. Then: "*Don Juan . . .* you're dripping on the floor."

I thought I knew what he thought life was like for *a man.*

Some of S.L.'s Jokes

"I have to laugh sometimes: people who look like turkeys think they look like angels—maybe they have their wings in their wallets. I had the face of an angel when I was young, and over prison walls I could fly. The daring young man on the flying trapeze. I would give you the shirt off my back, and a lot of good it did me. You didn't have to kowtow to me like I was God. I will say this: there is no appreciation in the world. Ah, ah, everything wears me out. Well, I always voted for a short life but a happy one. I wouldn't say it's been a happy one. I don't care. I'm the I-don't-care boy. How do you like them bananas? Well, you can all go to hell—not you if you're nice. I'll tell you the truth: life isn't good for you. Did you know I was a philosopher? I am but no one pays attention. It's not my fault I was always a sweetheart. I didn't make the world—there's a lot I didn't do. You are the light of my life—how is that for a joke on me? I guess I'm not too lucky, but I'm a good sport. I give three cheers because I have you in my life: you cheer me up: hoorah, hoorah, hoorah. I wouldn't believe everything I say if I was you—I wouldn't listen to me like I was *William Shakespeare. . . .* Listen to me like I was S. L. Silenowicz—that's enough for me. Give us a kiss . . ." He says, "I don't want to be listened to like I was a woman—but I sure as hell 'm not the man in the family. I'm down and out; I'm cannon fodder. I lost everything and I'm stuck. I'm stuck with you. . . ."

My sense of accident and darkness comes from him, from what he said in the weakened boom of his voice and how he looked at me, the expressiveness of his face, in the domestic light of his illness, of the time we spent together—bridal, two men in a room, a kind of early adolescent ceremony of education: I mean that being with him was to enter the world of men . . . "Learn to talk to me, and you can talk to anyone. . . . Believe me, I understand everything—everything. I'm the center of the universe. When I look up, there's sky all around, so I know I am the center." Him and his son more or less— Ah, God, you gave me a decomposing, local emperor, and the relentlessness of moments, death, actuality. "If you don't pay attention, I don't exist—do you hear me? If you don't understand me, I might as well be dead now—you're talking to a sick man, but I am a man . . ."

I was impressed by the efficient effect, the sense of truth (of a kind) that he conveyed to me in his talk, in his jokes, in his actuality. I listen and from time to time I actually *hear* him.

He says, with a sigh, "You have a way of sucking me in, little pitcher with big ears—the big pitcher—well, nothing ventured, nothing gained. I always hated old Jews: they smell bad and they think they know it all: they don't listen to anyone. You want to cheer me up? You want to make a career of this? Half the world is waiting for your sunrise. It's hard to love a man—ask me and I'll tell you the truth: I'm such a genius, I can do that. It's just my luck that you can't love anyone. Anyone asks you, you tell 'em, *S.L. said I couldn't love any-one . . . S.L. always defended me: people said I wasn't fit to sleep with hogs, and he said I was . . .*"

I remember the often ugly but thrilling melodies his voice had, the male implication, shameless-shameful, *men-in-a-garage*, his variety of talk. It stirs me in the bowels of my being—it reminds me of who I am.

"I don't want everyone spoiling you—anyone," he said. He often changed his mind midsentence. Pronouns and emotions flew around as did his sense of propriety, about what it was fit for me to know. "You're just a kid. Everything is hard enough without you making it worse."

His throat chuffs with obedient and disobedient breath in illness and intimacy.

"What I have to say is turn over a new leaf—actions speak louder than words. Give us a kiss. Who knows what a kiss means? Captains and lootenants—what would it take to get you to be nice to me, a real human being, day in and day out?"

(I said dully and in a pure voice, in some daring and self-protective and in some hurting-him and saying no and some scoffing way, "It isn't for sale, what I do.")

"What does that mean?" he said, outscoffing me. And adding a male more-than-a-schoolteacher knowledge of language. Also a social class thing, small-town, ruler-of-the-world thing. He said, "I know more than a schoolteacher does: what you say doesn't make sense. I know what sense is; ask me, I'll tell you."

I muttered, "Leave me alone." My eyes were not averted. My politeness; my refusal to be tough with him encouraged him.

"What? What is it now? You talk gibberish, Esperanto . . . pidgin . . . pidgin English . . . pidgin shit . . ."

Looking at him and feeling the express reality of my youth and comparative *freshness* (it is in the eyes and eyelashes; it is in the youthful skimpiness, *spindliness,* newness of nerve endings), I scowl, knowing that it affects him.

He winces. "Being nice gives people a reason to like you," he said encouragingly.

I was aware that if you were nice to him for *a reason,* that then he wouldn't consider it *nice*—he had a thing about love, about the paradisaical—always more and more complete and pure, more and more ideal, or nearer to it. I knew better than to say anything to him about him and upset him; he sometimes had spasms of heart fibrillation if I crossed him. It's interesting if you're thinking, if you have a thought or whatever, and you don't want it to show on your face, how the thought itself becomes nasty and more pointed because it is hidden: *He's being stupid.*

Anyway, my silences, my glancing away are part of our language which has problems because of the differences in our ages and in our minds—you know? You have to do it by feel and by eye—and you know misapprehension is built in—if I use an ideal measure, then he is not bookish. If he uses an ideal measure, I am not sonlike in the way sons act in movies or in daydreams—I am too fancy, too modern. To *understand* requires a physical sympathy, vaguely sexual, and an emotional sense of calculation. But when I manage it, it is like being dressed up and clean.

Then if Dad hugs me too intimately, it gets all fucked up.

As long as the gestures were sparse, then the signals, words, and breathing had precise musics or urgencies. When the sympathy grows more heated and touchy, then everything becomes gross. My side of the dialogue, already limited, is wiped out in his imposing this passion—or whatever it is—imposing it on us. I don't *feel* that stuff. It seems ruinous to me, ruinous of me. I mean, in the room, in the smell of dust, in the smell of sunlight, in the smell of the hour of sunlight in that room, in the nearby sense (and sight and odor) of my father's arms and chest, I was wiped out. Ugh. This made me skeptical toward his feelings. But if you're not going to be *destructive,* you have to be skeptical only in *the right way.*

I felt my existence had no merit in his eyes beyond that of to-be-devoured. I don't think there were many possibilities for him. The notion of infinite and different realities of meaning exhilarated and frightened me and seemed very secret, a *closed book.* But people felt I was an *open book,* which means young.

S.L., suffocating me, said, "You're a tough nut."

It is scary: the *infinite* time-bony extent to which someone touching you is an antagonist, casually ruthless, part of a delusion where *love* (and laziness) and surrender are entwined.

He said, "You're not so much fun as you think—you hog the floor. A real person has to make sense out of you. Your problem is you doubt people. You're no better than anyone else. . . ."

"You don't treat me as if I were the same as you."

That triggered his temper: "Shut up! SHUT UP! Hush! I want to hear my own voice for a change. I am smart by popular demand. I am good-looking in my way." Old routines he used to do at parties he and Mom gave. I kept wanting to understand *clearly* as when I read books. I knew his was love talk in a way.

But what was important to me—to my *soul,* if I might be permitted to say that—was that you couldn't film us. Or quote us as some kind of high, noble, *sentimental example.* The unordinariness and then the aura Dad has of his right as a full-grown man to have passions, the way he has so many ways of getting his way, the way he mostly runs things—you can't film that. He has a tactic of being in control impatiently; he has a fluster of *wicked* principledness. Male realism. *Glamorously* intent.

And that is always just about out of control in a *good guy way,* alive and human, and stinking and dark-willed in an invertedly and endlessly different-languaged world—his world. A stink of acrid nerves is in him as if he has been traveling day and night to this hug—traveling, ill in the moments . . . (His reactions to me were the basic medium in which I learned to swim.) Compared to the world—and in the light in the room—I was, at my young age, preeminently a change of subject for him, a change from illness and death, and from his own being, his own personality—that was the term back then.

Love for a son was part of an obscure rigmarole of a change of meaning which he, and only he, judged. I mean I had no say, or very little, and no social whatever constrained or guided him and certainly not Momma: no one had any say-so in what the meaning was. "I am a man. I am an American," he said. Momma said he was a *bossy Jew* and didn't know it. I rejected his definitions of things—he hadn't managed his life well—and I denied the reality of his principles and his ideas and ideals. But I was aware of how he breathed and the way he became sightless in the hug and was sighted inwardly with a sense of sensual-emotional *emergency.* I mean he affected me. The sensibility of the flesh, the hands, the backs of the hands and the palms like queer irisless eyes and his neck pulsing was a kind of sense—or judgment—so that he is what I know, his acts, these moments—his *obdurate,* anxious heat, an in-the-depths *heat,* a thing of being in deep water that took his mind off his dying.

The way you're loved really does shape your consciousness—do you know? The way it lays down paths or highways. I was unrehearsed, unprofessional, un*skillful*—a kid. I had a whole history of being his kid. In his arms, the moment is smelly and *poignant* and so familiar that it is sensually realer than language can easily say: it is as real and clutching as a dream insisting it is real, insisting on its own plausibility.

Comedy comes swiftly, the accustomed and unaccustomed torture; his hair tickles—I don't love him physically or as a father quite, or as myself in this time-gargantuan form, or in this other boy grown old and cagey form; but the torturedness in me is also sweaty and seriously hilarious, a familiarity of domestic flirting, unlaughing, the almost continuous, half-shocked hilarity of feeling—the evasiveness, half-scoffing, stupidly contemptuous—as the one who is being *loved,* as the son-lover, or whatever, just as in my blond childhood.

I am practiced at living on, at lasting for a while. I have lasted this long.

Finally I count aloud, "One, two three," and then I push him off me.

"You're a whole floor show, you are," Dad said.

His *reality* upsets me, and my reality upsets him—I mean the *feelings* and sharing the same address and then the eyes, the look in the eyes . . .

S.L. says, "Let your blond hair do your talking for you. . . . It's all a rat race. But keeping your mouth shut and being young, you hold aces. . . ."

You can lose your nerve about being loved. You can be bored to the point of rage. I was precocious: I made few, if any, confessions to anyone, ever. I am correctness itself among my errors except when I lose my nerve in the lit-up areas of this affection and the obstinacy of its *blind* unsuitability: love, *David the Psalmist.* Love between men is a strangely silent thing, really—

I want to talk to you—

I make a face in the ache of unsettled androgyny, in the degree of misplaced femininity he has imposed. I suppose he is repeating his adolescence, redrawing it in me, not him. The weight—and music— of what he does is recondite, nostalgic—forbidden. He is a dying man. The merit and sanctity of his life are greater if his definitions are the best ones, the absolute ones, the absolutely true ones. If both our lives are sanctified, what then?

If I am one of the electrifying boys and he is one of the grown rajahs and hidden-faced seducers, who are we then? His feelings. Well, was I regular-featured? Recessive? Pallid? *Juicy?* I don't really know. I suppose I had an exposed and plagiaristically awake look in the style of the time—*imitating nothings and nobodies,* he said once, despising how I wanted to be part of the time. Did my face have a heartbreaker's truth? Was it maybe a heartbreaking compromise as faces go? My role was that of the one whose *heart* is thrown away. S.L.'s was to have the *desperate* odor of a lover.

S.L. says, "You think you know it all."

What possibilities of story, the Know-all and the dying man. The Pretty Boy and the dying man's *happiness*—what is a dying man's *happiness* worth?

"Don't make a parade of yourself," S.L. says *paternally.*

"I don't make a parade of myself . . ." I say.

Dad's nervous odor, his saltiness are part of my mental sensations of youth. His responses to me aren't physically logical. Dad's moments *with a boy,* held breath and heroic tactics of eyelids: he is posing. Underwater. In the refractions, a man's eyes staring through a wet stain of feeling, I feel the oddly slick darkness of his interest. Male beauty is a heroic matter, the too-great commotion of that. "If you notice too much, you won't last long," he says.

Poems of Rejection

S.L. says, "You have no sense. You want to drive people away? Is that what you like to do? You have the wrong *attitude.* Me, I'm as smart as they come— You don't know a damn thing. Be careful," S.L. says with a lot of *silence* in his voice: "You want me to have the last laugh?" He says, "At least, I don't sound like a book. Try not to sound like a book. Don't lead me on . . . I'm not a Betty Coed—I'm a sick *man . . .* PERIOD. Well, I don't know who's going to teach you good sense. I don't claim to know every little thing: I'm not a Be-all and a Know-all like you. You ever put your head to the grindstone? Things are too easy for you. You're lucky you got a real lump in your pants. Try to be reasonable. That's in your favor: sweet reason. Some people are scum—don't be like them. I'm afraid you're no Tom Sawyer." Was that his real desire? "The rest of us have to live too. I wasn't someone who was there for the long count . . . I know my limitations. Don't try to understand everything—just be nice. Everybody's a thief—you know that? Don't look at me like I should explain everything—I'm not a teacher. Listen: I'm telling you secrets. I hope you appreciate it. Do me a favor, Wiley, and don't be a fool who thinks he's smart, don't be someone who thinks he's smart and doesn't know what's what half the time, don't be someone who doesn't have a Chinaman's chance in hell. Be nice to me. I've got no time to pity a fool. A young fool . . ."

And so on.

The ins and outs of Daddy's speeches, his underlying sense of its being hopeless that he will be understood, his lostness, his logics, his sense of power and the strain of his illogical sense of truth, his self-indulgent love of speech, his voice threading through his sense of things, his voices really, the idle exercise of subordinate or of superior speech— *At least, your dad talks to you, Wiley. . . .* Yeah but it is a difficult thing, this talk, strange and obscene, his life, his vision of things. It was strange and obscene to comprehend his loneliness, the unhilarious *despair,* the part that was not a joke. I felt what it was like for him when he touched me. Or when I listened. I comprehended with my restlessness, my butt—he said that once with the deadened smile of the supremacy of his experiences, the powerful rank of the domestic presence of death, the role of the male, the tiredness in him at that false citizenship in a harsh world, his jealousy and interest in the public histories of men. We are inside a protected silence, he and I. . . . The war was everywhere, nearly everywhere, but not here. I did somehow comprehend that men dreamed of usurping or matching the weird power of being beautiful and causing history the way some women did. It was like a myth to be in the room with him. And it was real: a lot of this showed on my face.

. . .

"Hard facts are hard," Dad said, wound up and ill, going on as if with mechanical delight—and slavery—to his life as *a good-looking* man. Nervous wit and loneliness. "I'm a lover. I do things whether I want to or not. I'll tell you a secret: everyone thinks he's God and wants to have a good time and his own way. That's the engine and the caboose."

"Am I a fool *all* the time?" I asked him.

"*All,*" he said with a triumphant, amused, huffy, weary delight. Welcome to our morphine-laced deadpan comedy. "They say people with my condition live longer if they have a good time. I'll tell you frankly, I'm not up to snuff. I'm a quitter. I don't care who knows it either. It's too much for me—I'll shout it from the window: I'm done in; it is all too much for me. I'm fair as they come. . . . At least I don't giggle when a man talks to me—"

"I'm not giggling."

He said: "It's baby gas. That's a riddle. Well, one lesson you learn is don't talk fancy if there's no money in it. . . . There's a word to the wise." He put his hand on my knee.

"I don't want to be a whore, Daddy . . ." I pushed his hand off.

"You have some funny ideas, a lot of very very funny ideas. You have too much imagination, more than you need. I'll tell you a secret about you—you don't know if you're coming or going."

S.L. is not, and never was, a *nice* person—"Gorgeous, yes," Lila said, "but he was a very, very bad person. Well, I say long live the rest of us." She stroked my arm which burned along the course of that movement of her now small-in-my-sight hand. Her touch in the fluctuations of my history is part of what I know of the fluctuations of history. We are a family of *whores.* In a sexual universe.

She said, "Do I give you conniptions? You're the hardest person to deal with I ever saw. *S.L.'s not a smart man where women are concerned.* . . ."

"Momma, I don't want to be a *whore.*"

Lila said, "You're someone who looks at everything and gets everything wrong. You can get away with that in school but you can't get away with that in life."

I said (about school and my life and my value-in-the-world): "I mostly
don't have to talk about it but I have to keep it in mind because the science teacher and Mr. Caulkins"—the school superintendant and my
realest ally—"say I can help win the war with what I might discover in
science: that's why *they're* interested in what I'll do next: they're being
patient with me." A somewhat muted *ha-ha* was in my breath: *I don't
belong to* you. "It's not easy; they expect too much from me."

Daddy said, "Don't aggravate me with your shenanigans,
Wiley. . . . DON'T EVER AGAIN LET ME HEAR YOU TELLING
ME OR ANYBODY ELSE HOW SMART YOU ARE DO YOU
HEAR ME THERE ARE SOME THINGS *I* CAN'T STAND AND I
DON'T HAVE TO STAND THEM *DO YOU HEAR ME AND
THAT'S ONE OF THEM . . .*" Guilt and jealousy in the shadow of
death.

"I was talking factually, Daddy. I get tired of pretending to be
Tom Sawyer, that's all . . ."

"People hide what they're supposed to hide. They don't hide
what's pretty. Brains aren't pretty." He had been a pretty man but
not known for his brains. He and I are talking in the shadow of his
death. Truthfully up to a point. Lying differently, at least. He got
pretty crazed at times with happenstance calculations—pain, torture, death. I was supposed to be afraid of him and for him—I mean
he wanted that. The oddity, Jesus, of all that he wanted. It was
eerie . . .

I didn't intend to accept his moody definitions or his helter-skelter
advice: and, yet, in my heart, I did. Anyway, he loved me at the end—
I could see it. . . . But it was his love.

He said, "There are some things only good-looking people
know—you're not really good-looking but you're young: it's all the
same thing . . ."

Near death, if you talk, you have to take carelessness as O.K. I
didn't trust him anymore ever. His mind reluctantly, abrasively
defined me, welcomed me. Wanted me dead.

He said, "You wish I was rich? It's all money. Everyone's a

whore . . ." He complained about the doctor: "Well, he's more interested in you than in me, and I'm the one with the disease. These fellas
wait their chance to win out over you—it's hard enough to die without having to watch everyone crow over me. I can live without that."
Then he heard my earlier speech or figured out the tactic: "AND I'M
TELLING YOU TO *SHUT UP*! SHUT UP SHUT UP SHUT UP,"
my father said. "I'M A DYING MAN," he said, taking pride in that
position, that fate, that reality of my inheritance from him.

DUMBNESS IS EVERYTHING

One time Ora and I were very drunk after a party in Bronxville—a large, milling, snotty-but-shy, defensive and prying and young and rich suburban Gentile crowd, with the usual party sexuality like a heated cloud. We were living down the road from Betty-and-Irving's, in what had been a farmer-caretaker's cottage. Betty was Ora's aunt, her mother's sister. Betty's mother and father had lived on this Westchester hilltop, the top of this steep ridge: and over the years they had bought up two or three more places to enlarge their own.

Betty's father was from Ohio and was a respectable sort, a front man for gangsters in the hotel and hotel-laundry business. Betty's mother had been a pretty woman, bright, afraid of boredom. This part of the neighborhood had not been fashionable. A Ziegfeld star had lived here, one who bathed in asses' milk. Two farms were still in operation. Most of the five remaining large houses belonged to Jews or to Ora's Mafia-allied grandparents.

Our cottage had no garage. We used the one at the main house, a wooden building painted very white and set at the end of a very short, steep, tightly curved driveway, overshadowed by oaks. We'd had the top down on the car. I'd put it up when we got near home, for privacy where we were known, as in the lighted gas station and by the local police who kept watch on the place when no one was there. I was too drunk to drive into the garage and I laughed at this and sat there in the car on the tarred apron—built up on one side to be level—in front of it. I'd taken off my jacket when we left the party and had unbuttoned my shirt a little so that cool air would help keep me control my drunkenness while I drove.

I'd driven soberly as an act of will—you can do that. You can stand outside your drunkenness just as you can stand outside the sentences and ideas of the decade. When the car stopped, when the motor vibration and noise stopped, and the wheels were still, the drunkenness shufflingly bulged and was dizzying, more than before—it pulsed in my head, stung my eyes and rang and banged—I felt encased in invisible water, drowning. I willed the drunkenness to be quiet. "We made it," I said. Ora and I had been stiff and as if counting the moments and miles, not certain this wasn't the night of disaster, of a wrecked car, perhaps of death or our being crippled.

Coming home, we had spoken a little about the party, about who made passes at whom. As it got later while we drove north, we began to speak to each other with the stiffest intellectuality we could manage, of the sort we had been taught in the style of the late 1940s at Harvard: we discussed Epictetus, Hegel, Santayana. We tried to make our drunkenness traditional, or something. We were living up to college standards. We spoke a bit of anti-Semitism and intellectuality—and we were alternately very grand, and we giggled often although not about being serious but about being drunk or about the mindless architecture of the highway, of how the Taconic Parkway was placed.

She was drunker than I was but when she was drunk she behaved with a rigid sobriety that was drunken only in a kind of underlying obscenity; she was a good-sized young woman and inveighed against things—some of it came from social class, as if she carried a horsewhip or a rifle. She was not ever at peace with that part of herself but had a refuge or retreat into an *obscenely* sturdy wildness of spirit, almost a rich girl's pretension, and her pet *dichotomy*—that was a word she loved—between life as boredom and life as wickedness. She had to piss often when she was drunk; but she was very good-looking; and the attempts on her were usually made in the back halls near the bathroom.

In the car she had been careful not to move much because that would agitate the saucepan and make it slop over. Still, we had stopped three times and then had settled into the endurance contest of getting home. Perhaps our realer home was the apartment in the city: I don't know.

The immensity of the view was behind us and to one side—we had an immensity of silence, an immensity of warmish wind, a breeze really but not stopping-and-starting, not made of individual hooks and curls, but, because of the great width of the night air, riverine, hugely animal and ghostly, a whispering dragon of a wind. Ora had taken her shoes off and she got one back on, a single high-heeled shoe. She turned her face toward me and said, "Kiss me. Do you feel sexy?"

No one was there, in the main house, or in the three smaller ones on the property. The trees were there, an immense copper beech snuffling in the breeze, and some larches and maples, firs and spruces. The slope opened to a view, sky and stars, distant hills and implicit valleys, farms back then, and comfortable small towns, soon to be suburb. The cleverest estates controlled their views; fools had chosen this high ridge. We had a scattering of lights above and below, stars and houses; the ones below indicated lives with less money to spend than there was up here.

"I have to pee," she said. "And I don't know if I can walk."

I put my arms under hers and kind of pulled-shifted her until her thighs were spread, until her legs were mostly in a sexual posture. She was usually verbally forward, the aggressor in speech, but physically she was passive and full of waiting—perhaps that was a style back then. Her heavy head, her marvelous skin, her hair pressed against my cheek. I lifted her skirt and got her panties off—over the one high heel. The night air, the bright albino watchface moon with its blurred random wholeness, the stiffly assaulting breeze, and my head ringing with drunkenness, of course—it is all a lost world now, those farms so near New York City and my youth and drunkenness.

The relief at not being dead and the social immensities of the time, the nearness-and-distance in the view of that vast, restless rural, semi-rural district and its local yeomanry, and the strangeness of the hour and of being in love. . . . Farming was merely part of what locals did; they worked, had businesses. Our escape, our elevation on this high ridge which was not fashionable—which was for outsiders (but it was beautiful, this land set so high) everything was fictional and touched with brevity and with a greatly skewed, faintly Gatsbyoid romance.

The warm wind, the moonlight, the strength of her body, the diminished dark as my eyes adjusted—in those days her face was never boring. Even she was not bored by her face. I helped her hobble across the driveway. No one could see us from the road; I mean the road was angled, and headlights would not illuminate us.

She clung to me and said, "This is too open." I held her up and we went behind the corner of the garage. A kind of warmth came off the wood of the garage and a damp coolness rose from the grass. "Are there any animals?" she asked. At the back of the garage was a stone wall, partly overgrown, and beyond it a field now young timber that had been farmed through part of the war, eight years ago, ten. You could hear the emptiness, you could hear and see and feel that no one was there, that few animals had survived. The moon illuminated part of the garage and then it was very dark. I held her and checked the grass with my feet. "Go over there," she said. She said, "Don't look."

I leaned against the garage. The feel of the paint and of the temperature of the wood came through my shirt and I loved myself both as a kind of machine of registry of such things and for being a little rich and for being young and on this hilltop—or side of a ridge—and I loved her more or was amorous or attached because of a thing of our minds being set at such angles that I let her describe me to myself: she expected me to love myself, to be angrily poetic, faintly savage. She taught me, kind of.

I took off my shirt so she could wipe herself with it but she didn't want to use it, so I handed her a sassafras leaf from a nearby sapling.

First, though, were the sensations of the wood on my thin-skinned, bare back, and the shirt dangling from my hand, and the sounds of Ora pissing on the grass, the wet whistling whisper of that. And the air. And then the heroism—sexual, too—of trying to live. Lechery stirred in a winged fashion; each element of the self is a fashioner of the air and of moments: the arms bathed in air, the queer onrush of sexual self-dramatization, you know, of how the two of you do it. The roles, the longing, perhaps the wish to use one's party self, the young woman and the boy-turned-young-man: "As long as you're squatting there . . ." She looked up. I partly undid my pants.

She always had a queer reaction to my doing things, a reaction of excitement to my initiating things: she was imprisoned and then not entirely freed. It was as if she slid deeper in a kind of burrow—that was, if she accepted the invitation: sometimes she hesitated. Still, some element of negotiation remained, and there was power present in her, too.

Is it power that stirs my now clearly animate flesh? Or is it a shuffling cowardice, fucking when we're drunk—moving within her daydreams, her ideas of sexuality? Is it a distraction of the will? Again I offer the shirt, the sassafras leaf. Ora uses her finger and some grass and stands—my bare arm supports her, touches her: she can stand and balance.

The weight of Ora leaning on me is sultry and real. I put my hand inside the loose-fitting, wide-shouldered blouse she wore. She is a powerful sexual presence.

The party had been partly for me, for signing a contract to write a movie for the youngish guy whose house it was. And Ora had dressed herself for playing second fiddle—a guy at the party, very drunk, said she was *the devil's Venus*. She had on a white cardigan, unbuttoned. The night slid and shuffled. Now her blouse was below her breasts. Her bra was absurd. The drunkenness made me alive all over my body as when I was a boy. Leaning on each other, pausing now and then to kiss, we crossed the back lawn in the silent and unlaboring moonlight. The path wound in the enclosed setting of lawns and flower beds past the main house and two giant beeches with their vaguely silver, shattered, moonlit faces and under some maples and past flower beds and hedges and a stone patio-terrace. Ora, weighty and real, solid-bodied, gleaming vaguely, leaned on me, permissively, negotiatingly as we moved drunkenly in the dark. Where the lawn is open behind the large house, she gripped my dong to balance out my soft, night-air palping and stroking of her bare breasts. Bare-breasted, sugary-breathed (from the alcohol), faintly wet-skinned, we share a snuffling drunken kiss under a murmuring, chattering beech.

The night spreads away below us.

"How far does sound carry?"

"I don't know."

"I don't want an audience."

I slipped my feet out of my shoes, got her shoe off with my bare foot . . . pants, her skirt . . . her cardigan . . . Now we're naked but in the moonlight—

"Can we be seen? Can anyone hear us?"

"Naw. It's just us and the spirits—" The booze and the black cupids of modern desire. I whispered, "I'm scared of the dark—"
Under the tree. A joke.

It is quite clear—as in a test—that we are not in any major way opposed to each other, physically or spiritually. It is strange, this tentative and yet, at least momentarily final alliance.

Ora's body is a landscape, a climate—or a kind of boat—for my feelings. She doesn't dance comfortably or wriggle or seduce with her body. There is some huge gulf between it as visible and affecting you and its inward or private reality for her as heat and that divergence is what you touch.

You touch the weird vivacities of the burrows of her body and their games of entry or hers; her body itself was the caryatid-columned porch of these moments. Perhaps I elected her body in something like the heavy way she elected me brute-of-the-moment, long-legged sexual demi-demon and commander. Not that I was or wasn't those things, but that was her sexual projection for me—a game, maybe. It was like being plunged into a dictionary of her life with secret moments in it written out, although not in language I could understand. The overweening handsomeness of her first guy in high school was part of what she conferred, maybe dreamily, on me. We are each in a category of desire relating to pride, which is not unusual but perhaps which condemns us, two spoiled creatures on the high, sloping, moonlit lawn among flower beds, some with wooden or stone statues in them, and the hedges like walls. Much of the event is lost inside a moment hidden from language: *We didn't make it from the car to the cottage—we fucked on the lawn.* Ora kept a diary in which she also wrote, *Perhaps this will be a famous diary. . . .*

What we have here is a shuffling set of drunken fields of attention, the phallus in night air—the white, faintly dry branch or self, unpriapic and then priapic *as hell,* a kind of silent violence of implication, the odor of grass and of lilies—*rich, rich,* the night murmured; the boy is inside the man: *On our country property as in a dream: but it is life. . . .*

"I owe you a good love poem, Ora. . . ." *I-uhahh—ohhhhhhhh-yooooooooooooooo-uh-uh-guh/id luh-uhvvv poh-immmm, Oh-rah. . . .* Laughing silently in the tenacity of my drunkenness, I stumbled and, boyishly, released her, rather than take her with me to the grass. And whirling and falling from my height and on the slope so that my head plunged seven feet, whirringly, me and my branchlike prick and me landing on my side and then turning on my back: ah, there are stars, leaves, night-yews, moon: the stink of grass: the grip of half-silent laughter, then loud, foolish laughter—"Hush—don't . . ." Ora bends over: oh the breasts, oh the breasts, oh the *oddity* of breasts, oh the weight of recurring innocence, of virginity returned: the weight again of present-tense ignorance and darkness, a kind of confusion: her breath, her shoulders, her head—a *timor felicitatis*—a fear of happiness and of its loss, a fear of her reality having power, a fear of moonlight and of my own desire. How I grip, with what ferocity, the thick, motionful sheaves of her long, handsome hair: how I own and control

fear of happiness

the dark, horselike moment, and am ridden myself by duty and pride, by her as audience, by her and me as audience—ah, ah, ah . . .

And the jolt of falling, traveling through my bones, did hurt my balls and my drunkenness-disdaining prick . . .

"Oh my God, I cannot *stand* being alive . . ." I said to her.

"Well," she said, slightly mush-mouthed, hand on my prick, other hand on my arm, then on my chest—exciting herself, owning me, feeling me, owning me inversely perhaps—"that is the way you are, Wiley . . ."

"Big-mouth—big-mouthed evil girl kisses Jew on the grass."

I never liked the way she kissed unless I directed her. On her own she kissed too *thickly* for my taste.

Drunkenly, I saw the usefulness of disliking her kiss, its usefulness as a plot device; it goaded me to roll on top of her, a little more down the slope, on the tickling, faintly harsh grass; I want to control the sloppiness of her kiss, turn it into sensual coherence. In disdain, to withdraw from the kiss, to rise to a half-sitting position, commandingly, as if punishingly—*ah, ah,* the extraordinary uninnocence of the event despite my being innocent and stupid, or stupid and—I don't know: somehow it was all of a piece.

Her hands, their touch, was often clumsy, detached from sexual meaning, from insinuation or rhythm or from submission but seemed left over from daylight stuff. I feel her hunger for—for what? For me and for Romance, for something knowable within the lingua franca of contemporary notions. I am so aware of her that I *feel* her hunger to know, to live what she has read, and I am aware of her distance from me and of her permission, and I am aware of her fake or counterfeit of self-loss. And I can close off that awareness and simply proceed or I can stay with it which is more sadistic in a sense.

I stroke her, in an aware way. I say, "Let's ruin your dress—" her skirt really, which I tried clumsily to place under her while mock-entering her.

"Here on the grass?" she says. She often complains that I am too blunt.

"Here on the grass—"

"The moon will see us," she said in the style of plays and movies she admired.

"Sssh," I said.

In our cottage, as in the apartment in the city, she went around pulling shades although we were not visible. She was afraid of envy—and she required privacy: she liked secret sexual perspectives or was imprisoned in them: the perspectives of a player and of an audience arousing the envy of the air, the spite of the night spirits. She objected even to the moon.

The omissively omniscient encyclopedia which is Ora is partly an encyclopedia of American Desires. This fine-eyed, astoundingly good-looking, strongly made woman loves her clichés. "I have a big brain—" she says. Then she abandons or loses the thought. She apologizes or masks herself: "I'm drunk—I like this. . . ." She said the last in a kind of college way: we met and first fucked at college.

Her thoughts are hidden from me behind the bones of her forehead, of her skull, of her great prettiness: walls of bone policed by will: her eyes in moonlight do not convey bodily acceptance but radiate attention from a different group of her congress of selves, her repertoire of attentions, of questions—her risks, her philosophies, her sense of fatedness in herself. . . . Her interest, her curiosity is in what other women have, and men: that envy and cleverness—that realism—it is a way of knowing real things. The boniness of her relents and what spills out from her in a kind of stink of promptness is sexual invitation to the burrows: that courage of hers, that thing of sexual readiness, that inert tension of whether to be active or still, but inviting anyway, I love that—I love it deeply. On the steep slope of the semi-mountain lawn, the trees, and me, drunkenly, reelingly risen over her, and the nursery dirtiness of our drunkenness: she says, "This will be a dirty fuck. . . ."

Perhaps she means *Let this be great sex . . .*

"Shut up," I said, from within the same fictional world—I mean it was me but I was playing my role. The moist ground and the moonlight: I was cautious and did not name myself: I was a structure of hiddenness—as she was but differently. Here, the circus trick, the trapeze thing is to be *logical* in a drunken moment on a sloping lawn with a specific woman at a specific moment in her life—in mine, too, and in a specific year: a specific fuck.

Ora says, with praise that is a little gritty with insult in regard to her *ambitions,* her fantasies—her fictional world: "You are a king— this is a king's garden—" she says pornographically, having a say: "It is a king's prick."

I whisper tyrannically, *regally*—I used to love my large white prick—"Hey, Ora, no propaganda, just fuck, O.K.?" She always hated my saying that.

To be logical is to recognize the free symmetries, where one act is free-willed, sort of, and the other in response is not as free to be unsymmetrical, directly or in undermeanings or overtones. The curious movements of the selves are *ambitious*—male free-will ignores her. Female free-will drifts off into fantasy or other absence: love and flight, the Eurydice thing, not blinking, not looking back, not holding back. To whatever extent I don't fantasize or withdraw into myself or respond to her direction, I hold her astonished physical gaze, but this depends on my finding her phallically exciting—a dialogue exists. She doesn't bounce or drift into feeling and then return: she is willfully present in a way that is unloving, but it is love as she does it. For each of us; she writes the dialogue, and I *astonish* her out of that daydream.

There are conditions and circumstances of touch and posture—the role you play in the kiss, in the licking—and elements of courage, of sexual courage, of wit and of sophistication of a kind in her that don't necessarily match my moods, my nerve endings. I like a kind of story-telling structure and a confession of who you are. When I touched or nuzzled Ora, she often couldn't do the dance of response, but she grew warm and welcoming. She seemed to be reacting to the drama, to what I did, but really to something inside herself. She was safe from me at the bottom of flight after flight of steps so to speak. Who she was—I mean the person and then the overlay of how she had been taught and how she had rebelled—was interesting to me, but not a lot since it seemed like a cage she was in. She never really confessed; she negotiated and did what she considered her part. I didn't like her notions of wildness or of routine stuff; her versions didn't permit much feeling or made feeling a curious thing surrounded by critical recognitions, little oh's and *ah, that was good, that was the goods.* She liked that kind of thing. I don't know how much that was her and how much was social class and a Gentile thing.

Sophistication? Well, each fuck is the edge of the end of the affair, of not caring, or being angry and set on cheating, or being mysteriously or unmysteriously set free—it's weird—and then that doesn't happen quite: you're not set free.

Well, drunkenness sets you free somewhat. At least to a flow of connections, undulations into modulations of mood: she was too movielike and not funny, so I said, meaning when we were on the slope, "Not here—there—" Rolling her over on the grass and rolling with her: "Roll you over in the clover . . ." It made her slightly dizzy, and she gasped and grinned, suddenly amused.

The odd, childlike submissions she would do were not like the stubborn things of her unresponse or the awed moments of frightened cooperation when her fright made her more sexual. She was more frightened of feeling than of me—of the loss of her powers of negotiation. But I didn't want to lose my male powers: we had these masks. Some of her fright was of losing me but it wasn't so great that fucking her was like dancing or a pas de deux: I mean she liked my presence, liked it steamily, but not as much as I would have liked from her and which I had had versions of with other people.

In a way, a life's story would be A Book of Fucks—wouldn't it? She wants me to let go of myself and do what I like: she says so. She means the two-character fuck—she is being generous and in her terms *loving.* I slap her butt sharply. On my knees I roll and tumble her smartly, and at first she laughs, but then she grows recalcitrant: she kind of grunts, rises from the waist, hugs me. She is strong-armed, wet-mouthed, wild-haired, something of a fake in the pouring moonlight; her strength and mind, her strength of mind, her head—she wants me to pose as the commander, to dance in the moonlight, be lightly brutal and grunt and plunge drunkenly; she wants me to show her my sexual secrets—my nursery secrets—my locker-room secrets.

We elude each other—but not completely. You can't assume a primary asymmetry of the selves: something in us fits with each other, the vibration of similar pain, similar selves in part, somehow similar. My mind doesn't lose its sexual attentiveness toward her but does to myself, which slows down the accumulation of that hot, luminous throbbing which indicates the nearness of orgasm. She stiffens faintly: it is a matter of seconds, she knows that quickly; it happens two or three times, a stroking, a manipulation of the breast; this affects her and registers in my body, in body heat and the smell of the sweat and in the drunken touch: we are now in the realm of secondary theatricalization—it seems like a moment of virginity because she is new to this.

I start to laugh in the night air. Women mostly know how virginal or unvirginal they are, but Ora is like a man in this, this other sense of consciousness, of being untouched, unpenetrated.

The moments of tumbling her and the moment of the slap on her large-ish, moonlight-whitened and moonlight-shadow-folded butt (and the sight of her marvelously beautiful back) were when I moved past her sexual experience and became the unvirginal, or dirty one, the priapic demon, the bad male. And she became the wronged, slightly angry—slightly huffy—well-educated virgin.

She laughed out loud, too—gasped maybe. Then I was alone— moonlight and the dark and the starlight. And in this moment she fled too, fled inwardly, either frightened or betrayed, a watching nymph—but a dirty-minded one, not a virgin—and everything got more theatrical and, as it were, mathematical, the two of us, minds and bodies, spirits and drunkenness.

Then it became a requirement, kind of in the sense of being the only good-*humored* possibility, to be violent and distant toward her, violent in a kind of dirty and knowing good humor, which is what she had tacitly asked for. She didn't always choreograph what I did, but if I was drunk or tired or tired of her, she did.

She couldn't recognize my experience if it was not like a book or like men she had known, if it was not in a category. She faltered in comprehension because I was like a younger brother or a cupid in some ways—I was actually a year and a half younger than she was. We were brother and sister in sin—sort of—sort of as in a story. But incest would be perfunctory and boring except for its being a sin because you knew the same things. Incest might not be such a deep experience but it would be easy.

I mean there was a kind of social class thing in Ora, a sexual social class thing, sort of *the inferiority of other people showed in the inferiority of their consolations*—she wasn't entirely sure of this but she was fairly certain. She had experimented—she knew the automaton reality and men who smelled of fear and eagerness and self-consciousness, and she had experienced some sense of inner darkness and of wrong invitation in the other: what I always felt as *a dirty landscape,* the dirty landscape of sex with its queer coils of space in one place, its queerness as journey and as instruction and as darkness and light.

When one of us failed in a moment, the other was often mysteriously symmetrical in failure but not always. I mean the symmetry wasn't an exact incestuous echo but a weirdity. You don't know where to put your feet—your prick, your sexual *anima,* or soul—and you hide it, you pretend to assurance. The moment opens up: and you see and feel your ignorance like blindness as everyone says, and you peer outwardly; your gaze flashes around the universe and comes back and is inward in some queer reciprocal fleshy elbow-and-knee and crotch-and-cunt geometry which is higher and less easily measurable than symbols on paper are. But you *see* that each freedom to act is a kind of prison demanding you act, that each iota of overlordship or privilege is a whipgoad of *do this, do that.* You see each reciprocity as a failure—

and goad—until orgasm frees you, and you see each refusal of
reciprocity as an invitation and a reciprocal thing somehow but in the
oh my God mode.

The very violence, or edge of violence, stuff is instinct with queer,
binding and blinding tenderness: blind girl, blind Samson, blind
Delilah. What we pull down—Ora is Samson, too—is concern for
other parts of our life. It is only us, drunkenness softening sexual vision
by deepening it like the moonlit-bright night sky with the thorns of
light on the lawn among the leaves and in the flower beds. Anyway, in
the depths of a moment, we're laughing and kissing, and I am kind of
active, and Ora is not; what is mostly there is ignorance, just like when
you're exploring philosophy, and the more ignorance you admit to, the
more sophisticated you are, provided the ignorance you admit to is the
right sort. Dumbness is everything.

I mean if Ora at this moment, drunkenly, refuses to admit her
ignorance but goes on being Sophisticated Samsonetta, she becomes
something like a tour guide. She fails to ascend the moment; she
avoids the fall into hellishness (not really)—the cunt obviously being
a gateway of sin for everybody. So the whole thing's a mess, but it's
juicy and tender. You know this by a kind of sensation or sense of
defeat, as if hitting her would solve everything, or at least ease the
defeat. I am looming over her, holding both her breasts. The demonic
and sour glee, the biting and choking stuff she likes, sort of *I am
strong, I am potent, I don't need anyone*—I don't do it much; I think she
is deluded. There is excitement in playacting it or in really dominat-
ing and scaring someone. Holding back becomes a complicated issue.

Ora knew it—or part of it. She said, "You are the daring young
man on the flying trapeze."

I said stupidly, "You are really incre-goddamned-fucking-dibly
beautifully fucking be-uuuuu-tiful . . . *God,* Ora . . ." She liked that
loosening of class lines stuff.

Pressing and rubbing, I knew, somehow, just how loud to gasp to
thrill her with shock, but not so loud it shocked her out of all her feelings—it's called being attuned: a kind of knowing guesswork . . .

I whispered, "We didn't make it from our car to the cottage that evening. . . ." The sloping lawn at a silent two A.M. I said, "We fucked on the lawn in the moonlight. . . ." I wasn't actually in her yet . . . God, we were young .... .

To propose reality as a story rather than a story as reality might at least remind you what a prior thing experience is. And how we hide it in stories. Ora hadn't in a long time done her condemnation thing, her invocation of *Goddamn, Goddamn this, Goddamn you* that she'd done once or twice sexually. I was scared of the lifetime's rage in each of us. She was as strong physically as a small man but she had all those complexities of overlay and training and much more delicate calibrations—it is an odd fate to be a woman. She was casually and wildly cruel (but not toward me) and yet calibratedly so toward the world; she was much more politically savvy than I was. Almost everything in my physical vocabulary became in relation to her even as the thinnest hint of itself, a shade, a shadow of brutality because the attraction was strong and we had stayed together long enough to know we would stay together longer. It irritated me profoundly, this eerie strength and weakness of attachment and corresponding freedoms and degrees of rule and permission, degrees, really, of finality.

Anyway, I liked to praise her. I like not doing the other thing, the thing of persecution by sexual praise delivered as condemnation and shrill invective. In a moment of withdrawal, of catching my breath (the thing of at-the-crossroads-we-pause in the moonlight), I saw around me hedges and trees, patient leaves in their kingdoms of air; and I felt in her, her impatience with me as a man, the anguish of love wasted on art . . . on ambition.

The grass ended and Ora's arm was flung across the grayish-dark salvia and ghostly artemisia and white lilies. The stink of dirt and of marigolds. There was her smell, Ora's breasts in the moonlight, in the clingingly half-warm air. I howled softly.

"This is a pagan fuck," Ora said. She tended to review things—nearly everything. She said, "Oh, Wiley, *you don't hate women!*"

She raised her arms and put them around my neck again. I have a
tendency to be fatuous, out of touch: "You already did this," I said
stupidly, peeling her arms off me. I helped her lie down again. I
couldn't help thinking, stupidly, that Quick Fucks were superior
because you hardly had time to notice your own fatuousness, or hers.

She said, "Let's have a baby. . . ."

"What? Here? Outdoors?" I said it into her ear. I didn't really have
to *say* it: we were body to body. You know that feeling? You breathe
breast to breast. She often claimed to be a nihilist . . . She said once,
*Nihilists can have a good time, Wiley—they just don't think it means any-
thing . . .*

I entered her; she helped. I thought things and didn't say them but
merely breathed them, pictures, words, pleasures, fuck memories,
drunken maunderings, drunken superiorities, all the guest stuff of a
fuck, all the stuff that the prick feels, the lower body, the pushily con-
tracting and stiffened and loosening butt. And all the smells in your
nose. And the rhythms—kind of, I don't know, *energetic* tenderness, the
Candide-naïve, the I-am-lost thing. She has stolen me, kidnaped me.

I don't think Ora ever told the truth, even a partial truth. Sometimes she claimed not to have a memory. But she loved lying, lying
and romance—she couldn't sing; she couldn't *hear* music. And I, well,
I am a writer and intrinsically naïve although not about people: the
truth-telling I did used to horrify Ora, sicken her, really. And all the
Edenic slynesses, the serpents in the eyes and in the crotch, the nests
of snakes in us everywhere—in naughty fingers, and in scratchy toes
and insteps where it's all feely now, and in the knowing and blinking
and inwardly twisting eyes, and in the sensation of my hair tangling
with her hair and my mouth on hers, and sweat prickling in tickled,
partly sour, excited pubic hair in the dark. The audience consists of a
separate room in each of us opening from a shifting set of other fields
and sensations—of the grass on her back, of the odors, of the weight
of sexual congress—it has nothing to do with acrobatics and only a little to do with the outdoors drama: it is mostly only that somehow we
are suitable.

Ora says it is love, and when she does I either deny it and tease her or burst out laughing: are we that lucky? What is clear, what is tangible is an angrily ambitious drunkenness, insanely flirtatious toward feeling (but somewhat resistant) so that it is hellish and celestial, and virginal and moonlit; and if other people let us alone this would not have to be judged. Well, it would be judged by us as audience, as our lives. The all-rightness, the fakery, the various meanings slide by, twistingly appear, slither away in darkness, as I pump and she, truly or not, grows *astonished* and far-off, celestial-secular and not unhappy. Each motion, each breath leaves a trail of light. Then I become a shoving elephant-kangaroo-snail, now moving slowly and a bit greasily (and saying, "Ah . . . Ah . . . Ah . . ."). My chest and head and crotch, enormous-seeming, become a shell over sensation and a luminous crawl in sexual space.

A slight disapproval or edge of male violence comforts her, but it cannot be real, since, as if in its absence, she eases off and drops the thing of the nearness of her mind and soul to the clutching, slightly off-putting *readiness* in her, in her thighs, in the cunt. She has loosened. She is something like an inward lawn. She floats out, in some female, *fantasy-is-real* way among the stars, a barge-borne Cleopatra-angel, half a whore, a *serious* young girl.

A sense of sexual consciousness in her and then my own, her sense of the irrevocability of sexual reality, which I don't have, her grasp is finer than mine, as is the dexterity of her fingers except sexually, rhythmically. The more aware I am of her the more, in alternate moments, I am aware of my own hands, my own pleasure. I am curious and as if entendriled in my own shoving and off-putting readiness to forget her and to plow ahead, chest and mouth and cock—cock-a-loro . . . My visitor's innocence compared to a woman's darkness of *genetic* spirit, compared to Ora's placative trafficking with hellishness, makes her want me to be guilty here—it is a rage here, in her, us as judges and responding or drying up—but we do respond. What is being allowed is some absence of loneliness, the exchange of meanings, perhaps of selves. In the mouth-stuff, in the mouth explorations we do of stuff, in the nuzzlings and licks and kisses, you can rushingly, briefly hear the electric runnings of the mind. A truth. A chance at some kind of grass-stained, fairly real happiness is here, not in a silly sense, but conceivably except that we know we will be blackmailed and owned by it if we admit to it. To any of it.

It is a peculiar bodiedness that the moment has, the attentiveness, the drunken distances blown liftingly or sinkingly—love: a farce? a tragic thing? Love of a kind. . . . what is it worth?

Not rhetorically. But really. I know better than to trust her sexually in the end stages of a fuck—she is anti-prick, silent, hidden, watchful, an enveloping presence of a fucked woman—it is sort of mathematical, her feeling, not mine, which is ashen and transcendent. Seeds of light break into rays and move otherwise as well, and ghosts of various sorts, a mirror flash of personal meaning and a constant sense of flesh, crystalline, statistical. Ungeometrically, almost knowably, one moves in the web of bribes.

Ora moves according to programs really, recipes of attention: *Do this;* then this; add this; then stir; then wait in the physically fiercer guesswork and ambition of curiosity about the next sensation, to see what it does. . . . *Now, add this, stir, and wait,* stir and blink . . . *Oh fuck!* . . . This fleshly wakefulness, Wiley's moment, large, slow, semi-recumbent . . . oh fuck . . . We are indecent creatures, brooding a lexical and emotional geometry as sophisticated as the white subtleties of the shape of an egg. So complex. "Go ahead: you come," she says—one feels a certain slickness of sensation, of one's own eminence, of light and meaning representing beauty: it does and doesn't represent *beauty.* . . . This is a gift Ora makes. Perhaps I steal it.

The real air is here, and the trance is half-dissolved. I can see why people prefer characters to have the abstract bodies of conventional reference, to be bronze in that sense, and not to be merely real and, forgive me, at sea on a lawn in the moonlight.

A GUEST IN THE UNIVERSE

What an odd game of subtractions and additions a life is. A thought passes through my mind like a cat walking on my shoulders behind my neck. The sensation of the cat's narrow ribs and finely tipped fur in motion ruffling my hair, lightly pressing against my skull is like the progression of a thought which then disperses. After the thought, it is as if the cat perches on my left shoulder, its small skull pressed to my temple, its body arched in taut balance.

At a party in New York City in 1956, twelve years after my father died, in a large room, I felt the self-conscious grandeur of the place as without an echo, as a *psychological* environment of extreme self-consciousness: Jewish figures in the arts. And the room's boastfulness was like a whisper without an echo, insolent and a matter of those-who-are-whispering-are-insiders: we are sophisticated and expensive: Upper Bohemian: *arrivistes.*

"*Nouveaux riches* but we're not *riche,* so it's just *nouveau,*" mad Moira said to me. The downy couch we were on was so deep Moira Kellow was practically horizontal. "We wanted a room you didn't have to sit up straight in," she said. "These couches *molest* you—isn't that nice? I like it. Have you ever played molesting-a-child when you fucked with someone? Ha-ha . . . You're so young, you're easy to shock. . . . You're just a baby . . ." Part of her style was to be warmly venomous.

Six oversize down couches, slightly grandiose, not *the real thing* (not the most expensive versions but very expensive Italian copies of the French thing) and covered in floral linens which I had been instructed by the woman I lived with, Ora, were the real thing. These couches were set among tables of all sizes and degrees of merit and value. A few of the tables were wood. "Wood is too English," Moira said. "I'm not English. I like Englishmen, though . . . ha-ha, ha-ha . . ."

The room had an amazing spirit of chic welcome, vases with charming fat or thin flowers, and books in small stacks on the floor; and small modern rugs and bare floor and large floral Aubussons (the room was big) and some glowing Persian carpets. But, all-in-all, by New York notions, the room had resigned itself to a kind of millionaires' *American* second-rateness in regard to *real taste* and to an inferiority to *real money:* a favored term in those years, like the word *grace.* Such terms and notions were common in books and magazines and even in some movies, and were paramount in Hemingway and Fitzgerald and Eliot, ex-Catholics and Protestant alike, the reigning male divas of English and the source of ideas back then. Anyway, piety and post-piety and romance and masculinity were for these divas of sexual terror *aristocratic.* Racial. Sometimes national. Masters of radically scintillant language when they were young, figures of greatness grown stale, they were determinative figures, images of instructive terror which the room's modesty—or the hostess's—acknowledged and against which the room offered itself as a harbor.

Three of the downy couches and three lacquered pale-orange tables (like memories of sunset) formed a group. The walls hold a number of poor versions of pictures from famous series: a damaged blue-green Picasso of a satyr-rape, five obscure Soutines, a large gouache of a screaming Pope by Francis Bacon. Food is laid out in the hall of mirrors, a Parisian elegant vulgarity of the time. The Kellows had a good chef of the second rank (twenty thousand dollars a year) who refused to work on Sundays: it is Sunday. On Sundays a Norwegian woman, an ex–registered nurse, who had been Moira's nurse during a bout of "terrible illness of the mind" (Moira and Brr often referred to Moira as *the new Zelda*), prepared more food to go with what the chef had left behind. This was mixed with what Brr called "Jewish smorgasbord." Moira has said to me, "I want to do what I want to do . . . I want to be *decadent; REAL money* gets to do what *it* wants to do, and I only get to do the best that I can."

We are lit by ordinary sunlight coming through a wall torn from a neoclassic intention by a series of enlarged windows that are unsettlingly *modern*. The wound of this is 1950s wit. . . . The old system, to judge from rooms in this apartment not so extensively rebuilt, was to have widely separated windows producing piers of light that fell wideningly in the strangely unrooted, semi-floating spaces of the altitudinous apartment at great intervals—fortresslike, shutting out the outside. The architecture had been an American imitation of an English variant of an Adriatic style, New York apartment house English Georgian but in yellow brick; the basic Georgian was derived from Diocletian's palace at Split and from the domestic architecture of Ragusa in what is now Croatia.

The idea in power at the time was that such historically bastardized and compromised architecture should be simplified, redone, should be *purified*. This was no longer identified as a fascist ideal. Anyway, now a wall of indirect light, of softened glare: the windows face east and it is afternoon; the direct sun is on the other side of the apartment: a wall of light partly broken by narrow brick piers and metal mullions and handsome, very expensive curtains; much of the room is glazed in almost a Greek wave of light.

We look out from the seventeenth floor; and to the right is the gargantuan stone-and-steel reality of the engineers' load-bearing webs (above mostly invisible-from-here gigantic masonry piers) of a bridge known for its ugliness: a stupendous framework of massive aerial beams and patterned light. When you go near the window or when you sit in certain couches and look out, it bursts on you and overshadows the pretensions and accomplishments of the room. It is witty that it is there, it is *wittily* horrendous, and the final pretension of the room is this alliance with nightmare: we are *"children of the age, rich garbage,"* one of the wits here has said; when you are in the torn room, you see in the flying enormousness of the structure of the bridge a mocking or hectoring ratio and proportion to what goes on here and to the people who are here.

It is a post-war *socialist* ratio, rude and smothering, that says the considerable style and brio of the room are, ultimately, shitty eat-drink-and-be-merry, as well as rich and cleverly thought out and in some ways genuinely pretty and aspiring. The quality of fashion is as if kicked by a very intelligent, gloomy, hysterical seriousness, more satiric and hysterical than reasoned, into a high gear, a *monstrousness.* The room offers a too-obvious lecture on the monstrousness of soul in people and monstrousness of fate and the monstrousness of forces of society and the monstrousness of genetic inheritance and of psycho-logical destiny—this is *deep* and yet fashionable and is a claim of art—and it does have force in the immediate moment on the gathered artists and figures: the tragedy of things in general in the significant form of monstrousness.

"People are always laughing about fashion, but what else is there? You can't live in a textbook," Moira says. "I read all the time but I have to come up for air. But what do I know: I'm nuts. If I could be anybody I wanted, I would be Kafka." She has an oval face, a very fin-ished air of style and mind, unexciting eyes, too-large teeth, and a truly extraordinary physical presence that comes from the degree of style and of madness—she is suicidal, enraged, self-aware. I know it makes no sense, but it was as if she had a brain tumor that caused her to be chic instead of inducing trembles or other forms of vertigo.

The absolutist, or dreamlike nature, of the looming bridge, the way it was there and was *looming,* the claim of deep meaning was rude and antagonistic; it was also childlike. The proportion of failed art and failed will, the size, the scale—this was before the 1960s argued that art didn't matter. The sermonizing and lamentation were *amusing,* but it was also the use of art as a bludgeon, a *who the fuck are you?* It is an attempt to be authoritative and deep in relation to truth-as-politics. But then the backlash of the noticeably failed genius or whatever of the place and its makers was something that affected the people there and formed a kind of cage of fixity and staleness of reference, not of art but of minor coquetry with truth so that the result was *merely* fashion. Which could be seen as psychological punishment or daily failure through the loss of God. But the chief use of art-failure and serious politics of the left or right is that in the end, obviously, one really isn't *overshadowed* by it except psychologically esthetically: Other people are overshadowed for you in their politics. It is just a frisson of the moment in the city.

Things in America are so much a matter of date and the onrush of flows of money that certain words and phrases used back then have in my memory a special air: they suggest the era and the Kellows and their friends and my youth: *witty, rich garbage, artists, artistes, socialist, pretty, serious, neurotic . . .*

Socialist meant genuinely human, not racially snobbish, sexually profound—really, it did for a while. It meant *Would-not-EVER-have-been-Fascist or Nazi.* It meant *is not now sanguine about the bomb.* It meant *is in no sense a killer but is richly human.* I suppose it meant that it was a lie and propaganda and it *really* meant something else. Have you ever seen a movie in which the flight of wooden arrows in a late medieval battle is reproduced along with the various sounds they make, the twang of the bows, the whirring in flight of the missiles, the thunk when they hit? One is as if caught in a warlike flight of a wooden rain of arrows, among actual deaths, failures, psychological collapses . . . *I was on the right side: I am ironic. . . .* It was that kind of era.

Moira said in her nervously aging, mad ingenue, toothy way, the tones of which got in your head and stayed there, "Oh (*uh*) I *ih*-hate it-*teh-teh* when *rih*ich people have me-eeee-an fayissis [*faces;* high-pitched voice and staring-eyed, rictus-grin] and don't enjoy theee-'ngs; ruh*itch* pee-uh-pill oh-utt tuh-ooo en*joy* thih-em-sell[deepened tone]ves: *I . . .* love having a good time . . . do you?"

A melancholic hysteric, recurrently suicidal: God knew what she ever *meant*—I mean it was as if a poet had written her speeches for her and meant them to remain obscure. She sometimes said she wished she could get a poet to fall in love with her and write things for her to say; she said she would like it if I came to see her early in the morning and "told me deep things to say. . . ." I had been ordained as *a poet* by some critics although I wrote prose; the term meant I was a Jew and used adjectives and was a smart-ass and it also meant that I was not politically identifiable. It didn't mean that I was a poet except with some critics, and by poet they meant eccentric and competent—no more than that. Yes, it did.

"The bridge is falling," she said and giggled, but she half-persuaded herself; and she craned her neck and looked toward the windows to see if the bridge or its shadow was bending. "It feels like the end. I dreamed about the ovens again last night. I am truly mad, you know: I come from New Jersey and that is just too much to ask of someone like me. Ha-ha. I have imperfect breasts and a lot of sorrow—a lot . . . I think we all should be good: we should all go and scrub out the temple and see if there's any oil left. . . . Or say Kaddish because it is the apocalypse . . ."

Everything in her was directed toward an unarguable guiltlessness, innocence at last. The 1960s were being bred or hatched here.

From where I sat next to Moira on a couch in a grouping near the wall of light, I saw the rapid, current-rippled rush of the East River, muddy eddyings seventeen floors down which were at moments in the light white-gilded. But there was no sound, I didn't actually hear the throatily murmurous noise of the water or smell the water stink . . . but they were there in *my head,* memories in the jumble of blown and lightly drifting, changeable, and itchy rays and intimately atticy old scenes and *feathers* . . . a lot of fancy-slanted impermanencies. The mind, more scarily and less persistently than a window or a river, is newly and stalely and stably and unstably itself every moment. *This aging junior world* is a spherical dervish in a half-sunlit path—I whispered that one sentence in Moira's ear. She giggled. Ora is watching from half a room away. And is jealous. Ora once dreamed she was a horseshoe crab scuttling in shallow water (in Maine) and a gull got her: *And the gull was you, Wiley!* It carried her aloft and dropped her in order to crush her shell; it wanted to eat her, Ora said.

It sounded to me more like gull equals girl and she was dreaming about the ecstasies and deaths in being female and she was blaming me, which I guess was to the point.

I told her, and she said, *Explain that to me, say it again slowly,* she said it to me with a kind of angry rapture of attention. At the party, in that particular present-tense moment—of teasing her (perhaps)—what comes back most sharply is how uninnocent I was: I feel my gull wings spread; I feel my *intelligence* like a very-hard-yellow-beak-attempt to tear at her, to turn her over. To make her momentarily helpless, sunny side up. And in her neck, her young neck, in the thin tendons of her strong young neck and her bare arms, in the dank womanliness of her postures—so unlike Moira's dryness, so unlike anyone: that patient, maybe sullenly amused *sweetness,* that *thin,* restless shell of patience, is life and resentment. It is clear even in the death-gamble of her beautifully boned, fine-eyed face—a face for stories.

But the resistance in her, the intelligence and yet the incomprehension—like a coil in a heater so that the electricity of the woman is joined to the electricity of the rage . . . the toughness. She glows darkly with anger behind the patience verging on the actual intention to betray and hurt and even murder, actually murder, the urgency to lie—she has a code of honor but no conscience; she is willing to go to hell and to be suicidal rather than be obedient, rather than listen to anyone, rather than learn.

And I know this genitally as well, that she is sexed up by this stuff. But with her sexuality is nothing ideal, nothing movielike, it's just Ora and her deep-womanly sexual shit, the Ora stuff . . .

And she shifts her posture, a vaguely semi-boyish stance of the legs—and a quivering abandonment of her breasts, a fleshly, dirty, runaway thing.

I am uninnocent. The papery now is astir as if with fire, with its merciless transience; motion is the substance of love. Anyone might wish for stillness, for an end to the eerie lawlessness of people in reality. . . . Oh, the restlessness of the light . . . I am a music of fireworks. Real truth is not necessarily meant for humans to see in human terms and might very well be lightless. One is a guest in the universe—I whispered that to Moira. We can spy but we cannot know. Blinking eyes and the reality of the sun are a bitter explanation of the condition of motion—geographical motion plus a continual efflorescence and dying, the tiny spiraling and flick of the gray, unnameable, undammable, damnable mumble of bustling unstillness in an un-named everywhere. Of course we are mad in the fixed-liquid-airy-wind, *The Breath of God,* I am sorry. It is pompous but I am half-consoled by this unmapped and emotion-laden condition, this ungeographical, seaborne, breathborn sense of God-as-motion. I don't know the moral weight or the consequences of saying that Time does not forgive us. Time offers no protection against *chagrin.* . . . Imagine all posterity laughing at your errors, cursing you for your errors, without bothering to remember you. What would timelessness be, Moira? Moira is nailed and fixed in place in psychic pain, in overwhelming meaninglessness, *crucified* by nerves . . . And I am *uninnocent as hell*—for the moment—but I do not intend to harm her.

"Do you feel you're on a strange planet?" Moira asks. She says to Harvey Deuteronomy of me, "He is easy to talk to."

I really do not understand time, but I feel myself as a young stalk of it stretching his legs on the couch, and goony with consciousness: one lives in the moments *wildly* no matter the austerity one attempts. My state is fringed with distances and exhaustion and doubt and voices.

The queerly swift shuffle and giant glides of the mind are part of a disbelieving rivalry with light. Moira (born Sadie) is real. Her real name is *This Moment,* is her sudden swallow of champagne. "Look: the sky is raw with time," she said to me. How strange it is, the moment of re-entry to the world. The city is so noisy it is like an echoing porch around this room.

Moira-Sadie says to me, "I see it in your eyes: you're someone who can use a little help. You're so sure of yourself . . ." She is clearly troubled by madness. Pain, when it gets bad enough, jealousy, say, things in the mind, things in the body, is a smelly lion on the path . . . I think she told me this; I think she made up the image; and I stole it and in memory I hear myself saying it.

But I think it was Sadie-Moira. Her mind, like mine is a cagey, broken rustling of bits of caught or fleeing attention.

Moira said: "I don't know how to behave with intellectuals. . . . Well, I'll just invent something." I realized how valuable in this world people's methods were to them since they had risen to this point, so I assumed she was talking fictionally. Whacko Williams, the elegant comedian-turned-television producer, moved nearer. Moira said, "Look: here is the Handsomest Man in the World—and the sexiest except for a couple of English bastards no one has ever heard of—"

"Oh," said Whacko, "those *duchess-eaters* . . ."

"Duchess-*eaters*," repeated Moira said with a sly *you-are-stupid-I-am-wicked* grin.

"They are *pussy* cats," Whacko said.

Moira giggled and laughed enthusiastically: "Oh let's talk dirty some more," she said.

"Pussy cool cats," Jeffrey Bestmann said, a tough guy, *promising* director. And yet a hanger-on.

Whacko Williams, a big-shot show business corporation figure in the business world of that decade, said, "I want to drink champagne from your slipper, Moira—"

"I'm a size eight," she said drolly.

Whacko, still in his making-love mode, said, "You know all there is to know. . . . You are a sexual *Britannica* . . ."

Natalie Bone, a ballet star once, then a movie star, then an ex-star, married three times, and well-married still, called a *great beauty* because her large face was streamlined, large-boned, Nordic, and *famous* in gossip for her bad temper, for her being a dominatrix, for her tormenting men who pursued her, said, "I hate champagne in the afternoon . . ."

"I always need a lift," Moira said pitiably and put herself as a rival to Natalie as someone agreeable and *feminine* according to 1950s Freudian analysis. She turned and said to a man on her other side on the couch, "Judy Garland is wonderful but she's stale. . . . Alden Whitto, he's really wonderful, he has a *dirty* purity. . . . He's not trapped in the middle class. . . . He's *escaped.*" She was an expert, a woman consulted by columnists and people writing for magazines; she knew a lot, encyclopedically, in the language of her particular world.

Thirty people are here so far. Ten are strewn in the couches that molest you. Some are walking around or standing here or on the balcony outside the windows. The younger, less famous, more decorative men sit on the floor in supple self-advertisement. Some are in the dining room.

"They get haircuts that look good blowing in the wind," Moira said of the people on the windy terrace: all were men. There are many more men than women; there are only a few women.

Harvey Deuteronomy was standing over us and looking down at us, and he said in a witty manner—a kind of cabaret comic actor manner: *wittily* as a trick of manner, as someone *pretending*—in a carrying voice, "Why is it like high school here—why is it I never escaped from high school—why are the grownups always someplace else? I think your bridge is giving me a *migraine.*"

"Isn't it *wonderful?*" Moira said with her giggle. She said in the high-pitched, slick voice she had sometimes, "The bridge is *nicer* in the morning. . . . It's shadows and *blur* . . ." She means with sunglare pouring through its beams. "We should have people in then, but I can't face people in the *mornings.*"

"I'm so gauche," Deuteronomy said *humorously,* sinking with a neurotic, tousled, gangling air into a couch at right angles to the one Moira and I were on.

American speech, with its transposed keys, its mimicries, its Gentile and Jew thing, its democratic and snobbish elements, is almost never used in books—it's too hard. An American conversational exchange is a peculiar thing, businesslike or like an encounter in a wilderness even if it is erotic. In general, you have to be careful because you are in contact with so many social and psychological categories of people.

Moira said, "The French are so *tiresome,* they think they know everything, such snobs; after all, I'm *gauche,* I'm hardly going to hold it against the men or boys who visit here: I don't want to be bored, but I don't care if you're gauche . . ."

And you had individual, current professional standing and marital standing, and current and former social classes, lied about, hidden, or exhibited; and gender attitudes—Natalie Bone was a feminist and a purposeful bitch: it was a *famous* style: she had done it in the movies and been apostrophized in magazines as a *goddess.*

Then you have educational differences and sexual attitudes hidden or paraded; and various kinds of susceptibility to intimidation— *What? you haven't slept with Moira?* or *You haven't read Camus?* Depending on how *innocent* and helpless you appear and on how powerful you are, then when you get things wrong—and how can you not when people's lives are so unliterary and sprawling in America—the person you're talking to maybe will set out to get you in order to prove themselves to be O.K. It's a kind of sparring and is a measure of wit-and-power on Park Avenue. Sometimes it's said that it is better not to listen too closely, that it's better to swing along like a playground swing, alongside and parallel.

Mostly in real life, American men don't talk—talk is a special trait with us, specially indulged in, men and women . . . Books use phony dialect or modified English dialogue, which is stylized to start with, and it suggests the characterization, not a real person. So does the theater. And the movies.

So this group sounds like movies. Pauses in the middle of a speech to think, changes of direction, hands over mouths, bold eye-stares are fairly theatrical. And do form an almost complete language. So mad Moira, if she wants to be a conversationalist, and if she imitates books, her druggy voice will be mannered for performance synchronous with Deuteronomy's, and influencing his songs and other work, as if Harvey and Moira were lovers or were brother and sister. She has her own style, but it is not eccentric but is derived from successful examples in her time.

Moira said, "I love my drugs— Don't mind me—I'm just making party talk. . . . I need a little help to get through the things I have to do."

"Be married to Brr and drink champagne . . . ?" Whacko said.

"Why not be superhuman if you can get a prescription for it?" Deuteronomy said. He was very sharp-witted, very bright.

Moira giggled. Then: "I never wanted an ordinary life."

A handsome, oldish man smiled at her, hearing a joke I didn't get.

Moira then complained that she wasn't a writer or a performer, she had no money of her own, she was dependent on Brr: "I'm not an artist: I'm mostly just hungover from all my wonderful pills. . . . Ha-ha." She gave a mad Bohemian toss to her magnificently tended hair. She said in another voice, abruptly other, "I used to think it would be worth selling your soul to get the hair of your dreams."

Deut said, "Brr, he do has he little ways . . . Brr knows how to get the hair of your dreams . . ." He is talented and strange—I don't think he likes being talented. I don't think he is possessed by it—he hasn't that kind of greatness. He was a huge new celebrity, a singer who wrote and sang *the new songs*—he led the next wave in the *American Popular Song*. He playacted naïve and bumbling but he produced his own shows and was already very rich. . . . He is maybe androgynous.

Deuteronomy said, "I *like* this room . . ."

Moira said, "Oh it's a stage set: it's so gloomy when no one's here I never enter it. . . ."

The room's anatomy glimmered when it was empty, unlit; I had seen it, a semi-vast social machinery of space and furnishings.

Brr said, "An arm and a leg . . ." His English is like that of his magazines, but when he is being personal, he leaves phrases off: this was a phase he went through. "I'm eaten *up* alive—"

"Keeping the ball in the air," Deut supplied.

"I have no time: I would like to create something before I die . . ." I *think* he was imitating Moira—as I said, we all stole from one another. "The only thing I can say of this room is that it photographs well—"

"I run away in it, in it," Deuteronomy said; he had a large, unarguable, naïve, deeply photographable, deeply feelable smile.

"A little bit," Moira said. "You can be comfortable here: you're among friends . . ."

Brr said, "It's for running away a little: You can be comfortable here: you're among friends." He tended to own, to hold a copyright on anything said in his presence.

He had a trait of looking sad when he subsided from his tough mode into politeness, a form of visiting his past, before he was so successful. His awareness of your style was the mark of his awareness—his own style was never discussed (he owned quite a few magazines).

Moira said, "I think it's *moral* to have a good time. . . . Oh look at the bridge: it's a big net and the clouds are little fish. . . . The sun is a big fish—ha-ha." She pushed her riffs quite far. Her laugh was unsettling, discreetly soft, but still looney and threatening: an *Oh God, I am so unhappy* laugh, a *fuck me . . .*

Brr said, "People always say Moira ought to be a writer."

"No one ought to be a writer—it's a dog's life . . ."

"They say she should just write the way she talks, just write down what she says," Brr said ignoring me.

If you listened carefully to the talk, if you noticed the real shape of it—the physical shape, the stirrings of meaning and intention, the breaths and the hysteria—Deut and Brr were stringing her along. I mean she couldn't write but she was, forgive me, *insanely* interesting (in a way). But they were cheating her, fooling her—was it hatred? I don't mean only in the overpraise, I mean in the ways they looked at one another, in what they understood and she didn't.

She said, "I wish we could afford a really expensive apartment but Brr says we're always broke, because of me . . ." She giggled again. "Brr is stingy . . ." She was fighting back perhaps.

Deuteronomy, at that time the most famous, let's say upper-
middle-class, entertainer in the world, said, in a slightly other voice—
a voice slanted some way: "It is a *clever* room. . . . I can't say it is
stingy," he said drolly.

The room was important in that decade: to some extent it defined
our lives, our careers: does a room do that?

Moira said, in a strangely evil voice, "It's a room for clever talkers."

Neither she nor Brr, who have, of course, influenced each other,
can go for long without making threats or demands as in this implicit
ukase that we be clever or forfeit our right to spend time here. But it
had a jokey tone, the threat.

"I come here to bumble," said Deuteronomy, privileged—he is a
star but it is more than that; he is close to Moira and to Brr.

"Bumble bee," said Moira. "I like the James writers, James Joyce,
Henry James, and James Jones . . . I like Noel Camtippy best because
he kisses my hand . . ."

Brr said, "He kisses her ass: he steals ideas from Moira."

Deut said, "The James gang. You left out Jesse . . ."

Brr seems young for his age, almost pre-pubic, as if he has been
able to stay close to being ten years old, as if he had never been
wrenched by puberty and physical size.

"Honey," Moira said to Deuteronomy in a complex New York
inflection: New York of the 1950s. She was addressing him with
unusual intimacy, and I lost my attention; I blacked out; I didn't want
to know about their intimacy.

The room was beautiful with handsomely radiant, softly glaring
light. The maybe-marvelous floral fabrics of the chairs bloomed
meadowishly. I remarked that I was "devoted to not spilling coffee on
myself." Then I asked Deuteronomy if he was aggressive. I meant
because he was a famous star. It was maybe half all right for me to say
odd things.

"Passive aggressive," he said. He had a kind of young innocence
that was part of 1950s style.

"You're aggressive," mad Moira said to me.

"You're interesting," Deuteronomy said to her with a different sort of smile, an encouraging smile, contingently intimate.

"*Life* is aggressive," Brr said.

"Books aren't," I said.

"We like books," Brr said.

"We steal our lives from books," Moira said.

"We depend on books," Deuteronomy said.

"We depend on and steal from books," Brr said.

"Ha-ha," I said, unable not to laugh. "Do you think the word *shtick* comes from *stichomythia?*" I asked.

"Oh you talk like a book," Moira said. She had a profound sense of the unfairness of things, social class and talent especially. She said, "We're acting just like Protestants . . ." *Wasp* hadn't become a social term yet.

Socially you are what people think you are. Sharply observed by these souls expert in our sorts of lives, the young man was in a state of cold visitation, of animal expectancy and naïveté mixed with youthful nerves.

"We get our routines from books," Deuteronomy said. In the webby thing of real life, they are talking for Moira but really for me— a seriocomic *normal,* with a normal surface.

"I hate it when everyone agrees," Moira said. "I want everyone to be *nasty*—and fresh—I love insolence in men. Englishmen are good at it. Although the French aren't bad." She leaned back still further on the couch and crossed her legs and did something with her torso, a sideways arch.

"Routines are the soul of America," Deuteronomy said sadly.

Brr said, "Sincerity is the key—you have to recognize that a lot of people are sincere."

In the 1950s Moira is Isaac on Mount Moriah, the child-creature who is to be sacrificed. The rest of us are busy. And have projects. She does not like being the one who is sacrificed. Harvey Deuteronomy said in his patter, in his show, that the secret appeal of religion was that it encouraged you to disembowel your children. Brr's children—

four of them from three marriages—he uses as evidence of his normalcy. He espouses doctrines of their sweetness; they have no room to be anything but saintly in relation to his worldliness. Being famous is attention-getting, soul-wearying stuff. But it is a party, and you use people.

"He sounds like Gerard *Manley* Hopkins," Deuteronomy said to Moira about me, an old joke between them used for other men. He speaks with his *famous* sweetness, sweetness of an order specific to him, to his public performances, Deuteronomy's.

"Oh I don't like him," Moira said and grinned evilly because I was so young and wouldn't be able to know if she meant me or the poet Hopkins. My blood ran cold with guest's fear and then with dismissal of her—and with hidden anger. I have a secret inner life not much like my outward manner. "Who?" I said stern-faced: a tall boy said it.

Deuteronomy said, "You know: all those college professors—those *biddies*—who talk about the priest writers as so *manly* and muscular . . . are peculiar." Deuteronomy disliked the Catholic writers. All the people in that room were better informed than I was.

Brr was rarely courteous if you were tall; he measured out such things with a curious exactitude, a form of beauty of manner; he said, going back in the conversation, "It's a compliment." He said it *courteously*—it seemed to me almost an admission that I was being courted and competed for by all of them. . . . A game.

I had no idea what any of them knew—or planned. Faintly drunk, bold, I said, "A RARE TRUE HOPPING TOUGHLY MANLINESS KINNY-KIN-KINS . . ." Much of the time (when I write or in company) I am being *funny* or making jokes, but few people notice. These were surprisingly unfrightened people. . . .

Moira said, shifting the intensity, "There is more happiness in a good movie than in all of New Jersey. That's why I left New Jersey." A special stink of time-riddled language as of old clothes, but Freudian-rebellious, sucked in, well-adjusted-by-rote, the word *happiness*. "We're just rich garbage. . . . I'm glad I'm not an artist . . . I'm an *artiste*—I'm a *socialist* . . ." She didn't want to talk books.

I think Moira was sexually profound in her self-destruction and in her destruction at the hands of men and of society, and in her vengeance, which was to spend money and to have style and to go mad: a form of intelligence and *real wit*. Not in what she said—but in her destruction. Perhaps it was a *narcissistic masochism* but I don't think so. . . . How strange everything was. . . . She said, in a kind of ugly way, sneering at Deut and Brr: "I like Chekhov. . . . And you know what he says? He said, *How are we to live?*"

"We are to live well," Deuteronomy said. *Living well* as a phrase and idea had a lot of meaning then but not Chekhovian meaning, but a weight of its own weightlessness. "*Seriously,*" he said in a droll way. *Serious* meant to attempt to be ultimate.

"Do you like the way we talk? Do you like New York talk?" Moira asked me.

"I feel we're floating around in the idea of the quotable . . ." I was trying to be interesting.

In Moira's house, it is sophisticated to be grudging. Also, a social get-together is a rehearsal, a part of preparation for worldwide performance—that's a kick. But my audience is smaller than theirs. Moira believes that *art* is as well-paid as it is for Noel Camtippy or Picasso, as in the small Picassos on the walls of her room, men she desires or likes.

The two ex–movie stars here are aging women of powerful presence and extremely pronounced views (on everything). Perhaps in some sense they are whores, as Moira has whispered. But they are universal whores. It is hard to *read* the signals of a person such as Moira. It is easier to know what the screen image of either ex-star means. Also present is another show-business corporation figure, a behind-the-scenes intellectual, who knows thousands of critics and writers and who gives parties and determines reputations and the gloss or glamour on them. Here is a fairly famous script writer often called The Jewish Noël Coward by well-informed movie reviewers who don't get to come to these get-togethers. He is a "famous" parlor wit and "famous" lover. Moira has said, "We keep score on Stanley." He is describing a movie comedian star: "No Funny Business" Martin Stone, "the shlong of destiny: he just puts it in and salutes Charles Darwin." Then he said, "Now that Noël Coward is old and Dorothy Parker is toxic drunk, I'm the quickest tongue in the non-Communist West, the daddy firecracker, the daddy *wisecracker*—"

God, I'm the poorest one here.

Moira said eerily, "Oh you won't sell out; that's not what coming to see us means." Moira said it in a little *hopping* voice, mocking everything. Peccinorda di Gustibus, the lesbian, is watching *Moira* carefully.

Moira had stepped on the summoning bell and a *manservant* had appeared and been sent to get champagne, "not the really good stuff," Moira said with a little laugh. "No one will notice."

Whacko came in from the balcony, knelt, and kissed her feet again.

To be here is as mysterious as hieroglyphics. It is like floating out to sea. I said something like that to Moira.

"A group is who is friends with who, and everyone has secrets, and I don't know, is this a good group?" Moira said, looking around—the style she was adapting was French and American, like one of those American women who spent time in Paris.

Did I say that Ora accepts the Kellows' judgments? So does three-quarters of the educated population of this country. Ora fawns on them—I can think of a dozen or two dozen women in whose careers Brr was the initial or secondary figure of discovery, who gave them public names, public existence, public roles as *women,* establishing the public image of the proportion of looks to style to brains. She is fascinated by what they know, and she is enragedly jealous—or fawning.

When he introduces Ora—who is of another social caste from the people in the room: exiled, upper-crust Maine—to someone, he says, *And this is Ora,* leaving off her last name. I think what he is doing is encouraging her in her magnetism and brainy good looks, her aura of power and heat, to be bitter; he wants her to cheat on me. He makes trouble for all the couples: he is known for it.

He is likely to take her arm and seat her next to Peccinorda di Gustibus, famous for being lesbian and brainy, and then he looks at me innocently. Ora doesn't want to be defined as The Lesbians' Darling—her phrase—but she likes those women; I often find a number of monocled and booted women, a lot of them European, with powerful haircuts and brilliant eyes, in the front room of our apartment; they look bruised emotionally—by Ora. Ora said once, *Well, sweet housewives aren't going to call me and ask to have tea anymore.* (They had at the beginning.) But now we were too famous, and she was dressed wrong for a housewife; she worked for Arestow, the photographer, a friend of Brr's.

Or Brr will seat her next to famous male lechers such as Jewish comic scriptwriters deep in analysis for their male nymphomania and who have written movies about *all their women* and who are notoriously *forward* and vital and suffering. They attract women justly. One has heard Ora in this very room say sternly, *I am not a schiksa, I am a person.* Also, she was totally not blond—I am partly blond but she is nut-brown.

Or Charles Pearl, the most popular movie star of that time who was also a famous lecher, and so maybe was the most famous fucker in the world at that moment except for Porfirio Rubirosa and Alden Whitto: *he* said to her, "Hello—my god, what nice breasts you have," cupping one. Ora, dark-eyed, vibrant in her dark youth, in her renegade Maine upper-crust avatar—and often coldly ferocious with people who mauled her, although she was as likely to become passive and victimized and tearful but scathing-mouthed and contemptuous. (Pearl also cornered her in the back hall near the bathroom; he said to her—he told me—*Touch me, just touch me, see what you do to me,* and Ora said, *No, this wasn't my idea—whatever you do, you do on your own.*) And saddened when professors did it or someone she wanted to know. Now she was confronted by a movie star whose work she admired and a man she would like to work with (if nothing else: I didn't know what her desires were in men), and she may have felt left out and betrayed by me and ill-at-ease in that group. She looked slick-haired and finely erect. Already a number of Brr's photographers had imitated Ora's look and exaggerated it—she herself was unphotogenic; she closed in when a camera was aimed at her—and then cried, "DON'T DO THAT! I HATE THAT!" Then: "I'M PRACTICALLY MARRIED to him!" And she pointed at me. This was when Pearl mauled her in the Big Room.

But she didn't push him away. I did that, and she berated me later: *I can take care of myself.* Well, she can and she can't; she can't within the frame of a monogamous affair; and she doesn't want me to sleep with (fuck) Connie Lewistein with whom I am making a small movie.

Or rather she keeps changing her mind, yes, no, yes, no—finally, *I will kill you if you fuck her*— She is really odd—everyone is really odd; it's a world of mad people: "New York is a looney bin," Moira announces gaily.

But Ora is the most odd: her father named her after the Latin vocative for *pray.* He meant her to be a virgin of light. She is, she says, *the dirty girl, the Wild Girl*—now in the big city, in this setting, a supernumerary: what will she do next?

A tubby, really famous, *serious critic,* also famous as a lecher, and resigned mostly to affecting women writers, not young, but old, tough-minded, dirty, moved to join Pearl and Ora, one hand out and cupped. I went back to Moira.

"Everybody loves everybody," mad Moira said with considerable disinterest to me: she was wearing a weird green-colored thing, a silken jumpsuit or version of it, a dress with pants, I don't know about such advanced clothes (but I am learning) and in her hair was a narrow pink ribbon, a quietly vivid unforgettable pink, that was the dominant color in the room. She was clever that way. She said with a laugh, "I don't know who I am when I wear *clothes . . .*" Famous clothes. "Brr likes it; he makes me wear *things . . .*" Famous clothes, famous at the moment. "I am designer designed."

"Oh my *goodness* I didn't *know,*" Pearl said to Ora in a hick manner, well below his usual enunciation. "Let me get you a drink. But I would like to screw you, you know." *Very* gentlemanly and *dear.*

Ora turned her face aside and, without thinking, raised her stiffened arm and kept him an arm's length away from her breasts. Ora was wearing a discarded black, sleeveless dress from Paris that Moira had given her and which was worn without a bra. Ora is genuinely beautiful often; her posture, the sloping, bare shoulders, and then the proud neck, and the great-skinned radiant side-and-front finely shaped fleshed out boniness of her face. But she was a *type,* gorgeous girl dowager, sadly fastidious but passive about it, something of a good sport resigned to *dirtiness* but so given to lies that if she liked Brr, she would deny these events had occurred. She wanted to be there. And she hated it. It was heart-stopping to see her. So good-looking and so knowing and so full of ignorance and so out-of-place there, although not entirely. And she didn't know how out-of-place she was. She was herself, and she didn't realize yet that for these *performers,* if I might call them that, everything was stylized.

"She's new," Moira said with condescension to me. "Well, you know what you're getting into when you come to *this* madhouse," she said evilly: "You're getting a madhouse! Tee-hee . . ."

The fat critic Walter Pauline Christian said, "No: I expect a very sweet evening when I come here—and good food—and pretty women—and *you,* Moira." He kept glancing toward Ora.

Moira said to me, "He's not bad in bed you know."

He was partly drunk, taut with party-nerves and social conceit, but he was also shy, teddy bear–like, arrogant, hard-working socially, sexually looney, and like most of the men in the room, he was quick to signal he had been recruited and used by Moira, that he had a sexual entrée.

Brr said to him, "Wiley is brilliant . . ."

This grated on Christian who was in his own view the Julius Caesar of literary reputations. "Brilliant? *Brilliant?*" he said: "Well, you have a backer," he said to me, backing down, uneasy at Brr's control of so many magazines. Christian was *charming* with a fat, smart man's practiced enticing curmudgeonliness. He said to me, "I have noticed that tall writers usually overwrite."

I couldn't afford to care or not to care, do you know? He was sweaty and red—like a eunuch washerwoman. Brr had stepped between Pearl and Ora. He said, "We don't want to upset Wiley—he's quite *crazy* at parties . . ." He winked at me. I had already confronted Pearl at that point; Brr was *playing a game.*

He had already told me privately: *It's unwise to be settled down with someone while you are finding your way in the THE REAL WORLD*—he tended to speak in an excited, magazine-captionish way. He meant you had to be available. He said, "Mad Moira knows all about it . . ." She was defeated by him but cruel about him; she'd called him Little Balls and Mr. No Love the Killer. This was when she was very high. A guy I knew and his new wife explained to me that it was part of being a good hostess and host, if you wanted to be famous for that, to laugh at your wife or husband or lover: otherwise, you excluded people, the people you were talking to.

Brr said, "Mad Moira says you are like an idiot—" Brr spoke very clearly as if to be recorded.

"Yeah?" I said.

"Prince What's-his-name . . ."

"Prince? Myshkin? The Dostoyevsky one: From *The Idiot.* I thought you were telling me Moira thought I was dumb."

"She thinks you're a big brain: she hopes you're big elsewhere, too. She says you're *heavy* . . ." Not light company.

"I'm sorry I'm heavy," I said. "Phallically, I'm maybe more the family economy size than giant."

After a moment, he said, "Do you think your approach works with . . . people?" He sounded naïve for a change.

I looked at him, big-eyed, meaning *I don't know.* I said, "Work how? For what reason?" I was on the defensive in his house.

"Don't you want to write a Proustian novel? And have a good life." Proust, in this set, was supposedly the best novelist ever.

"No. Do you? I want to write best-sellers like Jack London and Hemingway: sincere, popular—"

He caught on faster than I could talk: "You *are* an idiot," he said so quickly that it gave an interesting rhythm, I thought, to the dialogue, which struck me as intelligent dialogue, not because of what was said but because of the structure given to it by Brr, who was so alert and ruthless and such a captain of industry.

"But not saintly—not like Myshkin," I said.

"Yes," he said. His yes was like a self-conscious sentence, but it didn't require knowledge of sentence structures. He meant I was *weird.*

I was dressed in very dark gray flannel slacks and a good black cashmere sweater and a white shirt: it was all I could afford in terms of dressing up; and it was a sign of respectful effort toward people who cared about clothes. I don't know how this was taken except that after a few weeks, other people—some women—showed up, dressed the same way. Of course, in this social group of hard-working people, mostly *freaks,* to use Brr's word (*They're all freaks and their work is their masks,* Moira has said), I was given the role of someone *healthy*—a specialized form of ephebe, supposedly *a sexy man,* but the favorite of the house *for the moment.* Everything everyone did in this room was a signal, was semiotics because of everyone's careers.

Ora knew *other* people from her girlhood: the governor of New York State, for instance, who was the third-richest man in the world. We sometimes saw some of those people. They were often put off by me—and my clothes. What I'm trying to say is that what was signified wasn't clear at all outside its own context. The critic wanted me to talk to him and Ora; he kind of wanted to see if I would whore her. That kind of stuff can be done good-naturedly; in the middle of night sometimes back then when I couldn't sleep but had an attack of panic, I wished Ora was a cold-blooded, ruthless climber who did sleep around and get us places like many of the women we knew.

Calvin Higgins's wife—Higgins was my publisher—his wife was extraordinarily ambitious and pretty and charming but stupid, too, and pretentious; she was very jealous of our *knowing* the Kellows. She had a little high-pitched voice and short legs and she said to me in her kitchen, "I am Faustian: I made a Faustian bargain with my life when I married Cal." She said it in this little high-pitched, Ivy League woman student's voice, which made it all even stranger, and I felt cold terror.

She was sensitive and quick and mannerly and had money of her
own, but she was, in a way, high-bred white trash, hysterical and full of
calculation and not capable of much victory. She was really a supernumerary and exploited by Calvin, who was a small, nervous, determined
man, a great liar, and charmer—a heart-tugger once you got past an initial shudder at some clownish and very white physical repulsiveness he
had. He hinted at a tragic sexual past and told anecdotes of being
spurned—he managed to avoid mentioning which gender. He was so
thoroughly second-rate and so irresistibly sweet—but it was a lie; he was
ambitious; and his wife was nearly as imprisoned as Moira—that if the
sweetness didn't put your teeth on edge, knowing him put *you* on edge.

He wrote deeply sincere, very sweet social diaries about how
human and humane the ruling class was, but I don't think he knew
the ruling class; he knew some fine-drawn, well-educated, rich people. His books did gloat. He loved writing about maimings. He had
worked to establish my reputation.

Anyway, Higgins's wife, unlike Moira, *adored* Ora, her life, her
social standing which she recognized. Higgins's wife was from North
Dakota or Indiana. She had a Faustian woman's college dormitory
crush and she spoke of Ora as *such a big person, so brave, she goes out and
meets life halfway—I want to be like her.*

So at the party it was confusing to me that Ora was sort of disap-
proved of and not much liked. Ora said to me sotto voce, "I am humiliated when you defend me: let me defend myself."

"But you weren't defending yourself: you were crying."

"Don't live my life for me. Now everyone knows about me."

"Knows what about you?" Do you ever have talks with someone
that you think are utterly meaningless but that a day or two later you
see a meaning in, but you can't check it out because they don't
remember clearly enough and neither do you. And they don't want to
talk; their mood has changed.

"That I'm a victim and a fool—oversexed." She really wasn't. But
she was a brave, moving, sexual sight: a mother of dynasties. Among her
old friends, I was, if not disliked, distrusted and looked at askance, just

as she was here: I think it was the amused value I placed on myself that
upset the Prots she knew, most of whom were famous, just as the una-
mused, subcutaneous value she placed on herself upset the Jews here.

"Ora, I thought you were trying not to make a scene for my
sake"—because of Kellow's commissioning a piece from me.

"You think I'm weak—you think I'm a nobody—"

"I think you're a hero . . ." But then I went too far: "of the Third
Reich . . ."

"I am not anti-Semitic! I am as good with you as any Jewess could
be!"

"Ora, so help me God, I'm going crazy: you're absolutely nuts:
let's not have a scene at this party. God, you're driving me crazy—"

"You live in a dream, Wiley. You're so spoiled because you have a
brain—"

"Fuck off, Ora."

I hadn't any real idea what we were talking about. She was jealous,
I was a star there, in that house for a while. I don't know; I smiled at
her: the smile just happened—how frail and intimate real life is . . . I
mean the smile was uncalled for and had no subtext except amusement, partly at the horror.

The speed and dexterity of the man, Brr, the distance back from
the surface of his eyes that he stands and his sadly triumphal, tireless
(pilled-up) nature afflict me with vertigo. And *amusement*.

"I kiss your shoelaces," Sam Chonberg said to me in echo of
Whacko's kissing Moira's feet. Chonberg is semi-openly homosexual
as is Camtippy, but Camtippy, not a Jew, is much much more famous.
Moira said to me, "I love anti-Semitism—it just twists the whole
world into knots and fills it with lies." Gloria Peeler (my agent then)
said Chonberg offered ridiculous terms for me to work on a script of a
movie for him. *You can't lower yourself that way: you can't afford to yet—
you're too small potatoes now* . . .

Peeler is openly, and in the most friendly way, an S&M lady, sort of
Let's Tango, Let's Tangle—a famous Tough Cookie and *friendly* New
York presence.

I told Moira what Peeler had said, and Moira chanted, "Small potatoes, small potatoes . . ." Then: "That's better than itty-bitty balls."

Kellow and Chonberg and Deuteronomy and Christian (a Jew). Ah, *Kellow is pure Arabian Nights,* oriental; Chonberg is The Little German turned American Star. Peeler does what she does for *The Feminine Principle.*

Brr had earlier crushes on both Leonard Doetroch, who is, after all, kind of a very great commercial director, with pronounced elements of being an artist of some sort, and on Little Sam Chonberg (Kellow is a Jew who likes Jews) who is maybe a great comedian, who is at least very, very good, and who will never do comedy again. He is about to make a top of the line, top of the world movie in England, with Sir Edmund Buller and Lady Joan in it for class: "I can use extra dialogue—if you have any . . ."

Moira whispered, "That's a nineteen-forties wisecrack. We don't do that anymore." She said in a regular voice, "We do nineteen-fifties wisecracks," and she looked at Chonberg warmly. God, even that is an act of flirtation.

Chonberg and Brr have certain abilities in common: they are very good horsemen: I am a butcher boy when I get on a horse, without finesse or posture or sensibility: my procedures work but they're brutal and stupid. They both dance extremely well. They both burn with restlessness.

I am a counterbalance to Chonberg. If I get out of hand, Kellow will make his way to Chonberg's side. Actually, I think that Kellow intends to own me and this little movie I want to make with Connie Lewistein: that is, he expects it to reflect his world and to be about him. There is something about psychoanalysis that turns people into being almost General Terms: Kellow is Maneuver and Ambition.

Kellow pretends to a kind of (sexual) interest in Ora but actively dislikes her—he has "confessed" this to me. Chonberg has actually made a pass at her but doesn't really feel drawn to women so far as I can guess. Kellow, sitting on the arm of the couch, his arms folded, asks me *warmly,* "What do *you* believe?" I can't remember an immediate context in the last few minutes in which that would fit in. I look down at my hands in my lap.

In a voice of much more overt cleverness than Brr's, Moira says to Brr, "Ask him what does his smile mean?"

Brr said, "Chonberg has done a great piece for us on smiles."

Deuteronomy said, "You rarely smile, Brr. You part your lips and sparkle a little bit, and then you call it quits."

Brr looked at me, meaning he wanted my opinion.

"You have a different tonality of no-smile for each one of us: it changes so swiftly I get the feeling of wind blowing off you, to me," I said.

"You are very quick," Moira said to me.

"I thought that before and remembered it now," I said.

"You are like a rock," Brr said mysteriously.

"A quick rock?" Then: "*Épater* the rocks? It's a kind of agony being small-time compared to everyone else in the room."

Moira said, "You ought to make a real movie—with Brr—on your own, you analyze everything too much."

"My mind is a clutter of darkness," I said.

"Oh listen to the *child,*" Moira said.

Kellow wanted me to use in my movie a very small, very short, fine-boned Chinese actor, aged about eighteen. Kellow said the Chinese guy was the most beautiful adolescent model in the world. (This was a long time ago; being Chinese was exotic.)

"How can he represent freakishness?"

"Have him wear glasses. . . . He loves a girl bigger than he is: a blond girl with big breasts—someone who never saw a desert, who hardly even knows he's *Chinese.*"

"Is he greedy? Is he competitive? Why a desert in China?"

"What do you mean? The Gobi."

Moira said, "Is he bossy? Does he always walk faster than everyone? Does he set the pace? Does he always have The Best Gossip? Where did you learn to notice things?"

"In some ways, you always manage to have the last word . . . Wiley," Deut said.

I am of an indefensible order of the human. It is cheap and special to be like me: you never have to live, or know how people live: you never have to feel except as notes for scenes. I didn't want to spend my life like this, but then one isn't a boy for very long. So far as I know, someone's social surface is a lie as a mark of civilization. I am a liar too and a recent lecher, and not a river god or really a boy among the currents and artesian wellings of time. Style is a brooding patron of metamorphoses who gives you a liar's surface, partly as a privilege.

If you refuse social metamorphosis, refuse the riverine, and substitute the mental stroll and flight of *keeping track* you think all sorts of strange things such as that I am the child of my child self more than I am the child of my childhood. The fruits of Eden and the walled garden and the spirit that moved among the leaves and on the waters, how am I bound to such selves? How unfinal they seem, and the fragility of them, of one's past roles. Truth is as different from that as bringing a real tiger into the room—and releasing him: not a portrait of a tiger, not a poem about a tiger; but the complete thing.

I mean, if you're serious, and if you wake from daydreams about your life to a dream-tinged life, to wakefulness and a landscape of attention to parties, and with ideas of truth and of work you might do like a tiger in the room, hinted at, but invisible so far. I am someone my younger self would resent—although he would have been relieved that we have not turned out to be no one.

Brr stared at me, bug-eyed; he has a natural state of being bug-eyed, very insectlike, which he controls and hides and then reveals. He wants to know what I mean by my not saying anything about selling out. *Moira* approved of selling out; she was a *famous shopper*, she was mad and deep as a shopper—she said matter-of-factly (but with a giggle), "I've had visions while I was in Bloomingdale's—I never talk about them though. I have a thing about escalators." Then: "You'll write an unkind book about us, you'll see—I can look at your eyes and see right into your soul: I'm a *witch!* A Dostoyevskian witch—" I *think* she meant she was a Russian-Jewish witch.

Brr interpolated: "She's a reader! I'm not a reader at all . . ." He was rivalrous with her but also protective and he did a sort of public relations boastful thing about her.

Moira hurried on; she said to me, "You're The Idiot played by Gerard Philippe with a lot of Yankee Hollywood male ingenue thrown in but we all see the Captain Bligh and Stavrogin in you: I know it's Stavrogin in that other bad book I like so much although it's not *Crime and Punishment* and it's not *The Brothers Karamazov. The Possessed?* I love that title—"

"I do too," I said.

"I mean it literally: I *love* it. I know it's Stavrogin because I want to say Raskolnikov—so if I think Raskolnikov, I remember to say Stavrogin: my doctor has taught me to do this. . . . He taught me to be *personal* about how I use my mind. My poor mind . . ." She said she thought about these figures sexually and allocated sexual organs to them and love scenes and seductions. "*Raskolnikov* was a jerk-off with a little prick, one of those troubled lover-murderers who are round. But Stavrogin . . ." she gushed in pantomime. He was a sexual big-shot, a hot-for-damnation character, a figure of limitless danger, always staring at her in her mind, she said.

"Moira has the most expensive shrink in the Western World," Brr said quietly boastful. (Seventeen years from now, she will cut her throat and wrists and bleed to death while he is in the next room in a pill-induced sleep. That happened in the 1970s.)

Moira said loudly, "Stavrogin is more responsible . . ."

We are discussing the nature of trespass and social horror—how we harm others. But we are unclear in this. I said, "I like very strong people so that whatever happens is not my fault—"

"Well, that's deep," Moira said. Then, with an evil sort of giggle: "I never know what I think about deep things until I see my doctor. I *love* my doctor—literally. I think *he's* scary—he's a Stavrogin but not so mean—not so good-looking either. I'd love to marry him—he makes more money than God—and he's more interesting. I love guilt when it makes men, you know, English and *mean.*" She had a real ability to interest me, real power in her observations, a competence at being trespassed against: one implication of her manner was that she was having an affair with her doctor and was sleeping with Deut and Brr, and they all knew about one another.

"Moira's deep," Deuteronomy said sweetly. He was never entirely not onstage when I saw him.

"Oh, Moira's *deep,*" Brr said in a theatrically mysterious tone. It had to do with having power. Moira and Brr invented a kind of journalism. Moira maybe matters more in post-war culture than is known. She propagandized for this or that political or cultural idea, a mad duchess of pop literacy, a mad American Jewess—genius wife who changed the world. Somewhat.

It is fashionable and pungent and shitty and post-war that in this set they hold over one another's heads the sort of judgment that they are or are not *artists.* Almost everyone in that room will still be unforgotten fifty years later, but no one in that room except me has held the rank of *artist* in that time. I mean only that all the false dealing and swapping and buying of the term came to nothing. My rep may wind up being that of a swindler.

One of the directors there had made a popular movie about jazz—an interesting movie, kind of crude. He came over to join us, and Moira praised his movie; she said, "I loved all the dim light—" It wasn't insulting either. But I didn't understand it.

He said, "I don't like movies—I don't like jazz. I'm just a hired hand." He was drunk and wore cowboy boots back in the fifties when that meant *Time* magazine would think he was *avant-the-rest-of-us* (Moira's phrase). The way he said what he said aroused a kind of stillness in Moira: he was a viable and durable and influential sensibility: male, maybe more competent than talented and certainly strong.

Brr said, "A hired hand who does *great* work."

Brr said, "You know what Whitto said to *Life* magazine—" Whitto, iconoclastic and marvelously popular and sullen, was often in this set proposed as a source of prophecy, a mad young rabbi really. His quality of *truth* as an actor had the quality of a temporary religion. Brr has an idiot savant's memory for journalistic quotes and he reproduces Whitto: " 'Jazz is the great American art: it comes out of oppression. Jazz shows you how to react—if you have a good conscience you can have a good time among the criminal actions of your country.' " Brr was such a good mimic that it was as if Whitto were talking in the room, but Brr can't really *do* Whitto despite what I just said; Brr's version is stupid and noble and questionable, Broadway versus Hollywood—theatrical.

Brr has to run things. The purpose of his activity is to overcome you—he is *like a four-year-old,* Moira says. If he was not like this how could he run his magazines successfully? Each of his writers had theories and friendships and was calculating; he negotiated with agents and had a staff of photographers. He said to me once, *Everyone is in rebellion all of the time. I spend too much of my time being a policeman.*

"What do you think movies really are?" Brr asked, setting a topic. A few people in our group sighed at the classroom essay aspect, the thing of being used.

Moira told the jazz-movie director to pull over a table and sit on it: "It's less like a speech, it's easier if you're sitting." He was short and pudgy, very energetic and commanding in his cowboy boots, and kind of sycophantic in an offhand way—*cute* that was called back then.

He did pull up a table but he said, "You only fed me bagels and caviar: I listen to jokes for that, I don't answer questions—"

That remark of his had the quality of being applauded or nodded at good-humoredly. Brr Kellow as a laughingstock, him and Moira as jerks, as pushy users and jerks, oddly that was part of their having so much *style.* I don't know how people do that no-mercy and yet *sycophantic* thing.

In the long-drawn-out afternoon of Apocalypse, the ex–movie star women preen on a couch facing ours. Supposedly innocent professionalism is coercive, unstable, a plenum of rights claimed and enforced. It stains everyone that this is the decade of *perfect breasts,* wild brassieres that bestow weird, jutting bomblike breast shapes. Such lies make it difficult to be sane: sanity is social, somewhat Freudian. The idea of a fanciful reality and of people's secrets is built in to the local notion of sanity, of normalcy. . . . This is a group high in nervous breakdowns and charity. The men (but not me) have a frightening and fashionable idea of a universal but ideal and tireless and undemanding *fucker,* and they wear very expensive, impressive clothes.

The brute structure of being *cute* (in the youthful sense) and possessing a maybe bullshit veracity, and the semi-Baudelairean *corrupt* reality—behind these styles are the beliefs and terms of people who live in personal hells, me too, but mine is diluted in the middle of the supposed Eden of the U.S., a suburb of Hell. The eerie thrum of holiness in a given moment may have a homosexual tinge—that too is an issue.

Deuteronomy said, "Movies are what you have to see so you can stop hearing your mother's voice in your head say, *Don't handle yourself, Harvey . . .*"

"Simple stories for simple people," said one of the woman movie stars, someone I'd found attractive when I was thirteen: she was still attractive. It was strange how *known* to me she was, her voice, her mannerisms, some of the shapes of her body. An element of dream was attached to the memory of her.

Moira said in mad, sotto voce mockery, "Simple stories for simple people." She was often rude to women (a party as arena for unnamed championships).

The show business corporation head said, "Movies are how I know I'm unhappy because my life is *not* like a movie, but they make me feel good anyway because I know I am not as dumb as a movie. Ha-ha."

"Wiley," Brr said. He is *calling on me* to speak. The bastard.

I said, "I never knew a simple person. I don't think such a thing exists. So movies are simple forms for complex people, but then people want to be simple too, like ads and movies. They get competitive. Or they run out of ideas. Or it looks good—it's a victim-thing. I think movies are truly terrible simplifications, smothering. But they get their power from two things: what movies define is popularity for now. Movies themselves are operatic hallucinations with motions substituted for the music in opera—but simple: simple, dirty music. Like dirty talk it tends to have a limited vocabulary. Their force is derived from the way hallucinations become active delusions during masturbation. And in dreams—what makes you out to be handsome or powerful and kingly. They're in the genre of masturbation-accompaniment."

"Go on," Brr said.

"No," I said. But I did go on: "I mean it's interesting that movies are so fake, and we make them real. You are alone in your head in public, and you roar along with the crowd for God and community—I dislike the way movies bully and dominate the audience. What we *know* about sex—and people—never gets shown in movies. . . . Isn't that strange? Movies do dance numbers and scenes of women getting dressed really well. Maybe everyone wants to see faked, tamed stories of self-willed sexuality. I think movies are hard to do: it's hard to get the victim-thing, even only parts of it, right: and to palpate the audience and kowtow and to take the punishment the audience hands out and being made use of and also being adored. It's very tricky: it's all S and M and sexual terror and faking it all—"

The jazz-movie director said, "We're all downtrodden in Hollywood—"

Deut, who was tall, and who had a much greater public popularity at the moment than anyone else in the room, said, "Oh that: that's socialism—" A joke. "But, also, you're very short." Nearly everyone laughed. Brr was short and mostly liked only short people except for Deut and me.

I was tense from talking the way I did, kamikaze and without direct calculation: a role.

"It's getting too deep for me," said one of the women ex–movie stars making a play for importance in the room.

Deuteronomy said with great as-if-onstage charm, "It's the sibling rivalry tango . . ."

The short movie director had been Deuteronomy's (and my) predecessor as Brr's closest friend. Brr's dominance was because of his knowledge of style as much as because he controlled so much publicity. Also, he wanted it, and people granted it—it was Sunday.

Moira said, "Aren't we *heavy?*" *Heavy* was a term in use in New York then. "It's a relief sometimes to be *heavy.*"

"Touché," Brr said.

I looked at Ora who was some feet away, across the room, and silent; she was having one of her *Wiley-is-showing-off, I-can't-match-that* moments. I wanted her to be proud of me. Ora was the best-looking person in the room if you liked her style.

"Do you rehearse what you say?" Moira asked.

"I went to Harvard," I said.

"What else can you do?" she asked.

"Yes," said the short movie director; it was a job offer and a challenge. An offer of New Yorkish friendship.

"Yes. What else can you *do?*" said Moira again, more intensely.

I kind of went haywire. I said, "I can type and I can fuck, but mostly I'm a mess—I make a mess of things." I got enraged and looney from nerves.

The director moved in closer, but Brr said to me, "You want another bagel?" which I thought meant shut up, that he didn't want me to talk to the director and make friends. He and Moira kidnaped me. We left the big room, Moira and Brr and I without Ora. Or Deut. Moira's hip bumped the wall; she had a pretty body and a drunken-drugged pretty walk, kind of a trained walk, but she was ill and strange with the pills she took. She and Brr *liked* leaving their parties and then returning. Or had to, to breathe, or because of their states of mind. But they liked to tease as now. In the dining room, Moira sat me in the corner; and she and Brr went and filled dishes of food and Brr got a glass of champagne from the kitchen for me, and they came back with a napkin and silverware. They sat on either side of me: they interrogated me about my movie theories which I hadn't worked out, and they asked me about myself.

Brr said, "Now is what you're saying that movies are mostly sado-masochistic—S and M?"

"Well, the audience is masochistic and vengeful. The virtual destruction, physical and moral, of the star and of the character in the movie and of the producer and director and everyone else is necessary. In most movies and in movie careers sooner or later—"

"Alice in Wonderland," Brr said. The aftereffect of his making use of you is a passionate and troubled love and hate and punishment.

Moira wanted to know where the knowledge of sadomasochism came from in *my* life. She is at this moment insolent and domestically somewhat sly and socially alert and articulate and given over to big-time psychic violence—it is unsettling. "Were you a brute as an ado-lescent?" she asks. I nodded; I don't know why I lied; I thought it was sexy. Moira went on, "Your mother encouraged you?"

Brr was watching: it really always was a case of him *watching.*

"My mother was meant to be the mother of sissies— No, I swaggered in spite of her."

She wanted more: "Were you her victim too?"

"Sure—"

"But your mother loved you a lot, I can tell—"

"Mostly she liked to come first—she kind of *fell* in love with me now and then—"

"You have such a *romantic* way of looking at things," Moira said sarcastically.

"It was partly sunlit and it was partly that the sun turned black." I was misquoting Racine.

"I don't really understand you when you talk," Moira said, forgivingly.

"O.K. I was quoting Greek stuff." Then, courageously, I grinned at her: I didn't need her, and I wasn't really afraid of her.

Brr said, "What do *you* mean by S and M? Whippings? Or psychological *meanness*—"

"Oh *floggings*—sure . . ." I meant the imaginative thing in movies, old shipboard routines and British schoolboys and pirates.

He said, "No. I mean, hanky-spanky." The real thing in a bedroom.

I said, "It seems to be good for the complexion."

He said, "What kind of analyst do you have?"

"I haven't been analyzed: I don't have enough money."

"Well, if you're *suffering,* they *help* you and let you owe them," Moira said.

I said, "Well, yes, if your suffering is what they're writing about at the time. Otherwise not. I asked two analysts in Boston, when I was in college, for help but I had no money, and both had been sympathetic, but when I said I was broke, they said I was normal."

Moira said, "Oh. Do they ever say *that?* Oh, the innocent—" Meaning me. "I'm a paranoid schizophrenic—"

"That's a *secret!*" Brr said.

"I'm only it off and on," Moira said with a giggle: "It's the worst thing to be if it's full-time— You are so pure, honey," Moira said to me in a mad way now that the idea of her madness was in her; then she said to Brr, in a serious and exaggeratedly sane tone, a whole other accent, said of me elegiacally. "*He's* pure . . ."

Brr said, "Do you think of S and M as mostly *physical?*" The phrase *psychic violence* wasn't in use yet. But it was clear Brr suspected himself of it.

I sighed. "No. The worst is to be destroyed mentally." I made a face. I figured he'd take it as a challenge.

Moira didn't help: "Like me by Brr," she said among the lies and poses. And she giggled.

I hesitated and said nothing.

"Oh my God," Moira said. "You're such a baby. It makes you sad about me. Hurting people excites men: their whole self becomes an erection—I'm a femme fatale for some people—"

"Alden Whitto," Brr said to her.

I said, "Yeah, he's one of those beautiful, romantic shits."

"A shit?"

"Remember when you were little, the kid who put pebbles in his shoes or burned himself with matches and wanted to burn you?" Brr accepted Whitto as a prophet-of-sorts.

"No."

"They were really sophisticated about punishments. About handing out shit. They're like dark mermaids. They learn about this stuff; they can do it *intimately*. They always want to get even: they liked revenge—they're juicy, like caterpillars. I'm talking about kids, the kids' version—"

Brr said, "No." Then: "Were they freaks?"

"They were bright, not class-officer material, they were too mean. And they were of an absolutist cast, and the rest of us weren't—they had the one-God thing, the one class leader, the one smart boy, the one pretty girl. If you're one of these guys or girls you get to tyrannize in all sorts of ways in everything you do—"

"Where did you read this?" Brr asked.

"I observed it," I said, and shrugged.

"He read it somewhere," Moira said. "Everything's in books. Nothing new is possible. Are you a sadist, Wiley? It doesn't matter what he says," she said to Brr; "he's a sadist."

"Are you a sadist?" Brr asked me.

I shrugged. "Now and then . . ."

Unwillingly, with a true unwillingness, he laughed, "Ha-ha." I see myself as a comedian but he rarely saw me as one.

"The master of the erection is the master of the hounds," I said, taking refuge in nonsense, to discourage the talk. But, also, I turn foolish without warning.

He and Moira winced.

I sighed and explained, "You look into each other's eyes—you maybe let what's there make itself visible. Then you have it like a stone to carry: you're responsible for it. . . . It's not easy to bear the attention—it's like being naked in a torture chamber—I think you suffer differently if you're a sadist."

Brr said to me, "Is that sexy?"

"It doesn't explain itself—sometimes it's sexy: it depends on which direction the whip is aimed. It's better as an aspect of nature than as theatrical carryings-on—"

"I hate intellectuals," Moira said.

I stood up. "I'm in over my head."

Brr, standing up beside me, came to my shoulder. Fear or tension or whatever it was made me say in a shadowy voice, "Erections are like bananas in the marketplace, they're part of monkey business." I often say stupid things because I am often stupid. I hoped that would eliminate the short-man-tall-man thing between me and Brr. It is part of some sort of give-and-take to speak without sense.

I followed Moira and Brr back into the other room.

Deuteronomy, on the same couch, *fills us in:* "The talk here has gone from movies to books—are movies ever as good as books? And now the talk is about books: are they as good as sex?"

All the talk at all the Sunday brunches was like this.

"Ha-ha, ha-ha."

"HAHAHAH."

"HA-HA . . ."

Bray, rasp, snort, snurtle-chortle, wry smiles, the latest model for wisecracks.

Moira said with cold sexual precision, "*We* talked about *sadism.*"

"Well, you had the best of it," Chonberg said.

Faces turned; it was shocking: the faces move in separate tempos and with separate intelligences and agendas—we didn't use that word. Each face is clearly a kind of *vagina dentata.*

Well, don't think about it, don't notice, don't think about people's bodies, don't unzip anyone in your mind, don't unbutton any 1950s perfect-booby brassieres, promise nothing. The real subject is success. And meaning.

"Well, tell *us,*" Deut said.

"I don't want to," I said, a bit haughtily—sadistically. (I was joking.)

"Please," Deuteronomy said with his wide-faced akimbo onstage charm that so disconcerted me offstage.

"I have to think about it more."

The Jewish Noël Coward, Noël Schwearzen, said, "I've passed up fucks for books—" His wisecrack was in the style of *the hot poop.*

Moira spoke in a tone of cross sexuality to Schwearzen, "Oh you, you're an *artist . . .*" I have no idea if she was mocking him or not.

Brr and Deuteronomy flicked their faces and their eyes, almost like headlights, at me: then Deut said to Schwearzen, "Oh you, you're a *real* artist—" His timing and vocal dexterity were much greater and swifter than Schwearzen's. He went on with a stagy naïve smile: "I've passed up books for fucks."

Brr, still looking for magazine topics, said, "Why does a man's being an artist matter to women?"

"Hunh?" Schwearzen said. *Hunh*s were a form of wisecrack but Deut was the ace at them.

"Ha-ha," Deut said in his making-friends way but with a faint edge of ignoring Schwearzen as well.

Brr also said in a way that ignored Schwearzen: "But we *know* art matters . . ."

"*Sometimes,*" Deuteronomy said. He was rosy-cheeked, had floppy hair: light makeup and a wig, self-made, invented. He was running things, and he didn't surrender command to Brr now, which was interesting.

I had power in an eerie way that I didn't have with most people except in New York: power of this sort was also a form of weakness.

I said as if it were a quote, "And this was commonly, but not universally, said, in praise of men who were called artists, that it would mean something to a woman or to women that these men made things out of their own heads and bodies which then become a large part of the furniture of the mind."

Deuteronomy asked, "Where's that from?"

"Where do you think?" I said, feeling him throb a little. "Thomas Aquinas," I said, making it up.

"Oh he does nothing but quote," Moira said crossly, of me, I suppose. She was on a down slope from her drug-and-drinking high.

The texture of the silence then was wretched, at least for me. My face grew hot: "Brr introduces me to people and doesn't warn them about how I talk." Then I said: "I have to talk the way I do—I don't know why. I just do. Sorry." I often have the sense socially of being blindfolded with a gauze blindfold that I can almost see through: I am in a translucent haze and can almost see what I am doing but not quite.

Deuteronomy said, protectively, "The wisecrack meets the footnote."

All at once it was secrets time, a maze thing, the egos and attitudes—the thing that makes parties work sometimes. The people there were not scholars or artists, but they understood the market in seeing. Or something. The moment is penetrable by the force of physical logic, the grammar of motion, but we're not accustomed to doing that.

Mad Moira said, "Oh hell: why think? I can't think."

Deut said, "Fuck thinking? It gives people pimples."

Moira said with modesty, "I *am* crazy: I think you're funny."

The party was a whiff of battle—think how *human* everyone is, and who they sleep with, and then how surprised they are by death or by grief.

Moira said to me, "Do you have a tiger in you?"

Imagine the reality of a tiger inside you, the clawing restlessness and stretching and the stench, the carnival-colored predator.

Deuteronomy said, *apropos of nothing* (a phrase fairly popular then), "Why don't you write a play for me?"

The insistent, *insurgent* urgency of ambition—"By the time I try you may have begun to dislike my work." We were for the moment almost entirely ambition with only a thin rim of the human. "What kind of play did you have in mind?"

"Hunh?" he asked warmly, agreeably: a joke. "I wanted some young art—you know."

I had a small vocabulary of American boy noises. I made a naïve squeak and said, "I don't really like the young art bit . . ." Cal Higgins had told me, *Don't think, just sing like a bird*—God, he was awful. I said

to Deut, "I don't like the birdsong shit." People don't have to understand you; they'll ask you to explain if they care.

"What do you want to do?"

"I want to do *American* work but psychologically grownup—not
just daydream freedom-and-success shit . . ." Very unpompous in
manner when being pompous: that was politeness.

He had become still, physically. It is immodest to say so, but he
felt something in what I said, in the noise I'd made—he'd had a
glimpse of an idea like a glimpse of a deer in the woods, the whispering of the small *a*'s and *b*'s of an idea in the shadows and lights of his
mind of something he could use. I suppose it was as if I was doing
Moira's role but from an angle unlike hers.

"What you mean?" he asked in a voice so gently musical that I
smiled involuntarily.

I said, "I resent having this form of interest as *a young writer*—it is
like being a male model, one so handsome he can't act, his face is so
dimensionally suggestive that he can suggest little further: he can
merely carry the damn thing around and flicker, now and then, with
feeling, while others' dreams of happiness play on him. I want to be
sufficiently in control that I go to hell or heaven in the light of some
responsibility I have carried out on my own. I know how to be understood, but that means I say things in order to be understood: it is not
my real face: it is like a director's face, an invented face. I intend to
make a try at creating something American—but unexpected. I am
talking about young art, the thing of being young—"

"Yes? But the thing you want to create, *what* is that? What would
it *be*?"

How do you say enough to get them interested to the point they
give you money and a contract? Or do you just let go? Or do you go
off on a *serious* tangent that they can't use, although even a singer
like Deut can find a way: "Well, first, you have to know that the language we use mostly only points to what is there already in language, something in a book, copyrighted, something already said, a
territorial noise for a generation." We didn't use the word *media* yet.

"So it has a weird double nature as comprehensible and as *not-yet-sensible:* we know life is different from language. You have to go take a look—the herd of lions has to trot over the top of the hill and *see* the herd of okapi. And learn English to cover the exigencies of the hunt. . . ."

"I like okapi," he said warmly. But my weird little joke was a dud. It wasn't right for the 1950s.

"Language can have a predictive nature. Visual images are inherently worldly since their mistakes don't involve prediction. They simply misrepresent what is there or not, and if they do, that becomes the draw of fantasy, O.K.? I don't want to mislead anyone. Perhaps I could invent a way of dealing in more lifelike perspective—but what if this is just adolescent bullshit, you know?"

"Gosh, if I were you, I would do it. The thing about being young—you should do it for *people.*"

"Make a fool of myself." I said, "Well, it's a mastery tussle"— Deuteronomy let me go on being boastful; I mean his face was kind— and interested—"I see the United States as a series of adjacent legislatures with various bullies and systems of bribery and of voting: this is the nature of reason here. I am told, fairly often, almost daily, as a matter of fact, that if I would convert I could have the prizes, and if I was silent, silent about my being a Jew and about my writing being a Jew's writing, Jew-writing, I could have *some* of the prizes. Or none if I do what I want to do, do you follow me. I'm the writer who got the word *Jew* in *The New Yorker* the first time. I am seen as a *blind* kid. It's the second-rate who band together and who conspire. I mean in America it's the lone figure that matters, the lonely Neitszchean kid next door—you know what I mean? It's terrible here in a lot of ways . . . I am watched as a monster, a monster-bully, a sissy-monster-bully, minor, a Jew . . ."

Then I tried to, I don't know, show I knew what was going on: "Ideas, good or bad ones, mediocre ones, strange ones have a particular value in this country where no one is anything much for long. No matter how stupid I sound, it is a matter of ideas but not such intelligent ones that they aren't easy to modify." For popcult: we didn't have that term yet.

Brr and Deut were listening, and mad Moira put a blue-and-white plate of peaches on the table next to me where I slouched on the couch with a big sunflower: "There, that's Renoir *and* Van Gogh," she said, refreshed, re-pilled; she'd vanished for a while; her eyes were dead, her smile was sweet, her voice was rather eely . . . She wasn't jealous. She was offering me to Deut and Brr. Brr's nickname came from a *New Yorker* cartoon of a showgirl wearing a fur coat, who said, *I got it for going Brr in front of Bergdorf's.*

The last time Brr had taken an idea of mine, he'd given me a black-and-white sketch of me by a woman painter who was mostly only fashionable but had an interesting series of lovers; she suffered articulately and was willing to divulge everything on the telephone— she was a star on the telephone circuit. She later jumped out a window—we had a lot of suicides. The 1950s were hard on everyone: perhaps it was guilt. Or remorse.

What good would it have done anyone to love Deuteronomy—he reeked of sellout. Not just common sense but a whole, crass poetry of it. So did Moira and Brr. And Ora, my lover, tried. I'm not quick enough or smart enough to be king of the hill—if you take into consideration characters' behavior over a span of minutes, you get a different notion of character, as linkages within an enterprise, an agenda (not a word we used then). Why bother to act anything out when you can pretend nothing is real?

Moira said, "Oh you're a brilliant young man and you're having your hour—"

Brr said, "How does it feel?"

He was strange.

"You get cheated and used a lot," I said.

Deuteronomy said, "Come on: tell us how it feels." He and Brr thanked me at times for saying things or writing things useful to them. But they never did it in public. Still, Brr was *respectful,* and Deut was on an arc of sweetness that didn't obligate him; he was tougher than I am, at least toward the world. I don't know how evasive I was and how malicious he was. I know how malicious Brr was: it was an uncontrollable element in him, for him I mean. He had to cheat you. Maybe everyone is like that a little bit: a sly child-man.

I said, "It feels unusable as *example.* In public you become merely a phrase or some such thing, a political image, I think. But if I am actually good at what I do, then it is completely unusable as example. I feel famous and overinflated and not famous enough and underrated—I feel a lot of different things: it depends on details and on the time of day. You're more famous than I am. And no one is interested in seeing how style arises as moral choice out of the rush and charge of the multiplicity of moments."

He nodded. He got his ideas from everywhere but his notion of being young came from me—for a while. I was useful, which was dizzying.

Moira has said she would like to be hurt by a grasping Englishman or vain, arrogant Frenchman. She wants to be part of the background of her time. I guess I did too but in a different spirit.

Anyway, she seemed to understand my position or rank. I thought her vulgar and irritating in her interest in Pygmalionization: "We have to buy you some nice clothes—or who here is the same size you are?" Get the clothes free.

"I have already decided to wear the wrong clothes: it's a kind of privacy."

Deuteronomy naughtily said, "Brr dresses like you already. He says you *are* the next style." If he'd taken an idea from me, it was because Brr had suggested it.

I wear modified Harvard black tinged with *rabbinical* black— black cashmere with a slightly hoodlum tone.

Deuteronomy said, "I wore a sweater Brr liked once and he did a piece on sweaters in every one of his magazines: it was eerie going to the theater and seeing maybe a half-dozen men dressed wrong like me, only it was no longer wrong."

"Whitto does it now," Moira said smiling nicely, too nicely. Her smile was a mad headlight.

Brr said, "I got my style from Jouvet." A French actor of the 1930s and 1940s, very tall, very discreet in style, very different from Brr. So Brr was perhaps joking.

What I meant about Moira's vulgarity in her Pygmalion sense of clothes and stardom and psychoanalysis was that it was *a-song-and-dance, a whole rigmarole,* pre-suicide stuff—you lost yourself.

Moira mentioned a piece that Brr ran on Paris and the existentialists and Parisian women, "Lipstick and Nothingness" it was called, and she said the idea had come from me. But it hadn't. Part of the piece had been about the aging Coco Chanel, an ex-Nazi: did her guilt matter? Brr told me advertisers made him run that piece, which, like many others, was a lie, a *duty.* So much for my influence.

But he was on some sort of arc now; he took pills too but he managed them. He called in the youthful semi-butler and sent him upstairs to get a Chanel suit that Moira wouldn't wear but would lend out so I was to look at it to consider the *Pygmalionization* of Ora. Ora wasn't to choose; I was.

It was an extraordinary object, that suit, rough, nubby, navy blue fabric, workmanlike or vaguely seamanish, a uniform suggesting adventure and dutifulness and patience all at once in a world when workmen and barmaids were sexual objects. Or if it was a uniform, it was a uniform for a long sail across the universe, gold buttons and black braid. It seemed more fully an invention than any other such dress object I had, until then, seen.

"But she was a Nazi," Brr said, lightly stroking the suit with his fingerends. "A loathsome woman. *I* loathed her—"

"Brr dislikes a lot of people," Moira said.

"Ora, would you like this suit?" Brr said in a loud voice, in front of everyone.

To my surprise Ora said, "I had better try it on . . ."

Deut said, "Women trying on clothes are *very* sexy."

Brr said, "I always masturbate after Moira tries on clothes in Paris."

Schwearzen said, "I am a *great,* great, GREAT masturbator—"

Brr, who from time to time did sudden riffs, said, "I am a Napoleon of masturbation—masturbation is my *art.*"

"Oh goody," Moira said. "Now we'll have fun for a while. . . ."

Brr said, trying it for purposes of giving interviews, "Masturbation is the foundation of my work." (Moira said in an aside, "He's wonderful when he gets on a subject." She did look interested.) Brr said, of masturbation and the fantasies that went with it, "That's my secret life—I can have no women after Moira. . . . No woman compares with Moira. . . ."

(Most people figured he was *queer*—that's how we said it back then.)

Deuteronomy said of masturbation, "That's the secret of show business—but *I* love *Hollywood*—"

I said, "Masturbation, after all, after the first few times, is largely memory-lane plus amendments. It's interesting that you pay attention: you pay attention physically: *this is my prick, this is my abdomen, this my grown-up hand, these are* my *rhythms* . . . You keep watch internally—"

"That's really *true,*" Deut said.

"Childe Harold to the dark tower came—or *This is what I didn't do for so-and-so* (in the last fuck), or *This isn't what so-and-so did for me* . . . these steps to—whatever, the waste dump, the ash pit after—"

Deut said, "At least it is something I know how to do. I don't have to worry what someone else thinks of my technique. . . ."

Then I lost my head and didn't hold back: "No *heavy* reality of consequence overlays this act-and-physical-reality: going too fast, going too slow, being fat, being small-pricked, none of it matters. It's king-of-the-dream-of-final-power time. People say that it is just jacking off, or that so-and-so is just jacking himself off, meaning wasting time: the term comes from *Jack* and refers to *the common people,* to what ordinary people do—it refers to labor. The watery eyes, the slack mouth. The little jolts along the spine. Sometimes it feels like the doorway to suicide—a natural underlining to biological isolation. Sometimes, after a fuck with a lost orgasm, the kind of coming where it seems lost in a cloudy thicket, you know, I jerk off and the damned orgasm then brings tears to my eyes, but I'm ashamed—ashamed and embarrassed, ashamed and embarrassed and *defiant*—I wonder why. Well, I suppose it's cheating on lovers and parents; it really is kind of an exploration of being alone and self-willed—you know all those myths where someone behaves well and is given power and wishes and then goes berserk with the wishes? That's what it's like. Your body, your mind, you take them over. The desperate chronicle, the secret club and blasphemous thing of it, this sneaking off to the treehouse, the rebellion keeps twisting this way and that, and you don't have to notice, you can be quick and not look. If you slow it down or think about it driftingly, after, you can see that it twists and turns with strange beliefs, strange dishonesties—honesties, too. But it is rarely used in dramas—we don't see Hamlet jacking off and deciding to die. Or Lear doing it. Or Macbeth. You can find out that you don't love someone very much or even the world. And it's a chronic thing to do it—it's really not just sexual. Prometheus stole more than fire. Our jokes as kids were Aladdin and his lamp, djinni and the light brown pubic hair, Jack and the bean stalk, et cetera—"

"Don't say *et cetera*—it's not fair . . ." I.e., tell us everything.

"We had names for it from comic strips, Dagwood and Superman or Blondie and Mickey Mouse. I knew a guy who called it Swan Lake because of the neck of the swan. A lot was movies: Public Enemy Number One, Little Caesar, Gone With the Wind, Come with the Breeze—the weird one was Casablanca: I thought it was maybe Hump-free Bogus. But later I heard that *kazzo* is one of the Italian terms for prick, so it could mean *white prick*. Nothing is ever just Freudian-sexual, Freud was a sexual dud which is a kind of a good thing to be, romantic, you know, but we do lie a lot if we're like Freud. Writing, it's masturbatory, it's Jack and the bean stalk stuff, just you alone with the world with hallucinatory accompaniment. A lot of what we are in a democracy is a jerk-off society—you know what I mean?"

Kellow, although he's quite good-looking, is physically repellent. So is Deut. Brr is famously dapper and does very spruce, pretty
things with graphics (we said *with art direction* in those days) in his
magazines. He is fine-featured, well-proportioned, and has handsome hair; he knows about being attractive, he deals in this stuff
but, physically, he is accepted with difficulty—it's his nervous,
insectlike drive. It's *him.* Often you have to choke back real distaste
if you want his company. He is *repellent.* He is maybe spiritually a
cockroach. Or chaste. A *cockroach,* the waving legs, the foreignness,
the scuttling movements, the oddly unsettling shape . . . A famous
figure in art, after all.

Perhaps he was phenomenally odd-looking as a child or was per-
suaded that he was, and, so, became an expert in self-presentation and
in enraged disguise, in perfuming hidden stenches and the like—and
now he preserves by some magic or other his childhood ugliness and his
sense of methods and so is tremendously successful in the world, and is
caught by that success. He can't exist physically. He milks *the cockroach
aspect* and is appalled by himself and is sad and dangerous like someone
deformed and vengeful, like someone smart.

Deuteronomy said, "Do you find you want to get even with everyone for your being smart?"

"I'm not smart," I said automatically. I minded the doubleness of
what he was doing: the offering of friendship and the shoving me into
a sack, the warning he was issuing.

Deuteronomy said patiently (with acted out patience), "What do
you call what you just did, what you just said?"

"I only heard part of it: I was too busy saying it to notice it. I
would say it was a talent as in a tennis rally—I don't know what it is.
If I'm so smart, how come I'm not king of the world? My mother said
there was such a thing as being too smart: so you weren't smart at all.
Brr is smart, *pig-smart,* doesn't Moira tell me you use that word for
him? He uses everything; he finds everything useful: I mean, in running his magazines—as in seeing who will talk and show off. All I do

is show off in speeches. He makes faces at me and gets me to talk to see if I'm loyal—buyable . . ."

What I said wasn't making sense because I was trying to hide what I thought of Deut and Brr. I haven't much gift for intimate politics. But I can see what is going to happen, but that separates me, it doesn't help me join in.

Brr was heroic and caught in a psychological-social bind in relation to a personal pain since it guided him to success in mass market stuff, it guided him to a sense of the mass mind, or whatever. To go back to the it-began-in-childhood theories that he held, I saw him as a sly, unpleasant child whose embraces and attentions had been unwanted because of something *vile* in them, a precocity of powers of association and of courage in acting on those powers in spite of his being displeasing to his parents. He dealt in his own shit and had an appetite for *glamour,* for constructions of meaning and propriety because his family did, but he did it better. Years later, I saw some Arbus photographs, and I think Brr must have been a horror, or thought he was. He liked women because they were less violent and more interesting than men—this is seeing him in the third person, not the sort of third person that is oneself in dreams or in a mirror; but I'm trying to see him not in relation to me. This sliding in and out of one's self and trying to see him is strange, is as strange as looking at a cockroach.

He saw women as ugly-but-pretty—just as he was good-looking-but-repellent: there is a kind of odd stitching of sanity to be found in the embrace of reality, sanity as a style; but that isn't what he did—his sanity was desperate, his style was powerful and riddled with fantasy. If a man is attached to his own ugliness he might substitute being in the world of yearning for the actuality of his never having been a child-object of embraces and a source of comfort once upon a time. He faked the comfort he gave. He was not pleasant. He gained a tremendous energy from this, and his mental acuity was sorely tried; he wasn't as miserable as Moira was. This stuff represents the limits of my mind and feelings that year. I hadn't Kellow's gift for substitutive algebra. I figured that in him this stuff generated few emotions except for pride and a sense of what-is-appropriate and then the excited sense of what-is-not-appropriate-but-is-fascinating-anyway. I figured he felt those things *strongly.*

To be honest, I have a good time mostly, but life scares me.